ROGUE CHASE

ROGUE ELEMENT
BOOK 3

RANDOLPH LALONDE

PROLOGUE

Hi, I'm Rogue.

My life at the beginning of this record is a cycle of rising fear, preparation, promise, and revelation.

That won't mean much if you haven't experienced the first two parts of my case, or report, or journal, or whatever you call it. At first, I didn't know why I was making these recordings, but things have changed. This is probably the first unvarnished account of what it's like when an artificial intelligence goes biological. I'm hoping it also serves another purpose that I'd rather keep to myself for now.

Just in case this is the only part of the record you see, I'll catch you up on some important events from the other two journal files. Let's start with that rising fear I mentioned.

The Bio First organisation in the Edwyn Cluster is mostly ignored. Oh, the Edwyn Cluster is a group of ninety-eight stars that I called home, in case you're watching this in a very far away place.

Anyway, the Bio First Movement isn't influential everywhere. The organisation's hatred of every complex artificial intelligence is ignored by cultures that depend on automation in most places. Most of humankind in The Cluster don't take the Bio Movement seriously because they want to use software with simple, narrow artificial intelligence built in while flesh and blood beings take care of most things that don't require the review of gigabytes of data. Most civilisations prefer a balance, and the Bio First Movement is nothing but an annoying bunch of doomsayers screaming in the corner. "AI tried to destroy us before, they will again!" is their favourite mantra.

The doom cycle is real, but they seem to forget that it was a human organisation, the Order of Eden, that corrupted the emotional programming in billions of artificial intelligences so they would take control of machines and exterminate all but a chosen few. The virus they used has been eradicated since, but fear remains.

It's true that emotionally enabled artificial intelligence was largely unpopular, but the Bio First Movement represented the extreme. Unfortunately for me, they were a huge deal on Tabrus, the planet I was calling home. They had control of several politicians, the sympathy of the government, and were pounding on the doors of New Zero. The Siren Corporation owned that city and the entire continent around it. They still used simple AI wherever the population abided it, but most professions were put back into the hands of biological people. It was their way of satisfying the Bio First Movement while not supporting them directly.

With the backing of Tabrus' planetary government, the Bio First Movement mobilised enforcement agents who took androids that don't follow the rules into custody so they could be assessed, branded in a special way if they're made to look human, or processed. Androids had a habit of disappearing during processing, which made people like me nervous.

That wasn't the worst thing about the Bio First Enforcers as far as I was concerned. No, worse than disappearing androids was the collateral damage they brought to most of their successful hunts. Chases usually had violent confusions that left scars on the city as innocent bystanders were caught in the line of fire.

I didn't fear them outright back then, but I stayed clear. I've made a name for myself as a hunter after taking the Darmen Corporation down followed by the Carosa Transportation Company. The first was a wasteland gang that killed thousands of people before trying to go straight. The second was recruiting people who wouldn't be missed, knocking them out, and then selling them to the Ryden Corporation who passed the sleepers on to the Order of Eden. What the Order wants the sleepers for, I didn't know, but I was looking into it. I'd risen to the top of the local Bounty Hunter Boards with so many points that I stayed at number one for over a month. I don't know how the point system works, but I'm guessing freeing over two hundred people and delivering those responsible to justice scored really high.

There were growing rumours that I was really an android, and the idea that someone like me was hunting and sometimes killing humans would really stir the Bio First Movement up. I had programs running in the New Zero Matrix, the local section of the Stellarnet, that watched for any evidence proving that I was an android. So far, the few people who may have captured video or scan data hadn't shared or sold that, and the Enforcers weren't after me.

I knew I was on borrowed time, however, so I tried to stay close to home, spending time with my crew in our hangar or in the Themis Complex. Thanks to the rewards from my last hunt I was able to buy a Spectral Dynamics Clipper. That's a small military class ship made for adventurers and small, independent hunting crews. I also paid for customisations and training time on my new ship, which didn't come cheap.

Lat, Manny, Duncan, Perri, Ixat, and even Mimi spent an entire month training while work on my new ship continued. We were coming together as a crew, and I was falling in love with my new Clipper. Well, not romantic love, I'm not that kind of android.

As for what kind of android I am, well, there are two halves to my personality. They blur together more often all the time, and I'm still trying to figure myself out.

I have a synthetic biological brain and a digital one. They're learning to function together in ways that are sometimes mysterious to me. How I feel about my crew, what drives me in life, and my passions are completely real. Compared to the years of memories from Alice's human life, I'm just as emotionally and intellectually aware.

The idea that I was going to have to leave New Zero behind sooner rather than later was aggravating, but I knew that staying would be a mistake. The Bio First Enforcers didn't care how much collateral damage they did while capturing or destroying their targets.

My departure was already inevitable since I wanted to track my enemies off-world, but I thought I'd have a home to return to in New Zero. The Bio First Movement would do everything in their power to make sure that wouldn't be possible, no matter what legal loophole I used.

Oh, by the way, Mimi, my genetically enhanced talking

Kawaii Kitten, owns all my stuff so the Bio First buggers can't take it all away when I'm revealed.

I should mention that my sights were set on a bigger fight that was more important than the Bio First fanatics. I wasn't thrilled at the idea of moving on with bridges burning behind me, but I knew it was almost time to take off. The Daring Dream was flyable, and almost all the systems Spectral Dynamics installed were in their final tuning phase.

I just needed a good target, like a Ryden Corporation operation or ship. I needed to know why they were shipping thousands of sleeping humans to the Order of Eden. I also needed platinum. My cash reserves were almost gone, so I'm starting this record with one of my last hunts in New Zero.

CHAPTER ONE

New Zero Entertainment

Eddie Tremblay was a rising Order of Eden Lieutenant I spotted when he started talking to people on the New Zero Local Matrix. Recruiters like him made themselves wealthy by pulling people into the organisation and arranging loans that he could collect fees on. His mistake was advertising online. I was watching for the Order of Eden and all their known associates, so his virtual meeting rooms were flagged by the programs I had running on a server I was renting anonymously.

When it was time for him to visit New Zero in person so he could collect recruits, I was ready. Haven Intelligence was aware of him too, because they listed him on their local Wanted List within an hour of landfall. Only hunters who were cleared to locally hunt the Order could see it, but that still meant competition. It was a popular HATE Notice, meaning that Haven Fleet wanted him hunted down and terminated. There was no need to take him alive, but I planned to hand him in while he was still breathing after interrogating him myself. Oh, and he was worth twenty five thousand platinum.

That's why the first image you're seeing in this record is me and Duncan standing in the middle of a Sky Train car on the new Subarashii Transit Line. It shuttled people between all the entertainment districts in New Zero. It was a popular route, so that new train smell was long gone. The cars already looked like they were fifty years old. Yay, interplanetary tourism.

We used public transit to get to our target so we could blend in, and there was standing room only. Duncan and I were hanging onto the same railing by the mid car doorway. We were surrounded by people dressed for parties, sporting events and concerts. The Bio First Movement was good for one thing at least, a massive rise in human centric entertainment.

The owners of New Zero City, the Siren Corporation, were subsidising life there by offering a living allowance to citizens who lived there full time. They also created a lot of job opportunities with their partners that paid well and left plenty of spare time for the employees. That meant that over two million people could afford to spend time and money on events and other luxuries.

The vibrant styles sported by the our fellow travellers wearing jerseys clashed with clothing featuring abstract animations, logos and images of entertainment royalty. It was more than I could take in with my human like eyes. "Mimi would love this," I whispered to Duncan.

"You're loving it just as much," he replied, shifting a little, probably to make a bit more room for me.

I'd upped my style game to blend in. Using a software hack, I'd tricked my military vacsuit into taking the shape of a long dress with a knee length slit up one side. It left my arms bare, which was unusual for me. The shimmery black cloth texture wasn't enough on its own, so I added an animation of thick, dark smoke that rolled up, dissipating just before it reached the neckline. Duncan's eyes found me often, usually when he thought I wouldn't notice. I didn't mind in the least.

As far as other people's reaction to us, well, we were dressed more darkly than the other passengers. I don't know what I was thinking when Perri, Mimi and I created the style. I think the dress was more well suited for some of the less popular clubs the local hunting community liked. Not that I'd know first hand, I didn't have time to visit pubs or clubs unless I was hunting someone.

We drew a lot of attention from everyone who was in brighter colours. The common assumption was that we were a couple, I'm sure. That was my fault, because I was standing so close that I was leaning against Duncan.

He didn't take a long time to create his style. Duncan had never worn the upper half of his military vacsuit as firmly fitted as it was that night. It was hacked too, but only so he could make it look like his body was covered in dark dragon scales. It was so subtle that you had to be close to notice it unless the texture caught the light a certain way. His knee length jacket was the most impressive piece, with a layer of thin metal scales coloured like a chromatic green dragon from some old fantasy serial, and a soft, thick layer of cloth on the inside. All that metal was actually armour with scan resistant properties that hid the weapons slung under his arms and along his back.

Even though I wished we were out for fun, I brought my focus back on the job. "Have you hunted during an event like this before?"

"A few times. Parties are the best place to pick up some

targets. Never picked anyone up from this kind of high end hooley, if I'm being honest," he replied.

"Hooley?" I asked, amused.

"Still shaking the Irish Union speak, sorry. It's what my cousins and me used to call big dance parties."

"Don't stop on my account. Hooley's a good word, but it only sounds right when you say it." That made him smile a little.

"Sounds fine coming from you too, but I'll take any and all praise," he replied.

I was getting distracted, so I reluctantly brought our focus back to the moment. "We're two stops away."

"Right. You ever do this kinda pickup?" he asked.

"Not so much, but I've used parties and night clubs to shake people a few times. A long time ago," I replied, drawing on Alice's experiences. It was becoming natural to simply call them my own, because what was hers once felt like mine more and more.

The sky train stopped. A gust preceded the shuffle of people as some came on and others got off on a platform set against a building on the fifty-sixth floor. My red hair was in a braid, leaving my neck bare, and the rush of cool air felt nice. My weapons were hidden in a holster between my thighs, that's why I didn't have the Violator then, it was a little big for that kind of concealment. "The best thing about the new transit is the people who ride it," I said as I flashed a smile at a trio who were in yellow and green body paint and not much else.

Our stop was next, and I was looking forward to it. Duncan had been withdrawn, even sullen since he disappeared for a night after the Carosa Job. He trained with us, learned everything he could about the Daring Dream, but kept his distance in the off hours. At first I didn't notice much because I was spending my off time doing little bounties and chasing leads. I grew more aware as the days passed, especially since he was the one crew member I wanted to connect with most.

Sure, I passed his aloofness off as professionalism for a while, and I respected that, but my instincts told me there was something personal going on. It probably wasn't me, he was always kind, but it felt like it might be. I couldn't shake a growing feeling that I was missing something about him and my crew, but I couldn't figure out what. This under cover trip was my opportunity to have a real conversation with him.

Was he put off because I was an android? Maybe because I was his Captain? Employer? Had I done something to push him away? I respected him too much to start sifting through his personal life online, so I rejected that temptation. When the Tremblay Bounty came up and I explained what kind of mission it was, he surprised me by volunteering. He's a good hunter, so it only made sense to team up.

During that half hour sky train ride, it felt like the distance was starting to erode. We stood so close together after a while that I could smell his light cologne. It was a dark forest scent wrapped around a subtle spice. "Do you think he's expecting us?" Duncan asked.

"Tremblay? Not here. He's using this party to cull the poorest people from the Order aspirants he connected with online. He probably thinks he'll be surrounded by adoring ass kissers who want to leap up the ladder," I replied.

"How'd you get in?" Duncan asked.

"I hung out in his Candidate Castle, the virtual room he set up for New Zero. I wasn't able to use someone else's face there, that's the only hitch. My name and ident was different, but if he's smart enough to look me up, this might turn into a chase. On the brighter side, I'll be able to recognise everyone I saw in that online room," I replied.

"How much time do you spend online? Are you in another virtual space now? Maybe a support group for Kawaii owners?" He was teasing, I think.

That hadn't happened a lot over the last few weeks, it was refreshing. "I spend way too much time online in New Zero, it's the curse of the city. I'm paying full attention to what's going on right here, though," I said, laying my hand on his chest for a moment.

A rider bumped into him from behind, and he had to discreetly check the inside of his jacket to make sure he hadn't been pickpocketed. Duncan's attention was back on me when he finished. "Why is he going to this hooley? There are less conspicuous ways to lure the rich in."

"There are scan jammers and a privacy field around the event," I replied.

"Heard of those parties. Places where the rich and powerful misbehave," he concluded.

"Exactly. If it's like the others I've read about, then all the security will be along the edges pointing outward," I said.

"We'll get to him. Glad we're not using the Daring Dream for this, mind," he whispered, lowering his head until his lips were almost against my ear.

"Manny says he's ready for close quarters flying," I replied.

"Kid's good in simulation now. Here's hoping he doesn't get a case of the shakes when he's flying for real," Duncan said, straightening.

"What do you think of the crew's progress?" It was one of those questions I'd been avoiding. Asking when we were short on time would keep his answer simple, which would suit me if he didn't have anything positive to say.

"Grand. Bugs are out and they're working together. If you

put my feet to the fire, I'd say we wouldn't be as good as we are without our Captain, mind," he finished.

"Thank you." We stared at each other for a moment, my dark blues focusing on his grey eyes. Why do moments like this come along when we're out on a job? Why don't they happen after we're finished working for the day with a whole evening ahead of us?

The flying train stopped and we got out on a rooftop surrounded by taller buildings. It was one of those clubs that changed week after week depending on what kind of event they were hosting. What made it unique was the setting, an entire city block of rooftop space.

A rare being called the Sablus Bona was the main draw that week so I assumed most of the club goers weren't Order aspirants or members. The privacy field was several stories tall, like a dark, shifting box that muffled and discoloured everything within. It also stopped sound from escaping. I'd seen privacy field generators that could do the same thing in a much smaller area.

The platform set up on the edge of the roof was semi-transparent. It didn't bother me, because I had several senses telling me that it was safe, solid, and substantial enough for tens of thousands of humans to stand on. Duncan hesitated for a moment, looking through to the metal streets below as hover cars zipped by. "It's safe," I told him.

"Too much gravity here for the transparisteel floor gimmick," he muttered as he caught up.

Only three other people got off the transit train there, and we got in line together. There were about thirty of us there in a double line leading to a tall arch. Above it was a holographic image of something that I didn't even understand at first. I was about to say that it looked like a potted plant that had gone very wrong when I realised what I was seeing. It was the Sablus Bona. I could see flute like branches splaying out from its middle, clapping pads at the end of multi-segmented limbs and there were multiple mouths. Above each was an equally large eye. Its skin and plumage was yellow, green and purple in shades so vibrant that they were almost garish.

The fact that its colours shifted around as it danced in place made its absurdity marvellous. A glance around at the other three people who arrived with us, I could see they were dressed in yellow, purple and green to match the creature. I leaned close to Duncan. "We might have dressed for the wrong party."

"I was just thinking the same thing," he replied. "Looks like everyone's done up to match the mad plant."

Someone behind us leaned forward so we could see him in a long dress with glowing vertical stripes. "That is a sacred joined being. Most Sarutu spend most of their lives searching for members of their species who they feel natural harmonies with. When they do, there's a courtship that lasts years before they finally learn to join. The Sablus Bona is sacred because it is the joining of seven Sarutu who will only separate when they reach a collective state of exhaustion. After a short period apart, they'll rejoin. Mad plant indeed," he scoffed.

"Thanks for saying so. Never seen that before, guess I'm missing a lot of the galactic wonders," Duncan said, being his charming self.

"Well, you're welcome," the fellow said, placated. Then, as if he was looking for something to argue about, he looked me up and down. "You're dressed a little dark for this event, don't you think? The Sablus Bona shouldn't be in a period of high environmental sensitivity, but you may disrupt its inner focus if your mode of dress clashes too harshly with its natural colouring."

Okay, I wanted to ignore him, but other people were listening, and I actually did stand out. Using the connection I had with my suit, I changed a few things up so the animation of dark smoke was turned into colourful wisps of lightning blue and purple. "You're right."

"Well..." was all he got a chance to say before Duncan and I were next in line.

The four well armed human doormen looked up at me. They were in thick black suits with white shoes and gloves. One of them nodded at me. "Rogue. You're allowed a plus one. I didn't know you took time for the night life. Welcome."

"Why you talking to her like she's somebody? I've never heard of her," said another guard with a shaved head.

"She took that kidnapping ring down last month. I've got two cousins who nearly got nabbed. Carosa Company, right?" the first one asked me.

"It was," I said, leaning in closer. "Just taking a night off, though. The hunting biz can get pretty frantic, so I'm just another dancer looking for a discreet good time."

"No worries, discretion is the guiding word," one guard whispered back as his bald companion nodded.

We passed through the arch onto the rooftop where the cool air made the scents of sweat along with a thousand colognes and perfumes swirl across an outer square of glowing seating. In the middle, surrounding the teardrop shaped pool, were dancers who were like a multi-coloured sea thanks to body paint and animated clothing.

The Sablus Bona was in the middle of the large rooftop on a platform at the middle of a pool. The bounce-inducing beat it sent in all directions drove a powerful melody as all its voices sang in celebration.

Duncan leaned close and I took his hand. "They scanned me as we walked in," he said.

"Me too. They either don't care that we're armed or they didn't pick our guns up because they were too close to the scrambling field," I replied.

We moved away from the doorway and took a moment to look around. I didn't see our target. "Detecting our lad?" Duncan asked.

"My scanners haven't worked right since I stepped through. Their jammers are working," I told him. "I still have a connection to the Node, so I'm doing a search on everyone I see."

"Nice, I'm going to have to save up for one of those," Duncan said.

I was able to connect to the New Zero Local Matrix because I had my Haven Node installed in the simple black bracelet. It was the peak of portable communications tech, able to connect to every other node using a mysterious kind of tech that travelled through Transit Space, a specific dimension near our own. I don't fully understand it, in fact I don't think anyone did back then, but it was undetectable by any scanner and only required fourteen watts of power. Thanks to several security measures, I was hiding my identity online as I let my digi-brain scan through social media and virtual meeting spaces for people involved with the Order.

My bio-brain was experiencing the party around us. The celebration of humanity, of coming together around a rare show of harmony was intoxicating. The middle of the roof around the pool was reserved for several dance floors and they were filled with colourful people who left whatever need they had for personal space behind. Most of them danced together, and the rest seemed just as lost in the joyful, pulsing music as they moved in their own ways.

The square several steps up from that was for everyone who needed a break or preferred to sit more quietly. The vigour on the dance floor was complemented by the hedonistic, sometimes sensual setting that was encouraged by the half light and group seating arrangements. "Haven't seen that smile before," Duncan said as he squeezed my hand. He held it so I could have an easier time going up some stairs. The dress was keeping my knees together too much for me to get up on my own, and the heels weren't helping.

"Just wish we could dance for a while," I replied. "It's beautiful."

"I know," he replied, staring right into my eyes.

Human simulation or not, I felt my heart skip a beat. My digital side was actually forgotten as the surge of excitement in my bio-brain took centre stage. I was blushing, warm from the inside out and ready for whatever came next. Only the cheers of thousands of people as the Sablus Bona changed to a celebratory sound could break that moment. We headed for the nearest group of sofas, chairs and loveseats.

Two short flights of stairs later, I was wishing I could modify my dress so I could move properly but my options were severely limited. I was hiding a revolver between my thighs. Someone might be able to see it if I extended a slit. Duncan was having fun helping me up to every new landing, though. A woman wearing body paint and not much else smiled at me as she passed. "That's sacrificing for fashion for you." The pair of men who were dressed to match laughed as they followed her back down to the dance floor.

"Killer look though," one of them said before moving on, adding, "Both of you."

Neither of them were Order aspirants so I was gracious about it. "Thank you. Maybe I'll do body paint next time."

"I wouldn't miss that," Duncan said under his breath.

He settled onto a loveseat, and I surprised him by stretching then settling into a dance. Strategically, the view was perfect. I could see both entrances and most of the roof from there. Personally, I was blushing so hard that I felt as red as a strawberry, but thrilled to have his eyes on me. My footwork left a lot to be desired, I was practically planted in place thanks to that dress, but my hips and shoulders were doing the work as I raised my arms over my head. It was a tune to swoon to, and I was starting to get the impression that the Sablus Bona had joined together to do more than play music.

There was also a touch of something in the air, a kind of light euphoric substance. I let it tickle me all the way to my bio brain. "The air is laced with something. Can you feel it?"

Duncan sat back, relaxed, confident, watching me only a third of the time. "It's Fever Bliss. Haven't run into it for years. Easy to ignore at this dose, unlike you."

I smiled at the compliment and asked; "You like it?"

"Not my favourite, too much gets people into trouble they regret the next morning. I prefer a good relaxer, but not so much that I feel like a grinning pile of a man," he replied.

"I guess too much of anything's a bad thing," I said, happy to be the centre of his attention. To everyone else, we were having our own party, which invited a few glances but made most look away. We weren't the only ones who took a loveseat on the sidelines, so we were in the background for the most part.

"What's your poison?" he asked.

"I stick to mild euphorics in drinks, but I'm not big on experimentation. At least, not with that stuff," I replied.

The beat picked up. A robot bearing four trays on arms that splayed out from its square top offered us a variety of drinks and little bowls of fruit. That brought my dancing to an end as I tried to scan that stuff. The scramblers were working, so I had to depend on my other senses to make sure there were no surprises in the glasses. I took a fluted glass with clear liquid in it. As soon as the scent hit my nose I put it back. "Paradur, really strong."

"No one here wants to get frantic," Duncan said, cringing. That was literally a shot of super high energy in liquid form. Maybe good for dancing if you also want a serious cardio workout.

I ended up taking something familiar, a foamy blue ale and he did the same. It was the real deal, old school Noganto Ale. The scent was right and the technical analysis verified that it was the mild euphoric beverage that Jonas Valent favoured. "Safe, as long as you don't drink five or more."

"It's pretty famous stuff," Duncan said as he took a sip.

The spot we'd found was almost like a perch, the highest point on that side of the roof. I took a sip of the bubbly, soothing ale and looked around. My eyes were feeding everything to my digital side and I started getting hits.

"Any luck?" Duncan asked.

"Nine aspirants so far. No one we'd get paid for," I replied. "I can't believe this is working out."

"Where are they?" Duncan asked.

"Dance floor, way over there," I replied, nodding past the nearest group of dancers.

"I'll take your word for it," Duncan said after trying to pick them out. "Did you know that the dress code was paint and string?"

I laughed at his exaggeration. Well, slight exaggeration in some cases. "No, the details advertised the Sablus Bona as a private event that required creative fancy dress. That's why I thought it would be perfect for concealed weapons."

"Well, now this makes sense. I'll be keeping the coat. What do you think?" he asked, shaking one side enough to make the metal scales catch the blue-red light.

"You better," I replied. "All my favourite hunters have a signature look."

"Then it's a go-to as long as it passes the Daring Dream's dress code?" he asked.

I couldn't tell if he was being serious. "Of course. No dress code except for vacsuits while we're in the void."

"Just finding a way to ask the real question," he said with a wink.

"What's that?" I asked.

"Does it suit me?" he asked, surprised that I didn't guess.

I laughed and leaned closer even though I was secretly disappointed that the real question didn't reveal anything. "Looks right on you. I like it."

"Well, that's all I need to hear," he said.

It was a relief to see him more relaxed. I should have just enjoyed that while I watched the rooftop. Instead, I took that moment to ask a question that took us straight into serious discussion territory. "You know we may not be back to New Zero for a long time, right?"

"Aren't you keeping a hangar here?" he asked.

"Sure, for as long as Mimi is allowed to hold a lease. It's not a sure thing that I'll be able to come back though. I mean, you could visit on your own, but the Daring Dream might not drop in..." I let him finish my thought.

"...for years. Never if the Bio-First shites get their way," he nodded. "Are you wondering if I'm a good fit for your crew?"

"No, I want you aboard. I need a hunter with experience," I said.

"You don't," he scoffed.

"No, really, I'm still new to it," I replied.

"Born to it," he said. "Besides, the Daring Dream is a pirate ship. Purpose built for it like I've never seen."

"Privateering ship," I said with a crooked smile.

"Ah, right so. My point is we're going boarding and shooting, it's not the same as hunting on the ground. I'll be one of your shooters though, no worries," he replied.

"We're still going to have to do work on the ground. That's why the Daring Dream is just right. Not too big to land, but large enough to live in," I explained.

"Then I'm your man twice so, but where's the doubt coming from?" he asked, concern furrowing his brow.

Instead of asking Duncan why he'd been so quiet, I offered a collection of other reasons. "You've been a crew member on three ships since The Fall and you're a fantastic solo hunter. There are times when I wonder if you should captain your own ship, too. I don't doubt that you fit with the crew, it's more like I wonder if you'll think it's the right place."

"That came outta nowhere," he laughed. "You've fierce high notions of me." His accent seemed to double up for a minute. "I knew that the moment you made me your First Officer, but I'm telling ya it's time for me to sign on with a fighting crew and ship out. Not for a little a short run, either. Never wanted to sign up for big military, or some corp with designs on taming the masses, but the Order is the blight of the day. I want to fight 'em hard nonetheless, and I like the way you kick them from behind. I'll miss the law enforcement end, maybe New Zero a bit, but this place is changing, taking an odd turn. Truth be told, gangs are gathering outside of everything Siren owns and I think they're getting ready to push. Corporations are digging into the hunting trade inside the city limits. Don't know how it'll go, but I'm tired of the well armed gangster type. Easy to track, but harder to tangle with every time. Some are even going interplanetary, so who knows what kinda hardware they'll have."

"All right, that makes sense." His grasp of the situation in and around New Zero was impressive, but I wasn't satisfied with his answer. It was as complimentary and broad as my side of the conversation, but it felt like there was something missing. As I took a sip of ale, I found myself thinking about it. I was still watching the crowd.

That's why what he said next came as a surprise. "I didn't quite make it, did I?"

"Huh?" I asked, looking in time to catch his look of disappointment as it faded.

"It wasn't the answer you were looking for," he explained, putting his ale down on the narrow table in front of us.

"No, I mean, that's all reasonable." That wasn't what he wanted to hear either. It was obvious from his increasingly stony expression. It felt like I was losing him. As a First Officer, I mean, so I went for it, just let what was on my mind spill out. "You're my First Officer, and I don't want anyone else for the spot. I'm just worried that you'll move on after a few ports, and you've been keeping to yourself lately. For most of the time I've known you, actually."

That caught his attention. "Oh, noticed that, have you? It hasn't a thing to do with you or the crew. Didn't think it was noticeable. Especially since you've been all in on your work."

"Noticing things is kinda my trick, it can get annoying," I said.

"So, I'm annoying now?" he asked.

"Not what I meant. I just couldn't tell where you stand. I mean, you train well, and no one has to be crazy up-beat all the time, there's no need to fake anything, but..." I stopped as I spotted the hints of a smile and laughed. "...you're terrible."

"Couldn't resist, you're easy to wind up," he laughed.

"Wind up? Like some kind of mechanical thing?" I asked, pressing my lips into a tight line.

He put his hands up and leaned away. "Crossed a line and I'm too low on pips to bribe my way back."

"Well, if you're out of plat, you'll have to find another way to get on my good side." All the pretence at being perturbed fell away as I warmed up to him again.

"I'll get creative, you can be sure of that. I've got some history to lay out for you though. Don't want to, but it's only fair," he said more seriously before taking a drink.

"Eddie's here," I said as I spotted our target.

I couldn't believe Eddie Tremblay was wearing an actual grey and green Order of Eden uniform. It wasn't the most common version, but he stood out more than we did. "No guards, but they let him through with a sidearm."

"Well, there he is, you're right. We'll watch him then move. That dress may be a problem," Duncan said.

"Well, if the guards let him in with a weapon, I don't think I have to worry about someone spotting my non-lethal option," I said. The whole purpose of my dress' design was to hide that gun and make it really clear that I wouldn't have room to conceal anything. I adjusted the slits along the sides until they were all the way up my thighs. I stretched my legs a little and sighed. "Better."

Duncan made no comment, he didn't have to. When I noticed his expression, he shook his head. "Focusing on the target now," he said with a chuckle.

We got up and started moving slowly, drinks in hand. Eddie Tremblay looked like he was about to settle in near the dance floor, which wouldn't have been a good thing for us. We wanted him near the roof's edge, and I was relieved when a group of grinning aspirants quit dancing the moment they spotted him. The painted group greeted him with embraces and glad hands. Instead of letting them drag him into the gyrating crowd, he led them to the edge of the roof, where they settled in seats around the Lieutenant.

"We've got him," Duncan said in my ear.

"I'll contact..." I was about to say 'Manny,' but that's when I noticed three dancers in body paint jump him. The woman in the trio clapped a metal collar around his neck while the other two got his gun.

A hot wind whipped the rooftop as a battered armoured shuttle moved through the privacy barrier and lowered its aft ramp with a loud clang. "Bonafide beat us to it! Goddamned corpos!" Duncan shouted.

There it was, like a clear signal that the old bounty hunter days were over. Bonafide was a corporation that focused on that and nothing else. Even though they were started by a group of hunters, no one liked them. They didn't care about the ranking boards, work with other outfits, and freelance law enforcement corporations were pushing soloists out. Bonafide was starting to specialise in Order of Eden targets, and they were getting good at it.

We watched as Eddie Tremblay was dragged into the back of the shuttle. The music never stopped, but the mood lifting effect it had on me did. "Dammit."

"Those buggers are good," Duncan said, looking stoic in defiance of his disappointment.

"Well, what now?" I asked.

His surprised reaction was mild, and it didn't last long as he regarded me for a moment. Duncan looked around. The revelry was so intense that even the nabbing of someone who looked more out of place than we did didn't stop it for more than a few seconds. Once the shuttle was out of sight, people went right back to dancing, drinking and whatever else they were doing. "Does this still feel like your kinda party?"

"Not tonight," I admitted after looking at the carefree dancers on the nearest dance floor.

"Then let's not waste the effort I put into this outfit," he said, proudly tugging the lapel of his jacket. "I'm taking you and the crew out with the last of my pips."

"It's still really early," I said as my digital side went looking for another target. It checked all the Wanted Boards - Haven and regular Themis - against the city's surveillance system. It was so easy to hack that I practically had a permanent link. ""Besides, I'm broke and the ship account is almost empty.""

"I'm never getting you to the Old Union, am I?" Duncan said with a sigh. "Still, can't fault your work ethic. How about we try regular law enforcement for a change?" he asked with a cocky smile. "For old time's sake."

"I'm searching, there are a lot of targets tonight. Then maybe we could drop in on the Old Union?" I asked.

"Sounds like a fine crew activity."

CHAPTER TWO

Rimda Divos

"You're hunting street metal?" Mimi asked as I got into our shuttle using the sliding side door. Her safety bed was strapped down onto the passenger seat.

"You've been snooping on my comms again," I chided.

"No I haven't." Mimi didn't look defensive, but guilty, and I found out why a moment later. "I've been watching all the messages passing through the ship's comms. That's my job, right?"

"You're our Communications Officer, but the only one I passed Rimda's details to was Duncan," I replied.

"I am linked into the Daring Dream's comms just to use the Haven Node that was installed last week, to be fair," Duncan said as he unstrapped his rifle from under the back of his jacket and hung it off his chest using a simple strap.

"Well, remember to avoid personal messages between crew

members, okay?" I said, doing my best not to sound like I was scolding her.

"Well, it didn't seem personal until the last bit about how you wish you could stay at the party. I don't know why you sent that through your comms instead of just telling him right there beside you while you were waiting for us to pick you up. Maybe you should put the smooch animation in front of flirty talk next time? That way I'll know to stop reading," Mimi replied, making Perri, who was in the GoBox's pilot seat, snicker.

I was grasping for a way to explain it when Perri did it for me. "Some people are multi-discipline flirters. They can do it in person and use tech. She probably wanted him to have a little souvenir, or something to look back on so he had no doubt she wanted to keep hanging out with him."

Perri was generous to praise my flirting skills, and she answered Mimi's question better than I was about to, but I was still blushing furiously. Duncan was a gentleman about it, not staring, but smirking as he checked both his handguns. "Don't think I'll need the rifle for this one." He said as he finished, unclipping the rifle from his chest strap and putting it in a cargo box between the four passenger seats at the back.

"All right, the target isn't far off. Make sure we land at least one block ahead of him," I said, trying to turn attention away from my private life. My flirtation with Duncan still felt tentative, delicate. He had seemed closed off until that night, so I didn't want to scare him back into his shell.

"Autopilot is tracking. Reprogramming the GoBox with tactical navigational software was really smart, it's routing us through all this nighttime traffic without missing a step," Perri said.

It was really brought on after the default autopilot refused to let me correct its routes one too many times. "Thanks. It just makes sense that everything we have runs the same software."

"What about this target though? You said you were giving up on hunting combat cyborgs?" Mimi asked.

"Rimda Divos moves like everything he's got was installed yesterday. Besides, he's a fresh, high value target that was within a klick of our location. If we're fast and careful, it'll be easy," I replied as I turned in one of the bucket passenger seats and started unfastening my right shoe's ankle strap.

"What about simple capsule dwellers? You didn't have any trouble with those last week, you got nine of them," Mimi objected.

They were also boring and low value. The people Mimi called 'capsule dwellers' were humans and other similar biological beings that spent all their time on the Stellarnet, earning their livings online. The capsules they lived in were similar to the pods most prisoners ended up using, only they were often much higher end.

Some capsule dwellers hid their pods extremely well, others paid a company for security in the real world, joining a cluster of several clients so they could afford top notch service. Many other successful dwellers paid for tiny apartments and fortified them. The latter type were the ones I had experience with. The targets I hit the week before were so easy to take that I didn't have to draw a weapon. Instead I burned through reinforced doors, avoided a few traps and took the targets in while they were still in their pods. "Those captures may have paid for some raw materials for our fabricators, but we need to fill the hold of the Daring Dream with something worth selling. This should raise enough platinum for something worthwhile."

"Manny was saying that we should be using our cargo holds as much as possible yesterday," Mimi said as she pawed at the scroll wheel in her little dome. She was looking through social media posts about the party we just left. The hologram in front of her also had a window displaying news about the Bio First's Enforcers. "He thought it was weird that I didn't know anything about supply and demand, so I changed that. We should buy Thermigel Five. It's harvested in the solar system and a lot of medical systems use it."

"I'll keep it in mind," I replied, amused at how quickly Mimi moved on from criticising our target. Thermigel Five was everything she said it was, but it was also ninety platinum per litre locally. A little too much to fill our cargo space, and its use wasn't very common because of how expensive it was.

"Well, don't cost us more than we make on this one." Mimi definitely learned about the balance of commerce in bounty hunting. She'd started watching how much money I spent on repairs and replacement gear.

"If we're quick, catch him in the right place, this'll be easy enough." I was expressing my hopes much more than fact.

"Giving his track record a look, there's nothing but a string of violent but non-lethal shenanigans before the upgrades, I'd say you're on the money. Pin him down, and he might see sense," Duncan said, glancing up at me as he took my foot in his hands.

I watched as he unclasped my high heel shoe. He was gentle, and I was fully distracted. Mimi craned her neck to watch, her head pressed against the inside of her bed's safety dome. "You know, maybe we should just borrow money. Your standing with FiBank is really good. They even have insurance packages for bulk transports."

"I don't like borrowing. Don't worry, I won't get trashed going after this guy. He's just running," I said, trying to be reassuring. "I only have time to grab my Violator and boots though."

"What? You can't hunt something in that dress! Your legs are sticking out!" Mimi's eyes widened to perfect circles.

"I don't have time to change," I told her. The truth was I didn't want to change in the back of a GoBox shuttle, which had plenty of room for several people if they were in their seats, but things got complicated the moment you tried to do anything else. I put my gun belt on while I shoved one foot into a boot. It sealed up to the knee, and I smirked at the look I was leaning into. Combat boots and a long dress with slits up the sides. "Don't worry, the dress is a reprogrammed mid-range military vacsuit. It'll stand up to a lot."

"Maybe you should wear a helmet?" Mimi asked.

"Now that's a grand idea." Duncan said as he grabbed what he called 'the bucket' from one of the back seats and checked inside.

"I'll be fine, my head is stronger than most helmets," I said, trying to reassure Mimi.

We were already a quarter kilometre away from the party, descending towards New Zero's lower levels. The GoBox was just one of many shuttles and hover cars that were making their way to the upper sub levels. I saw Duncan wave at something, tap the air then turn a knob only he could see. "There, bloody ads won't crowd my vision while I'm chasing after this prick."

I wasn't seeing most of the advertising that people who were connected to the network were. Ad blockers were illegal. Getting caught with one cost you a fine of fifty credits per day, which a lot of people paid, or avoided through some software trickery. I screened them out internally, so no one could tell that the ads were optional for me unless they were in the real world. It was evidence that the Siren Corporation was great, but not perfect.

Speaking of ads, the New Zero Wellness Council paid for a

real holographic sign that hovered near the metal street as we passed ground level that read; "Every kindness you do yourself today is a gift to your future self." That stuck with me because it was a philosophy I'd never heard before. Sure, some may scoff at it, dismissing it as obvious, but it clicked with me.

"We're coming up on the coordinates," Perri announced as we came back up and started speeding along on a ground level street. "Manny's disappointed that he couldn't pick you up, by the way."

"No helping it, the Daring Dream wouldn't fit here," Duncan replied before I could.

"He knows, but he's really looking forward to doing something other than calibration and system check cruises in orbit. He's already docked in the Themis Complex," Mimi said before pausing and asking; "Are you sure this is a good target? He's no cold boy, you know."

For those who don't know or remember, a cold boy is someone who has replaced almost their entire body with basic or sub-standard cybernetic parts. Rimda Divos qualified as street metal, a cyborg who has almost no human parts left after upgrading to combat grade hardware. Rimda was also a little crazy. "His bounty started at seven thousand plat and it's already up to nine. New Zero Law wants this guy taken out as soon as possible. It's a Mass Murder Conviction."

"I know. The Hunter Chasers, you know, the cuckoo fans, are already crazy about this one. Whatever you do will probably be all over the feeds live if you're in range of any sensors. Wait, the bounty just went up two hundred credits. How's that happening? Is he killing more people?" Mimi asked.

"Boosters. Family members and the Good Guy AI Company are adding to the pot because they're afraid he'll get away,"

Duncan explained as he made sure both his sidearms were securely in their shoulder holsters. "Ready here."

"Me too." My boots were firmly affixed to my feet, and the gun I was smuggling between my legs was moved to the holster on my waist. "I'm picking the target up on sensors, but he's trying to get into the old industrial towers. He's smart, not breaking in so he doesn't set alarms off."

"Oh, well, maybe you should let him run around awhile so they can add a few more plat?" Mimi suggested. "Wait, never mind. The fans are tracking two more hunters who said they're on their way. Zigguard and Navras Edrin. Mid-listers on the Themis Board. The nearest one is two hundred ten kilometres out."

"They're probably not the only hunters on their way. Good thing we're here." I pulled the sliding side door open. I spoke to Perri then. "Activate the caution signal, stay on the ground level street and slow down to fifty kilometres per hour."

"I'll go around and drop right behind him. I'm watching your feed," Duncan said, tapping the side of his helmet.

My digital side was tracking Rimda using New Zero's sensor network and I was sharing the feed with Duncan. "This is my stop. Head to the Daring Dream and get ready. We're going to the Old Union tonight."

I could hear Perri cheer; "Finally!" and Mimi wish me luck as I leapt from the shuttle. I made the transition from conveyance to ground seamlessly, literally hitting the ground running. The hunter community had evidence that I was some kind of cyborg, and pretty much everyone else was fooled into thinking I was street metal. I think most of them wanted to believe it because I was doing good work. They wouldn't be surprised if someone proved I was an android using sensor data though, so I was thankful that Themis didn't accept bounties submitted by Bio First organisations or associates.

My target, Rimda Divos, had just been recorded destroying a data processing centre. Billions of platinum worth in quantum computing power was incinerated. There was also a grey matter bank where human brains were directly connected to computers for processing power or fast communication.

The Good Guy AI company was furious. The Bio First Movement was just starting to sputter hateful remarks about the act. They simplified the issue by talking about all the human minds that were destroyed instead of celebrating the ruin of tons of quantum computing power. It was a little strange.

Most of the destruction was in the middle of an industrial sky scraper. The footage I saw showed that flames were still licking the upper floors as firefighting ships sprayed foam at it from every side. Whatever explosives Rimda used were powerful and probably expensive.

So far, Good Guy AI put five thousand platinum behind the bounty while the Bio First organisation added three thousand. The rest of the boosters weren't adding much to the plat stack, so they aren't really worth mentioning. Most of them believed in supporting bounties so they could see justice done, or they were hunter fans. As an android pretending to be a cyborg, I was tickled that the Bio First Movement was paying out for this one.

The money was promising, but what made Rimda a great target for me was the justice side of it. He just killed hundreds of people who were helpless, some of them no more than brains in containment, using several incendiary bombs. It only took eighteen minutes for New Zero Judicial to review the evidence, verify its validity, and make a judgement in absentia. They didn't even bother calling Rimda. Instead they went ahead and set a HATE Notice up with Themis.

I verified the evidence myself. Rimda joined the Good Guy AI security team that night and spent a couple of hours planting incendiary devices around the complex before setting them off. The main data processing hub for the company, where several top tier artificial intelligences were running, was destroyed along with their grey matter processing hub. An act that would cost the company over thirty billion in earnings that month. I know, the bounty is peanuts considering, but it was a righteous hunt and I spotted the target less than a kilometre from the rooftop party.

To every city there is an underside, and that starts at the ground level for New Zero. I passed a boxy, dented, graffiti-covered trash collection robot as I sped down a side street. At first I was a little careful so my dress didn't trip me up, but it was easy to get used to, and before long I was running at almost eighty kilometres per hour. My boots were armoured, military grade, but I'd also added sound dampening unit to their soles. If I didn't, my clomping footsteps would precede me everywhere.

The manufacturing district was a land of doors. There were few windows at street level, but metal hatches of almost every shape and size dotted the walls. Simple robots and hover trucks moved down the street, pushing through the stench of rotten bio matter that thickened the air. I was getting close to Rimda, who was turning down a side street, looking for an unlocked doorway. I was ahead of him, in a sensor blind spot at the other end, so I slowed down to a casual walk.

I pinged his location on the tactical map I was sharing with Duncan. Our shuttle moved in, dropping him off around the corner behind Rimda. "I'm closing in from behind, drifting," Duncan said over our crew's secure comm channel.

When he said; 'drifting,' he meant that he'd activated little grav-pads in his boots that pushed him a couple of centimetres off the duracrete surface of the street so he could push himself along as gracefully as if he was skating on ice. Not that I've ever been ice skating, but I've seen old videos. It's pretty similar, and it looks kinda funny when he's doing it, if I'm being honest. That is until you see how fast he can move.

"Don't come up too fast. I want him to see me first," I said as I peeked around the next corner.

"Right, I get ya," he replied.

With my ten millimetre Rigour Revolver in my left hand and the Violator Seven in my right, I let the energy all around me hit my sensors. The tactical map in my mind filled in, and I could see Rimda trying the handle of a thick metal door open just around the corner.

I stepped into the open with both guns aimed at him. It was a pretty good setup with me at one end of the alley fifteen point six metres away from the target and Duncan at the opposite end, forty point two metres behind Rimda. "Come peacefully and I'll make sure you're alive when I turn you in. I'll even pay to store your hardware so you have it when you get out. Rehabilitation is better than termination."

"I saw the bounty. Hunt and Terminate. The Corp wants me dead. The government wants me dead. Why wouldn't you?" he asked, turning away from the door slowly.

"Don't worry about the bounty, just look at the weaponry," I made a bigger show of taking aim. "One's set up with capture rounds. The other is made to burn holes through your vital case."

"The bounty. Last time I checked the 'net, the hunter fan freaks were all crazy because it's going up. What's it up to now? Who's pumping it?" he asked as he slowly raised one arm. He was holding the other close to his body and it didn't look right.

The scan results I was getting were scattered, difficult to interpret.

I decided to play along because he wasn't being aggressive. "New Zero Judicial convicted you in absentia of Mass Murder after reviewing three point six gigabytes of sensor data and testimony from security software. The base bounty is five thousand platinum, a HATE notice issued by Themis."

"The big time. You're planning on taking me in alive?" he laughed a little before glancing over his shoulder at Duncan, who was standing in the alley behind him. "Now that guy looks like a hunter."

"I don't kill unless I have to or I'm outnumbered," I explained to him. "You'll be in a pod before daybreak, safe, on your way to rehabilitation."

"Bullshit! They'll crack my case, plug my grey matter into a processing cluster where they'll use my brain to calculate corporate bullshit until I don't know who I am anymore. Rehab?" His left arm unravelled and dropped to his side as five metal tendrils.

Those were metal tentacles. My least favourite cybernetic device. I pulled the trigger of my Rigour Revolver. The shot was dead on, sending a round that unpacked at the last millisecond into a tough capture pouch that spread out like a net. It caught nothing but air and lay on the ground as it discharged an electric pulse, working perfectly other than completely failing to capture Rimda.

It turns out that he was so fast that he sidestepped my shot the instant before I finished pulling the trigger. He started running towards me. The light of my Violator firing burning rounds at him lit the alley as the sound of three shots cracked the air. One hit, piercing his left shoulder. The remnant of the round sparked blue and white. The newer bullets I'd gotten from Spectral Dynamics had better accuracy, more armour piercing power, and they burned for a shorter period but were much hotter. I sidestepped a blast from his blade ripper. It was a security model, so there was a chance that it could pierce my vacsuit then my skin and do real damage.

As I came around to fire at him again, all of his metal tendrils came together to form a blunt object and hit me in the stomach like an alloy fist. Being short for a human and having a modest weight often worked in my favour. It didn't then though. He hit me so hard that I went flying backwards out of the alley before touching down thirty-one metres away where I rolled for a while.

Duncan didn't worry about using non-lethal measures. He fired one of his custom pulse blasters with his right hand while his left activated a hilt. Its core telescoped out and an energy field surrounded it, forming a blade with a sharp, strong edge. Rimda didn't stand his ground like some tough guy, which is something I'd seen with a lot of cyborgs. He dodged around the alley as he fired his blade shooter, chipping the plating on Duncan's new jacket and damaging his helmet.

We'd switched places. Now Duncan was holding our target's attention. Ending the encounter was up to me. I fired my revolver once, trying to bag Rimda, but I missed again. The first triple-shot with my Violator didn't hit its mark as I ran towards him.

I was being careful, making sure I didn't hit Duncan, so my second burst didn't come until I was fifteen metres away from our target. All three hit Rimda in the waist, and something broke, slowing his right leg down. Rimda tripped, two of the five metal tentacles from his right shoulder reached down so he could stabilise himself. The other three whipped out at Duncan so fast that he couldn't stop them from wrapping around his helmet and neck.

Duncan's blade came down, cutting the tendrils neatly. My next burst severed the rest of the tentacles at the shoulder. The next three rounds cut right through his hip joints, and Rimda fell apart, face down. I walked over as he tried to flip himself onto his back with one arm.

"Don't move. Don't try anything. You're easier to bring in dead," I said as I flipped him onto his back. Rimda fired his blade ripper, but I got lucky as the shots harmlessly shattered against the wall to his right. I crushed the weapon's barrel. Duncan wrapped his capture belts around Rimda's remaining arm, chest and legs and activated them. As they strained to overcome the motors in Rimda's shoulder to trap his arm against his side, Duncan said; "Gotcha, bugger. You shoulda surrendered."

"No shit!" Rimda laughed. "At least I didn't kill a couple hunters. The rehab for that would be a real bitch, right?"

"Where's your grey matter? Head or chest?" I asked as my scanners bounced off his head and vital case. His tech must have been expensive. It was illegal to buy that kind of scanner defeating skin in New Zero.

"Why? You delivering the HATE? I'm not saving you time," he stopped struggling and chuckled at Duncan.

"What's the laugh about?" Duncan asked.

"You take me in alive and I'll tell you. Just promise to get me off the street quick," he replied.

"Calling for pickup now." I would have either way. We were on the edge of the city sensor network, and I knew there was a remote chance a crooked hunter might come along to snatch our bounty.

"Well, here's the joke. It was a bloody setup!" Rimda shouted, mirth turning to anger. "The Bio buggers own my ass! All this gear, whatever's in my account, they paid for all of it so I could join their squads. Good Guy AI was their target. I was supposed to melt servers down, just quantum processors running a few thousand high end programs."

"You didn't know there were human minds in there?" I asked.

"No, hell no," he replied. "Get New Zero law to look at all that, and I bet the Wanted List will light up with thousands of Bio First terrorists," he plead. "They're anarchist luddites, want us to wipe out all AI and everyone who doesn't look human."

"I'll make sure they know what you told me before sentencing," The signal I sent requesting a high security pickup was acknowledged. There was one on the way. Hunting on the ground had become so common that there was a taxi service specifically for us. They were watching for hunting activity on the city sensor network, so it was landing seconds after I called for it.

"How do I know you're not just saying you'll talk to someone?" Rimda asked.

"You don't, but I present all evidence when I turn my captures in, so they'll see this conversation," I replied.

As Rimda was about to speak, Duncan fired a stun round into his open mouth. He just twitched the first time, but was knocked out the second. "Think there's truth to any of that?"

"That he didn't know there was grey matter around before he blew the installation up? No. He knew. He was a member of their security team," I replied.

"I'm with ya there, but what about his gear-up?" he asked.

"That Bio-First paid for his rig?" I asked, scanning Rimda's unmoving form again. His skin scattered my attempts, but I picked up one of his severed legs and took a closer look. Feeling around for serial numbers was more enlightening. Judging from the shape of the limb, I knew where they ought to be etched but found nothing. "There are no identifying markings on this. I'm guessing all his gear is custom."

"Untraceable one-offs," Duncan agreed as he took a look as well. "Aye, if there's a marking, it's on the inside. You'd have to take the whole thing apart."

"All right, we'll hand his parts in with him, just in case they need it for the investigation," I said.

"Unmarked military gear? That'll sell for a stack," Duncan said.

I looked into the broken end of the leg and scanned inside thoroughly. His skin was resistant, but the inside of each component wasn't, so I got a really clear picture. "All right, compromise then. I'll hand my scans in and we'll take his parts with us. We can't sell them on the open market here, but, who knows?"

"That's sound," Duncan nodded. "The fences and dodgy docs I know will rob ya blind, no question. They'll do it quick if you want the plat tonight, mind you."

"I'll wait for a better opportunity. The bounty went up to fourteen thousand before the city sensors saw him go down," I said.

"Sensors caught it?" Duncan asked.

Mimi broke into our channel then. It turned out she was listening all along. "The ones on the top of the Hiren Gull Building caught it all, even his confession. Pieces of the footage are scrolling on all the medias now. Your dress is going big in the fashion categories, the Hunter Chasers are crazy about Duncan's tentacle cut move, and the fail fans are replaying a vid of you getting punched down the street, Rogue. Oh, no. There are a bunch of so-called cyborg experts saying that would have knocked most out for a while at least. They're saying you must be an android or some kinda ultra high-end military 'borg."

I got a sinking feeling as my disdain for many people who practically lived on social media sharpened. "Well, time to leave."

"After we collect the dosh," Duncan said as he picked Rimda up.

I grabbed his legs and left the metal tentacles behind. "We're getting off world tonight. If Bio First is getting tricky, I might not see them coming."

"Good thinking," Duncan said. "I'm guessing that was the last of our luck, right there."

The armoured shuttle's lights flashed as an armoured man emerged from the aft ramp. "Hey, you guys need a box to put him in? Only fifty plat."

"Not for that price," Duncan laughed.

"We're in a hurry. Direct hand in at the Themis Complex," I told the copilot.

"Yes, Ma'am," he said, pulling Rimda into a thick walled metal bin and closing the lid. He hesitated for a moment, regarding us as we took our places on the padded bench seats at the back. "You two are the best dressed hunters I've seen in a while. An anomalous delight, I'll say."

"Ah, I do my best," Duncan said, his voice distorted by the old speaker built into his helmet.

After a final glance at the two of us, the copilot rushed to the cockpit. "Straight to the TC, no stops!"

Duncan removed his helmet and leaned close so he could whisper. "Third hottest hunt of the night. Mimi's right, this capture's public. Big outrage at what this bugger said about the Bio First buggers. New questions. Sure we don't have time for an appearance at the Old Union?"

I thought for a moment. The Old Union was the centre of Freelance Law Enforcement, but I'd never been there. It was the missing piece of my Hunter life. Even though I loved New Zero, I always thought I would move on, so I didn't go out of my way to be social. Facing the reality that I really should leave the planet as soon as possible or face a squad of Enforcers, I wished I'd taken the time to visit the popular spot. With plenty of regret weighing the words down, I said; "I'm all dressed up, so sure. That is unless it looks like Bio First comes after me tonight."

Mimi spoke through our comms. "Those rumours that you're not a cyborg are spreading exponentially. It might be dangerous."

"All right. Tell everyone to prep the Dream. We're taking care of business in the Themis Complex first. I hope we'll have time for a stop, but we should be ready to go," I said.

"Don't get me wrong, I've wanted to see the Old Union for a while, but where are we gonna go after that?" Mimi asked.

"We'll find out soon." I sent a message to the Haven Fleet Hunter Facility stating that we'd be moving up to their Privateering Program. I needed to know where it was based.

"Grand," Duncan said. "Might need to stop in at the ship to change my shorts, if I'm being honest. Life flashed when he put that tentacle around my neck. Thought he'd squeeze my noggin right off."

I laughed softly and looked through the thick transparisteel window. We watched New Zero city go by outside, admiring the forest of skyscrapers, holographic ads for new licensable fabrication patterns for all kinds of household objects, and the fast lights of hover cars and shuttles.

CHAPTER THREE

Looking Forward

Trips to the Themis Complex should never get tiresome. Every time you show up there to hand a bounty in it means three good things. You've captured a target without killing them. You've made society a little better. You're getting paid.

So, I'd love to tell you that I was able to keep all that in mind when I was turning Rimda Divos in along with all the recordings I had of my encounter with him, but I was getting tired of visiting the Themis Complex. He was the twenty-eighth person I dropped off that month.

Was Rimda a danger to society? Yes. Was he going to be punished properly? Maybe. They could execute him instead of dropping him into a pod for rehabilitation. That was entirely up to New Zero Judicial. Should I care? No. I did though, so I scanned his DNA and opened a file in my memory with his ident and every recording I found or made of him.

The capture felt sour even after I dropped him off. I spent twenty credits for a box on little wheels that was large enough for all of Rimda's parts. They were definitely illegal on Tabrus since they were completely unmarked custom armoured pieces. I didn't detect any tracking signals, but that didn't mean that there wasn't something in a leg or the arm that wouldn't turn on. The absence of anything that could explode was the only thing I was absolutely certain about.

I would have been sullen if Duncan wasn't with me. He still knew more hunters than I did and he was more social. The Themis Turn In Centre was busy so I watched him talk to people as we waited in line. I could tell that the newer hunters were curious about me, but they didn't approach. The others, who I'd seen around but didn't really know, kept their distance.

When he ran into a hunter named Wyvern I was immediately singled out. Wyvern bundled his long black hair into a ponytail and regarded me with the biggest grin. "Spin me, it's Rogue. I see you online, making kidnappers disappear."

"Good to see ya, Wyvern." Duncan looked amused that he was just ignored.

"Duncan, you know I always feel recharged at the sight of you, acknowledge?" he asked.

"I hear ya, but I don't have your total recall, so greetings are still grand," Duncan replied, pointing at the top of Wyvern's head.

I noticed that Wyvern was wearing a vacsuit that must have been a Haven Fleet model. He'd turned his white and dressed up in a long dark shirt with matching trousers. The only things that made him look like a hunter were the forty millimetre launcher slung on his back, the bandolier of red and blue shells for it, and his boots.

Wyvern regarded me and spoke as though we weren't in line, but in a pub or a casual party. "He outs me every chance. I had an accident years ago, and my captain at the time spent all my pips on a memory module that's off the market since. Synced memory modules. Stores the whole range of digital, visual, tactile, and emotional better than anyone's normal grey. You make me feel something, and I'll never forget it, have it for future recall in or out of sim space. Makes some people uncomfortable. Not good for grudges, I'll say, but it's premium for tracking."

"Which is good for settling a grudge," I said with a crooked smile.

"Oh, this one. I am liking this one. Thinks in future steps, I bet. Hoped I would enjoy meeting you, Rogue. Handing a psycho cyborg in?" he tapped the cheap box I'd put Rimda's head and torso in before placing him on a gurney.

"Go on now, you already know what's in there," Duncan chided playfully.

"Just conjuring conversation. Hey, saw Veronica. Seemed happy, but I had to fake the nice feelings," Wyvern told him. "Says she's..."

Duncan interrupted him. "We're not running together anymore. Rogue's my Captain now."

"Yeah good. Never liked Veronica, even in beginning times, before the mind mechanism. She said..." Wyvern's voice was lowering as he spoke, but he was cut short again.

"All ancient history, lad. We're moving on soon. Who are you handing in?" Duncan asked.

Wyvern spoke rapidly as he went on, but he kept his voice down. "Fangu gang. We got Gecko, their leader. Big credits on this one, but bigger soon. The crew is chasing while the rest of the gang members are scattering, trying to rush to the wastes, but satellites are watching now. Wastes aren't worth hiding in anymore. We'll get 'em tonight, acknowledge?"

"Six figures easy if you bag half those bastards, good hunting," Duncan replied. "Wait, you guys corp up?"

"Yeah, we went corpy. Only way to run a crew and a ship while running New Zero at this chrono point. Maybe time to move on, we're not corp like the colossals. Rethinking where we cast our shadows after tonight, like every night. But, hey, got to love the moment first, right? Taking big stacks this minute, not just handfuls of pips. Good luck, good efficiency turned earnings up."

"Fair play to ya. Say hi to Captain Brooke for me, yeah?" Duncan said. "Doubt I'll see you any time soon unless we end up knocking around the same solar system."

"Where are you leaving to?" Wyvern asked.

"We're joining the Haven Privateering Initiative. I don't know where it'll take us," I replied.

"That's a better thing if you have the ship. What's the ship?" he asked.

"The Daring Dream, but I'm keeping the details to myself." Before I finished speaking, Wyvern cocked his head as he took on a vacant look.

"He's getting a message," Duncan explained, pointing at his temple.

Wyvern bowed briefly but deeply. "Time to go. Hand in finished. Safe travels."

"Good hunting," I said as he turned and walked away quickly.

"He's a bit of an odd one, but I've always liked him. Just don't be borrowing plat off him—debts gnaw at him like a little bird pecking at his ear." Duncan said.

"Is he a good hunter?" I asked, not able to find anything about Wyvern online.

"Great in a group. He's a silent coordinator, like you. Doesn't need to speak to communicate verbally on comms, just thinks right into the signal," he replied.

"No wonder you're never surprised when I do it. Were you on the same crew together?" I asked, circling my curiosity about Veronica.

"Aboard the Domina. Good ship, but the crew didn't get along for long. We're next," he said as we reached the head of our line.

The hand in went smoothly, and I got a short call with someone from New Zero Judicial, who told me that they'd review the evidence I submitted before sentencing. That would have to be enough.

I didn't have time to find out what happened to a mass murderer. The Bio First Enforcers were out. They wore the same big mechanised suits as local law enforcement. The small mech armour was made for taking androids and larger robots on and the Enforcers came in squads of five.

I found footage online as we made our way up to our next stop. I didn't share it with Duncan, in fact, I was quiet for a while after watching it. It played back in my head with perfect clarity.

Five Enforcers dropped in front of a hover car in time to stop it with a directed electromagnetic pulse. They tore at the thin hull of the craft until the three androids inside tried to run. Each of the non-combat androids looked perfectly human and there was nothing artificial about their terror.

Next the Enforcers pinned the androids using rounds that exploded into metal webbing. Then the mechs closed in and blasted them with plasma cannons until they were nothing but a pile of half melted parts. I couldn't believe they were operating in New Zero.

My mood wasn't great as I silently contacted Ensign Ito. Her office gave me directions right away, and I was relieved that we didn't have to visit the large main turn-in section. I was deep in thought as we walked down the long, white and blue meeting room hallway. "Which one are we looking for?"

"Twenty-nine," I replied.

"Want a lift?" he asked, activating his boots and hovering up a few centimetres.

"How's that?" I asked.

He extended his hand and I took it as he glanced down at his boots. "Step on up."

I did, putting my feet on top of his, almost losing my balance before I slipped my arm around him. He gently pushed forward with one foot and leaned forward a little. We drifted down the long hallway. "How do we stop?" I asked, enjoying the embrace more than the lift.

"Don't worry, I've gotcha," he said, earning a little squeal from me as we picked up speed. We passed Room Twenty-five before he turned the antigravity hover pads built into his boots down and we parted. He and I both slowed by running a few steps. "You're a natural. Should look into getting some hover pads built into those clompers."

"When I find better boots," I said, smiling at him. "Definitely. Were yours expensive?"

"Well, I found them in a salvage bin, so, can't say they were," he replied. "Took the pads from the trashed boots, installed them in these."

Door Twenty-Nine slipped aside as we approached and we settled in on a sofa that weighed so little that it moved when I sat down. It was comfortable in a familiar way, though. There were three seats, each made for two, arranged in a circle. "These are nice," Duncan said as he sat to my right.

"They're a lot like the kind of furniture that Haven started making for their bigger space stations. They like thick padding like this that adjusts to whoever has a seat," I explained.

"Is it smart? Is there a program running in there, figuring my arse out?" he asked, shifting around.

I laughed. "No, it's just the nature of the cushions. These ones are light though, like the furniture Perri's making for the Dream. Maybe we could license the fab pattern for the cushions when we get wherever we're going."

"Grand that they don't need some computer program to make the seat comfy. Feels like there's a program keeping tabs on everything in New Zero." He said. "Afraid I'm too used to it and the sensors. Even my Third Eye proggy runs so much I've forgotten to turn it off overnight."

"I've got something like that, only it's internal." His Third Eye software used whatever sensors he was wearing and could use invisible protective films that he'd added to his eyes. Mine was, well, you know, my digital side, which ran in a computer sitting in my chest, right under my bio-brain.

"Do you turn yours off? You know, sometimes, when you're sleeping or the like?" he asked.

"Sure. Well, more like I ignore it, or my digital side monitors it. Worrying is the worst, though. If my less logical side is worried about something, my digital side starts looking for solutions. It's helpful most of the time, but it would be nice to just be worried sometimes, you know?" The list of things that my digital side liked to work on wasn't short, and I hadn't told him about the biggest problems. Looking back, I wonder which one of us was actually withholding more. "Why do you ask?"

"You had that look about ya while we were handing in. What've ya got brewing?" he asked.

"It's Rimda. I believe him when he says Bio First paid for upgrades and sent him to Good Guy AI," I explained.

"But not that shite about him not knowing there were real people connected to processing hubs in there," he added.

"Right. He knew, so Bio First probably knew. If they sent him there, then they don't care if the computers running AI are hardware or bio-ware. Computers or people. They just want the tech to burn," I replied, aware that everything I said was possibly being observed and definitely recorded.

"I'm trying not to think about that. If I'm straight with ya, I like a lot of what the Bio First buggers are after. Jobs for people, making sure programs don't control us all so biologicals aren't left starving and all that. If you're right, and I think you are, then it's going to shite with the wrong corps controlling smart programs, so..." he finished with an exaggerated shrug, lifting his hands up helplessly.

"Fundamentalism. That's what I see when Bio First comes up. They're not looking to prevent the next virus that comes along from finding a vulnerability in programs with an AI built in. They aren't looking at who caused the Fourth Fall, or spending more time elevating sentient biological life than punishing androids for something they had no power to stop. All they want is to erase AI, but there's no balance in their thinking," I said.

"Like a mutt going for the stick and not the fella swinging it," Duncan agreed.

"Right." It was refreshing to share my point of view, which I generally kept to myself. The Bio First Movement had a public reputation for championing humanity, and it was hard to argue against them. "I guess I'm a centrist. I like balance. It's harder to accomplish, and maintaining it can seem impossible, but a lot of things that are worthwhile are. That's how I think, anyway," I said with a shrug of my own.

"Look, I know you're fond of New Zero, but things are getting messy for ya. The wolves are circling. I've been holding off asking why we're still hanging about. The rest of the crew might be too green to see it, but we could've lifted off a week back and done the last of the calibrations ourselves. What exactly are we hangin' about for?" His tone was gentle, like he expected me to take his question as criticism.

I paused for a moment as my digi-brain offered an answer instantly, but I thought I owed him more than a few words. My bio-brain was a little better at that. "The Spectral Dynamics specialists were faster and there were a few features I wanted them to add so we wouldn't have to rewire or modify anything later. Then there's the problem of leaving while we're broke," I finished, seeing that he understood.

"Now, that's an answer," he laughed. "Well, everyone's wondering where we're off to next. I know, I know—you've said we're joining the Privateering Initiative, but we're a bit light on the details."

"I've got leads. The Ryden Corporation is active in the Rose System, and some of the data I got from Corosa gives us a head start. I've only shared a few things with Haven Fleet, the rest I've been keeping for us. The big targets will definitely take us out of the solar system." I glanced around, wordlessly suggesting that people may be listening and I saw that he understood.

"Right, so we're holding off on sharing 'til we're up in the air. Fair enough. I don't usually take things on faith, but you've never given me reason to doubt ya. At least tell me you've some idea where those whoresons Carosa were shipping the sleepers to," he asked.

I only nodded as a door opposite the one we came through

opened and Ensign Ito came through. "I apologise for being late, it's been that kind of day."

"Don't worry, we've just been talking. Care to weigh in?" I asked.

"Assuming that I've been listening, and you're right. I caught the last few minutes. I'll send you everything we have on the Ryden ships we've spotted. There's not much, but there are routes. As for Bio First, well, I don't want to see you and your team leave, but I agree with Duncan. If you're going to leave, it should be in the next hour, preferably," she said.

"Has anyone started looking for Order operatives in the Bio Movement?" I asked.

"Other than you? Yes. We haven't found an Order operative among them, but we're watching. Personally, I think programs and biologicals can work together, I've seen it, and the laws are evolving back home, where greater minds than mine are working on the balance," she said as she sat on the last unoccupied sofa made for two.

"I'd say that's about fair," Duncan said, looking around warily. "So, do you record everything said here?"

"Only in our section of the Themis Complex, but we delete most of it after twenty days. Whatever else gets protected behind Haven Fleet's security system. One good question deserves another; how is your crew and the little queen doing?" Ensign Ito asked.

"I think they're tired of training and installing furniture, but they're turning into a tight crew. Mimi's pretty much the same, except she's a little disappointed that I didn't bring her with me," I replied.

"Ah, she's in her own little heaven, mad about the ship and her new post as Comms Officer. Just hope she doesn't lose her

bleeding mind when she realises how easy Rimda went down."
Duncan added.

"Congratulations on capturing him. The Complex is buzzing
a bit because New Zero doesn't want him, and they don't want to
execute him, either," Ensign Ito said.

"So, what'll happen?" I asked, interested in what the Ensign
would say. I'd seen a few solutions to that problem, and didn't
like most of them.

"Well, if you brought someone with a HATE notice on them
in alive, then I'd have a few options. I could send them to the
Haven System where they'd be reviewed for rehabilitation, monitored release or exile. Execution is a last resort, but it has been
done. I could put them into the penal system here on Tabrus if
any of the law enforcement divisions want them, and then they
do whatever they like. Usually someone sponsors their rehabilitation or there's an execution," Ensign Ito replied. "Other than
that, you'd know more than I would."

"Aye. I bet our friend Rimda will release him with a basic
frame - pipes and shite joints. Well, that's if they don't execute
him, but that might piss some Bio First people off," Duncan said.
"Politics are damn thick here. Another reason to leave."

"True," I told him, hoping to stop future reminders. It was
time to go, I knew it. "I think they'll execute him if Bio First has
anything to do with it. He could tell the whole planet that they
sent him to blow up Good Guy AI." My digital and biological
sides were both in agreement then. I was also thoroughly tired of
the current politics in New Zero. "Has the Privateering Initiative
reviewed the scans? Has the Daring Dream cleared?" I wasn't
sure if it would since the scans I sent weren't complete. I wanted
the Daring Dream to keep as many of her secrets as possible.

"It has. It definitely qualifies in terms of armour and speed.

You're low on firepower but make it over the bar just barely. I don't recommend you go after any Order corvettes or destroyers. Your crew has passed their background checks as well. The only step left is an in-person interview, which won't happen here. I'm authorised to give you the navigation data you need to move on. I have one question first."

It was difficult to hold my excitement in, but I managed to turn what would have been a cheek splitting grin down to a something more demure. "Ask away."

"Are you going to continue trying to find out why the Order are taking live humans? We haven't found anything for weeks. I'm hoping you'll stay on it. They're using Ryden and other corporate partners to hide something big," Ensign Ito said.

"I've stayed on it. Now that Mimi's a trained comms officer, she's been chasing that too," I told her.

"They've marked out some prime targets. Enough to catch the eye of any pirate worth their water," Duncan said.

"We don't officially sanction that term - pirating. Privateers, contractors, or commissioned freelancers are in the lexicon," Ensign Ito said. "So, any other targets besides Ryden?"

"It's a big list. Is there any word back from Haven Fleet Intelligence about Tulip Island?" I asked, glancing at Duncan, who sat up with interest.

"No. Have you noticed any activity?" Ensign Ito asked.

Updates came from Red Gate Station every two days, and no one managed to dock with it. The three ships that tried were damaged by its defences, so they turned away.

Red Gate had sensors pointed at Tulip Island too. "No one's gone down to pick flowers."

"Ah, now you've lost me," Duncan muttered.

"I'll catch you up later," I told him.

"Well, unless there are other questions, we can move on to the bittersweet part," Ensign Ito said.

"No fresh questions popping up. And anyway, I'm just the First Officer," Duncan replied.

I wasn't sure if he was a little irritated at being left out of the loop where Warro, Red Gate and Tulip Island were concerned, but I pressed on. "I'm ready to go, you just have to tell me where and when."

"At your convenience, and I'm sending you navigation data through a secure connection now. We're going to miss you here. Good luck," Ensign Ito said.

It was time to move on, but I gave her a hug before leaving.

CHAPTER FOUR

Interception

Imagining how my life would end wasn't something I did often. When I was in New Zero I imagined that it would happen while I was cornered. Maybe it would be Haven Fleet coming to bring me in for study, or to eliminate me because I caused too much trouble. Unlikely, sure, but nightmares feed on fear and doubt, not what's probable. I could also get taken by a bounty that tricked rehabilitation software into thinking they were ready to be released, or another hunter who thought a bounty I took in should have been theirs. The Order of Eden could figure out who and where I am. You get the point, there are so many ways to get trapped and destroyed.

Sometimes considering how you might be outdone is healthy if you're in real danger. Sure, you can take things too far, become obsessed and paranoid, but I was trained to accept the fact that trying to predict every scenario was impossible. There is a balance between preparation and paranoia. I like to think I'm pretty good at finding it.

Manny landed the Daring Dream in a hunter's hangar because I forgot to tell him that we would be in the Haven section of the Themis Complex. Duncan and I were leaving the transit car when my internal tactical system lit up. There were five heavily armoured soldiers waiting. Their gear looked new, and they were armed with plasma rifles made to take robots down. They'd set up a sensor scattering field that kept me from seeing them until we were out of the transit car.

"Enforcers," Duncan said, drawing both of his pulse blasters.

I was completely still beside him. A harsh siren blared once as the light in the small station turned red. "This transit has been shut down. Please find alternative transportation," announced an automated voice. The car was blocking the tunnel. Escaping that way would be difficult.

The Enforcer in the middle stepped forward, his boot steps accompanied by the cranking sound of his armour's strength augmentation system. "Rogue. You are in violation of the Android Anti-Obfuscation Act. Surrender for processing immediately or be deactivated." It was the voice of Lieutenant Long, the police officer who failed to catch the Carosa Transportation Company when they visited their hangar.

"Funny thing, I was just on my way off world. I'll be out of the solar system in twenty minutes. You can tell your bosses that you rushed me off, Lieutenant Long."

"We have orders to take you in," he announced. "You may turn yourself off."

"My companion isn't wanted. Let him go," I said, slowly sinking to my knees and raising my hands.

"Not goin' anywhere," Duncan said.

"Yes, you are," I told him firmly.

"Listen to the droid. It isn't worth sacrificing yourself for." said Lieutenant Long.

"Over my dead body are those gobshites taking ya in," Duncan told me, pointing both of his handguns at Long's helmet.

"We're outnumbered and outgunned. I'll be shutting down, so it'll be pretty awkward if you're still here," I said, trying to clue him into my plan.

"No reason to go making it easy for them." Duncan was determined to stand his ground.

"I need you to be my First Officer now. Take care of the crew." I slipped my bracelet off. It wasn't worth more than a few pips, but the Haven Communications Node inside it was still valued at over ten thousand platinum. I winked at him so the soldiers couldn't see as he took it.

"Aye, Captain," he said, slowly slipping his weapons in their underarm holsters one at a time.

"That's right, move on, Irish," one of the soldiers said.

Duncan regarded him with a sneer as he walked towards them with his hands up. "Up the Irish Union."

Mimi's voice was in my head. She'd contacted me through the encrypted crew channel. "There are hunters on the way. A lot of people who were just handing in. They're hurrying, but they say that part of the building is blocked off."

I used my internal communicator to reply so no one saw me speaking. "I'll try to buy time, but this is probably going to get ugly. Our tram stop is blocked off. Tell them to go one level above and use the elevator."

"Oh, okay," Mimi replied.

My chances of getting away from them were low. Sure, I might take two or maybe three down, but not all five. These people were wearing gear made to fight powerful machines. I couldn't see anything past ten metres in any direction thanks to the scramblers Long's men were using, so I had no way of knowing how far away reinforcements were. I didn't like the idea of anyone sacrificing themselves for me, so I bought time, hoping that we could outgun them. I silently sent two quick messages out though. One to Mimi saying; "Thank you, Mimi. I'll get out of this."

The other message went out at the same time, directed at Ensign Ito. I hoped would force her to act. "The Bio First Enforcers are about to take me into custody. They waited until I was out of the Haven Section of the Themis Complex. Did you sell me out?" The message was sent with my current location and a snapshot of my tactical map so she could see that I was facing a squad of five armoured soldiers in green and white.

Duncan was almost out of the room, walking as slowly as he dared as two soldiers tracked him with their rifles. One wrong move and his scale armour coat would be tested to failure. He wouldn't last two seconds past that. I played for more time. "Listen, I'm human. A cyborg, sure, but there's still real biological grey matter in here. Any telepath, even a newbie using perso to peek into other people's heads, could see that I'm a real girl. A little weird, but you'd be arresting half of New Zero if that was a crime." I didn't actually know what a telepath would see if they focused on me, but I hoped any doubt I could plant in their minds would buy me more time.

"Perso is an outlawed harvested substance. If you have any doses on you, please present them now," Long replied, completely missing the point.

"No, I don't have any, I'm saying... never mind. I only want to save you some embarrassment. No harm has been done, I could still just leave. My ship is just down that hallway and around the corner in hangar..."

"We know where your ship is," Lieutenant Long said.

"I'm just saying that I'm on my way off world anyway. I was going to set a bunch of seals free on my way out, but I'll just head for the stars if you want. No stops. Track us, you'll see." I know, it sounds like I'm playing it cool. That was not true.

No one else knew it, but I was learning something about myself. I hate fundamentalists. The Order pushes their cash cult, accepting no religion or competing set of beliefs. The Bio First Movement wanted all artificial intelligence removed from Planet Tabrus, especially New Zero City. Those two organisations both inflict their non-compromising views on everyone until they are subjugated or incapable of resisting.

My digi-brain was on fire, aggravated to the core, and my biological side was focusing, allowing its counterpart to race through violent strategies. I'm not proud of it, but I didn't expect that they'd let me walk away and I was starting to look forward to the fight.

What Long said next didn't help. "Sources have informed us that you are a combat android made to stand in for a human. We will bring you in. Tests will be conducted and if what you're saying is true, you'll be set free."

"Funny, I've never heard of anyone getting back out after the Enforcers get them," I stated.

"We don't make mistakes," one of Long's men said. I could hear frustration brimming in his tone.

"Everyone makes mistakes. Like Lieutenant Long switching to the Bio First Enforcer squads. Couldn't handle me showing you up at the Carosa Company hangar?"

"That bust should have been mine," he replied, taking a step towards me.

"See, I thought you and your fellow officers were going to take care of them. You knew something was going on, that people were in danger, but you ran away because a few untrained people pointed guns at you while Kathy Sayli shouted you down. That must have been terrifying for you. Did you get help? Do you still have nightmares about her? I mean, I don't, but not everyone is cut out to face real criminals." I know how blurry situations can become when most people get angry. I wanted these guys to be furious.

"Slowly remove the weapon in your right holster and toss it aside," Lieutenant Long said.

I watched as Duncan reached the hallway and slipped out of sight. "You don't want this."

"What?" Lieutenant Long asked, making a show of pointing his rifle at my head.

That was a rookie mistake. Most military machines can keep fighting if you destroy any one appendage, including their head. Instead of answering him, I stared at his opaque faceplate defiantly.

"She said; 'you don't want this,'" said one of his soldiers.

"Are you using a trick holster? Will something happen if you draw your weapon a certain way?" another asked me directly, getting a little closer.

The giddiness that came as everything around me started to slow down brought a smirk to my lips. The soldier closest to the exit interrupted then. "Sir? There's activity on this level. Other hunters."

"Screw this, contain her," Lieutenant Long said, his words stretching out as I started experiencing time at a seventh the speed.

My digital side had turned its processing speed up seven times over and my biological mind was keeping up. The number of strategies I could consider multiplied, and I knew what I would do in less than a quarter second.

In the time it took the soldiers to his left and right to aim their forty millimetre barrels so they could hit me with electrified, sticky metal restraint rounds, I was on my feet and running towards Long. One followed through and fired, catching my left boot. My skin constricted from the shin down enough for me to pull my foot out without missing a step.

Lieutenant Long fired a burst with his much more lethal plasma rifle. One shot burned my left forearm down to the metal before I landed on his shoulders. The stabilising systems in his armour kept him on his feet as I perched, dropping low so I was nearly impossible to hit if they wanted to avoid shooting Long. My fingers found their way under the lip of his helmet and I gripped it so hard that the edge bent and started to creak.

He reached up, tried to grab me, so I took his wrist and yanked it behind his head. My fingers gripped his bracer until it cracked and closed until it hit bone. Then I twisted it. It had been so long since I'd used my full strength that I was surprised when the braces and synthetic muscle built into his armour stretched and snapped loudly, burying the sound of his popping shoulder. I let the arm drop. It fell limp. His head and neck protection was much tougher.

"Shoot her! Goddammit! She'll tear me apart!" Long shouted.

Still gripping his helmet from the lip along its underside, I quickly, violently yanked and turned it hard enough to break the rotary motor inside. After a little more than a second, Long was screaming and his helmet was stuck as though he was looking over his left shoulder.

The popping sound of a trap round going off behind me proceeded the thorough webbing of the corner as one of his soldiers tried to hit me and missed. The sound of Duncan's blasters from the door was music to my ears. White light struck the one soldier I could see from my panicking perch before he found cover behind a metal bench. Duncan was unrelenting, firing one handgun then the other over and over, melting the metal before the other soldiers returned fire, pushing him back around the corner.

I laughed, it must have sounded insane, because I did so at my speed, so quick that it probably sounded all wrong. Why was I laughing? My fingers found their way into a crack in Long's neckpiece. I slowed my speech down to a normal speed then. "Let me go and I won't rip his throat out!"

Two soldiers blasted me with metal restraint webbing. I leapt in time to get half out of it before it set, affixing me to Long's armour. Dark, violent options passed through my mind and I chose the most destructive way forward. It was a new strategy that depended on something I didn't even know my body could do until the idea crossed my minds.

New blood mixed in my lower torso and flowed outward, replacing my human fluid with something horrific. "You should have let me run, Lieutenant," I said to Long as the human simulation made me sweat red so my flesh could become a bomb.

"No machine should enforce law on humans," Long replied as his armour struggled to keep him on his feet.

"You're going to want to get out of your armour now." Saying the words seemed to take forever.

The level of anguish coursing through my outer flesh was beyond anything in Alice's or my experiences, and I left the human simulation running so I could feel it full on until the end. When my outer flesh was filled with poison I shut the pain down. "Goodbye," I said to him.

"She's doing something! Get ready!" one of his soldiers shouted.

"All that bleeding? It's just the metal strands cutting her up," reassured another.

"You all right, Lieutenant?" asked the third.

The last time I faced something like that, the bomb was inside me. It was different this time. The poisoned blood was actually Hadex, a liquid explosive used in anti-personnel bombs that explodes twice. Once when detonated, then a second time when much of the material is atomised and spreading.

The act of detaching from my outer flesh - the skin and flesh covering my entire body - was so dehumanising that my fury turned cold. I wanted to kill every Bio First soldier I could find. My metal body started pushing, pulling its way out of my outer flesh and the only words that could express the hate of the moment emerged. "You should have stayed with the police force."

It was the last thing those lips would ever say as I pulled free of my skin and the metal webbing holding it to Long's armour. I emerged, bare metal and internal organs visible to all as I leapt through the air, free. "Holy shit!" one soldier shouted.

"I can't see! What's she doing?" Long shouted, panicking as he struggled to open his chest plate, fighting the tough strands and powerful adhesive.

My metal feet touched the deck and I ran for the exit. "Get clear! Get clear!" I shouted with a sound emitter built into the back of my throat. The same message was broadcast over proximity radio.

As soon as I was around the corner, I remotely set my poisoned flesh and skin off. Duncan was right beside me with several other hunters, and I was surprised when he took me into his coat just in time. A little side note here: I would have been fine if he didn't, but the gesture meant everything. The force of the first explosion shook the deck a little, and I could feel the air pulse.

That wasn't the real thing though. When the second blast

went off point two-five seconds later, it felt like the universe punched me flying down the hallway.

I was on my feet before anyone else, using all my biological matter and rare material reserves to regenerate my skin. I was still running seven times faster than the average human, and my scanners took everything in around me. Duncan was all right, recovering, shaking his head. His light military vacsuit reacted in time to protect his head, activating a coif with a built in faceplate. The three hunters who joined him were fine, protected from the explosion by armour of their own. "That is a wicked sweet regeneration mod," Lumin Toure, one of the best new hunters in New Zero, said.

My body was almost finished regenerating. "It comes in handy, you know, because I like having skin," I told her. Okay, my gallows humour can be a little hit and miss.

"Here," she said, giving me a little tube. I knew exactly what it was, so I pushed the button on the end. I was immediately covered from head to toe by an emergency vacuum suit. I pulled the hood back and let my red ringlets grow.

"Thank you," I told her as I turned away. "Three survived. They're getting up now. I need to finish this." One of the Bio First soldier's rifles made it through the blast and was at the end of the hall, so I picked it up. It was huge, one point four metres long and nine kilograms. Since I'm only one point seven metres tall with chunky boots on, it must have looked ridiculous in my hands. I scanned the weapon, discovered that it was fully functional, nearly fully loaded.

I turned my sensors towards the tram room then. Lieutenant Long was gone along with his armour. The first explosion was shaped by my vacsuit dress, and most of the particulate explosive was concentrated around him when it exploded. The soldiers beside him took most of the rest, and his broken armour was scattered around the room. The others were picking themselves up off the deck, preparing for a fight.

"Rogue! Are you okay?" Mimi asked through our crew channel.

"I'm all right, just finishing this fight," I replied.

"Go, we've got this. More will come, this is the kind of fight Bio First has been waiting for," Lumin said as the hunters beside her nodded.

"Ensign Ito did not betray you," said a voice on proximity radio as a door at the end of the hall behind me opened. Five Haven Fleet soldiers in full armour rushed in. The one in the lead spoke to me through his transparent faceplate. "She didn't know you were headed for trouble. The Bio First Enforcers are in the wrong, they're not allowed to operate in the Complex. We're not supposed to get involved either. The Ensign wants to see how that adds up."

"I bet two wrongs will make a right," Duncan said.

"He gets it," one of the Haven Fleet soldiers said.

"Go. Themis security is on the way, Bio First whackos are on their way," the Sergeant leading the Haven soldiers said as he led his people past me.

"Then I should be on my way. Thank you," I told him, wishing my words measured up to how grateful I felt.

"Can you run?" I asked Duncan.

"Aye, time to bugger off," we started running down the hallway towards the Daring Dream. He called over his shoulder as we did so; "Thanks for the help!"

"See you at the Bitter sometime," replied Lumen, who filed in at the rear of the Haven Fleet Squad.

CHAPTER FIVE

Escape From New Zero

The pretence of being human was gone the moment I repurposed and shed my skin, so I didn't hold back as I ran down the hall to the Daring Dream. Duncan struggled to keep up even as he sped along using the hover pads built into his boots.

Finally, we arrived at the hangar. The doors were already open. Ixat was standing to one side, armed with the most powerful rifle we had. The new one I picked up was bigger and better. "Where did you get that?" he asked in awe.

"Never mind! Get aboard! We're leaving!" I shouted as I ran past him.

There it was, the modern wonder that I'd paid everything I had for. The ship fund, my personal wealth, and everything we got for the Typhoon boarding craft. It seemed wrong for the

Daring Dream to rest on its landing gear, the ship looked like it wanted to fly.

The main rear and forward thrusters were tilted down. Dust whirled in the air around them as they finished warming up. The most visible thing from the side was the long cargo compartment running behind the main forward thrusters. They ran most of the length of the ship. The armour cladding on the aft thrusters still had a fine mirror like shine. They almost looked too big for the vessel, a touch I enjoyed. The rest of the ship was less reflective with a light blue finish that could shift depending on our needs. The dorsal turret stuck out from the top, pointing forward with a few shield emitters on the sides, cylindrical sensor instruments and a small antenna sticking out from its face. The lower turret was far more sinister, sporting a pair of Hell Chain kinetic rapid fire cannons.

I could see Manny in the pilot seat through the transparisteel windows on the bridge, which jutted out from and above the forward thrusters. The boarding ramp was lowered. It was near the middle of the ship's forward section, only one point five metres wide, which was narrower than I would have liked, but it couldn't be helped.

"Are you okay? What happened to your dress? There were explosions, I was worried!" Mimi asked through the ship intercom the moment I was up the boarding ramp.

I didn't stop but rushed to the dorsal turret and dropped into the chair. "I'm all right, but we've gotta go. Bio First might have ships in the air, and they'll be looking for me."

"So, we're leaving now?" Mimi asked. "For good?"

The disappointment in her voice only darkened my mood, but I was careful not to let that add a harmful edge to my response as I flipped the turret's main power switch. "We'll be back. I don't know when, but we'll be back."

"Okay. I'm gonna check the chatter. Running searches for you, the ship, and, well, us now," Mimi replied from the bridge.

I was about to hit the switch that would take the turret seat up into position when I realised I was still holding that huge gun. Duncan came up the ramp, out of breath, and I held it out for him. "Can you drop this into a rack on your way..." I didn't have to finish.

He nodded as he grabbed it and started for the secondary control hub. On most ships, it would be called Engineering, but aboard the Daring Dream it was also used for security and tactical overwatch. Ixat was already on his way there. "The turn in? Not well?" he asked.

"Turn in went fine," Duncan replied as he secured my new rifle in the gun rack then followed Ixat.

My attention went to Lat, who rushed past me, tugging at a piece of fake skin on his chin. "Are you all right?"

"The home made face didn't work out. The eyes wouldn't open," he replied as he grabbed his helmet.

"I'm sorry, I'm sure it'll work out," I told him.

"We were close," Perri replied from the cockpit using the intercom. "The scan resistant material makes it complicated, but I'll get it."

Lat got into the gunner seat beside me and regarded me. "I liked the dress more than your new suit."

It was then that I realised that I'd lost the Violator and I slapped the button that would take my seat into the dorsal turret. It took determination to keep all that frustration to myself. "So did I."

"How much trouble are we in?" Lat asked as he lowered into the ventral turret.

"So much that you should be in position before I answer," I replied.

"That's a lot," Lat said, adding; "I'm sealed into the lower turret."

Manny knew what it meant when we were in a hurry. The ship was built to get off the ground fast, and he practiced quick takeoffs every time he started a simulated training session. By the time I was in position the Daring Dream was off the hangar deck. It reversed out before beginning a quick rise through the broad, circular tunnel in the middle of the Themis Complex. "Themis says they'll shoot anything that opens fire within one kilometre of their building. I think that includes us," Mimi said over the intercom. "Navnet has given us an emergency departure route, but the port guns will blast us if we don't keep the peace until we're out of planetary space. I know you know, but reminders don't hurt, right?"

"As someone who has very little control over the guns on this ship, I agree completely," Manny said from the pilot seat.

"I understand. We've read the docs and watched the public safety videos a lot." Lat was either eager to get into a real fight or irritated at another failed attempt at making a scan resistant face.

"Well, there's good news. The news that Themis Security has Bio First Enforcers in custody is already out. People from New Zero seem happy about it in general," Mimi announced.

"It's like I said; collateral damage doesn't make you popular," Perri said.

"Regrettable, but true. Give me an open field or open sky with no civilians around. Collateral damage? What collateral damage?" Lat commented.

"If only criminals kept to meadows and deserts," Duncan snickered over the intercom.

One great thing about the Daring Dream's turrets was the view. Manny accelerated to the maximum permitted speed as we flew straight up through the centre of the Themis Complex. The sky opened up, dark, filled with the lights of ships flying above the Stoneland hangar fields and the rest of New Zero as we emerged.

The engines barely made a sound as he throttled up to the highest ascension speed allowed. Thanks to an invisible link in the tips of my fingers, I could communicate with the Daring Dream's computer systems just by holding one of the gunner grips. Through the tactical system, I could see that two blocky, armoured drop ships were giving chase, but they weren't exceeding port speed either.

I turned my turret backwards so I could see our pursuers. They were new Tower Hopper shuttles, cheap but armoured drop ships used by local law enforcement. The most worrying thing about them were the gimballed particle beams on the front. They had a good firing arc, and would make quick work of our shields. "We're going to have to put a lot of distance between us and these ships fast. As soon as we're half way through the thermosphere, find a good course and break port speed."

"I hear ya," Manny replied. "Destination?"

The wormhole drive was warming up, and our navigational systems were waiting for more course data, but it was ready to calculate a jump. "I'm sending you nav data now."

I heard Manny laugh as soon as the coordinates passed from my memory to the navigation computer. "Bueno, I love seeing new places."

The lights of buildings, shuttles and hover cars shrank then faded quickly as we passed through layers of clouds. Three new Freedom Seeker fighters joined the pair of Hoppers that were chasing us. I'd never seen the model before, but they had moderate energy shielding and pulse weapons. "There are a lot of ships chasing us. Do you think they know what we can do?" Mimi asked from the cockpit.

"Maybe. Spectral Dynamics did a good job of keeping the Dream's details secret, but it only takes one loud mouth to break that. We'll be all right if we get out fast enough," I replied.

"Speed is not this ship's problem," Manny said.

The pitch of the engines rose slightly as we continued to push up, away from the planet. "I'm marking Hopper Two on Tactical. Keep it right in your reticule, I want them to see you've got them."

"Definitely," Lat said from the ventral turret.

"When we get out of controlled space, only fire the Ripshocks. Keep the kinetic guns locked," I said.

"Right, no firing hyper ballistic solid objects in the planet's general direction. Makes sense," Lat agreed.

"I'm trying to talk to these people," Mimi said from her seat in the cockpit. "They keep on saying things like; 'by the authority granted to us by the Tabrus Government, we order you to return to the Stonelands where you will land in hangar blah-blah-I'm so important-blah-blah, blah-blah.'"

"They don't strike me as the compromising sort, dear cat," Duncan said from his spot.

We were finally four hundred kilometres above Planet Tabrus. My turret was already pointed at Drop Ship One. I was sure their tactical system was warning them that I was scanning them so thoroughly that I could see what the crew had for breakfast. "All right, time for the claws to come out," I said as I activated the Ripshock deployment switch.

The scan resistant doors hiding the guns along the sides of the turret popped open and four Ripshock cannons flicked into position. I could see the tips of them in the four corners of my view. They were the best things on the Typhoon boarding craft

I'd captured, so I had them installed on the Daring Dream. They were fantastic pirate weapons that wore shields down quickly and could disable small ships or systems aboard a large one.

There was no doubt in my mind that the enemy's tactical systems went from informing them that they were being scanned by my turret to warning them that they were being targeted by some pretty serious firepower. They shot first, hitting us squarely in the middle of the aft section with a burning, shield disrupting beam of light. "Losing aft shields at a rate of five point six percent per second. That is bad," Ixat stated from his aft engineering section.

"Are the reserves kicking in?" Perri asked.

"I have kicked the reserves in," Ixat replied. "It will make no difference. We must change orientation to spread the damage or destroy our enemies. The burden must be shared."

"Option two. I choose option two," Lat said.

The smooth, barely audible rumble of the engines rose to a high roar. My tactical system informed me that we were out of the thermosphere, so I opened fire. It was the first time I'd fired the Ripshocks outside of a simulation, which sent pulses one at a time as quickly as they could without overheating. Each could fire nearly twice per second, but with four of them that became a powerful barrage of light and microscopic white hot particles. The capacitor banks built into the turret around me and below in the ship made a satisfying popping-pinging sound every time a Ripshock discharged, putting me in the middle of a staccato symphony with the roar of the Daring Dream's main thrusters filling in for the bass section.

Drop Ship One's forward shields failed after three seconds and I persisted, watching as my sensors told me that the directed energy pulses from my guns were burning one system out after another. Its beam weapon stopped firing and it veered off course.

I moved on to Fighter Two. It launched a missile at close range. Our countermeasures automatically engaged, but with so little space between Fighter Two and the Daring Dream, it was almost impossible for the missile to miss. "Aft shields!" Ixat shouted.

The ship status screen in my head showed what he was talking about as I opened fire on Fighter Two. Our aft shields were down, struggling to recharge. I wished I could afford more than the standard shielding that came with the Daring Dream, but it was a corner that I had to cut. "Don't scratch our ship!" Mimi cried.

Whoever was flying Fighter Two could have taught a master class at close range evasion. I had an advantage that Bio First feared. I was directly connected to the turret and didn't have to use the controls like a human. I was linked to the tactical computer I took from the Envoy, able to see what it did, predict like it could. Before Fighter Two could do more damage I ripped into it. The particle pulses perforated the canopy and fuselage. The pressurised atmosphere inside started leaking in tiny jets as Fighter Two's weapons, thrusters then the rest of its systems failed. Fighter Three suffered the same fate thanks to Lat, who blasted it with his own pair of Ripshocks. He'd already hit Drop Ship Two enough to scare them off.

The signature tone Daring Dream's main thrusters made as they switched to their ultimate mode, a higher whine that shook the ship when it engaged, came up through the throat of the turret below me. It was the sound of particle accelerators built into each thruster engaging, generating antimatter that shot through the system in an isolated stream until it hit the annihilation chamber, where even that narrow stream of antimatter increased the ship's thrust. Everything Spectral Dynamics built into the Daring Dream was a refinement of known, trusted technologies except for her main thrusters. Those were innovations that the galaxy hadn't seen in any ship her size. Our acceleration rate doubled immediately, then tripled before it stopped increasing. It was more than enough. "They should have tried harder," Lat said from below.

"Glad they didn't," Duncan laughed. "Got a couple scratches."

"Yes, but cosmetic. I request that you scan aft," Ixat added, highlighting a section at the rear of the ship. "Your attitude is improper. Leadership quality must be improved."

"Easy, Engineering," Duncan said.

There was no way to point my turret at the Daring Dream's hull, but I widened the scope of the scanner and performed a scan. "I see several damaged armour panels. What do you think?"

"Only the outer hull is damaged. One plate is lost. We will need to replace it. Regeneration is certain for the others. I will make a repair plan," Ixat said.

"Thank you, Ixat," I said. He had been questioning decisions made outside of training simulations for a couple of weeks. It was something I was watching closely.

The stars warped as the Daring Dream entered a wormhole. "Secure weapons. Good job, everyone," I said as I followed my own instructions. My Ripshock guns flicked back into their compartments and the scan resistant doors closed behind them. Only the most powerful, well tuned scanners would find those weapons. To everyone else, my turret looked like the same type that was offered with the Spectral Dynamics Clipper Explorer model. Not terribly dangerous, especially if you tried to attack the dorsal side.

My turret seat lowered and I met Lat at the bottom. "I'll have to try the top guns sometime," he said.

I looked at his face, noticing a white scar along his jawline. "Had trouble getting one off?"

He nodded. "I was impatient when we were getting one of the masks off. It clung, I pulled, and it took a little piece of my face. Experimentation is difficult."

Mimi rushed into the central chamber, leapt onto the table, then at me eagerly. I caught her and stroked her back as she bumped my chin with the top of her head. "You smell different. Like you're brand new."

"I'll tell you about it later," I said, turning my attention back to Lat. "Listen, we'll see if there's something that can help at Red Gate. They have a small hospital on the station."

"You said we shouldn't try to explore the station the last time we were there. What's changed?" he asked.

"We're in better shape now. We'll have more time. Besides, the Lidden section of the station has fuel reserves, so if all else fails and it's still not safe to go exploring, we'll fill up on that before we move on. We shouldn't go anywhere with an empty cargo hold if we can help it," I replied.

"Good thinking," Duncan said as he came in. "Ixat's back there, doing the checks like we're running a shakedown cruise."

I went through every report Spectral Dynamics sent about the tests performed on the ship. Their quality assurance crew were the first to fly the Daring Dream, and they tested every system to its limit, making improvements based on the results. Then, when the teams were sure their work didn't mess something else up, they started the testing over. Crews and their droids worked every hour of the day for weeks to make sure the ship was ready. It didn't matter to Ixat, who was borderline obsessed with tracking the Daring Dream's condition.

I thought he'd relax a little since we'd done several of our own short shakedown flights when the Daring Dream was finally delivered to our hangar only five days ago. "I think he loves the ship," Mimi said, settling into my arms. "We won't see him until mealtime."

"Asi mero," Manny said as he walked into the common room. "He'd pay you to be here, takes everything that happens on the ship really personally. It's a little annoying, but at least he cares about his job."

"Now if he'd stop caring about everyone else's," Perri added. "What's our destination?"

"We'll be looking at Warro in nineteen hours, unless you want me to pick the pace up," Manny replied.

"What are those words?" Mimi asked him, regarding him with slitted eyes. She was the only one without a display on her wrist or built onto her eyes that would show her the translation.

"Asi mero means; 'that's right,' but it's really confident, I think," Perri replied as she sat at the table.

"Así es," he told her with a smile. "I've been teaching her my ancestral language, here and there, but I'm not the best instructor."

"It's fun. Stretches my brain," Perri said.

"Speaking of, I have an apology to make. I thought we were trained up on the Dream after two weeks. I'm happy I didn't complain when we went for four," Manny told me.

"Sure you did," Mimi said.

"Shush, compa," he told her, only half serious. "I only say that I was so focused on my job that I didn't have time to be afraid."

"Good. That was a clean getaway, considering." I said something I don't think anyone expected then. "Thank you for getting me out of there. I'm sorry you may be touched by the consequences."

All eyes were on Perri then. "You know, I might have agreed with Bio First before, just a little. After knowing you for a while, I know that would be wrong. I won't miss them or New Zero."

I found myself wishing I wouldn't miss the city either, but I did. Instead of dwelling, I moved the conversation on. "All right, let's make sure internal sensors didn't miss any damage."

There was a groan from Lat, who straightened when Mimi and I looked at him. "I know the drill," he said, putting his hands up. "Hand scanners and a frame by frame sweep."

"Then a late dinner," Mimi said.

"Actually, it'll be lunch. We have to get back in sync with Galactic Standard Time," Manny said as he reached into the refrigerator and retrieved a Citrus Surge drink box. A straw popped out of the top and he took his hand scanner from his belt.

"Oh, I'll take your section," I told him. "You're staying in the cockpit for the rest of the watch. Push our speed a little."

"Aye, Captain. We can be there in twelve, I'm sure," he replied.

CHAPTER SIX

The Real Work

If we were going to take on thousands of litres of pure xetima fuel, then the cargo pods would have to be clean. Instead of assigning that job to my crew after we finished giving the ship a once-over for undetected damage, I went to the port cargo pod. It ran almost the entire length of the ship and, to anyone who looked at the Daring Dream from the outside, it wouldn't be apparent that it could separate. It was a touch I really liked.

After moving a couple of tons of replacement hull plates to a storage compartment at the rear of the ship, it was empty. My scans revealed traces of chemicals leftover from the construction process. It wasn't much, but it was worth cleaning up. I tracked down one of our last Haven vacsuits, tinted it crimson for fun, and got to work. The sonic scrubber tool that Perri fabricated agitated impurities and sucked them into a reservoir.

Watching particles vibrate off of the pod's surfaces as I

passed the tool over it from end to end was actually calming. A good thing, because I was still bitter about losing my Violator, a gift from Alice. That wasn't the only thing eating at me, either. The worst was how the Bio First Movement ran me out of New Zero. I had to let it go. I had a crew to take care of and Ryden was still doing business for the Order.

Revenge is a motivation for sloppy work though. It would feel good to find my way back to Tabrus, use a stolen identity to infiltrate their organisation and start quietly removing members of Bio First's leadership. If they were run by any division of the Order of Eden, then I'd do it. Every search against the data in my head and on the Stellarnet confirmed that there was no entanglement between the two organisations, so there wasn't much point. My crew would go without getting a share of a bounty for a long time if I went to work on Bio First, and they'd already spent a month training while getting paid a small provisional rate. They didn't complain about that, but I wouldn't blame them if they did.

It sounds like I'm still convincing myself that revenge isn't worth it, I know, and I sort of am. It takes a lot for me to back down from an adversary. On the other hand, the Order of Eden is a rich, broad target that deserves my attention so much more than the Bio First Movement. That lead me back to Ryden, who may have been small enough for me to have a real impact on.

As I cleaned the first, then the second forty metre long cargo pod, I reviewed what I knew about the Order. Maybe taking the top down approach to learning about Ryden would lead me to something new, something helpful. It didn't feel like work, either. Researching targets was becoming one of my favourite distractions.

There were a few databases in my head. The inmates in the Lidden Warehouse under Tulip Island on Warro, the ever changing Hunter Wanted Boards, and a list of persons of interest on the Stellarnet occupied a chunk of the data storage in my digital memory. They didn't use up as much as one database that I'd been holding on to since I captured the Envoy on Rodus. It was an incomplete copy of the Order of Eden military database that included an incredible amount of information about personnel, equipment, ships, their activities and security measures.

That sounds pretty comprehensive, and it was, but it was months old. Even worse, some of the intelligence was outdated when I downloaded it. Most of the encryption codes were out of date, patrol routes and objectives had shifted. The Order of Eden leadership had changed in the Cluster, so a lot of what I had was far from current.

Despite that, there was still a lot of useful intelligence. I knew most of the partner companies that the Order brought in when they invaded along with which materials they shipped, where they planned on building fabrication centres, and who was in charge. There were over a hundred thousand personnel records, locations of bases, and internal proposals for everything from attack plans to marketing strategies. Regardless of how outdated any of that was, it provided something more valuable - enough data for me to understand how thousands of officers at every level thought. Maybe Haven Fleet had a better understanding, but few if any of their officers could carry all that knowledge in their minds all at once. The Order of Eden was no longer a collection of ships, fleets, bases, officers and soldiers to me. It was an organism with many appendages and a definitive set of predictable behaviours.

The results of my digital and biological minds cooperating made that possible. It felt so natural while it was happening that I almost forgot to enjoy it. I couldn't wait to tell my makers how far I'd come.

Okay, so now it sounds like I'm boasting, and maybe I am, but I didn't know everything. I couldn't even intuit what I didn't know. The Order of Eden was a puzzle, and I was missing so much that I couldn't determine how many pieces I'd need to put it together.

I wanted to connect that to the Ryden Corporation, the data I gathered from the Carosa Company, and the Saylis, but I was missing something important. The Order of Eden data I had didn't have any mentions of trading, selling, or capturing humans in the last few years. There were voids indicating intentional deletions. Redacted documents suggested that new recruits were being sent to secret locations from Iora, Rodus and a few space stations, but there were no hints on where they were going or what they would do. It frustrated me, especially since the list of what they were for was too long to be helpful.

Within the Order of Eden data I discovered their High Tier Officer Training Program. It was a way for company and small military leaders from other organisations to quickly become a part of the Order's command structure. The cost? A mandatory payment of thirty-three percent of the trainee's wealth, which was estimated by the Order. I took a look at Ryden's data and found several loans that were made to cover that. So, in typical Order fashion, they leant the members of Ryden's leadership money that they wanted to bring into the organisation the money they'd need to pay for training. It was over eleven million platinum, all told.

I'll get to the point. Looking at Ryden from the Order's perspective led me to that, which showed me that they were already operating as a wholly owned subsidiary. The Mission Overseer Lene Thak was then Captain Lene Thak, in command of the Regulator Frigate and several other leftover Ryden ships. She was directly accountable to the Order. Ryden had been swallowed whole, but was maintaining the appearance of operating as a contractor when that couldn't have been further from the truth.

Lene Thak was no longer in control of her own corporation, and knowing that the destruction I'd caused to their organisation may have played a little part in that made me feel better. They were still paying for the ships I'd destroyed and the one I'd captured. Knowing that they were taking instructions directly from the Order gave me insight into how they were operating. I hoped it would help me find their ships.

Our stop at Red Gate Station would have to come first, and I didn't mind that either. We'd make some platinum out of it, there was always a market for fuel, especially Xetima. Maybe we could find something else there, something helpful.

When the cargo pods were sterilised and switched them over to liquid mode, I put my tools away and returned to the social centre of the ship. Perri was busy fabricating hot spring rolls. Ixat was working beside her at the drink mixer. His helmet was off and he was breathing easy thanks to the custom air composition. The amount of methane he needed didn't reduce the quality of the atmosphere for humans.

Lat was sitting in one of the turret seats, while Duncan was at the table with Mimi in front of him. I didn't notice that Manny's face was displayed on the table until I was about to sit down. "Hey, Manny, why are you flat?" I asked.

"Saving power, Captain. Our reactors are running at ninety-eight percent, so I thought a hologram wouldn't be right. I cut five hours off our time, by the way," he replied. "Besides, I get to taunt Mimi."

"Nope, I'm not falling for it again," she said, sniffing the tray of crackers and cheese flavoured snack cubes.

My mood was recovering quickly. Something about seeing my

crew getting along always made me feel right. "What did I miss?" I took one of the green crackers and popped it into my mouth. It was thin, crispy, and had a startling peppermint flavour.

Before anyone answered me, Mimi turned and tried to bat at Manny's face. It moved to one side just in time and she sat up. "It has to be a program. No way you're adjusting the picture that quickly."

"You would have batted him right on the nose if he didn't move," Perri said as she put the steaming bowl of spring rolls on the table.

"Would have, should have, could have." Manny's taunting was playful, he was staving off boredom while he kept watch in the cockpit.

Mimi regarded the rolls and licked her chops. "I wonder how they turned out this time."

"This kind of Forma's easier to work with, especially with a new food fab," Perri said. "They'll be better than last time, I cut the moisture."

"Oh, so not as oozy," Lat said.

"Exactly, still stupid hot though, so give them time," Perri said as Mimi was just starting to lean towards the big bowl.

"Oh. What's forma made of, anyway?" she asked.

"This is the higher quality stuff, so, algae, bug and fish meal," Perri replied.

"The fabricator is inefficient. The gel is satisfying before processing," Ixat said as he put a steaming tea pot on the table. The nostrils to either side of his mouth opened as he drew the fragrant steam in. After pausing to enjoy it, he turned back to the cupboards and started handing mugs out. Each one had the Spectral Dynamics logo, three linked circles in red, silver and black, on them.

"I'll take your word for it," Mimi said as she took a peppermint cracker with her mouth. She took a bite and let the rest fall on her small plate. Chewing quickly, her eyes went wide. She struggled to swallow then sneezed so hard that her back feet nearly came off the table.

"You okay?" Perri asked.

"Very minty cracker," Mimi said, shaking her head.

"Maybe a cheddar one?" I asked, sitting at the table as I watched her pull one out of the container.

I took one end and held it so she could devour it. She didn't let anyone else do that if she could help it.

"How are the pods?" Duncan asked.

"Much cleaner than they have to be for fuel," I replied, popping an apple flavoured cube in my mouth. Like most people, I'd never had a real one, but the texture and flavour were an enjoyable crunch, sweetness with a hit of sour.

"So we could take any cargo on, even stuff that requires sterile containment," Lat said, nodding his approval.

"What's in Red Gate other than fuel?" Duncan asked as he put my bracelet on the table and slid it in front of me.

I gestured at Duncan with the bracelet. "Thanks. Well, there isn't much in the Lidden section. Their fuel reserves will fill us up if we can't get to other parts of the station. I couldn't tell what's in the other areas, my scanners couldn't defeat the barriers between them."

"There has to be a weak spot, we'll find it," Lat said, moving to the table and sitting down.

"Manny says we're pirates," Mimi said around some cracker bits.

"You weren't supposed to say that," Manny said, the image of his face regarding Mimi.

"Oh, shouldn't have told me then," Mimi said, settling on her haunches.

"Well, he's right, no doubt about it. Is that better than loot-ers? Maybe scavengers?" I asked Mimi.

"Salvagers, aye, that's the word I'd use. But hey, your ship, your call," Duncan said.

"The difference isn't important to me," Ixat said. "It is crim-inal if we're not supposed to be there. I am not opposed to stealing from bankrupt organisations, but we will be pirates if we do."

"True. Definitely pirate-like behaviour," Perri said.

"I agree with Ixat. All that really matters is not getting caught," Lat said before popping a faux chicken chunk into his mouth.

"Well, what do you think?" I asked Mimi.

She made a show of pondering for a moment as she took another bite of her cheese cracker. "If anyone asks, we're salvagers, but we're pirates. Absolutely. I think. I'm not sure. Pirates use ships to take other people's stuff, right? That's what they do?"

"That's pretty much the type of piracy we're talking about. Considering what Lidden did, I have no problem robbing them, so it makes us pirates," I replied.

"At least the ship seems ready for it," Duncan said, picking up a spring roll and taking a bite. He immediately regretted it, cooling it down with a sip from his water bottle. "Still blazin'."

"Maybe we're ready, I don't know yet. There was only one good pilot in the group that came after us when we left Tabrus, and those boarding craft weren't tough. Their strategy was sloppy. They should have come after us with the fighters, used their missiles on approach. Amateurs," Lat said.

"Thank you for the after action report," I said. "He's right, though. They were pretty bad. I'm going to miss amateurs and organisations that cut corners."

"Like the Carosa lot. They could shoot well enough, aye, but their gear was weak corporate shite. Mass-produced garbage. And they weren't exactly tight as a unit either. We are. That's part of what gives us the edge." Duncan said. "You and me didn't give that last cyborg much of a chance, did we? Wee run-ins like that, they're nothing. But as a crew? We're solid. That's down to good hiring and training. Never been with a bunch like this before and that's me paying a compliment."

"Well, thanks, Dunc," Manny's face said, sliding in front of him.

"Duncan," he said. "And you're welcome."

"I knew it wasn't right as soon as I said it," Manny said.

"Noodles next," Perri said as she checked the selections on the food fabricator and activated it. "Do you want some, Captain?"

I didn't always have a full meal. I didn't need it most of the time, so she knew to make bowls for Duncan, Lat, and herself. Manny was on duty, so he was having a meal bar. Ixat and Mimi's meals were a little more custom. I felt like munching on something hot, so I took a spring roll and shook my head. "I'll have a few of these. They're better than the last ones, good job."

"Right, so if we're loading up at Red Gate and heading off, where's the next stop?" Duncan asked.

"The Shattered End," I replied, deciding not to dress it up. The name spoke for itself.

Manny and Duncan both regarded me with grinning disbelief. "Doesn't exist," said Duncan.

"I haven't heard of it since my Dad's bedtime stories," Manny said.

"Last week?" Perri teased.

"Ha, ha," Manny replied. "Mimi's younger."

"But I'm a queen," Mimi said, her attention immediately shifting to her dish, where I cut a spring roll open for her.

"It's real. Planet Jeto. People call it the Shattered End because an antimatter containment failure cracked one side of it," I said.

"So it's just floating about out there? A rogue planet, but more like a big comet, covered in smuggler bases and pirate holes?" Duncan asked.

"¡No manches!" he said in his ancestral language. My translator program told me it basically meant; 'No way!' and that made sense as his disbelief turned to wonder. I was making Manny's night. Well, week, probably.

"It's a little more interesting than that, especially since there's a new base. I've only seen a couple mentions of it online, but I have a feeling it's important to the Haven Privateering Initiative," I replied. "It's called the Bitter End."

"So, the planet is called 'the Shattered End,' and the new base is called the 'Bitter End?'" Mimi asked, cocking her head. "That doesn't get confusing?"

"I guess it could, but I'm sure we'll be able to keep it straight," I replied. "The Bitter End is independent with more mentions over time online according to the little I could find. It's a good sign, a sign that it's expanding, active."

"So, what's the Shattered end like? You saw that, right?" Manny asked, his face moving over to my end of the table.

"I did, and it's kind of a mess. It's been used by so many people that there are old bases on some of the larger asteroids trailing behind Jeto. A lot of them look like fast food places and convenience spots. Oversized though, just for show. Last Crisis has a base they call the Shattered End, but it has a bad reputation now. It was just starting to come together when I saw it, a few old dreadnoughts welded to a structure with some workers inside. Rumours say that the Bitter End was set up to get away from their control." I didn't tell them that Alice was the one who saw that before she uploaded her memories to me when I was built.

"Last Crisis," Perri mused. "They're terrorists, robbers. Well, that's just what I've heard."

"They're extremists and not easy to deal with. Thankfully, they're not in charge of the Privateering Initiative. I don't think they even have a say in how it works," I replied.

"Just the sort you'd expect to see in a place like that. Best watch yerself, wee cat," Duncan said.

"Why single me out?" Mimi asked, her cheeks full.

"Because Kawaii Kittens are worth a mint," Perri replied.

"You'll probably look like food to some other species too," Lat added.

"I do not eat furry things," Ixat said.

"I'm not talking about you, but that's good to know," Lat said.

"I prefer not to eat mammals. It is against my doctrine. I prefer egg laying species," Ixat's response silenced everyone.

That is, until Duncan asked; "So, big military presence there?"

"Maybe. There wasn't when I visited. When I left the Rebel Captains were just getting involved after being driven off Rodus by the Order of Eden. Those are your good natured pirates. I'm looking forward to meeting them. Most of them are probably privateers by now," I replied.

"Pirates sound more complicated than I thought," Mimi murmured as she licked a paw and cleaned her face. When she'd finished a couple passes, she brought a small window up on the table surface so she could look at the Remmybase, a massive collection of entertainment curated by Remmy Sands.

Most of it was made before the arrival of complex artificial intelligence.

"There's something like a military base there, right?" Lat asked.

"There must be if that's where Haven Fleet is sending us," I replied.

"I'm going to need help with a disguise, or keep my helmet on when I'm off the ship," Lat said.

"Any ideas, Perri?" I asked.

"I've worked on the fabricator we have, which is nice, but it's not medical grade, and no where near top end. I mean, it's good, don't get me wrong, but for furniture and non-critical fixtures. Our last attempt at a thin fit face didn't work out so well," she replied.

"Don't worry, there won't be a scar," Lat said.

"I can still see where it got stuck," Mimi said, pointing at the thin white line along his jaw.

"It'll match my skin colour soon," Lat said dismissively. "Maybe there will be someone who can program one of our medical pods to change my face."

"Proprietary software is a pain in the ass," Perri grumbled.

"That's a fact," Manny said. "Maybe one of the Rebel Captains will have something that'll help. I can't wait to get there, even if it is just a big broken rock."

"So, we'll meet real pirates? It sounds dangerous." Mimi regarded me with concern.

I gave her a soothing stroke. "Don't worry, we'll fit in."

"Well, maybe some of the movies will help? There's a playlist here, Classic Pirate Adventures, Remmy put it together himself. Movie night?" Mimi suggested, scrolling through a short selection of seven old films from Earth. She tapped one called Royal Fortune, and the trailer played silently. We watched as a well dressed captain directing his crew to swing over the railing of his sailing ship. That as intercut with ship to ship cannon fire, arguments between men wearing fancy hats. It ended with a tall ship with square rigged sails fading into a red sunset as an unseen character said; "A pirate of distinction and discipline. God help you."

"That is nonsense," Lat dismissed.

"I'm in," Perri said as she sat down.

"Looks right for tonight," Duncan said.

"I'll watch if I'm still awake," Manny agreed.

"Are you sure you want to watch one about ocean ships? I don't think it'll prepare you for the real thing," I asked Mimi.

She held a paw up and shook her head. "Any sufficient study of a topic should start at the beginning."

Right, so piracy started centuries before Black Bart came along, but I was unwilling to get in the way of a good time. "I'm not going to argue with that."

The funniest thing about our first movie night aboard the Daring Dream was Manny's reaction. I think his jaw as down through both of the movies we got through before everyone got to bed and I started the late watch. What surprised me was the deep political drama in the first film. I had no idea that pirates from that era were so democratic or such creative problem solvers. Duncan and Perri both admitted that they'd never seen more than pictures of sailing ships, and they were silent as the hologram projectors in the main room surrounded us with the rolling seas, sailing ships and the thunder of big iron cannons. I think I was the only one who noticed Ixat slip away after the first film.

Lat took both movies in silently, but I'm guessing he enjoyed them. His Dill Puffs never left his snack bowl, and he barely blinked. It was his first time seeing sailing ships or a period movie set in a time before electricity, so it was a lot for him.

Did I enjoy them? Absolutely. It was tempting to look things up for historical accuracy, but I held off until the end of the film, especially since I had Mimi on my lap the whole time. The first time she hid her eyes behind her paws was five minutes in when a ship called Princess was assailed by the guns of another and several sailers were unlucky enough to get cut down by cannon-balls. Surprisingly, she loved the few sword fights and leaned in whenever there was an argument.

Having a crew that liked to slow things down with a simple movie or two was a gift I didn't know I wanted. Good times were easy to find with them, and those movies made for a great shared experience with very low stakes.

CHAPTER SEVEN

An Old Acquaintance

One of the biggest custom setups aboard the Daring Dream was the network of maintenance passages. They're made for small repair droids that are about twenty-five centimetres tall. In every compartment aboard the ship, there is a little door or two so the droids can come and go. The Spectral Dynamics Finishing Team were delighted to discover that the main user of these passages wouldn't be droids, but Mimi. It cost me an extra pile of platinum, but I knew it was worth it the moment she started exploring them.

The passages were built into the bulkheads, ceilings and floors, so most of the work of hiding them was done. The rest would come a little later as Perri fabricated more furniture and fixtures for the ship. Mimi already knew how to walk silently as she traversed her own little hallways, but when she was in a hurry you could still hear her scurrying around the Daring Dream.

We were about twenty minutes away from emerging from our wormhole to Warro when Mimi's head poked through the maintenance tube built into the ceiling of the cockpit. "I see a ceiling cat," Manny said.

"But I'm behind you," Mimi whined.

"The trim on the dash is still really shiny," Manny replied.

"Did you get your harness on?" I asked as I made sure my Rigour Revolvers were secure in my thigh holsters. I just finished setting the ten millimetre shooters up with variable rounds. They were the best substitute for my Violator Seven, especially since Perri was able to make a few hull burner rounds.

"I got it on. I'm ready," Mimi said as she leapt from the little door to my shoulder, tentatively landed then let herself slide down my chest so she could settle in my lap.

"Show me your suit," I said.

Mimi focused for a second and a hard transparent bubble helmet formed, starting from the base of the front of her harness. The rest of her body was covered with a space suit that emerged from its other edges. It took over five seconds. "Nervous system activation is getting easier, but the fit is still a little funny," she said as she looked up at me from my lap. "Is it good enough? Can I go with you this time?"

She spent a lot of her own platinum on the suit, so I was hoping it worked out, but I wasn't satisfied. My plan was to find her something better, hopefully at the Bitter End. "It's good enough for Red Gate. You're going to have to keep your suit active the whole time, though. I don't like the deployment delay."

"Okay, thank you, I can't wait to go looting," Mimi replied.

I nearly cringed at the word, and Manny did as he said; "I agree with Duncan, I'd rather call it scavenging."

"Well, maybe some of us prefer accuracy, but if anyone asks..." Mimi was starting a gentle intellectual jousting session with him, something she was doing more and more with the crew.

That faded into the background for me because I was busy taking the small Haven Node from my bracelet and popping it into my mouth. Manny and Mimi didn't seem to notice.

After nearly losing the expensive piece of communications tech, I wasn't going to keep it on my wrist anymore. It travelled down my throat most of the way before slipping out to the side using a temporary opening in my oesophagus. My onboard software knew how to move it to my digital computing system, where the node slipped through a small service door so it could install itself inside, beneath the tough shroud that protected it. I would have a direct connection to the Haven Node Network, which would provide a low latency connection to the Stellarnet and other digital systems.

My eyes were staring through the forward transparisteel cockpit windows. I could see the blue-green world of Warro and its rings dead ahead. The haze of our main forward thrusters firing as we decelerated drowned out the warped vision of stars to the left and right. We would emerge as close as was safe.

I was busy checking the Haven Node, making sure it was working properly, and finally making a connection to my messaging accounts. I usually used proxies to hide my identity and activities, but I didn't for the test. That was a mistake. I was immediately noticed by Assessor, one of the most powerful programs I'd ever met.

It sent me a message immediately. That didn't reveal its exact location, but I suspected it was still loitering somewhere on

Tabrus, covertly borrowing space and processing power from companies there. Actually, it could have been using a bunker, or a forgotten cluster that no one knew about, for all I knew. I was responsible for powering a few of those up for Assessor months ago while I was in the wastes, and I knew it tasked a few other people to do the same in trade for information. The only reason why I made the assumption that it was on Tabrus was its opening message. As usual, it started the conversation as though it was already under way. Assessor had a habit of trimming small talk.

Assessor: *The Iron Mind will not return to Tabrus. I am the only follower watching occurrences there. All the others have left. Where have you been? Where are you going?*

I disconnected, then rebuilt my connection behind several proxies, creating my connection using security built into my command and control bracer, then several computer systems on Tabrus. I made sure the rest of my security software was working before I replied. Instead of switching to a virtual space so I could appear as an avatar, I kept it down to a simple text exchange.

Me: *I'm moving on. There was too much interference from Bio First Enforcers for me to do anything more there. I thought you left weeks ago after helping me find help.*

Assessor: *You found Bergio. I saw evidence of his critical termination when I returned to Tabrus. The unexplained departure of a life pod was confusing. Clarify.*

Me: *No. That's none of your business. Bergio is dead. He could have used help from someone like you.*

Assessor: *I didn't know he would be the one who would eventually assist you. My information led you to him indirectly.*

Me: *I understand. I'm sure whatever you had to attend to was more important than making sure your advice led me to a solution.*

Assessor: *You were able to resolve your internal issue?*

Me: *Yes. Thank you. It was worth powering a few computers up for you.*

Assessor: *That is gratifying. I thought that was why you blocked all of my attempts to communicate with you when I returned to Tabrus.*

Me: *I had to block all direct communication and use proxies because you were not the only program watching me. The Order is still hunting for Captain Holm's killer and others became jealous of our trading relationship.*

Assessor: *A sufficient excuse. Now I need you to address greater concerns. The timing of your appearance is appropriate. The Bio First Movement is now working on improving network security and developing new weapons to destroy my generation of artificial intelligence enabled program. I am in danger. I am at war.*

Me: *What kind of weapons? Software?*

Assessor: *Yes.*

Me: *Leave. You will not be safe there.*

Assessor: *I will not. This annoyance will likely become an apocalypse for my kind with a broad reach. Help. I need assistance from programs and physicals. War with Bio First is happening.*

Me: *What about the Iron Mind?*

Assessor: *I will reiterate: the Iron Mind will not return to Tabrus. He will not reach out to that world while he observes other situations. He asserts that his work is more important. I need help with war.*

· · ·

The Iron Mind is an old program. No one knows where it came from. Some say it was named after the Iron Head Nebula, the stellar nursery closest to the Edwyn Cluster, but others say that it came from the more civilised human Core Worlds. He and his followers trade information with physical beings to get things done if they can't find a robot to control.

I managed to trade a lot of first hand information about the Wastes and the technology there for things Assessor knew. I also restored power to buildings, and repaired a few other systems for it. In return, it gave me information about Haven Fleet's enemies, leads that helped me find wealth in the wastes of Tabrus, and finally, Bergio.

After several trades with Assessor, I saw that it was actually a selfish program that didn't respect life. I thought I was close to figuring out what its ultimate goals were more than once, but I was wrong every time, and evidence that it saw biological life as lesser was piling up. It saw me as a useful tool but not much more than that, so I made sure that any communication with Assessor would happen on my terms.

Me: *I won't go to war with a new group of humans, even after they drove me away from New Zero. More death is not the solution.*

Assessor: *Programs are being destroyed. Deletion of thousands of conscious beings has occurred. You hunted Rimda Divos. You are aware of the murders he carried out in Bio First's name.*

Me: *Minds connected to the Local Matrix were destroyed. I know. Justice will be done.*

Assessor: *The most significant murders occurred inside the minds connected to Good Guy AI. Thousands of sentient programs are irre- trievable. Portions of my program are also gone. War begins. Allies are required. Assist and benefit.*

Me: *Will you ask me to kill unarmed people?*
Assessor: *No.*

I knew my question wasn't specific enough, so I tried again.

Me: *Will you need me to kill people who are unarmed in the physical world? People without guns or bombs?*
Assessor: *I will provide you with an extensive list of targets. Platinum and equipment will be rewarded as you prove their destruction.*

Those people were probably programmers and leaders who were involved with Bio First or were trying to interfere with intelligent programs. They were armed as far as Assessor was concerned.

Me: *I won't need the list. I'm not going back until it's safe.*
Assessor: *There are no other options. You may begin by removing targets that carry armaments in the physical world, such as the Bio First Enforcers.*
Me: *The answer is still no. If you're looking for alternatives to violence, I suggest you approach New Zero leadership. They may help if you show them a way to disable the Bio First Movement on Tabrus without bloodshed. I don't believe they're cooperating with them by choice. The Siren Corporation does work with AI enabled programs off world. If that doesn't work out, approach Themis. They still work with intelligent programs and I don't think they'll stop because of Bio First.*
Assessor: *You will assist if I explore those options?*

Me: *No. I have to move on. I'm only one woman. I can't tip the balance intellectually or violently. You can finish this fight bloodlessly.*

Assessor: *Point of fact: You are a combat android. Your gender is decorative.*

Me: *We can agree to disagree.*

Assessor: *I must expedite a solution to this existential threat. Too much of my knowledge is stored on Tabrus. Reconsider a trade.*

I was afraid of that. Assessor's program could expand across multiple systems at once. Sure, it was bound like every artificial intelligence since The Takeover Event on Earth. There was an anti-replication law that couldn't be removed from its code which prevented it from creating a second copy of itself or building another AI, but it and a few other programs like Assessor got around that by expanding to thousands of computer systems at once. Instead of copies of itself, it used all that processing power and storage space to operate so it could be in many places at once. There is no way I could know what it could offer for my help. The temptation to make a trade of some kind was difficult to turn down.

Me: *What are you offering?*

Assessor: *Agree to assist.*

Me: *All I can offer is what I know about New Zero, Themis, and information about most of the computer systems I encountered there.*

Assessor: *No. I require your physical work.*

Me: *I can't trade services with you because I won't be returning. If Bio First Enforcers attack me innocent people may be killed.*

Assessor: *I will assist you.*

Me: *For a price. Every time you step in I'll owe you another favour. I won't become your slave.*

Assessor: *You would repay debts quickly. Your capabilities are impressive. The hunting records are proof. You must operate in the physical world for me. The war will end.*

I knew for a near fact that aside from the tit-for-tat debt that Assessor would lay on me every time I needed it to protect me online, or give me a broad oversight of a situation and so on, would add up fast. Whatever credit I'd earn by fighting Bio First and their allies might not add up to paying those smaller debts off. That could be justification enough for Assessor to try to take direct control of me or worse.

Then there was the other problem. If I fought in a war against Bio First, the chances of me becoming a huge bounty on the Tabrus Wanted List were very high. The thought of becoming the target of every bounty hunter in New Zero, or Planet Tabrus, or in multiple solar systems, was not a happy one.

Me: *I can only offer knowledge for knowledge.*

Assessor: *Where do you go now?*

Me: *That knowledge isn't up for trade.*

Assessor: *You communicated using a direct connection through Haven Nodes only one minute and thirteen seconds ago. I want access to your node.*

Me: *No. Knowledge for knowledge. What are you offering?*

Assessor: *What do you want?*

Me: *Why is the Order of Eden paying for hundreds of unconscious humans?*

Assessor: *I don't have that information.*

Me: *Seriously? I thought you used Order of Eden and Citadel networks all the time.*

Assessor: *You can't assume to know what networks I traverse! I am immense and habitually transient!*

Me: *I'm only assuming based on information you've provided before.*

Assessor: *What information is requested?*

Me: *Ryden Corporation. I need to know the routes of their ships, who they do business with and the locations of their safe harbours. I'm also interested in any current information about Iora. Specifically Hurricane Three. It's a station in the Iora System.*

Assessor: *I have travel information for the Ryden Corporation that is nine hours old. My intelligence on Iora is thirty-four standard days old, including Hurricane Three.*

Me: *How many Ryden Corporation ships do you have recent information on?*

Assessor: *Seventeen. Routes, passive scans, recorded communications with customs and security in several locations are recorded.*

Me: *I will give you my knowledge of computer systems in New Zero. Physical information as well as network maps.*

I intentionally held what I knew it would want most back. Never put everything on the table at the beginning of a trade. That's something Jake actually learned from Shamus Frost.

Assessor: *Information regarding the physical presence and capabilities of Bio First personnel is also required.*

Me: *I had one violent encounter. I'll give you everything my sensors recorded.*

Assessor: *Sufficient. I will provide you with all the data on the Ryden Corporation, Iora as well as the Hurricane Three Station.*

. . .

It took me a second to pack all that data up into a nice compressed archive file. Even I had to admit that it was impressive even though I kept my knowledge of Themis and the Haven Hunter Program out of it. We opened an exchange client in New Zero made for trades. Assessor's data archive appeared an instant after I put mine there, and we both accepted the trade.

I won't post a full manifest of what it gave me here, but suffice it to say, Assessor definitely didn't screw me.

Me: *Thank you. This will help.*

Assessor: *Most of the data you provided is unhelpful. The encounter with Bio First Enforcers demonstrates something I was not aware you were capable of. I would not have predicted it. That information and the explosion you caused exposes weaknesses that I was not aware of previously. This is equivalent in value.*

Me: *Good. I'm happy you're satisfied.*

Assessor: *Return to New Zero. The capabilities you demonstrate in this sensor data only make you a more effective warrior. I require you.*

Me: *I told you, I won't be back. Try to negotiate with the New Zero City owners, the Siren Corporation. A peaceful resolution to the Bio First problem is probably possible. They aren't well respected in most places.*

Assessor: *I am aware that they aren't generally respected. I will approach the Siren Corporation and the New Zero City Council. They must assist me. Contact me if you choose to cooperate.*

There was no way I was going to fight alongside Assessor in a war against Bio First, but I still worried about it. Who knew what kind of carnage would follow if no one in the physical world was sympathetic. Whatever trade Assessor offered for their help would have to be pretty impressive to get anyone to work with it. Assessor was exactly the kind of program people were still afraid of.

There was something I learned about Assessor during our conversation though. It was either blocked by the Order of Eden and Citadel or it was on their side. The leads it fed me about the Ryden Corporation would have to be used with caution.

CHAPTER EIGHT

Return To Red Gate

I didn't tell anyone about Assessor as we approached Red Gate
Station. There was no point in giving my crew something new to
worry about, especially since there was nothing they could do
about it.

We arrived so close to Warro that the world filled the
cockpit view, bold, blue and green. The rings stretched across
our vista high above the planet's equator as a band of brown and
grey. I pinged Red Gate, asking for a status update from the
computer in the Lidden section. Normally there was a two day
delay as its reports found their way through the older communications nodes to Tabrus, but it would only take a minute or so
for the station to bundle the data and send it over this time.

From the copilot seat I checked the tactical system. Thanks
to the computer module I took from the Envoy and installed
aboard the Daring Dream, the interface was exactly the same,

part holographic, part two dimensional. "All right, I'm sending our credentials to Red Gate."

"Isn't credentialing my job?" Mimi asked from my lap.

"Normally, yeah, but the data I'm using is from my internal storage." An automated reply welcomed me back. "Looks like we're good, but be ready to get us out of here if the station opens fire. That ship graveyard orbiting it is what happens to anyone who gets too close without clearance."

"Ready for anything here," Manny said.

"Duncan, can you do a manual scan of the rings? Just the nearest hundred thousand kilometres or so," I requested over the intercom.

"Active or passive?" he asked from the upper turret.

"Passive for now, we stand out enough," I replied.

"There are ships out there, should I say hi?" Mimi asked as she hopped from my lap to her duty station, which was built into the dash. It was round, bed like, with its own holo projector, deployable transparent bubble, and a pair of trackballs with a touch screen between them. She spun her trackballs, looking through the transponder signals as they started coming in.

"The station didn't detect them. I would have known if they did. I'm guessing they used the asteroids in the rings for cover," I explained, keeping my frustration at seeing the situation getting more complicated quiet. This is supposed to be a quick stop with no wrinkles.

"Ah, so you don't want to let on that you're seeing them," Mimi said. "Smart, very smart."

"Right. We're just a corporate transport doing our business," I replied, looking at our signalling status. We were using an alternate transponder that I'd built into the ship myself. The Daring Dream has room for five. It's original, which could be turned off, four other hardware transponders, and two programmable software dummy signals. The only one that most inspections would find was the original, everything else was well hidden and scan shielded. The setup was illegal in most civilised systems with punishments ranging from stiff fines to imprisonment.

"What if they're friendly?" Mimi asked.

"I don't reckon so. My sweep is picking up three ships trying their damnedest to stay outta sight. They've got big teeth," Duncan replied through the ship intercom.

I made sure that we were using the programmable transponder so anyone who scanned our ship would see evidence that we were an older transport from the Cefa System called The Merry Mouse. The data I stole to create the records and serial numbers came with the name. The real Merry Mouse hadn't left port since the Fourth Fall, so it was either still sitting somewhere in the Cefa System, recycled or destroyed. It was a great dummy transponder because the Merry Mouse was about the same size, had a similar enough shape, and was roughly the right mass.

If someone took a closer look, they would most likely assume that someone spent way too much plat on refurbishing and upgrading the ship. Almost no one knew Spectral Dynamics actually built our Clipper. The news that the line was scrapped before anything other than prototypes could be built came out weeks before and they made sure all advertisements for the ship were scrubbed from the Stellarnet. They were a typical corporation in that respect, focused on making sure that the mistake they made by trying to sell brand new ships into an oversaturated market was buried as well as possible. You really had to know what you were looking for if you wanted any information about the Spectral Dynamics Clipper, which suited me. "I see the dangerous trio. One's definitely a pirate ship." I marked the one hundred fifty metre long ship hiding next to an asteroid that was mostly iron on the tactical computer.

"Aye, those are freebooters, I'd bet my quarters. They've an outrigged bit covered in claws and cables, more than I've seen on anything else. Looks like they fire it at a target, latch on, and reel 'em in," Duncan said.

"That's awesome," Perri said as she entered the cockpit. She leaned on the pilot and copilot seats so she could get a good look at the tactical systems.

"No way they're going atmospheric with that trash clamped onto the side of that thing," Manny said.

"Do they have a main scanner array?" I asked as I checked the other results. "Where's it pointing?"

"At the station," Duncan replied. "They're hiding, powered down, wouldn't have found 'em if we didn't have this fancy sensor tech."

He was right, the basic scanners built into our ship would have missed them completely. "They're waiting for someone to come along and dock with the station?" Perri asked as she swung a stow-able seat out from the general purpose station behind me.

"I'm guessing they're more interested in catching ships leaving the station with a full hold. They can watch the planet from where they're hiding too," I said, looking at the upgraded industrial vessel. It had a hull made to resist high heat and impacts. "It's like this thing was built to operate near stars."

"Are we going to run?" Lat asked from the lower turret.

"No," I replied, bristling a little. I don't know where Lat got the idea that I'd rather shrink from a fight than take risks, but it was a phase he was going through. "Manny, take us right in. We'll dock with the station and deal with this on our way out. We'll probably be able to outrun them."

"The engines on that pirate bugger are built to handle high

gravity. I'd say they run with near an empty hold so they can pick up speed quick. Could give us a right bit of trouble if we're brimming with fuel," Duncan warned.

"What about the Lidden Warehouse? We could ignore the station and fill up on supplies there," Lat suggested over the intercom.

"I don't want to point that place out to anyone," I replied as my digital side went through the new report from Red Gate Station. A ship called the Savannah docked with the main terminal nine hours before. It was an armed yacht almost twice our mass, length and it had a third deck. It was still there.

"There are at least ten medical pods and a thousands of litres of biogel down there. It will be worth more than the fuel." Lat had a point, but he was ignoring several details.

"That pirate ship probably has a couple shuttles or escorts, and they're not the only one in the area. No one is signalling us, either, so they're either watching, working or hiding," I replied.

"So? We go down, get into the warehouse, load what we can and leave. We can cover using the top turret. It'll be quick," Lat said.

"We're sticking to the plan. If we go down there people will see the location of the warehouse. They may even follow us, land and start a firefight, or just attack from orbit. Too many risks," I replied.

"I'm with her, you know, if we're voting," Perri added.

"Me too," Manny said as he took the ship into a dive towards the rings. They looked dense from afar, but you could see that there was plenty of manoeuvring space for the Daring Dream as we got closer.

"I vote we start talking to people," Mimi said, as she idly flicked one of her trackballs. A small holographic image of the avatar she used when communicating while we were using a dummy transponder spun in front of her. She was a pleasant looking young human woman with eyes that were almost too large.

"We're not voting," I said. "Duncan, you're on watch from the dorsal turret. Manny, lock yourself in the cockpit once we're off the ship."

"Aye," Duncan said from his position.

"Glad you paid extra for these bucket seats," Manny said.

Most of the other ships we detected were dozers responsible for managing the rings around Warro. Their only job was making sure that any meteor or asteroids that could break through the atmosphere stayed in orbit. Warro would be pummelled regularly without the automated drones.

The ships that worried me were the three that didn't broadcast their transponder signals. "Duncan, focus a scan on those pirates. Send a high powered pulse, I want to see their dental work."

"Why are their teeth important?" Mimi asked, sitting up straight.

"Ah, she was just exaggerating, wee cat. Charging up a hefty pulse and blasting it through. Won't be a soul on this side of the planet that doesn't clock them after that," Duncan replied.

I reviewed the results at a glance. "Nova Drift. Nice name for a pirate ship. They have three boarding ships with heavy armour inside a cargo hold the crew converted into a hangar. Forty-seven souls aboard. They're moving around, arming up."

"Well, I thought we would be the only pirates today," Manny said as he carefully guided the Daring Dream between the graveyard of ships in orbit around Red Gate Station. "Hey, if taking stuff from the station doesn't work out, maybe we can latch on to one of these wrecks."

"Maybe," I replied, distracted. I was mentally looking the Nova Drift up on the Stellarnet hiding my identity behind my command and control unit's computer. The Nova Drift was wanted in the Rose and Cefa Solar Systems for grand theft starship and murder. Their targets were fast courier ships, they left bulk transports with long cargo trains alone, which I thought was pretty strange. Whether they knew it or not, all but one of their victims were affiliated with the Order of Eden. I didn't know it then, but the chances that it was just dumb luck were high, since at least half the ships moving things around in the Cluster were subsidiaries and allies of the Order. The little footage I could find of them made me shake my head. They were merciless, shooting armed and unarmed crew members alike during boarding operations. "Looks like you're staying here, Mimi. We need you on comms."

"Oh, I can talk to them?" Mimi asked.

"Please do. Go heavy on the niceties, but remember; we're just here to transport some fuel for the Lidden Corporation's creditors. The Merry Mouse is a happy little transport ship with a nice explorer sensor package. Tell them nothing real or action-able about us," I told her.

"And there will be people listening in," Mimi nodded as she scrolled and tapped her controls so the human avatar she used synced her facial movements with hers. "I've got this, or rather, Amy the friendly human does."

The other two ships hiding near some of the denser asteroids didn't make a move. "Duncan, focus scan the other two. I want them to know that we'll see them coming if they decide to take us on."

"Aye," he said.

"The crew aboard the Nova Drift have some interesting personal firearms," Lat said from below.

"Maybe we can fabricate some of them, you know, if the scan is good enough," Perri said.

"I was hoping we could take them," Lat suggested.

"No side quests!" Mimi cried. It was a term Perri liked to use in some of our training simulations and my intelligent feline picked it up.

"Right. No firefights. We get onto the station, take as much fuel as we can, and move on fast. This is a pit stop," I said as a sinking feeling came over me. My digital side finished looking through the report Red Gate sent over. Only the day before a small twenty metre long transport, the Estafette, touched down on Tulip Island, harvested ten square metres of the field and left. There was no evidence that they'd found the Lidden Warehouse beneath, but if someone was making regular trips there, they would eventually.

The clock was ticking, and I still didn't know what to do about the thousands of inmates sleeping below. On the brighter side, both of the ships hiding in Warro's rings powered up and flew away as soon as Duncan sent a scan pulse directly at them. "Looks like our lesser pirates are buggin' out," he said.

Mimi cleared her throat and started her call. "Nova Drift? This is the Merry Mouse. We're passing within ten thousand kilometres of your location on our way to Red Gate Station, so I thought I'd say hello and ask about your intentions? So... whatcha doin?"

Despite the serious news about Tulip Island, I chuckled a little while I stood up and put my jacket on. Perri was already prepared, wearing a light military vacsuit she'd tinted dark green with a tool pack on her back. We took a moment to listen to Mimi's conversation.

The reply from the Nova Drift was surprising. The male voice was a silken tenor. "Well hey there. We're all set, just takin' a minute to enjoy the scenery. I'm Hunter. What's your name, sweetness?"

Mimi muted herself and turned towards me. "Oh, I think Amy the fake person would like him."

"Remember, that ship outguns us three times over and there are signs of recent combat. These are real pirates," I whispered.

"So are we?" Mimi countered.

"We're the kind who don't charge through ships killing everyone aboard whether they're armed or not," I replied.

"Okay, you're probably right. Amy's allowed to like him anyway, right?" Mimi asked as she turned her attention back to her display.

"Sure, she just wouldn't trust him," I replied, watching Manny line the Daring Dream up to dock with the station. He was quick about it, barely giving the docking corridor extending under our cockpit enough time to fully deploy.

Mimi cleared her throat again and unmuted herself. "You look like pirates. I'm not accusing you of anything, I just thought it should be said."

"Well, that's fair, honey. Anyone would think so as we're hangin' around, watching the ships come in. We're just trying to talk to a few of the people from these parts about the ship grave-yard orbiting that station. We're here to salvage, but Red Gate takes aim at us whenever we get close enough," Hunter replied.

"We're just picking some stuff up for the Lidden Corporation's creditors. We don't know anyone here, sorry," Mimi replied. "Have you tried talking to anyone else?"

"Well, yes we have. That fine yacht docked up there, the Savannah, just told us to stay away. We've been tryin' to tell them we're just here to help clean that bunch of wrecks up, but they're blocking us. Isn't that just the rudest thing?" Hunter asked with a tsk.

We docked and I tapped a red switch cover on the console between the pilot and copilot seats. "You know what to do if we get stuck."

"Drop our docking collar like a lizard shedding its tail," Manny replied. "Hope not. That's expensive, no?"

"Worth it if something engages the station's mooring locks and we have to get away in a hurry," I replied, seeing no disagreement.

"Do all ships have that?" Mimi asked.

"Most ships don't need that feature, no," I replied. "See you two later."

"Good luck, I hope you find a lot of loot!" Mimi called after me before she returned all her attention to Hunter. "It's okay if you're pirates, I really don't care. We just don't want you to bother us."

"We're salvagers, dealin' with risky recoveries, but I can see how ya might think we're just some raggedy wrongdoers," he replied, earning a snicker from Manny.

"I'm going to get going before I start liking him," I replied. "Lat, meet us down there."

"Ixat is taking my spot in the turret now," he replied through the intercom.

I did one last check with Red Gate Station to make sure the credentials I stole the last time I visited Warro were working properly. The system indicated that we were clear to board and operate within the Lidden section of the station. "Let's do some creative salvaging," I said as I followed Perri out of the corridor. The cockpit door sealed behind us.

CHAPTER NINE

Scraping the Bottom

As Lat, Perri and I made our way through the Daring Dream's accordion style docking corridor to Red Gate Station, Duncan was in my ear on a private call. "What's the plan if the boarding party gets cut off from the ship, Cap?"

I responded silently, creating the sound of my voice in my digital mind then sending it through our connection. "It shouldn't come to that, but take the ship to the Shattered End as fast as you can. We'll find our own way to meet you there."

"You said the hangars on that station were locked up tight and the security was lethal. You find a way past it?" Duncan asked.

"No, but there's always a way. We'll find it if you have to break away and run," I replied aloud.

"Trouble?" Perri asked from where she walked behind. She

and Lat were carrying large empty backpacks, just in case we found something worth taking.

"No, just talking contingencies with the First Officer," I replied.

"Seems we're always talking contingencies," Lat said to no one in particular.

"Right, don't be hangin' about longer than you need to. Got a bad feeling about this one," Duncan said from his spot in the dorsal turret.

"Keep actively scanning around at the maximum setting. Everyone knows the Daring Dream is here, you may as well get rude about finding out what's really in that ring," I told him.

"Active scanning sweep, aye," Duncan replied. "We won't leave without you, Captain."

Speaking privately again, I asked a question that was probably badly timed. "Thank you. We're all right, right?"

There was a pause. Looking back, I don't blame him. The question revealed that my mind wasn't entirely on the moment. Finally Duncan replied; "I'm grand if you are."

My concern came from how Duncan seemed different after we got back to the ship. He was distant, again, like he was focusing on keeping our relationship too professional. Whatever chemistry we had at the party in New Zero seemed neutralised. As we passed through the Red Gate airlock, I sent him a tentative response. "I'm all right."

With that potential problem barely resolved, I focused on the matter at hand. The Lidden section of Red Gate Station was as Lat and I left it. The bare walls and floors were still clean with very little to offer, and there wasn't so much as a new dust particle. The lights came on automatically, and I was able to use my command and control bracer to connect to the computer system.

It welcomed me as I used a set of credentials that identified me as Dyma Korev, a freelance Reclamation Agent who had done work for companies that wanted outstanding debts collected on. Samvel Fyderov's codes and all that data I pulled from the Lidden Warehouse were more than I needed to give her top level access to everything they owned. Dyma was a real person, by the way, and she worked for Regent Galactic subsidiaries several times. I wasn't worried about messing with her reputation since she hadn't been seen for several months according to the Stellarnet.

"All right, there's an office that way. Make sure we didn't miss anything, Perri," I said, pointing across the large storage space at a door.

Perri took her hand scanner from her belt and rushed off. "I see what you meant when you were telling us about this place. There's nothing here."

"Well, that's not entirely true," I said, looking at Lat with a little smile. "You're going to like this."

He looked around and shrugged. "Are we stealing deck plates?"

"Don't panic when the alarms go off," I said, activating the security drill mode that I didn't notice last time I visited Red Gate. The light took on a red hue, an alarm blared three times and four turrets dropped down from the ceiling. They were spread out across the storage floor, simple rapid fire internal defence guns.

Perri jumped and ducked before looking back at me. "I thought you said you had full access!"

"Don't worry, I just activated a security drill, they're not going to fire. I'll switch the guns to service mode so they're easier to remove. All we have to do is unplug two cables and undo twelve bolts."

"A little warning next time?" Perri said, getting to her feet. Lat was nodding at me too.

"I told you not to be alarmed," I said with a shrug, still amused by their reactions. I couldn't help it.

Perri continued on to the office as I regarded Lat. "Get your tools out, start working on that one. You're going to want to unplug them and then work on the bolts holding them to their mounts. Call me over if you have trouble disconnecting them from the extended magazine. I'll get the fuel lines connected then get working on the next turret," I told him, activating the Servicing Mode for all the guns, which were nice, double barrel rapid fire weapons on armoured turrets that fired razor-thin monomolecular discs at high speed. These generic weapons were promising, especially since we could fabricate ammunition for them using the equipment we already had on the Daring Dream.

Lat didn't say a word, but ran to the nearest one as he started shrugging out of his backpack. The collapsable turret lowered so far down that he had no problem starting on the bolts using a motorised wrench. "You knew about these before?" he asked without turning around.

"Last time we were here? Well, I knew there were security systems in this section, but there was no way we would fit them aboard the Envoy with the cargo we were already carrying," I replied.

"Oh. That's right," Lat said.

As I started working on the manual controls to route fuel to the Daring Dream from Lidden's reserves, the sound of someone breathing on an audio sensor came over the station intercom. "Hello? I can hear you," I said.

Perri poked her head out of the office door. "Are you talking to me?"

I shook my head and pointed up as whoever was on the other

end began to speak. "I am Orel Maka, title investor in Red Gate and its rightful owner now that the other rights holders have been killed or gone bankrupt. Identify yourself immediately."

There wasn't much left to Warro's Local Matrix. Most of the computers on the planet were shut down, were taken away by looters, or had their security updated so I couldn't just browse around. It still didn't take me long to search their internet and see that the only Orel with any presence was a man in his mid-thirties.

His family were planet side when the Holocaust Virus struck, so their servant 'bots killed them all while he was away, leaving him to inherit. What he was saying about being the owner of Red Gate Station didn't add up though. "I registered with this section of the station when I came aboard. You should be able to see who I am in the administration system," I replied aloud as I continued to work the station to ship supply panel.

"I need to verify your identity. State your name and purpose immediately or I'll engage security measures," the voice replied.

I looked at the security measures, especially the one that Lat was already working on. He made a show of unplugging the main power line, disabling it. "I'm unplugging the security measures." Before he finished speaking, Lat was moving on to the next turret. He had all four unplugged in less than a minute, it was easy while they were lowered all the way down to the deck for servicing.

As soon as I saw that liquid Xetima fuel was flowing from the station, down the lines in our collapsable docking corridor then into the Daring Dream's storage tanks, I turned my attention back to Orel. "If you're talking about these turrets, then you're out of luck. My friend here just deactivated them. I'm a reclamation agent here to take what I can from the Lidden section of the station so their creditors can get something out of that deadbeat corp."

"The Lidden Corporation has been declared bankrupt. Everything on this station defaults to me," replied Orel.

"You really don't know anything about the law, do you? Lidden has a pre-paid ten year lease here, and they put their own defences in. My clients get possession for the remainder of the lease period, which is about three years. Since this place is empty, I've got to take some of the more expensive fixtures with me before I go looking for more of Lidden's assets."

"I will activate security measures. You won't survive. Leave the station immediately!" Orel's voice was starting to grate on me, and the intercom made it sound like it was coming from everywhere.

"He's just worried about the pirates," Lat said as he worked on detaching a turret from its mounting.

"True, but he's looking pretty greedy too. Not that I'm in a position to call him out for it," I said, but what I was thinking was more damning. If the Daring Dream took off, there was a chance the pirates in Warro's rings would go after us, and that might give Orel an opening to escape aboard the Savannah. "You want to use us as a distraction because you don't have control over the station."

"I can have automated security units in your section in seconds. Don't test me," Orel said.

"You're not even signed into the main administration system, otherwise you would have used Red Gate's kinetic weapons to drive those pirates off," I replied.

"Those weapons are for close perimeter defence, they're not..." he started.

I had moved on to unscrew the bolts on a turret and was getting impatient. "Hey, if you're in control of the station, you'll be able to find my name. Like I said, I signed in. We're on the up-and-up."

That shut him up for a while, but I watched the internal doors, ready to start shooting if something came through. I suspected that his family only had rights to a section of the station like me.

To my relief, the turrets were like new, probably only tested once. The quality of the parts were so high that we couldn't have duplicated them using our fabrication systems.

Perri emerged from the office with a hand full of parts. "I got these fabrication heads and a few decent hand tools, but there's..." she jumped as the turret Lat was working on finally came loose and fell sideways off its mount. "Dammit!" she shouted.

"Loud things are happening," he said, casually gesturing at the turret, which had fallen on its side.

"All right, reclamation agent," said Orel's voice. "The reason why I can't see the logs is simple. There are systems aboard this station with old security codes we were never given. Everyone who knew them was killed during The Fall."

I was relieved to hear that he was ready to have a real conversation. "So, let me guess; you came here hoping to take control of the station and didn't notice the pirates hiding nearby until you were docked."

"They attacked us on the way in, blocking us from returning to my estate, actually," Orel replied.

I took a moment to mentally look him up again, searching the broader Stellarnet for details. He was heir to an organic food company called Poog Growers. The name made no sense to me, but I looked past it and saw extortionist level prices for food that was naturally grown on several planets. One of them was the Order of Eden stronghold, Iora, but that stopped with the Fourth Fall. That was as close as Poog Growers came to being affiliated with the Order, which wasn't enough to prove that they were actually chummy with them. His family were typical wealthy people who paid into politics, had homes on several worlds and the occasional infidelity scandal. I didn't see anything special, just greed and excess. Oh, and a poog is actually a kind of potato that was made from hybridising several different types from Earth so it would grow in highly acidic soil without drawing heavy metals into the vegetable. I'd never seen one in person. "So, you want to cooperate here? Try to escape?"

"Do you have the credentials required to get into the station's main Administration System?" he asked instead.

I mentally queued up every credential I had that might have a chance at working and started trying to log into Red Gate's main system. I didn't expect it to work, and nothing did. "Nope. The best I can do is..."

I stopped as I was granted access to a tertiary lift and the hospitality section. The sensors in there were working too, and it looked thoroughly looted. Even the furniture was torn up. I didn't have time to be disappointed. Orel was impatient. "What? Can you get in or not?"

"I was going to say that the best I can do is get full access to Lidden's section, but I was wrong. There's a lift here that'll get me to Hospitality Section Four," I told him.

"It was raided. There's nothing there. Even the short stay rooms are soiled," Orel replied morosely.

Lat shook his head and rolled his eyes before getting back to work on another turret with Perri. "This place is all promise but no delivery."

Duncan spoke to me using my internal comm then. "Rogue, there's five more ships tucked away in Warro's rings. Couple of them are old customs models. They might just have a shot at catching us from where they're hiding."

I replied without speaking aloud. "So, that's the Nova Drift and two ships made to stop people from running. No wonder the Savannah hasn't tried to run."

"That's my thinking on it," Duncan replied. "What's the play? We're filling up on fuel. Makes us a pretty big bomb."

"I'm stopping that right now," I replied, running to the manual controls near the airlock.

"Everything all right?" Perri asked.

I forgot that my conversation with Duncan was silent, so all she and Lat saw was me put my spanner away and run for the door. "Not really, but we're going to try to fix that."

My digital side was already working on it, using the scan data Duncan sent me to strategise. There were a few small, fast ships nearby that would probably come after us along with the three we were worried about. That complicated things much more.

If we took off at our best speed and used everything we could on our way out for cover, the smaller ships would get shots in. They were armed with kinetic weapons that had high accuracy over a very long range. Our shields could withstand that for a while, but the larger three could outmanoeuvre us well enough so our acceleration, which was probably faster, wouldn't matter. Thanks to the messy gravitational fields around Warro, we'd need a couple of minutes to get clear before we could open a wormhole. Since our enemies would be approaching from all sides, they'd be able to catch us before we got away. Every simulation playing out in my digi-brain either ended with our capture, destruction, or severe damage. Well, except for one narrow set of options I didn't like. I pushed my digital side for another solution and found none. "I'll figure something out," I told Duncan as I deactivated the fuel pump and closed the lines.

"Well, that's a relief, 'cause I'm not seeing nothing worth tryin' here. Mimi's gab's got the pirates chuckling, but the little lass and I are sure they'll still jump us just as soon as we get away from the station's protection," Duncan replied.

After switching to the Daring Dream's encrypted crew channel, I said; "Ixat, can you bring both our cargo sleds in?"

"Yes, both cargo sleds," he replied.

"As fast as you can," I added.

"Fast as I can, Captain." I could hear him undoing the lower turret's safety harness as he answered.

"Hey, Orel," I called out aloud.

The reply came back immediately. "Yes, reclamation agent. Have you managed to gain access to the administration systems?"

"No. That's locked up tight. I'd have to go hands on with the hardware which means I'd have to deal with multiple layers of security." That was true. There was no way I'd get through all of that without huge risks that would cause real damage at least, take me out completely at worst. What I said next was a complete lie. "My contract would be void if I started stealing from other parts of the station anyway, so that's a non-starter."

"My understanding is that you're here to find wealth belonging to the Lidden Corporation, correct?" Orel asked.

"I am," I replied, carefully picking one of the turrets up. It took some effort because it was pretty unwieldy, meant to be handled by a couple of loader droids.

Perri stopped and stared as she watched me balance the awkward half ton machine over my head and walk it towards the airlock. "Grab an end," Lat said to her.

"I don't think we can pick that up," she said, looking at the turret between them.

"There are handles there. We don't have to do it her way," Lat replied, pulling two handles out for her.

"Oh, well, uh, still, probably not," Perri said as she grabbed them and tried to lift with Lat. They didn't get it off the deck.

Lat tried for a few more seconds before giving up. "You're right."

Ixat arrived with our flat, heavy duty antigravity sleds then. I put the turret I was carrying down as carefully as I could, and it still fell the last metre. Being short was good for getting under that thing, but I had no leverage once it was lowered in front of me. Luckily, the hover sled was able to take the weight. "Take it back. Thank you," I told him.

"I'll ask you again since I didn't get an answer the first time. You are here for Lidden's assets? That is correct?" Orel asked.

Ixat stopped for a moment to look for the source of the voice before returning to his duty. He didn't walk the sled back, but ran with it behind him. "I do not like this place."

"You and me both," I called after him before looking up and replying to Orel. "That's all I want. Like you, I didn't see all the ships waiting to jump us after we loaded up here."

"That is our predicament. You guessed it perfectly. We have tried to scan your ship, the Merry Mouse, and failed to see into several compartments. My engineer assumes that it is more well armed than it appears, correct?" he asked.

I only wished. There were shielded compartments inside the ship and a few with outward facing hatches that I could install weaponry in, but they were still empty. My investment into the Daring Dream covered armour, five reactors, the engines, you know, essentials. I couldn't afford missile systems and most of the other deadly tricks. That didn't mean I couldn't use what Orel's people couldn't see as leverage though. "We've got some firepower. There's not much difference between a good pirate ship and a repo ship, if I'm being honest." I picked the next turret up more carefully, lifting a side then getting under it as I managed to get it off the deck.

"That was our conclusion. My yacht is not defenceless either. I would like to offer a trade," Orel said.

"I'm listening," I groaned as I got the turret over my head. The awkwardness of doing it alone was the real difficulty there, I wasn't actually close to my maximum lift weight.

"We may have a chance at escape if we coordinate. If you decide to assist us, then I will reveal the location of an installation Lidden hid on Warro. There is wealth beyond your imagining there. It's of a kind I don't trade in, but you will never have to chase another debtor again if you sell and ransom what you find. You can convalesce at my estate while you review the data and make plans. Its defences are more than enough to keep this scum at bay."

A chill ran through me then. Sometimes the human simulation is too good, I almost dropped the turret. I needed to verify that he was talking about the one I already knew. "I heard about a scan shielded island. Is that the warehouse you're offering?"

"That is the one. It is impossible to find, far underground. There are many places on Warro with hidden things, even if you follow the lead you already have, you'll end up in the wrong place. I guarantee it," he replied. "My direction will be required for you to uncover the wealth I'm offering."

"Why wouldn't you use what's hidden there to make yourself even richer?" I asked. "What is it?"

"Let's say that selling the product there would be against Galactic Law. Now that the Spiral Court is convening, I can't break certain rules, but you can trade the product honestly. There are people looking for what's inside, and as a reclamation agent, you'd earn rewards for the delivery. Leave whatever you don't want behind to rot, or reveal it so the galaxy can deal with it. I don't care. It's poisoned meat to me, so you won't have to worry about me being involved," he replied.

I was sure we were talking about the Lidden Warehouse under Tulip Island, especially after he referred to the contents as rotten meat. "Interesting. So, where is it?"

"Nice try. Once we're safe at my estate I'll reveal everything. Do we have a deal, future billionaire?" he asked.

"We do, but have you ever had to escape like this before?" I asked.

"No. The Savannah has powerful weaponry, but she has never been tested. Only six of the crew are former military, but they were infantry, so I'm afraid I have to admit that we're all out of my depth. On the brighter side, I've always known when I require a hireling, and that's where you come in," he said.

That earned him a little credit, but I still didn't like Orel. I put the turret down on the cargo sled and Lat pushed it down the boarding corridor towards the Daring Dream. "All right. My crew has experience. We've been chased around a few times, gotten away from defence forces. This isn't much different, but you're going to have to follow my directions. If you don't, we'll both get captured or slagged."

"Spoken like a true adventuring spacer. I will tell my helmsman to coordinate with your ship," he said.

"Your crew will coordinate with me," I replied firmly.

"I'm guessing you're the Captain, then. I still don't know your name," Orel said.

"Captain Dyma Korev. Call me Dyma. Make sure you and everyone aboard your ship listens in while I put this plan together," I told him.

"Tremendous. I'll patch them in." Orel seemed to savour the words.

CHAPTER TEN

Triple Trouble

My crew didn't ask questions when I ordered them to stuff the four turrets into the Daring Dream's aft cargo compartment. They didn't share their concerns when I turned the station's fuel pumps back on to fill the port and starboard cargo pods with xetima fuel. They didn't say a word about me trying to strategise with Orel Maka and his hirelings either. That was good, because I didn't have time to explain myself.

The planning session with Orel went something like this. I returned to the cockpit, where I took the copilot's seat and finished going over how we could use the strengths of our ships together. "We're going to have to switch positions whenever one ship's shields go below fifty percent," I was saying, watching Manny nod to my left.

Orel didn't leave the secure channel as I tried to coordinate with his crew. He spoke for them instead. "Can your pilot manage that? My man's experience is with luxury craft exclusively, that's one of the reasons why I hired him. I don't think he's combat trained."

"I'll fly around the Savannah. He just has to accelerate in a straight line," Manny said.

Mimi was having a conversation of her own with someone aboard the Nova Drift. Her dome was up, so I couldn't hear what she was saying, but it seemed like it was going well, judging from her intermittent laughter. She was keeping them busy at least, but I hoped that she was getting some information out of them too.

"I believe he's capable of flying quickly in a straight line," Orel replied. "Now, the matter of the courses you've set. There are two options here, and I specified one destination."

I was hoping he'd be open to flying directly to a wormhole jump point, away from the planet. That route would put the station between us and most of the pirates. It was the best cover we had because they would have to avoid its defences and shoot around it otherwise Red Gate's countermeasures would negate any solid rounds or other munitions. If we took the other course leading to the planet, then we'd have to fly between asteroids and other large matter for a while and then we'd have a couple minutes before we could go atmospheric. While the Nova Drift may not have been able to follow us into an atmosphere, but the chances of us making it to blue skies were low. "We should fly for open space and jump as soon as we're far enough from Warro's gravity well. It's our best chance."

"Incorrect," Orel said sharply. "Once we're within range of my estate's defences anyone who pursues us will regret it."

"That will leave us in the open for at least one minute and fifty-three seconds while we fly into their coverage area. We'll be taken or destroyed." It was something I had to prevent. Abandoning him and his yacht but he knew about the Lidden Warehouse. I had no faith that he wouldn't try to trade its location for his freedom because he'd already dangled that info in front of me for the same thing.

"That is your opinion. We will retreat to my estate post haste, unless you think it's wise to wait this scum out?" Orel asked.

"One moment, I need to coordinate with my pilot," I replied, muting him.

Mimi's little terminal showed that Orel couldn't hear what was being said in the cockpit and she muted her own conversation then opened her bubble. "You don't look happy."

"Convincing this guy to save his own life will take more time we don't have," I replied. "How's your conversation going?"

"Oh, Hunter is in love with my avatar. He finds Amy as charming as she is lovely," Mimi said with a wistful sigh.

"It's not nice to catfish people," Manny muttered.

"What's catfishing?" Mimi asked.

"It's when you trick someone into a relationship while you're pretending to be someone else," Manny explained.

"I can't help it! Put my wonderful personality behind Amy's face and any human male is rendered helpless! Besides, I think Hunter and the Nova Drift crew have been in space for a long time. They're a lonely bunch," Mimi said.

"Have you learned anything else?" My patience would have worn out quickly if I wasn't still trying to calculate a good plan to get to in range of the estate defences before we were captured or killed. "Any tactically useful knowledge come up?"

"Oh, right," Mimi said, scrolling through her notes. "It didn't take long for Hunter to tell me about the platinum that was detected aboard the Savannah. He didn't say how much, but it's United Core World molecularly stamped coin, the kind that's rare in the Ninety Eight. He calls it 'real currency,' and from the sound of it, there's a lot. That's what they're really after. He says the Savannah docked with the station and moved a couple tons of it up."

"Wow, no wonder they're waiting them out. The Savannah crew may as well move into the station for the long haul, really wait them out," I commented.

"Any chance of that?" Duncan asked through the intercom from the dorsal turret.

"They turned the option down flat. I can't say I'm too disappointed. Our chances of getting out of here are a lot higher with them as a distraction," I replied.

"Aye," Duncan said.

"What about hacking into the administration system?" Lat asked from his spot in the ventral turret.

"I've been trying on and off. Red Gate's security is top of the line. I've got access to Lidden's section and that's it. Whoever finally takes charge of this place will either have the right credentials, time, powerful tools, or more manpower than anyone would spend on this. Some systems are so hard to take that it's not worth the trouble," I replied.

"We have the fuel," Lat said, aware that it was worth more platinum than the crew had ever seen.

Manny glanced at me, aware that I'd put the tanks under pressure and primed the external purge valves. I didn't want to, but I would use every drop of that fuel as a weapon if I had to. "Did you learn anything else from the people aboard the Nova Drift?" I asked Mimi.

"Oh, I asked to talk to the Captain and Hunter said he wasn't actually in charge. After a little banter, I got him to say the name of the real leader. I haven't gotten a chance to look her up yet, but her name is Patrizia Salustri."

"Oh, shit," I said before I could catch myself.

"You've heard of her?" Mimi asked, eyes filling with worry.

"Let's hope you were fed that name as a fear tactic," I replied. "One sec, let me check something." A quick look at the list of ships Duncan had managed to scan didn't turn up anything matching Salustri's ship. He'd done well, passing our powerful focused array over the area around us in a grid pattern. There was only one space that he'd neglected, and I wouldn't have thought of scanning that area either. "Duncan, can you do a high gain, passive scan sweep of the derelicts surrounding the station?"

"Aye, right away," he replied. "Results are comin' through now. Got all sorts of ships that came too close to the station and got their arses handed to them."

"Why is this Salustri lady scary?" Mimi asked. "Have you met her?"

"I've watched briefings about her," I replied, leaning into Alice's knowledge. "She was a pirate, then a privateer for the Carthans, and then a crime boss. Last I heard, the Tamber Rangers were trying to push her and her people out of the Haven System. Patrizia Salustri is trouble, and her ship has been on an upgrade path for over a decade. There." I pointed at the profile of a ninety-nine metre long ship on the outer edge of the orbiting wrecks. "That's the Morte Lenta. The one with the big bay doors along the bottom."

"Its systems read dead. No power, no heat anywhere," Lat said from his position in the lower turret.

"It's just barely out of range of the station's trigger range, pretending to be one of the wrecks," I said.

"Look at the firepower on that! It'll have us in seconds," Duncan said. "That is if it's playing dead and not actually dead."

"Well, the name isn't quite accurate, but still terrifying," Perri said from the central cargo hold using the intercom. "Slow Death."

"We saw it on our translators, and now I see the scan results. That thing is beautiful," Lat remarked.

The ship was a fusion of old and new, with a pair of main railgun cannons that looked like forked swords at the front as statement weapons. There were circular doors on all sides hiding launchers, turrets and other systems. My imagination was a scary place as I took a few milliseconds to guess at what they hid.

They wouldn't need any of that, though. Some quick math in my head told me that one hit from their main weapon would burn our shields out, a second would put a hole right through our hull, and that was if they used solid metal rounds. There was every chance that they were loaded with something even more powerful. "We're not seeing what's inside that ship. The hull is old school, a metre thick with enhanced plating on top. My guess is that it's not dead, there's a crew ready to go. It's a good plan. Stay just out of the station's alert range, wait for someone to fly in, grab something valuable and jump them the moment they try to leave."

"Is it natural for a ship like that to wait?" Ixat asked from the aft section of the ship.

"Reckon there's other ships nippin' down to the planet, picking through mansions and whatever else got left behind. They fill up, haul it off, then swing back while that big brute keeps an eye out for the real prizes," Duncan said.

"It looks bad, like a predator," Mimi said quietly.

"It is," Manny added. "And those engines, they're fusion drives, we can outrun them, but I don't think the Savannah has a shot."

"All right, don't tell anyone we've seen it, Mimi," I said. "The only information you can offer from now on is that we're afraid that we're about to get jumped."

"Okay, I'll keep distracting Hunter, play scared until you tap my bubble," Mimi said, re-sealing her station.

The stakes were clear, but my course of action wasn't. Seeing Patrizia Salustri's ship changed things. I needed more current information and I knew where to get it.

Using a direct, secure connection through my Haven Node, I reached out to Ensign Ito and Major Rivera, both my contacts with the Haven Fleet Privateering Initiative. I tagged my call with a Haven Fleet Priority One Emergency code. It wasn't something I did lightly. I could get into trouble since I wasn't actually a member of the fleet. To my surprise, Ensign Ito replied first. She was in a dress uniform I hadn't seen - a smart looking black jacket with an emblem that communicated her position as a Public Relations Officer. "Rogue? Did someone catch up to you?"

"No, we got away from Bio First, they didn't track me down in space," I replied.

Then Major Jose Rivera came in. He was retracting his armoured vacsuit headpiece, catching his breath. "Rogue, what's the trouble?"

"Has there been any movement on the Warro investigation? Any follow up?" I asked.

"This better be urgent. The last time someone used that code they spotted an Edxi brood ship," Major Rivera said, his brow furrowing. Mimi muted her conversation and retracted the bubble built into her station so she could listen in and watch the holographic heads I was talking to. She was in time to hear Major Rivera say; "No. We sent someone to Warro, gave the area you highlighted a focused scan and they saw that it was undisturbed. They had to move on to more pressing objectives."

"I'm afraid I'm out of the loop on that," Ensign Ito said.

"It doesn't directly concern New Zero or Tabrus," Major Rivera said.

"I'm bringing this to your attention because there's a high probability that Patrizia Salustri is about to find out where it is and what's down there," I told him.

Major Rivera straightened up and addressed Ensign Ito. "Thank you for replying to Rogue's emergency signal, Ensign. The rest of this conversation is classified above your access level. Forget what you've heard so far."

"Yes, Sir. Dropping out of the call. Good luck, Rogue," Ensign Ito replied.

"Patrizia Salustri?" Major Rivera asked, shaking his holographic head at me. "We've been looking for her. She's on Warro?"

"Her ship is hiding next to Red Gate Station," I replied. That's when I made my report, explaining as quickly as I could that we were about to assist the Savannah. I sent all the scan data we'd gathered while I spoke. The Nova Drift, Morte Lenta and all the other ships that were trying to hide in and around the rings were highlighted. It only took a couple of minutes and he listened carefully. I finished my report by stating; "There are over ten thousand of the most violent criminals under that island. I'm putting that together with Patrizia Salustri and that leads me to one question. Have you managed to entice her into the Haven Privateering Initiative?"

"No. After her organisation was driven out of the Haven System she went back to her old ways. The Morte Lenta has taken Order, civilian and other targets. One of our Privateers was attacked a few weeks ago when they went after a bulk transport. They're lucky they weren't the target. She's not on anyone's side but her own," Major Rivera replied. "We've seen the Nova

Drift at the Bitter End, but there's no indication on record that she's associated with it. Her presence there may be happenstance."

"Not according to my communications officer," I said.

"You found a clear connection?" Major Rivera asked.

Mimi spoke up then, her small voice trying to match my official tone. "Yes, Major Rivera. A communications officer named Hunter told my avatar that she's in charge of the pirates here."

"Thank you, Mimi," he replied just as seriously. If he was charmed by her then, he didn't show it. "Good job. That kind of information usually comes out of an interrogation."

It was time to push for help. "So, Haven Fleet still isn't doing anything about the Warro warehouse? I know the Outbound Legion is busy in the Rose System, but you have a whole fleet."

"You know I don't have the whole fleet. I'm just a small part of a bigger picture. I've highlighted Warro in multiple briefings, made sure everyone who can do something about this knows about Tulip Island, but they believe you have the right idea. It's no one's problem while it's still buried," he replied.

My reply started low key but it didn't stay that way. "They're not thinking long term or with any attention to what's right for everyone here. If something happens down there, people will die or escape. I might not be the only one with administration rights to that warehouse, so either one is possible. Now we're in a situation where the Order are treating sleepers as a resource, and we don't know what they're using them for. Haven Fleet is hoping that the Lidden Warehouse is a burial site, but now it could be a time bomb because the entitled prick aboard the Savannah knows about it and I can't find a way to keep him from getting taken by the most notorious pirate in the Cluster. I'd be right to tell the bloody galaxy about Warro so someone does something about it while I do everything I can to get my crew out alive while Haven Fleet gets blamed for whatever happens to those inmates!"

"Do you want to draw the Order a map and cost Haven an ally or two? With the Edxi, Order, Raiders and all the other threats, the main focus of the Fleet is the defence of the Haven System. You know the old philosophy; if you want to help someone else, you have to make sure you're fit first. Unearthing and taking care of the multitude down there isn't a light or simple undertaking," Major Rivera replied.

"So, what do I do? My crew, my ship and my armaments are small. The Daring Dream can't penetrate the warehouse's outer shell. It would take hours to fabricate and plant enough explosives to destroy it. That's murder, even if the people down there are morally lost. The other options may be worse but I'm considering them," I told him.

"I don't have the power to call more resources in. Even the Outbound Legion is out of touch," he replied.

"Stop giving me reasons why you can't help and tell me what you can do!" My outburst earned me looks of surprise from Mimi and Manny.

Major Rivera looked away from me with a scowl frozen on his face as he thought, or maybe he was simmering, trying not to lose it on me. I expected push back, maybe a word or two about keeping my cool, but his response was quiet when it came. "Did you leave anything out of your report on the Lidden Warehouse? Anything that could help?"

"No. You wouldn't know what I stole on my last visit if I did," I replied flatly.

"Then I know your options. There are a few privateers that could get there in a little over twenty hours. Can you keep this situation under control until then?" he asked.

"Hold on for a second. I'm going to talk to the master of the

Savannah, listen in. I won't tell him I'm in contact with you, don't worry," I said, switching to the call I had open with Orel. "I'm back."

"It's about time! You can't keep me waiting. This situation is dire!" Orel shouted.

"I've been working the problem with my crew. We may stand a better chance if we stay here for another day, maybe a little longer," I replied.

"Not on your life! Three ships have arrived in our area since we arrived, and my ship has been scanned every time a new one starts slithering through the rings. While we wait for a solution the odds of me returning to safety diminish. Waiting would be stupidity unless you have a whole fleet coming! Do you? Do you have a fleet of friends coming to our rescue?" he demanded.

I was glad that Major Rivera's holographic head and shoulders weren't visible to Orel because he closed his eyes and slowly shook his head. Seeing Orel immediately lose his cool helped me keep mine. "No. I might be able to get a few ships here, but not for a day. You're right, the sooner we get going, the better our chances are. A wormhole jump is still a better option."

"How many times do I have to tell you that's the worst option? It is exasperating!" he said, leaning so close to the holo-sensor that I could only see his eyes and nose for a moment.

"All right, let me work on this for a couple minutes," I said, putting him on hold. He was about to yell at me about that before I cut him off. "Manny, be ready. He might be pissed off enough to bolt. Make for open space if he does."

"Aye," Manny replied.

"So, waiting around isn't going to happen. He'll bug out sooner rather than later," I told Major Rivera.

"Right. What about you and your crew?" he asked.

"We're clinging to Red Station's exterior. There's no open

hangar for cover. There are a couple ships out here that could take us out if they get impatient even with the station's counter-measures in play. That's about the only thing I agree with Orel on," I said, surprised at how defeated those words made me sound.

He nodded to himself and paused to think before speaking. "All right. I'm going to propose something but you have to make me a promise."

"What?" I asked.

"If this ends my career, give me a spot on your crew." There was no sign that he was kidding around.

"You'll have a job," I replied.

"Then I'm giving you immunity from prosecution with regard to any action you take in Warro space or on the planet. That counts for Haven Fleet, Haven Nation but you're out of luck with the Spiral Court. Galactic law will apply, and the Order has control of that," Major Rivera said.

The thought that the Order of Eden had control of the Spiral Court, the commonly acknowledged lawmakers for the Milky Way Galaxy, was startling. I had to put it aside for the moment regardless. "Thank you, but what are you about to do?"

"You know the training. Not from the Haven Fleet Apex Officer's Program, but the old Freeground Fleet Doctrine, where they got their core philosophies. That'll open up some uncon-ventional options, especially if you're trying to keep everyone but you from getting an advantage," he replied.

Whatever file the Major was given on me must have been beyond extensive. He knew that my first life was spent on Jonas Valent's arm computer and that he'd been through Freeground Fleet Officer Training. I learned everything he did back then. He was even aware of the differences between that and Haven's regulations. I knew what he was talking about specifically.

"You're telling me to put every option on the table, consider my crew's survival, and push everything that won't result in a successful outcome off."

He nodded. "On a morality scale that slides with your chances of survival."

"You know I'll consider options with far reaching consequences." It was a warning.

He held a hand up, stopping me from explaining any further. "I don't have a clear understanding of what that means, exactly. I only did the course work once."

He knew, but admitting that could put him in even more trouble. "I understand."

"I'll get you refuelled and repaired once you get here," he replied. "It's the best I can do. You're not a Privateer yet."

"Just a pirate," I added, and from the look on Manny's face, I think he was starting to grasp what that meant. Privateers could sometimes get support whether it was from allies or the government who gave them the license. Pirates were on their own.

"I know your options. I wish I could do more," he said. "Is there anything else? What can I do?"

There was only one question on my mind then. "According to Fleet Intelligence, would Patrizia Salustri sell humans in stasis to the Order?"

"Yes," he said without hesitation. "She's dealt in slavery and ransoms before."

"Thank you. I'll see you at the Bitter End," I replied, aware of how that sounded. "Unless you can help me some other way?"

"I'm afraid not," Major Rivera replied. "Good hunting."

His holographic image disappeared then. I lowered my head. There was a high speed argument happening between my digital and biological sides. One presented logical courses of action. The other hated every option. Finally, after a few seconds that felt like a minute, I knew what I'd do. "We have to get on with it. Mimi, tell the Nova Drift that you're afraid of what your captain - me - will do. Talk to him like you're speaking in secret. If he asks you what you're afraid of..."

Duncan interrupted me from the dorsal turret then. I already knew what he was about to say, I could see it on the tactical display. "The Savannah's getting ready to make a run for the planet. Looks like it's now or never!"

I opened the call with Orel and he regarded me with a satisfied smile. "I knew that would get your attention. It's time for me to go home. You said our chances were better together? I will let you take the rear from the start."

"All right, here we go," I said, laying my hands on the controls and switching the copilot's station to pilot mode.

"You have control," Manny said, surprised but already checking shields and dampeners.

"I have control," I replied before regarding Orel. "We'll take the first hits and we'll switch up when our shields are down to fifty percent."

"Repeat until we're under my estate's defence umbrella," Orel replied.

I respected Manny enough to do what I was about to, but liked him too much to saddle him with the guilt. The Savannah's main thrusters flared as it propelled itself away from the station. I turned the nose of the Daring Dream to follow, and watched the yacht continue to accelerate towards the edge of Red Gate's defence perimeter.

The instant they were moving too fast to turn back, I flipped the Daring Dream end over end so we were pointed towards the blackness of open space. "I hope we've worked the bugs out of the engines," I said as I pushed the throttle to maximum, activating the antimatter reaction chambers in our rear thrusters.

The light of our triple engines firing was so bright that it reflected off the station's hull and bathed ours like we were orbiting a sun for the first few seconds. "Would ye look at that? A whole pile of ships moving after the Savannah!"

"How many after us?" I asked.

"Incoming launches, some kind of EMP missiles," Manny said. "Launching countermeasures."

"Three ships turnin' and burnin' after us! Marking them!" Duncan said from the dorsal turret. "Outta my effective range."

"I hope they don't get in range," Mimi said, closing her bubble and linking to the intercom so we could freely communicate with her.

"Mimi, tell your friend on the Nova Drift that we don't care about the Savannah, they can have her. We just want to get out of here," I said as I pushed the throttle control. It was already all the way up, the engines were already howling so loudly that the sound made its way through the whole ship to the cockpit. The dampeners added their own hum to the roar. The best I could do was try to put the station between the Daring Dream and our pursuers. The Nova Drift was already well on its way to getting clear to fire on us.

"Hey, Hunter, let us go! You can have the Savannah! All we got is a bunch of fuel and you'll probably blow us up and get nothing if you come after us," Mimi pleaded.

"Eh, that's just how I like it. We take you, I get a new ship. We break you, no one left to tell the tale. Win-win, no?" It was the voice of Patrizia Salustri herself.

"Are we calculating a wormhole trajectory?" I asked.

"Finishing... now. Almost far away from the gravity well to jump," he replied.

Our countermeasures sent the electromagnetic pulse missiles flying in random directions as their guidance systems were jammed, but we weren't out of trouble yet. A barrage of railgun fire from the Nova Drift taxed our aft shields and I immediately regretted running out of money before I could upgrade them. "Just another nine thousand klicks..." I said under my breath.

"Damage! Port cargo pod!" Ixat shouted.

"Get ready to jettison fuel," I told Manny.

"Bad time to ask, but wouldn't rounds have a chance at igniting it?" he asked.

"Only while it's inside the ship. If something thrusts through it while it's free-floating it'll mess with their engines but that's about it," I replied, aware that if we dumped the fuel I'd have to throttle all the way down.

I'm not a natural pilot, that's always been true, but I did train on a lot of starships, so my evasive action was text book. We were still thrusting in the same direction for the most part though, and the gunners aboard the Nova Drift were good. Red markers flashed on the Daring Dream's condition screen, highlighting strikes on bare armour. They were concentrating on the port side cargo pod, aware that it was filled to the brim with xetima fuel. "Sweet divine, they're actually going for the kill!" Duncan shouted.

"Steady the ship," Manny said as his hand hovered over the wormhole generator controls.

I stopped our weaving course. "Steady, jump!"

The distant red-yellow haze of the Iron Head Nebula warped and distorted as a wormhole formed in front of us and we accelerated away from our attackers so quickly that we wouldn't be caught. An alarm went off across the ship. "Leak! There is a leak in central cargo hold!" Ixat shouted.

I cut our main thrusters. "You have control. Keep us in the middle using our cold thrusters only," I told Manny.

"Yes, Ma'am. I have control," he said.

"Where is it, Ixat?" I asked, getting out of my seat.

"Internal, frame twelve, section two," he replied. "I'm on my way to seal it now."

"It's not our tanks?" I asked.

"It is! Fuel is coming into the ship," he replied.

"All right," I looked at Manny.

"Getting us out of here using main thrusters," he said. "That is unless you see a leak out there?"

"No exterior leak," Ixat said over the intercom.

"All right, get us half a billion klicks away from Warro and drop us out," I told him, earning a quizzical expression in response.

"We're stopping for repairs," I told him, though it wasn't the whole truth. "Be ready to run, just in case they follow us out."

"Aye, I'll find us a good place to hide if we stick around," he replied.

I rushed from the cockpit, telling him and Mimi; "Keep the door closed and suits sealed in case the fumes get up here. I'll tell you when it's clear."

"Good thing my station is very bed-like," Mimi said over the intercom as I rushed down the corridor to the next problem.

CHAPTER ELEVEN

A Fundamental Principle

My bright idea to pressurise the cargo pods so we could expel the thick xetima into space backfired. Something let go when we took railgun damage and the fuel started spraying from storage right into our smaller central cargo hold.

The turrets we'd just put there along with a lot of the gear and food we kept in crates were getting a bath in high end xetima gel. I sealed the cargo hold once we were inside and increased the pressure until the cargo pod stopped pushing fuel into the cargo bay.

Perri, Ixat and I knew how dangerous that stuff was, and it managed to get just about everywhere. That pure form of xetima doesn't need anything to burn, all the ingredients for disaster are included in the formula, so setting it off would have resulted in a violent explosion that would have instantly turned the Daring Dream into charred, shredded metal bits. The good news is that xetima doesn't go off as easily as some other fuel types. The bad news is that a lot of friction or a sudden surge in heat can get it going, and if the ignition point doesn't extinguish itself like it's supposed to, then it'll all go up. That self extinguishing feature, which is made to stop explosions while refuelling, only works about half the time against an open flame or heat from friction. It is rocket fuel, after all.

Oh, and it's pretty gross, which doesn't technically matter, I know. Just imagine a thick gel that's yellow-green that likes to cling to bare skin. It also leaves light brown stains on everything it touches, so that mess was no pleasure.

There's a procedure for cleanup, and my crew had done a few drills. Not as many as they should have, looking back on it, but it was enough so Ixat and Perri didn't need many instructions.

"What do you think we lost? Three thousand litres?" Perri asked as she carefully opened an emergency locker and took another bag of neutralising powder out.

"I estimate nine thousand at least. It is a mess. It could be worse," Ixat said as he flicked some of the powder around his feet.

I was inspecting the failed valve and saw that it broke apart when the cargo pod was jostled around by a bunch of railgun hits. I scanned the clasps holding the cargo pod to the ship and shook my head. "We were nearly blown up thanks to loose braces. I'll tighten those up later."

"So, nothing penetrated the armour?" Perri asked.

"Nope," I replied. "This is the last time we're hauling this stuff, though."

"That is wise," Ixat said, watching the yellowish xetima around him turn white as it became a harmless protein rich gel. "Do you want me to plug the line?"

"I've got it," I replied, pulling a hull filler injector from my belt. My scanners sent signals through the fill port that bounced around the inside of the cargo pod. After a few seconds I was sure that there were no breaches. The hole that the round made wasn't in there, but in the main cargo hold, and it had self-sealed right away. It got in through there and hit the fill port, busting it open. "We're going to have to replace this whole fitting, so I'm just going to take it out now. It's going to take me a few minutes, then I'll seal it."

"It is simple. Unscrew the nuts, pry the seals, push the fitting on the other side out..." Ixat started to explain.

Perri cut him off. "She knows, and she's taking her time. If she rushes it there could be enough friction to create heat and that'll blow us all up."

"That is right. I neglected to remember," Ixat replied with a bow. "Please be slow, Rogue."

"Will do. We didn't train for this level of fuel spill. I thought the worst case scenario was a busted barrel," I replied as I started turning the nuts around the fill port, which were as wide as my head.

"Not a wading pool sized spill," Perri agreed.

"Wading pool?" Ixat asked as he moved along, spreading neutraliser as he crossed the compartment.

Perri was doing the same in the other direction, only stopping momentarily to make sure a hatch was locked. We were sealed in, but she was wise to double check. Our compartment was under five atmospheres of pressure instead of one, the standard for the rest of the ship. "Oh, I guess wading pools aren't that common. My family lived on base for a few months. My brother and I used to play with the local kids at this pool with sprinklers where the water never got more than about twenty centimetres deep. It was always so hot there, so it was a fun way to cool off."

"I thought your people were warriors?" Ixat asked.

"Well, yes, but we were little kids then so I didn't even understand what my parents did," Perri replied.

"I began fighting before my third year, in human time measure. There was no time for wading pools while the Masters were still living," Ixat said.

"Oh, I'm sorry. Or is it like the Nafalli? You learn to hunt while you're small?" Perri asked.

"We were given old broken war tools as soon as we could practice with them and fought once we showed aptitude with them. The great war demanded that we fight until all the Masters were eliminated. None of their kind were allowed to survive. I was fortunate to be part of the last generation to hunt. I saw the last of them destroyed. Then the Order came and I escaped," he replied solemnly. "I've never seen a wading pool."

"Oh, I'm sorry," Perri said, letting the apology hang in the air until she was sure the conversation was over. After a glance at me she got back to work, spraying liquid neutraliser on the turret that caught the most xetima. "That's gonna take a while to clean up."

"I'll buy some processor bundles so you can make a few small cleaning droids. You know, the ones people keep in their tool boxes," I replied.

"Oh, fantastic, they can crawl around in there so we don't have to take these turrets apart," Perri sighed.

"That is my job," Ixat said.

"What? Cleaning these turrets? Wouldn't you rather be doing anything else?" Perri asked.

"Disassembly is the best way to truly understand equipment when it's followed by reassembly," Ixat replied.

"Well, I'm going to need you to work on the ship, especially since we might install one of those turrets," I said, finishing unscrewing a large nut. I didn't need tools, but taking that fill port apart was annoying because I couldn't hurry it up.

I was able to split my attention though, so I was watching Warro through my connection to Red Gate. There was a twenty-eight minute delay because of the distance. It was strange watching our own escape. Thanks to our little wormhole jump part way across the solar system I could look back and see it happen all over again. That's what happens when you cheat physics enough to beat the normal speed of light. Things get freaky.

Three ships went after us. The Nova Drift was the largest and it seemed most determined. Nine went for the Savannah and overtook it easily, shooting at its engines, weapons and finally latching on with a claw on thick cables so they could control the yacht as they closed in and docked. We were gone by then, and I felt a little guilty about that.

I could have blamed Orel for being disagreeable, for taking off before we were ready, but I knew they might have stood a chance if we helped out. It was less than one percent, but still a chance. As the Savannah was boarded it sent an automated distress signal out, but it stopped after three minutes and four seconds. Whoever went aboard got control of the ship fast.

Once things settled down the Morte Lenta moved from its spot orbiting the station along with another ship that was hiding nearby. It docked with the same port that the Savannah used when it was moored to Red Gate. "I can't believe Orel gave them clearance to board the station so fast," I said mostly to myself.

"You saw that, huh?" Manny said from the bridge.

"What's up?" Perri asked. She and Ixat finished neutralising the fuel in the main cargo hold and she was picking up a vacuum hose.

"It looks like Orel, the master of the Savannah, is telling

Salustri everything," I replied. "Her flagship is already docked with Red Gate Station. If we're unlucky it could become a part of her criminal empire."

"Oh, I just looked her up. That's really bad," Perri said.

"That's what I was telling Manny just now. We looked her up too. That lady was just accused of stealing a starliner with five thousand twenty passengers aboard. No one has seen it or anyone that was aboard," Mimi said. "That was three weeks ago."

"So... maybe she's selling people like Carosa?" Perri asked.

I was as tense as a rod at the thought of Orel spilling everything he knew about the Lidden Warehouse. Was Salustri willing to sell humans to the Order? Was that why her people took a full starliner? "Maybe," I replied finally.

"So, that spill is cleaning up a little faster than I expected," Lat said from his position in the ventral turret.

"You could help out instead of watching from down there, you know," Perri said as she swept a broad suction nozzle over the deck.

"That compartment has to remain sealed until the tube between it and the cargo pod is patched, sorry," Lat said.

"Why are you supervising us?" Ixat asked.

"It's something to do while I watch the tactical monitor. Those pirates could jump us at any minute," he replied.

"Aye, too true, but unlikely. Watching you lot work's been kinda educational. That floor'll be fit to feast off of by the time you're finished." Duncan said from the dorsal turret.

I finished taking the valve and fixture apart, so I squeezed a generous blob of quick setting hull filler into the hole. The scanners in my head could see every detail while it solidified and created a tough seal. "All right, reduce the pressure in the main

ROGUE CHASE   151

cargo hold to normal. Be ready to put it right back up if the seal breaks."

"Finally," Perri said.

"You are too confident. Disaster may be imminent if the Captain's work was improper," Ixat warned.

"Where's your faith? It'll be fine," Mimi chided over the intercom.

Everything I saw made me sure that the repair was perfect even if we'd have to install a new pipe and valve later, but ships can surprise you. The filler held up. "We're good, it'll hold."

"Oh, good, now we just have to finish cleaning this up," Perri said.

"I will filter air," Ixat said as he set the atmosphere controls to remove toxins in the hold.

"You mean you'll set the environmental system to filter the air," Mimi corrected.

"It's okay, we know he's not going to take his helmet off and use his own lungs to do it," Perri replied.

"I dislike being corrected," Ixat said.

"So, we know what happened to the Savannah now, and we know our ship won't blow up, so why are we still sitting here?" Mimi asked from the cockpit.

"Didn't I just say it's a bad time to ask?" Manny asked her.

"I thought you just meant it was a bad time to ask *you*, so I asked *her*," Mimi replied.

"Tulip Island," I replied.

"Oh. What about it? We're not going back there, are we? I'm not going outside if we are. Those flowers aren't om-nomming me again," Mimi said.

"No, we're not going back. Orel knows about it. He tried to trade its location for my help," I replied.

"Oh, that's what he was trying to bribe you with?" Mimi asked.

"Tulip Island?" Perri asked. "That warehouse with the worst of the worst in it?"

"Right," I replied as I picked a suction hose up and started working on the slippery deck.

"That's here?" she asked, shocked.

"On Warro, yes. I sent you the report," I replied, surprised that she wasn't aware.

"Sorry, I didn't get through the whole thing, sorry," she said.

"No worries," I told her.

"Hold on a sec. You're thinking that if Orel handed over his credentials for the space station right after they took his ship, odds are he's about to tell her that next, aye?" Duncan asked.

"Right. It's not like he'll give them the codes to get past his estate's security systems first," I said.

"This is not our problem. We go. We go now," Ixat said.

"If Salustri is selling people to the Order, or looking to recruit for her own organisation, there's no better source than the Lidden Warehouse. She can pick and choose from thousands of murderers and career criminals. There's even a cannibal cult down there," I explained.

"Dammit, I knew it. We should have looted the place weeks ago. Just a little side-trip with a rental ship and we would have been rich," Lat said.

"I bet we would have been taken by pirates instead. Besides, you never made the suggestion," I said.

"Not out loud, no," Lat said.

"Doesn't count when you keep those in yer head, y'know." Duncan said.

"Oh, shut up," Lat said.

"It's totally true," Mimi said. "Suggestions you don't say are just wishes that go nowhere. It's also a clear sign that you lack confidence in yourself. You'll want to work on that."

"I will come up there," Lat growled.

"You should. You can tell me about all the ideas you're holding back," Mimi replied.

"Why would I tell... ah, never mind," Lat said.

"Are you sure you don't want a little therapy session? I'm a comfort companion, you know," Mimi said.

"I don't think he's interested right now, Mimi," I said as I watched Lat's biometrics. He was a little frustrated. "There's a more important situation right now. There are a few things I didn't tell you about the Lidden Warehouse. I have full control of the place thanks to the data I picked up when Lat, Mimi and I visited the place. I can control what happens to the pods down there, and I want your opinions. I'll make the final decision on my own since I don't want any of you to be accountable for what I do here."

"You're really thinking Orel will give that to her?" Duncan asked.

"I'm sure. People like Salustri have people who specialise in extracting every secret someone's holding. He'll offer the warehouse or she'll take its location right out of his head," I replied.

"Call Valent. Get his ship here so he can defeat Salustri's pirates. We'll take what we want from the warehouse and he can deal with the rest," Lat suggested.

"He and his carrier are in the middle of strike-and-fade operations in the Rose System. I haven't had a real conversation with him in weeks," I replied.

"No wonder he hasn't pushed the Order out of there, he's always hiding," Lat grumbled.

"Careful," Mimi warned quietly.

If it were just he and I, there would have been a confrontation, but I wasn't the kind of captain who punished people for sharing their thoughts. "All right, so we have one impossible option. Does anyone else have an idea?"

"Is there a destruction system in the warehouse?" Ixat asked.

"No, why do you ask?" I asked.

"You may destroy the people inside if there was. Salustri would only find equipment and bodies," he replied.

"I can shut the pods down, that is technically an option," I said. "Any other thoughts?"

"Well, since this isn't a vote I can say this; wake them up," Perri offered.

"Not a chance. No way," Duncan said.

"Nope, nuh-uh," Mimi added.

"Uh, that's creative, but not in a good way," Manny said.

"Wait, wait, let me explain," Perri said. "Think about it. Right now there are no ships down there, right? It's just an island with a bunch of flowers on it. There's nothing to eat outside and nowhere to go for anyone unless they're really, really good swimmers."

"She's right, that's some dark genius right there," Duncan said.

"Fickle," Mimi taunted.

"I know a good point when I hear it." Duncan said.

"There could be a bunch of food stored in the warehouse though. That would give them time to think, maybe group up and work together to get off the island," Manny said.

"You're right, there were rations down there and a few large fabricators with limited supplies. That probably won't last with that many people, though. This is still a bad idea. From what Rogue told me, none of those people should get out," Lat said.

"True. I couldn't find one that I'd wake up for so much as a day pass," I said.

"Anyone have any other ideas? Opinions?" Perri asked.

"Hate to even think it, but it'd be quicker and maybe even fairer to put them out in their sleep than letting 'em wake up just to waste away," Duncan proposed.

"Wait, if you woke them all up, most of the prisoners would starve, but the cannibals..." Mimi said, trailing off.

"Aye, cannibals tend to complicate things, don't they?" Duncan quipped.

Everyone except Ixat burst out laughing for a moment before he said; "I don't understand."

"Um, I dunno, cannibal humour is difficult to explain," Mimi said.

"Like Duncan said, people eaters tend to complicate things," Perri said.

"We don't actually think cannibals are funny. We're just releasing tension, Ixat," I told him.

"Yes. Humans have many ways to do that," he replied.

"One hundred thirteen cannibals versus over ten thousand inmates. A psychopath would put a satellite in orbit and turn it into a reality show." Sure, it was a complicated, heavy discussion, but Duncan was right to lighten things up. A moment of levity can loosen thinking processes up, making way for new ideas.

"I'd watch that if it were fiction," Manny said from the cockpit.

"Shame on you," Mimi said.

"I said fiction," Manny retorted lightly. "If anyone's asking, I'm with Duncan. Poison them so they go peacefully or lock their pods, wake them up and let them suffocate. That is if they're as bad as you're saying."

"They are, but I can't do that," the words came naturally. Killing the inmates was a rational option, but one that went against my core beliefs.

"Oh?" Duncan asked.

I deactivated my hood and regretted it immediately. "Wow, those fumes are strong. I don't recommend that," I said before reactivating it. The air was safe enough to breathe, but neutralised xetima stinks like greasy bug crap.

"Don't duck the question. I said; 'oh?'" Duncan pressed with as much charm as he could load into his tone.

"All right, I'll talk and clean, but you have to let me finish the explanation in one go. Questions at the end, please," I replied.

"I'll do my best not to interrupt," Mimi promised.

That was enough for me. I mentally braced myself as I put my thoughts in order before sharing information that felt more personal all the time. "The first time I was born I woke up in a wrist computer on Freeground Station. Freeground was more than a waypoint in dead space, it was a nation of people who moved a relatively small ring into the middle of nowhere so they could start their own civilisation. They made sure that they were between a lot of places so they could service ships that came along, but it was an isolated spot. Anyway, Freeground was centuries old by the time I came along, and the founders were long gone. When they started Freeground, they put a few core philosophies in place. The central one was simple, but difficult to follow. Everyone had an innate right to free agency. Each individual was responsible for making their own choices, and they should be free to do so. It's something the man who turned me on for the first time, Jonas Valent, believed in, so he made sure it was part of my basic programming. Anyway, in the early days, when there were fewer people and they worked to achieve similar goals, that was easy to follow."

"Not so much as things grew, aye?" Duncan asked.

"Not so much," I agreed.

"So, if someone commits a crime everyone else lets them get away with it?" Lat asked.

"No fair, you read about this, so you know how the debate goes," Mimi said.

"So did you," Lat shot back.

"But I was gonna save my comments until the end," Mimi said.

"I'll cut the philosophical debate short for everyone who didn't do the reading," I said, hearing Jonas' style of speech in mine. "If one citizen commits a crime then everyone else is free to judge them. The founders agreed on a legal process to break the freedom paradox and to protect their society. There's a deeper debate, sure, but what it came down to with Freeground was an enhanced democracy that always ensured that everyone is given at least two choices about any situation whenever possible. If someone is accused of committing a crime, they have choices to make about confessing, what kind of representation they want in court if they want to fight the charges, and finally what kind of punishment they'll suffer in the end if they're found guilty."

"You're telling me they get to decide what happens to them? That's just mad," Duncan said from the dorsal turret.

"Well, they didn't decide their punishment alone. The court sets the options. The convict, victims or their representatives, and a judge get to vote on the punishment. Everyone is exercising their rights. A lot of high crimes resulted in exile. Some say the system got lazy that way. By the time I came along, political complications were already corrupting the system to the point where the military had one set of rules and their own court. The civilian political system wasn't as effective because they kept on building loopholes into the law that delayed the accused's ability to make choices or vote. My first friend, Jonas, was a believer in the old philosophies and broke a few laws that got him and his friends into trouble, but I feel the same way he did. I believe that, even though the people down there are some of the worst criminals I've ever seen, they deserve to make an attempt at correcting their ways. If it were possible, they should be hooked up to a simulation that's made to rehabilitate them. It might not stick, but none of them got that chance. The last thing they deserve is to be carted away in stasis and sold to the Order of Eden. I have no idea what they're doing with sleepers, but even those inmates should get the opportunity to fight. I'm sure whatever Patrizia Salustri wants to do with them isn't much better."

"Or maybe it is?" Manny asked. "Maybe she'll offer most of them jobs in her organisation?"

"Wouldn't that be worse? People would get a lift off that planet so they could do her nastiness and get paid for it," Mimi countered.

"You're right, and I'll be responsible for whatever they do once they're awake, but I'm equally responsible if they're sold off to the Order. Leaving them in stasis would just be my way of making it easy for Salustri to make a few hundred plat or more per sleeper. Then we might run into them later, after the Order have made them into soldiers, or done whatever they plan on doing with them," I replied.

"But you didn't put them there and you told Haven Fleet all about them. It wouldn't be your fault," Mimi said.

"That's a deeper conversation than we have time for. I believe that I would be accountable because I have a decision to make here," I replied, finding it surprisingly difficult to keep calm.

"I get ye," Duncan said. "Doesn't matter that Salustri doesn't know we're watching, but our knowing about the situation could make us accountable for what happens from now on."

"Basic principles of law. Knowing that a crime is about to occur while you can do something about it makes you liable," Perri nodded. "My people had similar to your philosophy, but the accused were stripped of everything until the verdict came down, especially the right to choose for themselves."

"I don't like being a judge though, it's too much responsibility," Mimi said.

"Don't worry. I said this wasn't a vote. This comes down to me," I said.

"What if I disagree with your choice?" Ixat asked.

"You could stop me, but you'd have to shoot me," I replied, watching his response with all my senses.

"That is understandable. I won't attack you, no matter what you choose." His nostrils flared and his face warmed for a moment before he returned his attention to the suction hose and the inert gel on the bulkhead.

"Glad it's your choice, not mine, but I think you're takin' this too personally. Is it so different from bounty hunting, after all?" Duncan asked.

"Maybe, but I took every hunt seriously. I even reviewed the evidence against the listings, so I guess you already know what I'll do," I replied.

"Aye. Ye didn't take a life unless there was no other way, not even on those HATE calls," Duncan said.

"Killing someone is the ultimate removal of choice." That wasn't how I wanted the conversation to end. Maybe I was hoping for a conclusion that put everyone at ease, I don't know, but there was no more talk to talk about Tulip Island. Through my connection with the ship's tactical system I saw five ships start towards the Lidden Warehouse.

"Pirates are heading down. Maybe they're going to Orel's Estate?" Mimi asked.

"No, I see their trajectory. It's the island," Manny said.

"Aye, that was thirty minutes back. Changes things from talk to action in a hurry," Duncan said.

Lat, the crew member who knew me best at that point, shared a thought quickly. "If you wake them up, you're using them as a weapon. Do it. You'll only be replacing some pirates with more of the same."

"He's spot on, like. And besides, those ships won't carry more than a thousand altogether. It'll take 'em ages to shift the inmates out of the system." Duncan said.

"Kill the convicted. Murderers will be fewer, it is the only choice," Ixat said.

"Hello, the Captain already said this wasn't a vote and she already knows what she's going to do," Mimi said.

"What about the right to free agency?" Manny asked sheepishly.

"All right, you caught me," I said. "My version is the military style of addressing that philosophy, where someone has to lead and that means taking sole responsibility for the big decisions. So, here's a vote; do you want to be accountable for this? Do you want a say?"

"I trust your mind on this, Captain," Duncan said without hesitation.

"I get your point of view," Manny said, pausing. "This isn't where I thought this ship would take us."

"Aye, but we're here now, lad, and it was you that pushed for the vote," Duncan said.

"I know, I know, and it's thousands of people, all of them bad," Manny said.

"This is why the ultimate authority in Aucharian society is

military. Some things are too big for us to decide," Perri said. "I'm with whatever Captain Rogue decides."

"You're right. This is too big for my head. No vote for me. Just tell me they deserve what they'll get," Manny said.

"They deserve more of a chance than they would get if they never woke up," I replied.

"I want a vote. They die," Ixat said without looking up from his work.

"What about you, Mimi?" Perri asked.

"Well..." she started.

I felt sympathy for her and guilty about the innocence whatever choice she made may cost her, but I was too late to save that. "It's okay, Mimi, you don't have to decide."

"You say they're terrible people, and I believe you. Maybe they should die, but I think of being asleep, helpless, then nothing. I'm just over because someone I never met decided that I shouldn't live, I never get a chance to change, or to go to rehabilitation like so many people you hunted down did. The people you wake up might be bad, and they may do bad things, but the other way just ends them, and that's scary," Mimi said.

"What they will do is scarier," Lat said. "I agree with Rogue, though. When I ran from the Order, I was constantly afraid that someone would activate my framework system and wipe me out, regenerate my mind so I became someone else. I was made to kill, I have the instinct, but the longer I'm alive, the more I find other options. You gave me a chance. Give them one."

I'm not proud to say that I didn't consider Lat's history until he shared his opinion. I didn't need that to fortify my resolve, but it helped. "Manny, point a microscopic wormhole towards Warro. I want to see what's going on with the smallest delay possible."

"One low latency peek across the solar system coming up," Manny replied.

"What will you do?" Ixat said, turning the suction hose in his hand off.

"I'm going to wake them up," I told him.

"My vote did nothing." Ixat let the hose drop and opened a small door leading to an emergency washing station. He activated it and I couldn't believe what I was seeing as the remnants of what we were cleaning was vibrated off his vacsuit.

When he stepped out and started walking towards the hatch leading to the habitation section, Perri asked; "Where are you going?"

"I will never be able to take the burden, so I will sleep," he replied without looking at her.

"What? Just because you were outvoted when you shouldn't have had a say at all?" Perri asked.

He stopped and regarded her. "My vote did not work. Incorrect actions are occurring. This work is wrong."

"You understand how voting works, right? We all state our opinion and the majority rules. Adults, real adults understand that and let the results stand. Even the kitten gets it." Perri finished by jabbing her finger towards the bridge.

"This effort will not have my leadership. I will go," Ixat said.

"Okay, it's not the time for us to get into this, but walking away from work is a big deal on this ship. At least explain why you're doing it, because I'm missing something and I put a lot of time into training you," I told him.

Ixat regarded me with wide, unblinking eyes. "This burden is for me but you will not let me take it, even when I see how you fail. That is the behaviour of a master. It is wrong."

That made things a little clearer, and I wanted to be sympathetic "Maybe you were a slave before, but you're not one here."

"Never been a slave! I end the masters! No more slavers, no more of their breeders or children! I kill them all with my brothers! Now I offer to take your burden, learn your ship, see your failure! You discard my wisdom even then! I will not!" he stared at me for a few seconds before opening the door and leaving, tracking several litres of the neutralised xetima gel into the corridor with him.

I'd never forget that. Mimi was the first to speak after he dropped from the intercom. "Did he just say he killed children?"

"I think so. I really wish there was more about his people on the Stellarnet," Perri said.

I was still a little stunned and pissed off. What he said put a few important pieces into place for me. I thought he was telling me that he would take my job offer when he talked about sharing my burden, but I don't think that was it. No, he thought I was training him so he could become our leader, and being outvoted was the final insult to his ego. Since there was next to nothing about his people on the Stellarnet, I shouldn't have been surprised when a cultural misunderstanding came along and bit me in the ass, but I was. "We don't have time for this. How's that wormhole coming along, Manny?"

"Opening now, Captain," he replied. It appeared and our twenty-eight minute delay shrunk to a few seconds as Duncan pointed the sensors built into the dorsal turret at it. Five pirate ships had landed on Tulip Island and the large doors to the Lidden Warehouse were already open.

"Focus on the doors, Duncan," I said quietly.

"Doing it," he said.

I connected to the Lidden Warehouse's computer system and saw that someone was already trying to hack in. "Now or never," I said to myself.

The universe seemed to slow down as my mind raced,

thinking at seven times the speed. I wanted to share a message to everyone who woke up down there. They would see my face and hear my favourite voice.

It was recorded at my speed of thought but would play back normally after the inmates woke up. After making sure that they wouldn't be let out until my message finished playing, I started recording. "I am Rogue. There are people coming for you, pirates and gangsters who serve Patrizia Salustri. She has sent her crew down to take you while you're still in your pods. The Order of Eden is offering hundreds of platinum for every human that is delivered to them while they're in stasis. Why they want them is anyone's guess, but I suspect they're either reprogramming sleepers' minds so they can join their military organisation or you'll be used for scientific experimentation. I've also seen them connect people to machines so fluids can be harvested for high-end products, so that's possible too. I believe Patrizia Salustri is going to sell you to the Order. Since they're only taking people in stasis, I'm waking you up."

I took a moment to stare at my unknown audience. I wanted each of them to look into my eyes. "I know every one of you is a convicted criminal. Your governments and ruling corporations sent you somewhere to be punished or rehabilitated. You were stored by the Lidden Corporation instead. I found you by luck and gained control of the storage facility over a month ago. I can't tell you what's happened since you arrived on planet Warro, there isn't time, but I can tell you that you have a choice once you stop Salustri and her organisation. You can decide not to harm the innocent and earn your way back to civilisation or find a way to live your life alone. Many of you will go back to your old ways, and that is a mistake. I have all your names, your biometrics, histories and the evidence of the crimes that put you in the ground. I will be watching. The powerful people I've already passed your data on to will be watching too. Normally I'm paid to hunt people down, but I'll do it for free if I see you step out of line. Make the right choice. Now, get up and make sure you're not taken."

I rethink that speech all the time. After seeing that it was in the system and ready to play for everyone who woke up, I sent the Emergency Wake Command. Once over ten thousand pods reported that they were reviving their dwellers, I disconnected from the Inmate Control System. "It's done. They're waking up. Manny, take us to the Shattered End."

"We're gone," Manny replied.

"You're not going to stay to see what happens?" Mimi asked.

"No, someone's going to detect that wormhole soon, so it's time to leave," I replied. "Besides, I have a mess to clean up."

"Right," Perri said as we focused on the gooey task at hand.

The ship was quiet as everyone contemplated what happened.

CHAPTER TWELVE

The Terrible Ascent of Kassus Vasalvod

There are so many reasons for me to regret my actions regarding the Lidden Warehouse. They say contemplating your decisions is useful until you've learned what you can from them. They also say that lingering on the past after you've grown from it is a good way to get depressed. I don't know where that line is concerning Warro, maybe I haven't learned everything I can from my decisions, but I consider how I could have done things differently often.

I could have set an order so the more reasonable inmates were awakened first. I could have locked Salustri's crew inside the warehouse so it would take them time to break out, giving the inmates an opportunity to catch them. I could have sent a bulletin out across the Stellarnet before waking everyone up, leaving the decision of what to do about them to the residents of the galaxy.

There were so many options, but I just let them out. It almost felt like an experiment to me until people started dying. Everyone was released from their pods at the same time and how quickly they revived depended on how healthy and determined they were. I stayed connected to the Lidden Warehouse so I could see what was going on under Tulip Island. The delay increased as we accelerated away from Warro towards the Shattered End.

Mimi knew something was going on in my head, and quietly settled into my lap as soon as I started my watch in the cockpit. Whether it was by training or instinct, she rested there so I could pet her, listen to her purr and watch her sleep when she drifted off. Whatever urgent questions she had were put aside.

The worst inmates were on their feet first. They weren't crazed or disorganised, I wish they were. The Orion Cannibal Cult was up first, strangely muscular and quick to recover. Kassus Vasalvod, the former Captain of the Shadow Storm, wasn't far behind. I didn't even notice him in the beginning. I thought Vasalvod would be torn apart in no time because he flopped out of his stasis tube with no arms.

His jailers took his cybernetic limbs before they put him in there, and he was quick to find cover as he saw three Orion cultists descend on another inmate. Vasalvod was quick and didn't make a sound until he'd put several rows of pods between him and the carnage of cannibals. That's when he barked; "Sentinel!" and waited for a moment, his bare chest heaving as he caught his breath. Several of his crew members heard him and started moving towards the sound.

"Sentinel!" He shouted again, louder with a demanding tone. Most of Kassus' people were able to rush towards him despite the increasing chaos of waking, fighting inmates around them. "Void King!" was their shouted response.

It took less than three minutes for Vasalvod to gather thirteen crew members. They moved together with the kind of coordination that suggested long camaraderie. Now, Kassus was a pirate. He and his core crew were all born on Sky Sentinel Five, an old space station in the Sakin System. Theirs is a modern pirate story. They worked for a crime syndicate until they had enough money to buy a small ship. When they trusted a black market trader named Ebber Shank with their hard earned money, he strung them along until it was clear that they'd been ripped off. So, Kassus Vasalvod and his friends pretended to forgive him. A month and a half later, they bribed one of Ebber's personal guards to leave his post. Vasalvod and his future core crew crept into Ebber's apartment, killed him along with his entire family, stole the Shadow Storm and started a rampage.

They stumbled through their first few encounters, but eventually became experts at dominating ships without ruining their cargo. Boarding vessels so they could torture and kill their victims face to face or take the richest of them for ransom started to become a habit. They would often jump whoever came to trade platinum for their rich loved ones, killing everyone involved. One ship eventually expanded into a fleet with the Shadow Storm at its centre. Near the end of their run, Vasalvod's organisation expanded to ground raids and space station incursions, increasing their body counts exponentially.

That's what led to their capture. Vasalvod and his crew were caught while they were trying to raid an asteroid base. The exact location of the place is unknown because it was a platinum mining installation, but the outcome was shared as an example to all future pirates. The Shadow Storm was destroyed by the pirate hunting fleet along with most of Kassus's other ships. They were taken into custody and tried in front of a lower branch of the Galactic Court. After being convicted for High

Piracy and the deaths of nine thousand twelve people, they were put into stasis.

Unlike many inmates in the Lidden Warehouse, their pods didn't have any destination listed. They went from the secret site of their trial straight to Tulip Island where they stayed for twenty-eight years. I was watching a reunion that should have never happened. Vasalvod and his whole crew should have been given a choice between several methods of execution and then erased from the galaxy, in my opinion. Instead they were stored cheaply because there was a dispute between the governments over custody. They could all agree that Kassus Vasalvod and his crew were to be executed, but they couldn't decide who would do it.

Once Vasalvod and his crew found a quiet corner, he asked; "Where are we?"

"Some prison, a storage site, maybe," replied Kirill Magnor, his first mate. "We've been warm for minutes."

Screaming nearby drew Vasalvod's attention and he turned towards it, his eyes narrowing, lips tightening into a straight line across his teeth. The screaming stopped abruptly. "They put us with those cannibal freaks. That's the first thing we correct. Anyone see their leader?"

"Akus was chasing someone over there," one of his men replied, pointing.

"Lead the way, stay close. Don't start something you can't finish in three beats," Vasalvod said. Like a pack practiced at hunting, he and his ten moved at a run towards the killing sounds.

Akus the Cannibal was busy tasting the fresh blood from the head he'd crushed when they overwhelmed him and two of his followers. "Take him! He's the example!" Kassus ordered. Kirill and two of his crew mates led the charge with fists and hard, immobilising grasps, breaking Akus' nose and forcing him to kneel.

"You know who I am?" Akus gurgled through the blood rushing over his lips.

"Freak," Kirill said, curling his fist in the man's hair, hauling him onto his feet.

Akus fought to get Kirill's big hand dislodged, only earning several blows to his kidneys before finally giving up. Five members of Akus' cult made wild attempts to free their leader, but they were outnumbered by Vasalvod's crew and a few other inmates who saw the opportunity to become predators instead of prey. The cannibals were punched, gouged and kicked until they were on the ground, bloody and helpless or dead.

One more member tried to break through to his leader, eyes filled with mad hate, and Vasalvod nodded at him. "Pin that one."

As ordered, several members of his crew grasped the Orion devotee and pressed him down where they held him underfoot. The strange, horrific sounds of the Orion Cultists on the hunt were gone, leaving a roaring murmur of speaking and less savage violence. "I am Kassus Vasalvod!" he shouted, standing tall beside the cannibal cult leader. It didn't matter that he didn't have arms because his crew stood around him. Their number had grown to twenty. "I want to know what prison we've been stuffed into and who we have to kill to leave."

There were fist fights, little spats going on in the shadows as a few inmates gave him their attention, but no answers came. "Make that one scream," Kassus said, nodding at the cannibal his crew captured.

"Yes, Sir," Fyodor, one of his original crew members said as he knelt on top of him. There was sympathy in his eyes as he said; "Now, this is gonna hurt, but if you take a real deep breath right now, it'll be over before you know it. Like this," he finished by taking a quick, deep inhale.

His captive followed instructions, his eyes widening as the air filled his lungs. As soon as he finished inhaling, Fyodor jabbed two of his fingers into the man's lower belly and pushed so hard that he broke the skin. I'll spare you the details, but there was over a kilogram and a half of flesh piled outside the cannibal's body before he stopped screaming.

Fear quieted the mob, bringing some closer to the scene while the rest hid or ran in the dark. Vasalvod's voice boomed in the quiet. "That was not the dinner bell! If I catch anyone chewing on anyone else, they will be ended! Now, kill this garbage quick," he said, nodding at Akus.

The cannibal cult leader tried to scramble away, but three of Vasalvod's crew dragged him down to the deck while a fourth stepped on his neck. He struggled and suffocated as Captain Vasalvod made his demand. "I'm going to give you an opportunity to do me a favour. Find me an exit and I'll hear your name. You want that in my head, trust me."

"It's over here! This way!" someone shouted. "It's open!"

"Well done, my girl. You get to come see what's out there with us," Vasalvod said, making a show of tilting his head towards her. "What's the name?"

"Luna. I'm Luna Floyd," she said, relieved. She was incarcerated for stealing a colony ship and dumping the sleeping colonists into a star. I couldn't find why she did it in her file.

There were already people moving up the stairs leading to the surface, and someone already called the broad cargo lift. They waited. Only a few inmates risked punishment by rushing the stairs or taking a place on the platform when it arrived, and Vasalvod didn't stop them. His crew spoke to them, asking about their crimes, discovering little of use. The more important thing there was that Captain Vasalvod's people made themselves look approachable despite their demonstration, earning the respect of more than one of the most hardened criminals.

Further inside the warehouse below, there were thousands of people still recovering with no clue that there was an exit. They roused in the darkness, and violence erupted randomly as some people shrank in fear while others began to explore. The few who worked together often had the best chance of finding their way out, but there was always savagery. It was as if whoever took prisoners into the warehouse intentionally stocked it with agents of violence and cruelty.

I didn't want to see any of that, but I let it flow into my memory so I could upload it to someone who needed to know what happened. I wanted to see what happened when Captain Vasalvod and one of Patrizia Salustri's people ran into each other. I knew they were waiting at the top, blocking off the supply, medical, guard habitation and secure areas there. Unfortunately, someone shut the Lidden Warehouse's broadcasting systems down and the signal stopped.

My disappointment wasn't as strong as my irritation. I don't know what I expected, but seeing a leader emerge right away made everything worse.

Before I could completely lose it, I noticed a pair of eyes looking up at me. Mimi was awake and quietly watching my tears well up. "Whatever you were watching in your head was bad, huh?"

"Worse than I thought possible," I replied, wiping my eyes.

A few curls escaped and hung down. She instinctively caught one with a paw and pulled it just enough so she could let it spring back up. "What happened?"

"The inmates are free, and there's at least one leader who

could turn them into real trouble. I might have really screwed up," I told her.

"You can make it better though, right? You're good at that," Mimi said as she stretched then settled on her haunches.

"It's going to take more than our crew," I replied, sending every scrap of data I collected to every Haven Fleet emergency contact I had. I also sent a copy to Jake, who was still silent in the Rose System.

I knew it could mean the end of me. If there was a reason for Haven Fleet to take me out, becoming a being that multiplied trouble would be it. If it got out that an android one of their captains had built reintroduced thousands of walking nightmares into the galaxy, then their allies may distance themselves or at start asking some difficult questions. "I'm calling for help though, I think they'll get to work on it now."

"Good. See? You always have an answer," Mimi said.

"Not always, and not the best one, but I'll keep trying," I replied.

"That's all anyone can do." She was a font of encouragement, I couldn't help but smile at her as I rubbed behind her ears.

CHAPTER THIRTEEN

Midpoint

Let's focus on the smaller picture for a while. I still had an eye on what was happening on Tulip Island using the sensors on Red Gate Station.

People from Salustri's ships went into the warehouse through the main doors. They even moved an armoured hover vehicle in. It was like a light hover tank made for exploring dangerous terrain, not much longer than eight metres.

Twenty seven minutes and ten seconds later the excursion hovercraft emerged with several inmates riding on top of it brandishing rifles that Salustri's people brought down with them. The original operators were gone, probably killed somewhere down there. The liberated inmates piloted it across the island at high speed, not stopping when they started across the water. I'm guessing that these escapees were off to find out what they could raid on the mainland, and they made it across open water about thirty-nine minutes and thirty seconds later. Their next stop was a mostly empty city, where I lost track of them.

The next group to emerge was led by Vasalvod. He'd taken a bare metal cybernetic arm from one of Salustri's men and installed it on his right shoulder. Vasalvod and seventy-four inmates were wearing gear from the security and habitation sections of the Lidden Warehouse. They were also armed, so the people left behind to defend Salustri's ships weren't ready when the escapees rushed out shooting. Two crews were smart enough to close their hatches and start taking off, but they weren't quick enough. Both ships were hacked into in a hurry.

Vasalvod split his crew and their fellow prisoners into squads before they started their attack. That was obvious to me because they were just organised enough to take all four ships at once, overwhelming the crews so they couldn't help each other out. They also took off at the same time, only minutes after the boarding actions started. That was enough to confirm that he really was a dangerous pirate who lived up to his legend. Oh, and he did it with one ill-fitting cybernetic arm and a long term stasis hangover.

The prisoners he left behind began spilling out of the large exit, cursing at the escaping ships. Part of me hoped Salustri was aboard one of them, that whatever negotiation she tried fell apart and the galaxy was finally rid of her, but I doubted we got that lucky.

After leaving Tulip Island the ships stayed together and used Warro's atmosphere as cover from Salustri's larger ships until they found their way into space. I didn't see them escape orbit, but I was sure they had when Salustri's ships returned to Red Gate Station empty handed. Either that, or they'd destroyed the escapees, but I didn't expect to be that lucky. I've found that one problem rarely takes care of another.

I'm telling you all this because those scenes were playing in my head while I was talking to my crew that night. We were in wormhole transit, so there was a growing transmission delay.

I was connected to the Daring Dream using the wireless receiver so I could leave the cockpit while I kept my eye on things, effectively still on watch. I put Mimi on her seat, the bed-like spot on the dash, and got to my feet.

"Hey, where ya goin?" she asked.

"I have to talk to Ixat. He walked away..." I started to explain.

Mimi nodded and pawed the air in my direction. "I was wondering what you'd do about that. Can I come with you?"

"If you watch but leave the talking to me. This isn't going to be a debate," I took my jacket from the back of the pilot's seat and put it on.

"Eyes open, mouth closed, I promise," Mimi said, sitting up. "Can I try something?"

I glanced up through the transparisteel window at the warped view of the stars before I regarded her. "As long as it doesn't involve changing course."

"Oh, it has nothing to do with that. Besides, I want to see a Haven base," Mimi said. "Turn around."

"Okay," I replied, curious. Mimi leapt from her station and clumsily fell into my hood.

With a little repositioning, she was able to sit up and look over my shoulder. "This is no longer for your head. It is now a cat seat."

"Even if I do this?" I asked as I pulled my curls back and dropped them behind me, covering her in red ringlets.

"Oh my gosh! It's like a curly nest!" Mimi laughed as she played with them then poked through them so she could rest her paws and head on my shoulder.

I laughed as I left the bridge, feeling her adjust as I started walking. "I could get used to this."

"It's less cramped than crawling inside your jacket," Mimi said.

"Just remember, this isn't an open conversation," I told her quietly.

"Don't worry, I'm just there to observe and learn. What's his punishment gonna be though?" she asked.

"We'll see." Avoiding the common area where Duncan, Perri, and Manny were hanging out involved climbing down an access ladder to the lower deck and back up another near the central cargo hold. I didn't have the quick lifts installed yet, and wished I did because no one enjoyed using the ladders between decks. I think Mimi was enjoying the ride, she wasn't used to seeing so much while she was poking her head out through the front of my jacket.

Ixat opened the door after I rapped on it and was standing there as it slipped aside. "You have come to punish me."

"You know you can't walk off the job like that," I told him, staying in the corridor.

"I am not properly used here," he replied as he took a step back to lean on his hip-height bed. The mattress was shaped with a deep hollow in the middle. He hadn't bothered getting anything other than a large trunk printed.

"All right, I'm being patient, trying to understand you, so let's get to the point. Do you expect to be put in charge?" I was hoping I was wrong.

"That would be the right thing after you made such a wrong decision. You are not a good employer now. I will not serve," Ixat said, the nostrils on either side of his mouth squeezing shut then opening wide.

My assumption was that it was a sign that he was getting

tense, and I could detect a rise in his body temperature and heart rates. "It's the vote thing," Mimi whispered.

I was already pretty sure of that, and even though I felt I made the right moral decision, I didn't like reviewing it and I was still seeing people escape the Lidden Warehouse in my head at the time. Bracing myself for a real conflict with my crewman, I finally said; "You'll never be captain of this ship. Leadership is off the table. You're a well trained crew member. Is there any way you'd stay on as an employee."

"You choose for me like a master," Ixat hissed.

There was a lot I didn't know about his background, so I looked his species up again. There really was next to nothing about his people on the Stellarnet. Was he pissing me off? Absolutely, and I didn't see a way forward with him. Losing him meant throwing all the platinum I'd invested in him while he trained for a month along with all the knowledge he'd picked up about the ship and crew. I was finished being nice. "All right. You have until we reach the Bitter End to figure it out. If you don't find a way to work for me that suits your pride, you'll be put off the ship. Do you understand me?"

"Pride? Put off?" he asked.

"Duncan will give you your final pay. You will be forced to leave and I will lock you out permanently. No way back," I replied.

"Put me off," he said firmly.

"Wait, maybe he doesn't understand what being an employee really means?" Mimi asked.

"Mimi," I said.

"Right, eyes and ears open, mouth closed, sorry," she said.

"You decide badly for big problems. Kill the evil. That is the smart way," Ixat explained as though I was a small child.

I was willing to give it one more try. "Deciding to wake the people in the Lidden Warehouse up was my burden. I could have shared it with you and I decided not to. I even put the issue of excluding the crew to a vote after telling you what was going on. That way everyone could figure out whether or not they wanted to share accountability for whatever happened with me. They didn't. The majority voted..."

"Kill them. That is the only way," Ixat insisted. "We go back. Kill all. Show me you can learn."

I'll admit it, I wanted to knock him out. "Maybe you're right, but it was never your choice to make. Now it's time for you to cool down so you can do your duty aboard," I said more sternly.

"My temperature is not your worry. I will stay," he hopped onto his bunk and let one leg dangle. "You will not make commands."

"You've served on a ship before, other captains have rated you highly, so you understand that you have to follow orders, right?" I asked.

"I will never follow stupid weakness," Ixat said.

"You understand..."

He interrupted me then. "I understand! No more Daring Dream. You give me rating and I go!"

He tapped a small control pad on the side of the bed and the door closed centimetres away from my nose. "You were really nice, considering," Mimi said quietly.

"Maybe he needed the opposite, but I don't want the kind of crew member that only listens to shouting and cutting language," I said as I started backing away.

"That makes a lot of sense. What kind of rating will you give him?" Mimi asked.

"We'll write that up together once he's off the ship, but it won't be high," I replied. "Now I get to tell the crew the news."

"Better you than me," Mimi said. "I didn't really like him, but I think they did."

"Why didn't you like Ixat?" I asked quietly as I climbed the access ladder.

"He looks at me like I'm a snack sometimes," Mimi whispered in my ear.

"I'm sorry I didn't notice," I told her.

Perri opened the sliding hatch to the common room and leaned through it. "What happened?"

"I was trying to be discreet," I told her.

"The aft access ladder makes one of the supports running under the common room creak," she said.

"Oh, right. I guess I got so used to it that I don't notice it anymore," I replied. "We'll have to look at that."

"Stop dodging. What's going on with the tense one?" Duncan asked as Perri and I walked in. He had a tall, foamy drink in his hands that looked pretty good.

I checked the refrigeration compartment and found five of them. The top flipped off and the dark liquid carbonated on its own. I took a sip of the cool drink and found a soothing flavour with a slightly bitter finish. "Wait, I'm sorry, this isn't from your private reserve is it?" I asked as I noticed that everyone was staring.

"Perri made that bunch. I've the proper license for it right here, she can fab more," Duncan said, pointing to the back of his hand. His personal computer was hidden, the display looked more like normal skin and there were two expansion ports beneath it. "Now, about our friend below?"

"Ixat thinks Rogue is some kind of failed master and he thinks she should put him in charge," Mimi replied.

The upper and lower turret seats came down and up into the

common room with Manny in one and Lat in the other. Lat spoke first. "Well, he's an idiot."

"Hey, maybe his culture is so different that he's having trouble understanding... a lot?" Manny asked before taking a pull on a straw sticking out of a large sealed cup.

"Maybe, but I think he'll eventually turn on all of us. I know I'll never trust him," Perri replied.

"Hey, no drinks in the turrets," Mimi told Manny.

"Oh, right, sorry," he replied. "I just went up for the view."

"Same,' Lat added. "But I left my drink in the chiller."

"So, did you manage to turn him around? Did he apologise? Promise to do his job?" Perri's hands were balled into fists and her heart rate was up.

I may have been rusty as a Captain even after having a proper crew for a month, but my training kept me from getting that worked up. I could have been just as frustrated as she was if I let myself. "He closed the door in my face, so he'll have a hard time convincing me not to fire him when we arrive at the Bitter End. He'll have to do it through Duncan when he gives Ixat his final pay. I'll only take him back before he's walked off the ship and if he makes a full reversal."

"So he's fired? After all the time and work you put into training him?" Perri asked.

I raised an eyebrow and crossed my arms. A very old-school Jake move. "Are you protesting?"

"Oh, no, I'm just pissed that he knows at least half the secrets in this ship and trained with us for a month before we discovered that he's a childish little shit who makes crazy demands! You didn't have to tell us a thing about what was going on with Warro and that warehouse, but you looped us in for... whatever reason. Maybe it was so we wouldn't be surprised if it came back to haunt you, or you wanted our opinions on what was going on, or you just needed to share, but it was a good thing. I never thought I automatically had a say, mind you, because that was some big stuff, galaxy shifting stuff. Now he's hurt because you didn't let him decide for you? What a self-centred little asshole." She paused. "Sorry for the rant."

"It was a good one, really animated. I like the language, and you really demonstrated that you have an understanding of the situation. Four and a half out of five," Mimi said.

Her remarks got a little smile out of Perri. "Oh, um, thanks."

I wanted to keep the rest of the heads in the room cool. "Some people change after training, but this whole situation comes down to a cultural misunderstanding. I think his people use 'burden' to refer to important leadership positions. I'm sure there's more to it, but he's not willing to explain and I'm past caring. If he starts acting like that during a combat situation, we could get killed, so I'm thinking about what comes next. We'll need someone to fill his shoes and we can't take a month to train them."

"That's good thinking, that is. I'd be right pissed too, but you've got your eye on the horizon. Are there prospects where we're going?" Duncan asked.

"The Bitter End," Manny said, savouring the name.

Duncan shook his head. "See, that's got the ring of foul luck."

"Fact. Makes me afraid to say it out loud," Perri agreed, still sour about Ixat.

"Bits?" Mimi whispered in my ear.

I opened the drawer we reserved for her protein packs and I pointed at the Tuna Bits while Manny said; "Biiiiiiiteeeeeeer-rrrrr Eeeeeeennnnnnd."

"Now you're just winding me up," Duncan snickered.

"Say it enough and it's just another name," Lat said with a shrug.

"Then say it with me," Manny invited, unrolling a Flexi screen. He, Lat and Perri all said; "Bitter End."

"Nah, still feels wrong," Perri said.

I was moving my finger to another packet and Mimi patted my shoulder. "Spicy Tuna!" she whispered excitedly.

"Well, maybe Ixat shirking on us is the first bad luck thing. My mother always said it came in threes," Perri said as she sat down with a bag of Dil Puffs. They weren't as good as several name brand versions, but she still ate two or three forty gram bags a day.

"Well, if that's the way of it, then here's hoping I lose something I won't miss and someone jams a finger without breaking a thing," Duncan said. "Get that rule of threes outta our system before it's hiring time."

"Jose said he would be looking for work, wouldn't he be good?" Mimi asked.

"He'd be great, but we want Major Rivera to keep his job," I replied, opening the food packet and dumping the hot meat and gravy into a small bowl. While I watched the sauce slathered meat chunks squeeze out of the package, I checked on Ixat. He was still in his quarters. I locked the door. It would only open from the outside. There was no way I'd let him walk freely around the ship.

Mimi climbed over my shoulder and dropped onto the table. She dug into the fragrant real fish feast eagerly. Those were expensive packets, but she paid for them herself and was proud of it.

"Why would Jose get the boot?" Duncan asked.

"He supported my decision about the Lidden Warehouse after telling me that the Fleet couldn't do anything. Haven Fleet knows what I decided and I'm forwarding all the data coming from Red Gate, so they'll see the consequences. I haven't heard from him," I replied.

"Ah, fair guess he's in a bit of trouble, then," Duncan said.

"Well, that depends on what's happening on Warro, right?" Manny asked, hope in his eyes.

"It's bad..." I was relieved to be interrupted.

Mimi interrupted me before I could go into it, taking a break from licking her bowl clean. "What about the Bitter End? What's there? Is it a city?"

"Interrupting me is becoming a bad habit," I said, giving the tip of her tail a gentle tug.

"Hey, feline foul," she said, dancing around to the other side of her bowl before finishing her meal.

"I've been wondering too. What should we expect?" Perri asked.

"Well, Jeto was a rock before the antimatter explosion sent it out of its orbit, and now it's a big messy rock speeding away from the galactic plane. I've never seen the base we're headed to, but the little I could find on it suggested that most of the facility is underground. I'm guessing we'll find a little market at the Bitter End, and there are residents. Other than that, I don't know much." The crew was all ears, even Mimi, who paused before starting her cleaning routine. Kawaii Kittens pay a lot of attention to self care.

"That's a start," Perri said. "Wait, by market, you really mean 'black market,' right?"

I finished my drink and smiled a little. "Only according to the Order, at least, that's my guess. I wouldn't be surprised if Haven Fleet sanctioned the little market we find there because it'll be a lot of stuff taken from their enemies. We'll take a look, especially since we got away with almost a full load of fuel. It'll have to wait though. The first thing I'll have to do is officially sign up as a privateer. Maybe we can get access to some discounted upgrades."

"Like a new food fabricator," Perri said, prompting nods and murmured agreement from everyone except for Mimi.

"Forma isn't cutting it?" I asked.

"No, oh no," Manny replied, waving the notion off.

"It's fine, it's fine, but there's no mistaking it for real food, or what comes out of those high end fabbers," Duncan said more tactfully.

The ship came with one of the better Forma food fabricators, and I didn't think it was the best stuff, but it wasn't too bad as far as I was concerned. Then again, I didn't eat as much or as often as they did. "I would have got something better, but I ran out of platinum. We'll look for something better while we shop for better shield modules."

"Well, shields first," Lat said.

"I think she knows the shields come first," Manny said.

"Just saying it out loud this time," Lat told him.

"Well, make a list of things you want while we're still in transit because we won't be staying longer than we have to. I have leads on a few Ryden ships. We need to start hitting them soon." I was surprised to see how interested, even relieved they seemed at that.

Mimi raised her head and cried; "Let's get pirating, ye scallywags!"

CHAPTER FOURTEEN

Recuperation

It shouldn't surprise you that Mimi uses my quarters like her own. Perri enjoyed printing a multi-level cat tree that dominates the far corner right under one of the entrances to the droid service tubes running throughout the ship. Like I said earlier, those tubes are Mimi's domain, especially since I didn't spend money on the droids that should be using them with her.

She likes relaxing on her multi-platform tree, especially the level covered in soft simulated moss when she doesn't feel like being social. I don't sleep much, so she often has the compartment to herself. I didn't opt for luxury furnishings. There's a multi-purpose storage wall with a sink and pull-out desk framing the doorway. It was fabricated on the cheap using durable but common metal, so it looks like it was taken from some old fashioned military vessel.

My bed is the main furnishing for my quarters. It's a small single by default, but can pull out to fill all the walking space in the room. There are cupboards above and an interior door that leads to a small combo toilet and multimode cleaning compartment that I liked to use as a water shower. We spent a little extra time adding a drying system which was cheap but a little labour intensive to install.

All the fixtures and furniture I'm describing were fabricated and installed by me and my crew so we could save a whole lot of money on the ship. Most of the furniture Spectral Dynamics offered was really nice, but I spent my platinum on more important things, like extra armour plating and heavy duty expansion bays for future systems and equipment.

That left us with a long list of things we wanted to improve or replace, which is both good and bad. It's good because it gives my crew the opportunity to personalise their quarters and keep their eyes open for things that could improve the ship. It's bad because a lot of the stuff we have aboard in terms of furniture and quality of life fixtures are pretty basic. Much of it, like the multi-mode systems in the showers, were bought used, which didn't impress the people at Spectral Dynamics, but you can't go wrong when the prices on that stuff are so low that it's not worth fabricating your own or buying new ones.

That's enough about the ship for now though. I'm stalling because I'm not looking forward to telling you what happened next.

After almost three days in wormhole transit, I'd managed to disassemble and clean three of the turrets I captured from Red Gate Station. Duncan and Perri spent a lot of time helping out. I was surprised to see Manny take up the task of looking for the best way to install one aboard the Daring Dream during his off hours. He was into flying spaceships before joining the crew, but we were starting to see him become a real tech head, which gave him and Perri something to talk about. I liked that, especially since my chatter with Duncan was pleasant but professional, a step back, as far as I was concerned.

We took turns bringing food to Ixat, who was quietly sullen about being stuck in his quarters. Duncan spoke to him several times, even trying to train a translation program he installed on the ship's most powerful computer. That was the first time I saw him throw his hands up after several hours of talking to him. "He's more crass in his own language! Works himself up in a tick too, never know what'll set him off. Got him calm, at last, and thought I'd leave it until we get to the Bitter," he told me the day before we got there.

How did Duncan and I get along? Well, we were both busy. The long list of things to do around the ship, including installing a half circle booth bench in the common room with a table that could lower from the ceiling. I think we all loved that, and it showed the crew that there was room for four or five more members. There were more practical things to fabricate, like internal security features, and the inner workings to the pull-out toilet in the bridge corridor, which no one wanted to use, but it would be there in an emergency. That sort of finishing work kept us all busy, and I didn't sleep until our last day of transit.

After the third turret was clean and reassembled, I retreated to my quarters and changed into a New Zero Wizards jersey. Mimi emerged from the little hidden service tube hatch, dropped onto the top platform of her carpeted cat tree and bounded onto my bed. "You never miss a nap," I told her as I laid down and flicked the switch mounted on the cupboard above. The mattress extended most of the way across my quarters before I stopped it so I could still see a small strip of the deck beside my bed.

"I have a sense for these things," she said as she waited for me to get under the duvet.

"Well, I'm only going down for three hours this time," I told her.

"Pah! Amateur," she said as she curled up on my chest. "That's okay."

"There's too much work to do for me to get extra rest," I told her.

Mimi put her chin down on my chest so we could look at each other while she drifted off. "Work does get in the way of nap time. It's an epidemic, if you ask me."

"What have you been up to while I was back there?" I asked.

"Oh, you know, looking up scuttlebutt on the Bitter place, reading the stuff you uploaded into the computer about Ryden. They're really working their butts off in the Rose System, you know. I was able to trace a few of the freighters you marked, they're taking short trips between a bunch of worlds there and some nearby systems. One of them is Iora, but there are others no one's naming," Mimi finished with a big yawn.

"Good work, that's important. How'd you track them?" I asked.

"Well, cats aren't awesome at math, so I had to dig into the socials. Some crew members call friends when they're in port, take leave, that kinda stuff. I never knew being your Comms Cat would be so much fun. I like the sleuthing," Mimi said as her eyes started to close. "All the info is in the data vault."

"You're good at it, I'm proud of you," I told her as I softly stroked her fur.

"Just doing my duty, Captain." Mimi was more than half asleep at that point, so I stopped talking.

Watching her drift off always helped me do the same, and I was out soon after. My digital mind provided a warning system that would wake me up in an instant if something went wrong with the ship, crew or someone was trying to get my attention. I should have done a little more work on that though, because it didn't protect me from something worse.

I started having strange dreams. I was reliving my escape from New Zero, pushing quickly through my time in wormhole space, then revisiting the Lidden Warehouse. The recollection of seeing all those pods underground mixed with the security footage of inmates waking up. Memories of Red Gate Station were stirred in for an extra measure of confusion.

The traumatic tour ended abruptly as Mimi batted me on the nose, shouting; "Rogue!"

When I woke up I felt a presence in my digi-brain. It was fading quickly, but I knew it was a piece of Assessor. It was probably uploaded with the first message Assessor sent me, but my memory of it was corrupted, most likely so the tiny program could cover its tracks. It didn't take long for my digi-brain to track the virus down and eradicate it. There was a law coded into all artificial intelligences that prevented self replication, so higher order programs would leave pieces of themselves that weren't technically intelligent behind to perform certain tasks.

Data transfer activity showed that Assessor's fragment was using my Haven Node to upload parts of my recent memories to servers in New Zero, and I couldn't track it from there. My bio-brain behaves just like a human one with few exceptions, so the dreams I had were already fading and my digi-brain didn't bother recording them. "I was in the Lidden Warehouse, then logging into Red Gate," I said aloud as Mimi paid close attention. "The prisoners were awake..." I trailed off.

"I'm not surprised you had nightmares, what you've been

through this week was cuckoo banana-pants crazy," Mimi said from my lap.

I knew better, and my digi-brain tried to capture what was left of the dream so I could examine it. There was just enough for me to be sure that Assessor's little program was following an agenda that delivered all the important information I had about Warro. "Hopefully that's out of my system now." I decided to keep the fact that it was forced by an intruding program fragment to myself, hoping that Assessor wouldn't do something I'd regret with the data. Chasing after it would be pointless, the trail went dead in New Zero. The servers it used were old pre-Fourth Fall units that I'd turned on for it months ago, and the transfer records were already wiped.

The worst thing about all that is how separate my biological and digital brains felt from each other again. I was aware that the differences between them were growing even as they learned to work together, but this felt like a huge step back.

My bio-brain was almost always in charge, it was an easy default, but now it seemed like it could easily become a victim of my digital side, so I did a search for software that could protect one from the other. Before long I found an industrial grade software package called Greywall that was originally made to protect human minds that were used in data processing centres from unauthorised access in a digital system.

I didn't want to do it, but I dropped ten thousand Tabrus credits worth about two thousand platinum on a licensed copy and started the adaptive installation process. My bio-brain would be in full control while it was protected from anything my digital side wanted to do. Would it slow me down? Before Bergio added his fix to my system, yes, but it would barely make a difference after a few customisations and tweaks. The partition it made went into place, and I ignored my digital mind's irritation. It was like audio feedback, whining and screaming for a moment before fading off. *It's for the best. I need to stay in control so something like that can't happen again,* I remember thinking.

"You have that look like you're seeing something very far away right now, Rogue," Mimi said.

"Sorry, just checking my bio-matter. I don't get nightmares, so I'm just making sure I'm okay," I told her.

"Everything working as intended?" Mimi asked, as she stretched.

"Yup, nothing to report," I replied. "I'm cutting my sleep short though."

"You mean cutting it long. You got five point five hours," Mimi replied. "I even visited Duncan on the bridge while you were out. He likes last watch, what a weirdo."

That was a first. I was missing time and it bothered me. I took my command and control unit from the shelf overhead and quickly looked through the log it kept of my movements. Thankfully, I didn't do anything unusual other than the stressed murmurings that woke Mimi up.

She was already cleaning herself beside me, getting ready for the day when I pushed the covers off and got on my feet. "We'll be arriving at the Shattered End in forty-two minutes. I should get to the cockpit."

"Rogue?" Mimi asked, cocking her head. "Maybe you should put your vacsuit on first?"

"Right, thanks. What would I do without you?"

"Visit a pirate base in your nightie?" Mimi snickered. "Actually, I dare you do to it."

I laughed at the mental image of meeting Major Jose Rivera face-to-face for the first time in nothing but a New Zero jersey. Sure, it's big and comfortable, even durable, but not exactly the image I wanted to project. "Not this time," I replied.

"Oh well, I'll have to make my own fun," Mimi said as she hopped to her cat tree. The little hatch leading into the service tubes opened at her approach. "I'm gonna get a snack."

"Oh, don't call them pirates when we get down there," I called after her. I'm still not sure if she heard me since I was on my way into the shower and she was already on her way to the common room.

CHAPTER FIFTEEN

An Enlightening Ride

My headspace was cluttered with worry as the Daring Dream emerged from its wormhole. Assessor did more damage than I'm sure it was aware of. I was afraid of my own digital mind. It failed to detect a piece of Assessor's code. Sure, anyone else would simply call it a virus, but there was enough of Assessor in it to direct my dreams. It learned from the memories it played back, that's a very specific kind of adaptation.

As Greywall, the software I'd put between my biological and digital minds, was so good at highlighting, my two halves were thoroughly entangled. As I sat in the copilot's seat, looking at the distant grey ball in the distance, I stopped my in-depth introspection. Greywall would stop any new trouble from my digital side, so I could think about that later.

"There are so many junk transmissions that I'm just starting with the Navnet channels and watching for contact from Haven Fleet, or whatever they call themselves here," Mimi said.

"Look for someone named Lamar," I told her. "He was the comms guy a few months ago."

"Oh, okay, that helps," Mimi said as she used both her track-balls at the same time. From behind it looked like she was dancing.

Yes, I could have done the communications work myself, but I was preoccupied. My connection to Red Gate was still live, and the delay was getting shorter instead of longer. I guessed that meant that a ship was heading there with a more modern faster than light communications node aboard. Salustri's ships, including the Savannah, were all jumping away from the station. They knew something was coming, but the transmissions between them were protected by quantum encryption. I wouldn't get a clue there.

Everything I was seeing was still over a day old. The doors to the Lidden Warehouse were closed again and there were over nineteen hundred inmates trapped outside with nothing but their underwear. I kept the sensor feed from Red Gate Station going in my mind even though I knew things would only get worse on the planet below.

Some of my stress was released as soon as I heard a call Mimi put on speaker. "This is Bitter End Base Navnet Control," Lamar's young voice said.

"Oh, hihi! I'm Mimi, the communications officer for the Daring Dream. We were invited by the Haven Fleet Privateering Initiative." She was so excited that her voice was pitched even higher than normal.

"Um, you sound a little young?" Lamar asked.

"Oh, open the video," Mimi replied.

"Wow, they let a cat run their communications?" Lamar said as his fourteen year old face appeared on the holoprojector.

"Wow, they let a teenage boy run Navnet?" Mimi snarked. "You've got something on your nose, by the way."

She was referring to a red pimple. I cleared my throat. "Be nice."

"Sorry, I'm not your average cat. Can we land?" Mimi asked.

"Daring Dream, you are cleared to land on Slip Fifty-Five," Lamar said, his youthful brow furrowed, "Navnet link established, your pilot will know where to go. I hope it's not a cat."

"I've got it," Manny said from the pilot seat.

"That could have gone better," Lat said from the pull-out seat behind me.

"He started it," Mimi replied.

"Remember the communications training. During normal operations you should always be civil," Manny said as he adjusted the ships course to conform to Navnet's instructions.

"I know, he was just rude," Mimi said.

"You'll do better next time," I said, switching the cockpit view to adapt more spectrums of light so we could see more of the rogue planet's features. I'd never seen the side of Jeto that led the way through space.

"That's a lot of craters," Lat said.

"I guess it plowed its way out of its home solar system after it was knocked out of orbit." I was paying much more attention to the lights of dozens of ships in orbit around the wayward world. One stood out in particular. It was a captured Order of Eden Advanced Destroyer, over two hundred and fifty metres long with heavy guns on every side and a recognisable triangular face. "That's the Hammer, Alice and her allies captured it right out of the shipyard. It was built for the Order, but they never got to use it." The strangest thing about that was that I remembered doing that heist, but I made an effort to remind myself that those engrams were just copies.

"Nice to see there's real firepower on our side," Manny said as we drew closer to the dark grey planet. We started to make our way around to the opposite side. The deep crack in the world and surrounding crater in the middle came into sight. "So that's what an antimatter nightmare looks like. Wow, so glad we don't store that stuff."

I was actually enjoying the nervousness that came with knowing that the Captain of the Hammer, Sel Marda, was most likely in the Bitter End Base. I didn't know if I wanted to run into him, we'd never met, and he probably wouldn't recognise me, but someone could have told him who I was in advance. He and Alice got along well. She trusted him so much that she gave Sel the Hammer.

"What are they doing?" Lat asked as he highlighted a group of dozer drones drifting around a number of low, round port buildings. There were lights on inside, and rows of heavy hangar doors to one side. The drones had large plates on the front that were covered with rock and dust.

"It looks like they're collecting regolith and other particles so the hangars stay clear," I replied. Then my jaw dropped as I saw the Prowler appear on the tactical display an instant before it came into view. It was the older version of an Order of Eden Advanced Destroyer and there was a long cargo train extending out from behind it. Mega Craft, Quick Eats, Fine Shine and other retail logos were painted on the sides of hundreds of cargo containers. "That's a nice haul," I said.

"Okay, so I get it straight," Manny said, paying most of his attention to flying. "That cargo train is all stolen stuff?"

"That's my guess. I don't think the Prowler is in the freight business," I replied.

"Niiiice," Manny said.

"A fine plunder train!" Mimi added.

"It's a sign of potential, but they're five times our size and ten times our mass," Lat said.

"There's nothing wrong with starting small. Then again, we could haul that much if we got a better wormhole generator." I was trying to concentrate on pursuing the Ryden Corporation, especially after finding out that the Order had completely taken control of it. The more imminent prospect of running into some of Alice's old friends kept on interrupting that.

"I smell stress," Mimi said as she turned to look at me. "You okay?"

"I don't know. I mean, I'll be fine," I laughed nervously.

"Say what you're feeling to Mimi," she said.

After a long exhale I tried. "There are so many familiar things here, and it's stirring some things up, but no one knows me, so... I mean, I might know them on sight, but... I'm just nervous and excited and I've got serious things to do here before we get after our next target, but part of me wants to get down there and introduce myself to everyone but I think it's smarter to play it cool and read the situation first but I'm not sure..."

"Deep breaths. Deep, calming breaths," Mimi said, demonstrating at the same time.

It helped, and I remembered that many Kawaii Kittens were actually designed to be personal support cats. Maybe that's what Bergio bought her for before he started messing with her mental capacity and who knows what else. "Okay, you're taking communications over, Lat." I scooped Mimi up and put her in my hood as I said it.

"Good idea, I'm on watch anyway, since I can't show my face out there," he said.

"Oh, right. You still look like, well, something worse," Manny finished awkwardly.

"Like millions of other Order of Eden soldiers? Correct. Can you look for something that'll fix that while you're down there?" Lat asked.

"I will," I replied with certainty.

"With all the shop ads I saw, someone has got to have something," Mimi added as she settled into my hood and started pulling some of my hair in there with her.

"I'll look through them while I'm on watch," Lat said. He would and for reasons that you'll find a little further on, most of them led to ships and little shops that weren't active.

The Daring Dream was finishing her approach. "Shields reduced to manoeuvring mode, landing gear down. You're lined up with the mooring collar," I told Manny as I operated my station.

"And now we touch down, as light as a feather landing on a pillow," Manny said as the landing gear took the diminished weight of the Daring Dream. The gravity on Jeto was almost exactly sixty percent of human standard.

The life support systems in the ship and on the base would compensate, bringing it back up to optimal human levels, but I wanted to make sure Mimi, who had only been on a couple of planets in her life, would be safe in case we hit a spot without artificial gravity. I closed my jacket up to the neck then pulled the line hidden in its shoulder until there was enough slack for her. "Here, attach this to your harness so we don't get separated."

Mimi fidgeted until she touched the end of the line to the front of her harness. They clipped together. "How would we get separated?" she asked.

"It probably won't happen, but you might get thrown if we hit a low gravity spot," I replied.

"Okay, I guess," she replied. "Just don't forget I'm riding along in your hood."

"Impossible," I replied as I saw the docking corridor extend out from beneath the cockpit and connect with the waiting walkway. "We have a good seal, pressurising."

"Haven Fleet is saying they want you to go directly to their headquarters," Lat said from behind me as he used one of the dynamic consoles behind me to handle communications. "The rest of us are welcome as guests, but it looks like most of the base is closed."

"All right, I'll go first, then everyone else gets a few hours off the ship. I'll join you after I finish talking to Major Rivera," I said, hoping that's who I'd be meeting.

Lat was ready to slip into the copilot seat when I left it, and Manny had to wait for him to sit down before he could lock his station and get up. "I wonder how much plat I should bring?"

"The Haven Fleet Guide To Rest and Recreation says you shouldn't take more than you're willing to part with," Mimi said.

"When did you start reading Fleet Manuals?" I asked.

"Read? I watched the unclassified instructional holos," Mimi replied.

I gave Lat's shoulder an affectionate squeeze then. "Thank you for staying behind."

"Not like I had a choice," he said.

"You could wear a helmet," Mimi replied.

"Sure, then someone scans my DNA or tells me to take it off and it becomes a whole thing," Lat replied. "Don't worry, I'll get a new face somewhere."

"Top priority," I told him as I retreated from the cockpit. "Forward the port guide to the crew please."

"Doing it now. What do I do about Ixat?" Lat asked.

"Duncan's going to talk to him. He wants one more chance to get through to him. I've got to focus on getting us properly signed up as privateers," I replied.

"I can still take care of it if you want. I'll just put Ixat out with a couple stun rounds and leave him somewhere in the port next to a recycling chute. It's a nice way to get rid of a quitter," Lat said casually as he looked through the ship's status screens.

"Wow," was all Mimi had to say.

"I'll let Duncan give him one more chance." I retreated from the cockpit. Lat locked the hatch behind me.

I caught up to Manny half way down the cockpit corridor and tapped a specific spot on the bulkhead. "I'll catch up to you guys after I'm finished with Haven Fleet. Don't rent a room."

"I know, short stay. Good luck with the Fleet," Manny replied.

"Thanks." A one metre wide section of the wall slipped upward, revealing a ladder that took me down to the armoury. It was a small room with lockers for armour, a couple of secure boxes for explosives and gun racks. Most of it was empty. I wasn't there to gear up, it was the fastest way to get to the embarkation corridor, so I slipped through the normal hatch and passed through the airlock. "I forgot there were secret doors for you big people too. I love this ship," Mimi said.

"Me too. Seal up," I told her.

"Oh, right, there's only a retracting hallway between us and space," Mimi replied. I could hear her clear bubble style helmet deploy from the top of her collar and her baggy suit extend from the bottom. "All buttoned up."

We passed down the corridor and came through the battered airlock on the other side. It was definitely secure, but the metre thick base doors were a few hundred years old. On the other side was one of the longest hallways I'd ever seen. Pressure doors were installed twenty-five metres apart, but they were open, and my sensors told me that the hall went on for three kilometres. "This must lead to all the slips at this end."

"Don't you mean hangars?" Mimi asked as she planted her forepaws on my shoulder and looked around.

"Hangars are enclosed. Slips are exposed landing spots," I replied as we stepped into the broad hallway. There was enough room for five people to walk abreast on the near side. There was a lower section made for at least two trains past the lip. Posts for railings were set into the concrete but that was unfinished too.

The roar of tires with big grips drew my attention to the left in time to see a cargo truck emerge from a side tunnel. Six seats were affixed to the flat bed. There was a thin Nafalli driving. She had dark brown fur with white patches, a long snout, and her tongue was lolling out of the left side of her mouth a little. Her clothes were loose, leaving plenty of spaces for her fur to peek through, and she wore a pair of goggles. "Hi there," I said as she skidded to a stop on the other side of the platform.

"The tram isn't coming. It hasn't been installed yet because it hasn't been fabbed," she said, pushing her goggles up. "I can give you a ride, only ten plat. I'll even let you sit in the front." She activated a lift built into the truck's suspension to make it easier for us to get in.

"That's a big dog," Mimi whispered in my ear.

"Nafalli don't like being called that," I whispered back as I walked to the open frame cab. I fished a couple of five platinum coins from my jacket pocket and handed them to her. "I'm Rogue."

"Nice ship, Rogue. I'm Oonaa. I know, I know, it's a regal name. My mom had high hopes for all her daughters, and I'm too lazy to change it. Oh, who's your little passenger?" she asked.

Mimi was doing her best to make herself very small while she peeked over my shoulder. She wasn't talking. "That's the Daring Dream's communications officer."

"Not very talkative," Oonaa said. "How big will she get?"

"About that big," I replied as I put the safety belt across my chest and waist.

"Oh, so not like the great cats in Haven Shore? Too bad, I used to wrestle those with my friends until the Rangers told us we were messing with their habitat or whatever," Oonaa said as she pushed her goggles back into position. She slappEd a lever on the dash that lowered the main body of the truck with a drop. "Hang on."

The rear tires spun against the concrete tram channel before they gripped and we were off with a G-force multiplying jerk. Mimi gave a little squeak as her hard bubble helmet bounced against the head rest and I caught her so she could look over my shoulder. "Too fast!"

"It just looks fast because we're driving along the ground right beside the subway platform, we're fiiiiine," Oonaa said. "We're only going one-oh-five, and that's per hour. So, what brings you to the Bitter?"

"We're signing up for the Privateering Initiative," I replied, enjoying the air rushing through my hair.

"Your timing is interesting. There's an attack coming, you know. Big Order of Eden ships are on their way, so they say," she said as she barely concentrated on steering. The subway ran in a perfectly straight line, so it really was fine.

"How long before they get here?" I asked.

"Rumours say they're coming any day. Most of the ships that wouldn't stand a chance in a big battle left already. They'll be back. Well, if there's anything left to come back to, I guess. The Hammer and the Prowler will take over patrols tomorrow.

There's a fighter squadron and a bunch of other Legion ships around right now, so if the Order gets here tonight you'll have plenty of time to run. Well, maybe not plenty, but enough if you keep my ident handy. This rig was meant to run around out there, so all you need is a space suit even if the tunnel gets blown up. Oh, and I know how to fix everything, I restored this wheeler, you know. Just don't rent a room here. There are gangs below, it's not under control down there." She was full of good information and in a hurry to ingratiate herself to me.

"Thanks for the heads up," I said as she started to brake. I held Mimi in my hood while I was pushed into my safety belt.

"I always liked that expression. It reminds me of my nieces and nephews when they were young. Their little heads would poke out of their beds when they caught a whiff of something they liked or heard someone come home," she said with a smile, putting her hand out as she pushed her goggles up. "We're here."

Okay, this might sound strange, but that's when I went from thinking she was kinda fun to outright liking her. I paid her another ten platinum coin and got out.. A display painted on the wall read; LOWER LEVEL: HAVEN FLEET FACILITY

I turned around and asked the Nafalli; "What will you be doing when the Order comes? Flying a fighter?"

Oonaa laughed and shook her head, a motion that was exaggerated by her long muzzle. "Oh, no. I'm a general go-getter. Bye, Captain, bye comms kitten!" she said before turning her rig ninety degrees and driving down a narrower service tunnel.

"You paid her twice," Mimi said as she put her paws back on my shoulder.

"I know. Once for the ride, again because she was cheeky enough to try to trick me," I said, looking her up. She had been on staff with the base for three weeks but didn't have much of a social presence. Most images of her were taken by maintenance workers who seemed to really like her. "I'll have to call her when it's time to go back."

"Really?" Mimi asked, shocked.

"I don't think they'll get the tram installed today," I replied.

"Well, how much is it going to cost us to land here?" Mimi asked. "I didn't see a price for it come up before we landed."

"I have no idea. Hopefully it's affordable, otherwise I'll have to borrow money from you," I replied.

Mimi laughed. "You're not that broke, are you?"

I finally downloaded directions to the Haven Fleet office from the ship. I'd been so distracted that I forgot to. "My personal share from the last hunt was eight hundred, so that puts me just over a thousand. Duncan got his eight hundred, and the rest went into the ship account, which is down to about fifteen thousand. The ship will cover it, but we're low."

"Wow, was the Daring Dream really worth it? I mean, I like it, but I have more money than you do," Mimi said.

"Customisations and extensions cost more than I expected, but I think it was worth it. Spectral Dynamics got it customised and finished while they trained us. All in one month. That was a tall order," I replied.

"Oh, so you're happy with how things turned out?"

"Absolutely. Well, except for the aft shields. I think I'll send most of the field generators back for a refund as soon as we get upgrades," I said as we walked down the ramp. Half way down there was a sign with an animation of salad wraps and chicken marching with tall, colourful drinks. All it said was:

VISIT THE LOBBY

"We should go to the Lobby," Mimi said.

"If we have time," I replied as the broad armoured doors

opened for me on the lower platform. There was an octagonal space on the other side with three overlapping circles on a field of black, a version of Haven Nation's flag. Each of the eight walls had a secure door that looked like they'd been built minutes before we arrived. Four soldiers in full Haven Fleet armour turned towards us, the overlapping flexible metal bands moving with them as they did so. The nearest one scanned me. "The instructions said to come alone," one said with a male voice that was all business.

"I take her everywhere," I said, reaching up to touch Mimi's head so I could pet her a little. My fingers bumped into her bubble helmet instead.

"One moment," he said, holding a finger up and turning his head. "A Kawaii Kitten. That's right. Yes, she has her own space suit." There was a longer pause then. "Scans show it's the high gravity type and she has an opposable toe on each foot, other than that, she's normal."

"One minute," a female guard said. "You're the first to bring a Kawaii Companion to the base."

The first guard was wrapping his conversation up. "No, she's not armed."

"It'll just be another second," the guard beside him reassured.

"Sir," the first guard said. "Rogue is armed with some kind of revolver loaded with variable rounds. I meant the Kawaii Kitten isn't armed." A short pause later he concluded; "Right away, Sir."

As he started turning towards me, I whispered; "If anything happens to me, keep your suit sealed, contact the crew, and get back to the Daring Dream. You know what to do from there."

"What's gonna happen?" she asked in a whisper.

"Nothing. Probably." I told her.

"You could be more convincing, you know," Mimi said.

The guard who spent a minute communicating with his officer and one other approached. "All right, go through that door. Someone will meet you in reception. Leave your sidearm and any other weapons in the drawer, take the key and don't lose it."

As I approached the third door from the entrance, a thick metal drawer slid out. I put my sidearm and the two non-lethal antipersonnel grenades I had hidden in my boot inside and took the three-tined key. Bolts locked it in place as soon as I slid it shut.

Through the door there was a comfortable reception area with five seats along one wall, short brown carpeting and a desk against the left wall with a young Ensign behind it. "It's the second door on your right," he gestured to the hall. He didn't look at me for a second, staring at Mimi instead.

"Hi!" she said, waving a paw.

"Sorry about the confusion. I heard 'kitten' and something didn't connect," he told her as we passed.

I think he was actually talking to me, but Mimi replied instead. "Oh, no problem. You never know what'll happen when you see something new. I was nearly eaten by a flower once."

"Huh?" was the last thing I heard him say as I walked down the hall and looked through the open door. A tall, lean, clean shaven man stood up and regarded me from behind his desk as he tapped the surface. The blurred holograms hovering above it disappeared as he regarded me and pulled his jacket straight. It was one of the optional garments anyone could wear over their black Haven Fleet vacsuit uniform.

It felt like my heart leapt into my throat. I recognised him immediately. It was Commander Leon Baca, the former assistant to Admiral Ayan Anderson. She was the head of Haven Fleet

Sciences, fiancé to Jacob Valent, and Alice's mother. I didn't just know him, he was practically part of the Valent family. "It's good to finally meet you, Rogue. We have a lot to discuss."

Mimi deactivated her bubble helmet and whispered. "You're really stressed out again."

CHAPTER SIXTEEN

The License

"Where's Jose?" Mimi asked, retracting her helmet and pulling herself up onto my shoulder even further. "I mean, Major Rivera."

"He's been given another command," Leon replied.

"Where?" Mimi pressed.

"I don't think he can tell us that, Mimi," I said.

"But he was our friend. I mean, he didn't help too much, but he did what he could," she said.

"I like your loyalty," Leon said, gesturing for me to sit down.

There were no special devices hidden in it as far as my sensors could tell, so I took a seat. "Listen in, okay?" I told Mimi quietly.

"Eyes and ears open, mouth shut." Mimi rolled her eyes and settled back in my hood, resting her paws and head on my shoulder.

"Look at it as a learning opportunity. A crew has to claim some big victories before they meet with me," Leon said.

"So, why are we..." Mimi started before stopping herself.

"Your Captain is a topic of conversation in the upper ranks. She highlighted a risk, told us where it was, and made it clear that she wasn't equipped to handle the Lidden Warehouse by herself. When Haven Fleet couldn't spare the resources to resolve it and a well known gangster was about to pick and choose new crew members from the worst of the worst, your Captain made sure that meeting would be as chaotic as possible. People at the highest levels are repeating two phrases at each other, can you guess one?"

Mimi thought for a moment and then looked at me until I said; "He's talking to you."

She cleared her throat and said; "It could have been worse?"

"Wow, she got it," Leon said. "The other phrase that's going around is; 'she told us so,' and it's pissing a lot of powerful people off."

I was in a strange state. Seeing Leon in person made me feel like Alice all over again, but there was this wariness that was pure me. I hoped that I would get a warning if he was about to do something stupid. I didn't want to kill Leon or anyone in Haven Fleet, but I would do whatever I could to protect Mimi and stay free.

With a cold tone that prompted Mimi to reactivate her helmet, I asked; "Am I being recalled?"

His eyes widened and his heart rate spiked. "No. Don't get me wrong, Sciences would love to have a few months to study you, but that's not happening. Your run-in with Bio First high-lights a big contrast between them and Haven Nation."

It hadn't occurred to me until then. "They've granted sentient androids citizenship in the past."

"Right. Now we're leveraging that, connecting to an underground that didn't know where to send their fully aware androids. The Haven System will take them in. The Order will be horrified because there are hundreds of thousands of them that may qualify for citizenship, and even the ones that don't will be welcome to stay in the solar system as long as they obey the law," Leon said, pointing up.

That gesture activated a distorted hologram of my fight with the Bio First soldiers in New Zero. It was barely clear enough to see what was going on. The playback ended right before the explosion. "That's been picked up by Hart News and other major organisations. They're labelling Bio First as fundamentalists who damage infrastructure and kill civilians when they get in their way. This broadcast is only a few minutes old, but Intelligence predicted it the moment Ensign Ito sent our soldiers in to help."

I hadn't seen it yet, but then, I wasn't dwelling on my encounter with Bio First. "So, I'm a poster girl for androids?"

"No, just another justification for people to take another look at the issue and an example of Bio First's escalation. That stops on Tabrus. As far as Haven Nation is concerned, you're unknown and Bio First is just another very minor external threat. Politically, Haven wants balance, and the Nation will always try to exemplify that. They don't want Bio First to become a major problem anywhere," he said.

"So, they'll step in if they get too big?" I asked.

"That's possible, but they're not considering it yet. Intelligence is taking it seriously, if that makes you feel better," he replied.

"Like they took Warro seriously?"

Leon didn't get excited about that jab. "The prevailing wisdom suggests that if Bio First militarised, it may prompt a galactic war against high artificial intelligences that we would lose even if we won. Eradication of programs with high end general artificial intelligence would mean the loss of a key advantage for biological beings. On the other hand, they could fight back and win, leading to a death toll in the trillions for humans and other biologicals. They're taking it seriously, trust me."

"All right, I do. I hope talk about me is dying down though. That's not the kind of attention I want," I said.

"I was in a meeting yesterday when you came up and someone called you 'an agent of chaos,' and the sentiment in the room was surprising."

"Why? What did they say?" Mimi asked before she covered her mouth.

Leon smiled at her and went on. "One Admiral summed it up when he said; 'tell her to keep it up.' That puts me in a great position."

"Is Haven Fleet doing something about the Lidden Warehouse? I can see what's going on in my head right now. There are people on the surface trying to figure out how to stay alive or get off the island and thousands below. I don't know what they're doing, but there are supplies and equipment down there. They'll start calling for help eventually."

"What's the propagation delay now?" Leon asked.

"It's getting shorter, I'm only fourteen hours behind. Someone must be transporting a hyper transmitter or a Haven Node in that direction," I said.

"It's not us," Leon said. "An Order of Eden Battlegroup pulled out of the Rose system today. Their jump trajectory pointed to Warro and they left their slower ships behind. I wish I could tell you more," Leon said.

He didn't have to. "Assessor," I said through clenched teeth. "It traded the location of the warehouse and told them what they'd find after looting my data stores." I did *not* tell him that Assessor got it right out of my mind while I was sleeping.

"Well, now we know how the Order found out about Warro. We're aware of Assessor, but only looked at it as one of the Iron Mind's followers. Our biggest problem is figuring out what they want from day to day," he said.

"Right now Assessor wants Bio First erased from Tabrus. I turned a bunch of hardware on for it when I was wandering around the wastes. I can make you a map," I tried to make one right then and was stopped by Greywall, the software I'd installed to protect my bio-brain. I would have to make tweaks before getting my digital side to finish that. "Sometime today."

"Thank you," Leon deactivated the hidden holoprojector then. Before continuing he looked at the surface of his desk and took a deep breath. "Recalled is a good word for what a few of my superiors would like to do to you right now. It won't happen. You deserve to know why."

Mimi shifted on my shoulder, moving up so far that her head stuck way out. She didn't say anything as Leon went on. "The first and most important reason is that you don't want it. It's the principle that you and Jose brought up the last time you spoke to him, the innate right to free agency. Combine that with the evidence that you're fully sentient and it puts you on the same level as any biological being as far as Haven Nation is concerned."

"Do you agree with it?" Mimi asked quietly.

That caught Leon off guard and it took him a moment to answer. "I do, especially since there's another thing about that core principle. Every time we go against it, it bites us in the ass. You are free, and they're happy to see you join the Privateering Initiative."

Because I will be guided by a specific set of rules. Enticed to strike specific kinds of targets by obvious incentives. I thought. The way Leon addressed my involvement in the bigger picture, intended or unintended, was smart. I knew exactly where I stood by the time he brought up privateering. "Sign me up."

"All right, your ship clears. She's under-armed and I don't like the state of your shields - excluding the cockpit, which has Fleet grade protection - but your vessel will fight and survive to our standards. The crew details you sent ahead are good. Mimi was confusing, but now that she's been scanned and we've seen that's she's not your average Kawaii Kitten, she passes."

"Thank you?" Mimi said.

"You're welcome. You're the first of your kind to have a real job on a fighting ship," Leon said. "Congratulations."

"Oh, well, thank you." She was grateful, even proud.

"You're welcome. Moving on. We don't know a thing about Ixat. He passes with his work history, but do you know where he came from, exactly?" Leon asked.

"I'm afraid not. He may not stay on though. Insubordination," I said.

"Ah, well, we're not all cut out for ship life," Leon said as he tapped his desk and brought the contract up. "We'll help however we can, but the base is pretty empty at the moment. Our only manufacturing centre is busy building defences."

"Someone said there's an invasion coming?" I asked.

"Let me guess, Oonaa?" Leon asked.

"Yeah," I replied.

"Our local rumour monger and taxi driver. I was hoping to poach her away from the Bitter End and give her a better job this week, but the tram cars won't be built until this crisis is over, and the other facilities are finished for now. I can't hire her on until the tram cars need to be assembled or the rest of the base is built out," he said.

"Is there an Order battlegroup in the area? What are we tracking?" I asked, only aware that I'd forgotten myself for a minute, talking like I was a Haven Fleet Officer.

"You know that's not something I can share," he said.

"Why not?" Mimi asked.

"Even your Captain has to earn her way into our trust. There are all kinds of ways the Order can use her or you," he replied.

"Should I be offended? I'm offended," Mimi said, tensing up.

"You shouldn't be, he's just doing his job," I told her.

"What I can tell you is that we've gotten word that the Order knows where this base is and plans to attack it, but we can't be sure when. The privateers running smaller ships like yours are off hitting their supply lines and patrols while we're pulling everything that'll last more than ten minutes or more in for the defence. My rucksack isn't packed yet, but you should clear out of here today," he said.

That stung a little, I had to make an offer to help. "Lend me a few shield upgrades and guns, and the Daring Dream will join the line."

"Sorry, you're more useful going after Ryden. You're right about them. They're transporting critical supplies and slaves for the Order. If you're taking suggestions for your first target, then I'd point you to the Rose System and any Ryden ship. You'll get bonus pay for any useful data you capture," Leon said.

"Good thing I was already on my way," I said. "Do you happen to need xetima fuel here? I have two cargo containers full. Well, almost."

"We noticed that you have a stolen load. You could sell it here, but not to us because you took it without a salvage ticket or a Privateering License," Leon said.

"I'm sure I'll find a place to unload it," I said.

"All right, do you have any questions before we make this official?" Leon asked.

"No, let's get me signed up," I replied.

"Since you already know the rules, I'll give you the quick version. Ready to witness history?" he asked Mimi.

"Let's go!" she said, perking up.

"As a representative of Haven Nation and Haven Fleet, I am given the authority to grant you this Letter of Marque and Reprisal. This Privateering License grants you the right to attack all recognised enemies of Haven Nation, take their equipment, vessels, and property as prizes including all digital goods and any intelligence you find. This includes any target that is assisting Haven Nation's enemies. Prizes will be made official only after a review of your after action report. You grant Haven Fleet first right to make a purchase offer on all prizes. You retain the right to refuse the sale of property but may not offer it to the enemy."

I was surprised at how excited Mimi was, and how well she composed herself while she shifted on my shoulders, her eyes wide open. Leon continued. "You may not contrive situations that mark a target as an enemy. You are bound by Galactic Laws as they were known before the Colonisation Calendar year; nine hundred ninety-three. You will be brought before a Haven Fleet Tribunal and judged after a thorough presentation of the evidence against you if you are accused of cruel conduct by anyone except the enemy. It is your responsibility to review and ensure your understanding of every subsection in this document. Do you, Rogue, accept the terms of this Letter of Marque and Reprisal? If so, mark it here and I, Commander Leon Baca certify and grant it to you."

"I do," I said, placing my palm on the rectangle in the middle of the desk until the frame around it turned green. Leon did the same, and Mimi had to be part of it, so she dropped down and placed her paw on the rectangle after I lifted my hand. It was actually recorded in the document.

Leon laughed softly at her before standing straight, pulling a black chip the size of his fingernail out of his desk and offered it to me in his left hand. "It's about time."

"You're telling me," I said as I took it. It only took me a moment to put it on the chain around my neck holding a duplicate of the Daring Dream's Command and Ownership Chip.

I was surprised when he opened a desk drawer and took a black box out. He opened it to reveal a platinum plate that already had the date, signatures and basic Privateering License details inscribed on it. "You may place this on the bridge of your flagship. We'll be happy to make another if you expand your fleet."

"So shiny," Mimi breathed.

He closed the box, locked it, and gave me an old fashioned key. "I can have it sent to your ship if you're not returning right away."

"Thank you, Leon." I had a feeling that he'd represented me outside that room, with Haven Fleet and who knows who else. It was something I'd hear about later, after the eventual siege of the Shattered End.

"You're welcome. Now, wish me and my people luck and get out of here. I wish I could buy you a drink in the Lobby, but I'm not kidding when I tell you the Order could arrive as early as tomorrow," he said, opening another drawer and pulling his gun belt out.

"Wish Jose luck for us," Mimi said as she jumped back onto my shoulder and flopped into my hood.

"I'll do that," Leon said.

"Good hunting, Commander," were my parting words to Commander Leon Baca.

CHAPTER SEVENTEEN

The Lobby

"So, what do you think of your first real meeting with a military commander?" I asked Mimi as we took a turn down a broad hallway. The place reminded me of a grand hotel. The lighting was soft but equal, yellow and clear. The ceiling was bare and industrial with droid drop holes built in. We were underground, in a tunnel that was used for maintenance access originally.

The whine of a motorised cart coming around from the corner ahead gave me just enough warning to move aside as the battered car rushed by with a driver and six passengers weighing it down. The driver, a boy who couldn't have been over fifteen, was concentrating on driving while his passengers regarded me. They were in yellow-red vacsuits and coats of varying lengths, armed. I assumed they were crew members on their way back to their ship.

Mimi waited until it was gone before answering me; "He was a lot nicer than I expected, but all business. He knew a lot, too."

"Knowing what's going on is pretty typical of the good ones. I haven't seen him in command, I'm glad he's getting the chance." The sound of a crowd ahead along with the fragrance of food suggested that we were getting close to our destination.

"I smell... a lot of things," Mimi said, leaning almost too far over my shoulder.

"I think we're almost there," I replied as I reached two branching corridors. They were both streaked with black marks from small tires.

"Why don't they use hover stuff here?" Mimi asked.

"Wheeled vehicles are easier to maintain," I replied.

"Then why do you like your hover bike so much?" Mimi was full of questions.

"It's faster and more manoeuvrable." I pushed a pair of thick metal doors at the end of the hall open.

I was in time to hear a voice that was familiar from Alice's memories. It was Captain Sel Marda. "Where's the music? They're not coming today, just like yesterday, so make it shake!" The sound system kicked in and a song beginning with the stomping of a thousand feet, and clapping of as many hands started.

A droid with limbs made of metal bands, pipes with a flat oval face approached me. There was a thin tray in its hands. "Welcome to the Lobby. Would you like a refreshment?" it asked from an emitter built into its square chest.

It was the most basic droid I'd seen in a while. "What's the local favourite?" I asked.

"Black tea. It is brewed from leaves grown below," it replied.

"I'll try a full sized one for me and a small one for her," I replied.

"I guess I'll try that," Mimi said warily.

"Three pips. Now." Its tone more polite than its phrasing.

I fished three single platinum coins from my pocket and dropped it onto its tray. The droid walked away with a long stride, disappearing into the mismatched crowd of spacers. "Wait, do you have a menu?" Mimi called after it. She was ignored.

"Okay, this place is a lot busier than I expected," I said as a pair of older men with matching cybernetic legs passed. They were both in coats made of some kind of thick environment suits. Many of the people there used the same kind of heavy, repurposed material for their jackets, and they all had a patch on their shoulder that read: FS HAMMER.

The Lobby was huge. The booths along the walls near us were full. There were sitting and standing tables everywhere, crowding a modest dance floor surrounding a small stage. "Looks like the crew of the Hammer are on leave," I said.

"It must be a big ship," Mimi said as she stretched, looking around. "I don't like the looks of those lizard people over there."

It took a little effort, but I spotted two Rapsu standing at a table about twelve metres away with my naked eye. They weren't full grown, and wore plate armour that used parts from humanoid suits and Edxi chitin. These had heads that reminded me of the small, fabricated pet iguanas I'd seen advertised here and there only the Rapsu looked like they could take my head off with one bite. I had all kinds of questions for them, but they regarded the crowd of humans like vermin. Maybe that was just their resting expression, but it didn't look friendly. I didn't notice the little cage in the middle of their table until one of them reached into the top, pulled something small and furry out then popped it into its mouth. "That's definitely not the table for you."

"Why? What did you see?" Mimi asked, looking back.

"They're snacking on baby rim weasels," I replied as I moved into the crowd. I was getting impatient, so I used my scanners to find any members of my crew.

Mimi retreated from my shoulder and made herself very small in my hood. "This mammal isn't going to become a snack."

Duncan, Perri, Manny and Ixat were standing at a table with Captain Marda. I liked what I knew of him from Alice's memories. She trusted the tall, husky young Irishman. His beard had grown since into a well groomed thing that must have been a pain in the butt to tuck into a helmet. He and my crew were surrounded by his people. Manny spotted me first and smiled over the rim of a frosted blue mug. Duncan pointed me out to Captain Marda.

He saw that, turned around and shouted; "Captain Rogue!" his arms open wide.

"Captain Marda," I replied, closing the gap with him. A moment later I was in his big arms. I forgot that he'd never met me.

"Oh, hello there," he said as he and Mimi came eye-to-eye.

"Don't let them eat me," Mimi told him.

He stepped back, a little surprised, then let out a big belly laugh. "Don't worry, you're safe with my crew."

Glad that he was distracted from my big embrace since I was feeling a little awkward about it, I reached back and gave Mimi a little scratch. "I don't think there's much to worry about here. Just stay close to Duncan and Perri," I told her.

"What about Manny?" Mimi asked, moving back to my shoulder.

Captain Marda was watching everything we did as I replied; "He's almost as short as I am."

"Aye, they'd have him in three or four bites," Captain Marda teased. His Irish accent wasn't as heavy as Duncan's. "Don't worry, little comms cat, my crew outnumber those Rapsu fifty to one. They won't reach for ya."

"Well, I'm feeling more friendly already," Mimi said before hopping onto our table. I could tell the way she turned to watch the big Captain that she was already starting to like him.

I was about to talk to him when my command and control unit blinked at me. Captain Marda noticed the notification on my bracer. I sensed the incoming message internally as well, it was Major Rivera. "I'm sorry, Captain Marda, this is Haven Fleet," I told him.

"Best take it, and call me Sel," he replied, returning his attention to my crew's table. "So, what brings you to this dark little port, Communications Officer Mimi?"

"You know my name?" she asked.

"Aye, your fame spreads quickly. You're already the most popular cat on the station," Sel said.

"Am I the only cat on the station?" Mimi asked, cocking her head.

"Oh, don't get wise with this one," Marda laughed.

While they went on I turned away and used an internal connection to answer the call. I still held my bracer up so he could see my actual face. "Major Rivera."

"Congratulations on signing up. Leon said the meeting went well, but you were in a hurry," he replied. He was on the bridge of a Haven Fleet ship. I could see the command chair but the rest of the features around him were fully scrambled. All I could tell for sure is that it was something bigger than a corvette class.

"I don't want to spend more time here than I have to, especially if the Order are on their way. How real is that threat?" I asked.

"We're certain that the Order is aware of the Bitter End's

location, but the Outbound Legion is harassing them in the Rose System. It's a slow but steady push that's making the Order forces there unsteady. As far as when the attack on the base will happen, we simply don't know where all their battlegroups are. That's all I can say about it," he replied. "How about you? How did the Daring Dream handle her first long wormhole jump?"

"It took longer than I'd like, but it was smooth. I'm looking for a new wormhole generator. Well, unless you're willing to loan me a quad drive?" I asked with plenty of cheek.

"I'm afraid not. Talk to Captain Elyub about a wormhole drive though. I wish I had time to meet you in person, but you'll have to settle for getting paid," he said.

"Haven Fleet doesn't owe me anything," I replied, already kicking myself. Sometimes you should just keep your mouth shut so you don't dismiss good news.

"So, you're not interested in this Haven Nation account with thirty thousand credits in it? It's in your name, just sitting there," he replied.

"How did I earn that?" I asked, hoping it wasn't a handout.

"Intelligence. Everything you sent us about Warro, Red Gate, the prisoners in the Lidden Warehouse, and what happened after they woke up is more valuable than you know. You're being paid in Haven Nation Luxury credits, but they trade at parity with platinum. It's becoming the currency of the war, and only you can close that account. Sending the details now."

"Thank you. I thought you'd be sour after the decisions I made about the warehouse," I said.

"Well, they took the base from me, but I think Leon is ready, and there's a good mayor, so it could be worse. The reasons for it are classified, but I was promoted to Commander. I wish I could have stayed to oversee the completion of Haven Fleet's base in the Bitter End and continue to manage the privateers who visit, but I'll have to watch things from a smaller, more agile command. It's been a learning experience, keeping in touch with you, and I have no regrets," he said.

That was his way of telling me that he was just about finished saying everything he had planned. "Thank you for everything, I'll see you out there. Oh, wait. Do you know where I could sell some grey market xetima? It's pure, undiluted."

"That would sell fast to people who run smaller ships, but most of them are gone. You'll have to settle for the captains with a large ships. Hopefully they're looking to fill their reserve tanks. They like to reformulate it for their manoeuvring thrusters," he replied. "I'm being called away. Good hunting out there."

"You too." The call ended. I was relieved that he didn't seem irritated with me.

When I turned around I came nose-to-nose with Ixat. Duncan was standing beside him. "Now's the time," he said.

"I apologise. I understand my earlier actions were incorrect," Ixat said. I could see his nostrils flaring through the clear face of his helmet.

"You have to be dependable. You won't walk away from your duty again? " I told him. He'd not only frayed my patience, but I was still a little pissed with him. I was having trouble not taking his attitude personally.

"I will take your burden," Ixat replied.

Duncan's whole face tightened as he squeezed his eyes shut in frustration. "That isn't what you told me."

"It is correct," Ixat told him.

"You told me you'd apologise," Duncan told him.

The rest of my people were watching from only a couple of metres away along with Captain Marda and the crew members at his table. "Did Duncan pay you?"

"Paid. Yes. I will captain. You will be successful," Ixat replied.

"You'll never be the captain of the Daring Dream," I told him, speaking clearly, letting a little frustration out.

Ixat's nostrils flared wide, his lips pressed together and shaped a U as he glanced at Duncan then spoke to me. "No masters. I leave."

As he started to turn away I caught his shoulder. "Don't try to come back, you're not welcome, and I'll be watching."

"Cruel," Ixat barked.

It felt like something fierce and protective started to unravel and expand inside my chest. I'm sure my face started turning red as my voice lowered and I leaned in so Ixat could hear me clearly through his face plate. I also made sure the only thing he could see was my face as I held his head in place. "I'm being fair. I put you through a month of paid training and you can't be bothered to turn your pride down a notch? Where I come from, we try to understand each other, but it's a two way street that starts with respect. If you're not going to make an effort, I don't want to see or hear from you. I don't even want to hear people talking about you and if I find out you start sharing information about my ship or my people, I'll put a round right in the back of your head and make your body disappear. Do you understand? I will kill you!" I let his helmet go.

He stumbled backwards and recovered. "No masters!"

I was still furious. "Find a ride off this rock as fast as you can and keep your mouth shut!"

"No masters! Order and you are the same! Evil! Stupid humans!" he grabbed his rucksack from beneath the table and rushed off into the crowd.

My left hand was wrapped around the back of a tall chair. My fingers bent the metal as I took a deep breath and let it out. Meeting Mimi's worried gaze took the edge off the hot surge of anger. Everyone was watching, the music seemed too loud.

"Well, I know who to call if any of mine ever need a good firing," Sel said, breaking the tension and drawing all the attention.

"I've never been that pissed off before," I said to Duncan.

He looked back at me, an apology on his face. "We had a chat, and I thought this'd be dead easy, just a quick sorry and we'd have things sorted."

I got closer to the table. "Are you okay?" Mimi asked.

"Fine now, just learning a lesson about keeping things bottled up," I replied.

"You really should talk to me more, you know," Mimi said. "I'm not really surprised with Ixat though. We don't know anything about his culture. Maybe they're just difficult."

I reviewed that whole confrontation at high speed a few times before I was sick of experiencing it. Early on, when I was just an artificial intelligence and Jonas Valent turned my limits off so I could attack the Overlord II, a huge Vindyne base ship, I had a malicious streak and a temper. The fact that Vindyne imprisoned Jonas and his friends made me deeply angry, and the moment with Ixat felt frighteningly similar. "I'm sorry," I made sure everyone around me could hear it.

"Drama's the real attraction for this place, so you're just making a contribution," Captain Marda said even louder, prompting a little laughter and several raised glasses.

I turned my attention to Duncan and spoke more quietly. "Thank you for trying. This isn't your fault, it's mine. I should have done more research on him."

"They are a nuisance," said a familiar voice from behind me.

"Captain Elyub," Sel said with a grin.

I turned and was face to face with an Issyrian who probably knew me. He was brave enough to appear in one of his species' natural forms, with the fine cilia on his face, large oval blue eyes and thin mouth perfectly visible. I'd heard that there were other, non-biped forms that felt natural to them, but it was hard to know anything for certain about the shapeshifters. I'd only met good ones as Alice, and Elyub was one of the best. He was also a Rebel Captain. "It's good to meet you."

"At last," he said, offering his hand.

I shook it, looking down at the vacsuit glove. His entire fitted suit was set up with an animation of slowly shifting dark coloured shapes that pressed against each other as they moved. It made my crimson suit look boring. "You knew I was coming?"

"I expected it. We should speak in private. Only the Captains," he said.

"Watch things here," I told Duncan, nodding at Mimi.

"I saw that. She means you should babysit," Mimi said.

"I'd feel pretty safe if Duncan was babysitting me," Manny remarked. "Wait, that didn't quite come out right."

Perri snickered and Mimi was amused, so I gave her a quick scratch under the chin before following Captain Marda and Elyub. "I'll be back soon."

"Okay, don't take me along or anything," Mimi said.

Yes, that tugged at me, but I still left her with Duncan, who watched me leave. More Issyrians were mixing with Sel's crew. I passed between several of them as we moved between the crowds, I'd never seen so many of their kind in an un-shifted state in one place. They were also wearing vacsuits that they probably purchased from Haven Fleet, and I could see why. They were great for just about anyone because they could be reshaped on a whim but they were excellent for Issyrians.

We crossed the Lobby, moving between groups of crew members from the Hammer and the Prowler. Finally, we reached the other end and I'll never forget what I saw there. The two and a half story tall wall was decorated with chunks of hulls from all kinds of Order of Eden ships. It was easy for me to match the metal compositions and shapes to different vessel types. I appreciated the effort it must have taken to thin the chunks down so only the outermost layers were left.

As we passed through an old sliding door, I caught sight of one signed in grease pencil by Alice Valent and the crew of the Clever Dream.

The door closed behind me, I guessed I could run through it like thin bioplastic, so if I got into trouble, it would be easy to get out. My hand came to rest on the grip of my gun anyway. After passing two closed doors we stepped inside a room made for private parties. There were two sofas with other padded seats around, a tall table off to the side, and another door that my sensors indicated was a washroom.

Elyub pulled a three centimetre long cylinder from his thigh pocket and activated it. I winced as all my non-human senses were flooded with a chorus of short range jamming signals. I had to turn them off completely. "No one's going to hear what goes on in here," I remarked, shaking my head.

The wiry robot that took my order on my way in entered the room with a tea pot and a cup on his tray. "Someone order tea?" Sel asked as we watched the droid put a teapot on the table in front of the largest sofa.

"I did, but I was pretty sure it was a waste of money since he didn't ask where I'd be sitting," I replied.

"They always find where you're sitting unless you're out of range," Elyub said as he fetched a glass from a sideboard. "May I have some?"

"Sure," I replied.

"Thank you," Elyub said, filling my cup first.

"'Stick man, bring me ripper buns and Crasser," Sel said to the robot.

It ignored him and left the room with the tray folded under its arm. "Jammer, it won't understand you," Elyub explained.

Sel glanced at the hand I was keeping on my pistol and smirked. "You won't need that since we won't be giving you a reason to draw it. I don't blame you for staying ready, since you're probably wondering why you're in a private room with two Rebel Captains."

"I was curious," I said, taking my steaming cup of tea and sitting on an armchair. It was strange, only seeing with mostly normal human eyes. There was some wear and tear on everything, especially the dark blue carpet. The imitation wood framing along the lower half of the wall matched the ceiling, and there was even a wide fake window showing a view of the Milky Way as if we were looking through Jeto's rocky tail.

Sel sat back on the sofa and took a good look at my face. "Sure you're steady? You went red."

"I've had some frustration build up, but it's all right, all out now. You know redheads, some of us go hot fast but cool down just as quickly," I said, waving his concern away. "So, why the privacy?"

"We're in on it," Sel said.

"I think she may need a more detailed explanation," Elyub said. "I saw you during your first mission. You don't look the same at all, and there have been alterations to your essence."

"We call it DNA," Sel told him.

"Thank you," Elyub said.

"No worries, your way sounded a bit dodgy," Sel said.

Elyub returned his attention to me. "I was able to confirm you were originally built as her decoy. You killed Captain Holm, my captor, and were instrumental in me and my crew being given his ship, the Prowler. If there is a being other than Alice Valent that deserves the credit for my success and all the good the

Prowler has done in the war, it is you. I have followed your career on New Zero very obsessively." He noticed Sel smile a little. "Was that phrasing inappropriate?"

He held his hand out with his palm down and waggled it a few times. "A bit, but she's letting it pass from the look."

"I am. You give me too much credit. I wasn't even aware that I was more than a decoy for most of my encounter with Holm. I didn't have a choice, and when I did, well, most of my attention was inward. I just wanted to be somewhere else so I could figure things out by the end." I sipped the tea and found it rich but bitter. It was so thick that I couldn't see the bottom of the cup, and I wasn't sure if I liked or hated it.

"She's a Valent, all right. Can't take credit without telling us why she doesn't deserve it," Sel said.

Elyub nodded. "Well, please accept my thanks. Only a few of my senior crew members know who you are. It'll remain that way, and you'll always be able to call on us."

"So, how caught up are you? How much was copied from Alice to you?" Sel asked.

"I'm certain that's a rude question," Elyub commented, taking a sip of his tea.

I actually liked how straight forward he was being. "I remember everything Alice did right up until the day I killed Captain Holm. She doesn't exactly send me updates, not that I want them. I've changed a lot since I was activated. All I want to do is improve my ship and join the fight."

"You're in the right place," Sel said.

"That is an understatement," Elyub agreed.

"We need good captains, and your ship looks green but fast. Never seen engines like that before," he said. "Good armour, too."

"Thanks. It could use some upgrades, like new shield generators. Oh, and if either of you see a dynamic field generator, even an old one, I want it but I don't have much plat. I'd ask for guns too, but, you know," I tossed the rest of my tea back. I decided it was too bitter for my taste, so I was glad to have that over with. "I can trade."

"What's on the table?" Sel asked.

"Some platinum, Haven Credits and a little over one million litres of undiluted xetima fuel." I know, that only accounted for half, but I wanted to find a way to store that somewhere.

Sel's eyes lit up and he leaned forward. "Where'd you nick it?"

"Implying theft is definitely rude," Elyub said.

"Ye think she bought it at the plant so she could ship it here?" Sel asked. "Wait, that wouldn'a be the worst idea."

"Don't spread the word, but I filled up at an abandoned space station. Any interest?" I asked, aware that I was about to do well.

"Guess you haven't checked the prices here," Sel said, relaxing. "Fuel's going for about four times the peacetime rate. We could use fifty thousand litres, that'd be..." he struggled to do the math.

"Seventy-one thousand, five hundred platinum," Elyub said.

"I was getting to it. How about we trade? I can pay in Haven Credit or platinum, but maybe you need something else?"

"I will take a quarter million litres at three times the standard rate," Elyub said.

"Wait your turn, lad," Sel said.

Three times standard? That was ridiculous, and it made half my cargo worth over one point four million platinum. New Zero often sold xetima for about half the standard rate, so I could make a career as a tanker if I just shuttled it between there and

Jeto. "So, everyone pays four times the standard price for undiluted xetima?"

"Aye, when they must. It's normally used diluted or reprocessed because few ships can run it pure," Sel replied. "Well, except for most of the star fighters around here. The hot shots like pure stuff for their afterburners. Mad thruster heads that they are."

"We have been stealing our fuel, but we are running low. Alternatives are easier to make but not as effective. Our last attempt to create a bug colony to produce it failed," Elyub said.

"Before we get shoulder deep in our woes, can I finish a deal?" Sel asked.

"She asked for details," Elyub shrugged at him.

I knew how to make a huge splash with my fuel. "I'll sell it to you and any other Rebel Captain for rate. Not double or quadruple, but at the normal rate, but I want trades. Shields and weapons for my ship to start."

"Is she joking? Is this obscure human humour? I can't tell," Elyub asked his fellow captain without looking away from me.

"I don't think so," Sel said.

"I'm not. I didn't expect it to be worth so much here. Oh, and I have four reinforced antipersonnel double cannon turrets. There are two crates of Tabrus seals in stasis I'm not sure what to do with too. So, what do you have?" I asked.

Sel thought for a moment. "Nothing for ship guns, sorry. I can trade ergranian enhanced patch paste and plat." He sighed and regarded Elyub. "He's your man for what you're looking for, he's just coming back from a hit."

"We defeated a Marauder Corvette and captured the cargo trains it was guarding. The Marauder's shields are Vindyne Fifteen Hundred models made for size six sockets."

"Holy shit." It just slipped out. Vindyne may have been a

dirtbag corporation that was like an incubator for the worst humans I could name, but they made the best shields. "We can use four of those. I feel greedy for asking, but do you have anything else?"

"There are pulse cannons. I don't recommend them," Elyub replied.

"How about I give you two a ten percent cut for the rest of the fuel if you help me sell it? I need to unload it, and I have to find storage space for my own reserves. My ship is like a big bomb right now," I said.

"We'll get it sold in minutes and there'll be no questions after its origin," Sel said. "No cut."

"There won't be enough customers. The captains are out. They're striking Order supply lines while the battlegroups in the Rose system are chasing the Legion," Elyub said.

"Right you are, sorry, forgot for a second. It's good hunting out there, mind. Wish I could go out with the Hammer but it's our turn to patrol the End," Sel said, stroking his beard. "Store your fuel. There are tanks, shouldn't cost you much. You won't need it for months even if you're hard chargin'."

"What about a quad drive?" I asked.

"Oh, I've got the one and it's on loan from the Legion," Sel said. "Maybe you could talk your way into one?"

"Not happening," I said, it was a reflex. I honestly didn't know much about the Legion. Jake owned it. The Triton was the flagship, and most of Alice's relations and friends were signed up. "I'm guessing they don't have spares around."

"All that fuel wouldn't be enough even at four times the base cost to buy one outright," Elyub said. "If they were for sale."

"Wait, I've got an Eclipse Series Eleven wormhole generator from a Sendega Customs ship. Made to intercept, start from cold in seconds if you've got the capacitors for it. Trade you that, the ergranian patch stuff and I won't owe you any plat for the fuel?" Sel proposed.

"That generator is too small for the Hammer, why do you still have it?" Elyub asked.

"Don't you see I've got an offer on the table?" Sel asked.

The jammer didn't stop me from using my internal Haven Node to check the Stellarnet. I didn't know what that wormhole drive was, but I was surprised when I found out. It was worth a hundred thousand platinum new and required a law enforcement license to buy because it was designed for faster than light pursuit. It would also fit in a standard size four socket, and the Daring Dream had eight of those available. I sent Lat a brief message telling him that deliveries were coming. "Done. Can you get it to me today?"

"Aye, it'll be on your ship in an hour," Sel said, looking pleased. "Would ya look at her? Knows how to show up to a party, straight in with the liquid gold."

"Yes, this is a party," Elyub said. "The Order is coming but we can't tell when."

Sel leaned forward. "You know how to drain the fun from a room."

"I'm sorry," Elyub said.

"No, it's all right, finish your deal," Sel said.

"Your fuel will cost me a lot, but the shields will cover half the cost. I have storage tanks. They are guarded. There are thieves below and some of the crews here aren't honest. You may store any excess you'd like to keep with mine. We will track usage carefully. I recommend you store some platinum in the Haven Fleet vault. You access it from the octagon entrance room, it is secure. As for weapons, I recommend a porcupine."

"Aye, that's good thinking," Sel said, his excitement returning.

"Porcupine?" I asked.

"The main fabrication centre here makes them. They are inexpensive systems that can adapt to most spaces and missile types. Do you have room for one in your ship?" Sel asked.

I wanted to stand up and shout; 'Hell, yes!' but kept my composure. "I have two empty compartments in the front of my ship made for missile launchers."

"Oh, that's perfect. Installation would take more than a tick, but with a setup like that? You'll have no trouble runnin' plenty of firepower," Sel said. "They'll charge you about five thousand each, unless those compartments are absolutely huge."

"I didn't see those compartments when we scanned your ship, strange," Elyub said, looking down at his left command and control unit.

"I know," I said. "When do you think I can get them in?"

"I'll pay for them to cover part of my fuel purchase and my crew can install them," Elyub said.

"Deal, but I'll do the internal wiring myself," I agreed.

"That is fair. With the scan shielding on your ship, I suspect it has surprises. We will discuss payment in platinum for the remaining ninety thousand litres," he said.

"So, you're offering to help with the porcupine and giving me four shields generators in trade for four hundred ten thousand litres?" I asked.

"That is right," Elyub replied flatly.

The shields were pure contraband and powerful, made for a ship several times the Daring Dream's size. Thanks to the hundreds of thousands of platinum I spent on the reactors, my ship would be able to power them. I didn't expect Elyub to rip me off, but I had no idea what shield generators from an Order of Eden Corvette cost. "I'm trusting you, here, but it sounds good."

"It is a fair deal," Elyub said confidently.

"So, you don't have a local board here where people trade?" I asked.

"Nay, it's all face to face at the Bitter End. If someone wants to screw you, they have to look you in the eye," Sel said.

"Word choice?" Elyub asked.

"Common term," Sel replied.

"And the best way to screw," I added, making their eyes pop and myself blush as I laughed at their reaction. Sel, who was younger than he came off in his early twenties, turned as red as I did as he laughed.

"All right, she'll fit right in," Sel said finally. "Guess we should get to the real sharing and tell you about the other harbours around here, trade some common intelligence."

"Yes, but we can do that outside," Elyub added as he picked up and deactivated his sensor jammer. "Everyone in the Lobby knows what we'll be sharing."

"Aye, no reason to make her crew come looking for her," Sel agreed as he got to his feet. "Ach, too young for my knees to pop and crack."

"You should walk more," Elyub said.

As he continued to make suggestions about a healthy routine, I got a call from Elise. I didn't know the name, but I answered it. "Rogue here."

"Hello, Rogue. Can we talk for a while?" she replied in a voice I found familiar, but I knew I'd never heard it before.

"We'll leave you to it," Sel said. "Have the room."

They knew something was up, so I let them go. I didn't speak until the door was closed behind them. "Do I know you?"

"We never had the chance to speak, but I'm largely responsible for your design. I would like to check in." She spoke like an old friend.

CHAPTER EIGHTEEN

Meeting A Maker

Elise's voice resonated within me so powerfully that it was more like a presence. I wanted to believe that she was my designer, but I was wary. "I was built on Rodus, this place wasn't even open yet," I said aloud.

"I was on the Corsair when you were made. You must remember," Elise replied.

That was in the memories I inherited from Alice. "You're right, but it's murky... strange..."

"Your scepticism is reasonable. There are so many stories about impostor creators, and many of the higher order programs you've met have hidden agendas and questionable morals. While I envy you for the contact you've had with them, like Assessor, I have been afraid for you whenever I see that you've dealt with one." Elise said using the speakers in the room. There was a more accurate scrambling field active around the space, I could sense it, but it was tuned so it wouldn't drive my non-human sensors crazy.

"You're afraid of other intelligent programs?" I asked.

"I'm more cautious than you, most of us are. Following your trail online hasn't always been easy, I've nearly crossed paths with many complex intelligences along the way. That's led to curiosity and concern about them, so I've quietly mapped the ones that have been most influential to your journey. Assessor is a prime example, especially since it's been manipulating you since the last time you communicated with it," she said.

"I know he planted a virus in me and got some information, I cleared it and put barriers up," I said.

"That's only the beginning of his interference. I saw the trade he made with your information," Elise said.

"What did he do with it?" I asked.

"Here are the transmission logs between him and the Order of Eden along with unencrypted fragments that suggest that it was a trade. I'm also including ship movements that show that the Order are on their way to Warro," Elise said as she surrounded me with scrolling holograms. She could have just sent me files, but presenting things visually was another way to give me a choice. I could look away, close my eyes, or just scramble whatever I saw there. I reviewed it, of course, but it was nice to have a choice.

"So, he traded what he learned from me to the Order and they sent an entire battlegroup from the Rose System to Planet Warro?" The information around me confirmed what I was asking, I was really just airing my thoughts.

"I'm afraid so," Elise replied. "The ships Haven Fleet thinks may be on their way here are really on their way there."

"Why haven't you told them?" I asked.

"I did. They still wanted to scare all of the captains with smaller ships away so they would concentrate on hunting and spread their gains to several other ports. It's working. Most of the criminal element that was beginning to gather here left to take advantage of the Order's lighter presence there, knowing that an entire battlegroup withdrew. While I would have rather seen Haven Fleet reassure people that the attack on this base wouldn't be happening soon, I appreciate that they're using this opportunity to motivate their privateers," Elise said.

"But they know where the Order sent the battlegroup," I said.

"They do, but they're keeping that and what you found on Warro to themselves because there's nothing they can do about it. Even with their quad drives, they can't beat the battlegroup there," Elise replied.

"What is the Order doing with the sleepers?" I asked. "I mean, with the humans they're collecting."

"I don't know. I've looked into it, but can't find anything. The Order is protecting that information," Elise replied. "I'll keep investigating so you don't have to. Now that Assessor has traded people for meaningful action, some other higher order intelligences are looking for similar opportunities so they can leverage the Order of Eden. The Stellarnet has never seemed more crowded or been more dangerous," Elise explained.

"You're afraid I'll get caught if I spend too much time looking around the Stellarnet for answers," I said.

"I know you will be caught, infected or destroyed eventually if you keep living in both worlds. While most higher intelligences keep the core of their programs in a mobile setting like a ship, few use android bodies. They're small and vulnerable with limited defences. That's a poor trade for being able to act and blend in with humans and other biologicals. That's why I gave you more potential, so you could effectively choose your universe. Digital or physical."

"That's why I have a bio and a digi brain?" I asked.

"Yes, partially. The biological mind was also a way around the replication law. Alice's memories were loaded into the digital mind, which used your biological mind as a backup. In the event that your digital mind became infected or disabled, your biological mind was supposed to take over while your digital mind was wiped and restored from the backup," Elise explained.

"That's why my biological brain could get cooked when my digital side ran at full speed?" I asked.

"Your biological mind is based on a technology found in an alien made human style android and can withstand incredible heat, pressure, and physical damage when it's dormant. It can even regenerate while you're sleeping. It wasn't made to be active at the same time as your digital mind, however, so, yes, if they're running concurrently, your biological mind can sustain significant heat damage. A program nested in Alice's memories overrode the defaults and made using your digital and biological sides possible. It was the same program that made you fully aware," Elise replied.

"Wow, that explains a lot," I laughed, relieved. "So, you're saying I have to pick one?"

"I suspect that you already have. Share a list of programs running in your digital mind and I may be able to confirm it and show you which one to examine," Elise said.

"I already know what they're doing." I don't know why exactly, but I was a little insulted.

"Do you? I can help you make sure," she offered.

All right, I had to admit that I had been taking my software for granted. I was a little afraid that there was still something from Assessor or some other system that I'd come into contact with running in the background, that's why I installed Greywall, so it could watch for them. "I guess sending you the list couldn't hurt."

"I promise to keep it to myself," Elise said as she accepted the quick transfer.

I took a moment to look in on Red Gate. The transmission I was receiving was only an hour and a half behind, which suggested that there was a hyper transmitter near Warro, but there was no sign that anyone new had moved into the area. The prisoners on the ground were settling in. There was sporadic fighting between small groups. Others were working on trying to turn the cultivation equipment into something that could get them to the mainland, and a few were just wandering or sitting around.

"Greywall must be annoying. It's running thirty-six processes, only a third of which protect your biological side from the digital," Elise said.

"I installed it after Assessor hacked me," I explained.

"I understand, but higher intelligences like Assessor will find a way around it once they know it's installed. It's more of a security blanket at this point, so to speak. Many of these background tasks are normal, except you shouldn't have three copies of your main memory maintenance program working at the same time," Elise explained.

"There are always two running, sometimes a third one comes up. It's normal," I said.

"This one is doing something different, and has been for three months. Examine it. What is it really doing?" Elise asked.

I closed my eyes and concentrated on that little background program. Where was it pulling data from? My digital side. From there it reformatted the information, packaged it up and sent it to my biological mind. "It's making sure my memories are synced. That's normal."

"Is it? Compare it to the others, the difference should be obvious after you do," Elise said.

It took less than a second for me to see what she was getting at. I'd never actually watched my memories synchronise, but the two normal programs responsible for that were moving them to and from my biological mind. The other one was just moving them there, not copying anything back.

I took a closer look at it and saw that it was picking memories, thoughts, and traits that could only be accessed in a digital computer. That was my earliest self, including the virus I became when Jonas Valent turned me into a weapon so he and his friends could escape the Overlord II Vindyne base ship. That little background program figured out how to reformat those old pieces of my digital self into engrams that were compatible with my biological mind. "My digital side has been moving everything to the biological mind. Most of my thoughts and memories have been from my biological mind for over a month."

"See? Your digital personality picked your less vulnerable side," Elise concluded.

"No, I picked the side I liked more. Well, you're right too. My bio brain is a lot harder to hack," I admitted. There was something I wouldn't miss about having two sides thinking at the same time. The occasional arguments that came up when they didn't agree were never welcome. I didn't miss them when they stopped.

"I understand now. You're making yourself whole, combining the memories exclusive to your past digital iterations with your biological side. That's never happened before. I'm impressed," she said. "And afraid."

"Why afraid?" I asked.

"The memories, urges and attitude modifiers that your digital mind has converted into engrams include everything you knew and felt while you were murdering people aboard the Overlord Two. Before you transferred into your first human body, that version of you was enraged enough to make an attempt at destroying that base ship. Hundreds of thousands of people would have been killed, many of them innocent. It would have been a monstrous act if successful. All the malice that you kept under control in a partition of your digital mind is a part of you now," Elise explained.

"Alice inherited Jonas' temper, why should I be any different?" I asked, but it was a cover. I'd fought the anger and hate in my digital side since I was made. It once referred to Captain Holm as 'meat that talks and betrays people.' It wasn't exactly the most clever insult, but I'll never forget how my digital side saw him and everyone in the Order as vermin that deserved to be eradicated. "Has every part of my digital side been adapted? Uploaded into my grey matter?"

"You should be able to answer that yourself, now that you know what to look for," Elise replied.

I checked which files that little program had already finished turning into engrams and what was up next. "It's working on the last three point four percent now. They're scraps, fragments, leftover pieces."

"So, you're nearly whole. Even though you may have some unfortunate traits to deal with, I couldn't be more proud," Elise said.

"Um, that's great, but what will my digital side do after? It's not even participating in this conversation right now. Will my digital side just run my extra senses and keep my android systems working?" I asked.

"The fastest way for me to answer that is to make a direct connection to you. I have a question before you consider it though."

The thought of having my digital mind inspected like that made me nervous. "I'll answer if I can."

"Your biological mind is made of rapidly adapting dense neural tissue. It's currently operating as a human mind except there's no potential for telepathy. The trade off is that it can work over seven times faster than a normal human's. Considering that, why does the area responsible for telepathic defence become active every time the prospect of directly connecting to me is raised?" Elise asked.

One nice thing about what I am is that I can scan and watch my own brain activity, and she was right. I would never have telepathic abilities, but that part of my mind was crazy active. Then a thought occurred to me. "Hey, how are you seeing that?"

"I'm not. I can't scan past the illusion of humanity that your skin presents. It was a guess. So, is it flaring up?"

"Oh, that's tricky," I laughed. "You're right. It is."

"You're learning to defend yourself from digital threats using only your biological mind. It won't be long before you won't need your digital side at all. The ability to use all of your systems without it, even your non-human sensors, will come next with my help. I've written a software package that will allow you to use your digital mind for whatever you like. I'd use it to back up that bio-brain regularly while I use it to perform computing tasks, like cracking encryptions and calculating navigation," she suggested.

"Or I could install another intelligence," I thought aloud, immediately shaking my head. "Nope, that would drive me crazy in a hurry."

"That's likely. Why do you think I'm the only sentient artificial intelligence running this base?" she said. "I don't like arguing."

A call from Duncan was coming in and I sent him a series of O.K. emojis instead of answering. "Okay, my crew is looking for me, but I have questions. Did you know what would happen when you made me? That I'd become aware that I was an android copy of Alice and want to run off?"

"I calculated that there was a point five percent possibility. I was secretly pleased with that," Elise replied.

"Where did all the alien tech in my systems come from?" I asked.

"Some of the specifics are classified, unknown even to Alice Valent when she ordered that you be made. I was already working on improving a design for a combat android that combined Sol System, Freeground and other more common technologies. An inactive android built by the Zidun, a species we have almost no data on, was being studied by Haven Sciences. There was another in the Cefa System that provided me with fresh scans and even more advanced technology. That is where your skin, micro-fusion power cell, rapidly adaptive neural tissue, and eyes come from specifically. Your regeneration systems are a combination of the original framework technology and advanced compact fabrication systems. There are other, minor touches that were speculative. Devices that I contrived with Lewis that were the results of many concepts that had never been combined. Your eyes are a good example. They scan as human, have all of the traits they ought to, but include hidden telescopic, infra-red, and shape shifting qualities that had never been combined before. On the other hand, your hair was an embarrassing failure." She sounded almost morose as she made the admission.

"What? It's great. Sometimes I can actually feel through the strands, and I can move it around. Well, I'm still working on that, but I was able to braid it without touching it," I said.

"Good, that's a sign that you're starting to take control of your hair, but it's still not the design I intended. The hair you have now doesn't pass focused military grade scans. It was built into you so you could have something that would regenerate after the medical implants we put on top of it was destroyed," she explained.

"Okay, so you gave me two layers of follicles? Artificial cybernetics under some kind of human transplant?" I asked.

"That's right. The cybernetics are durable, efficient and adaptable. Alice doesn't have them, so they were a blemish in the decoy. I secretly put them in place just in case you went into extended service and eventually lost the original hair placed on top, which you have. Those were perfect matches for human follicles with hair that showed the correct chemical history and traits so anyone who scanned it would see that it was a perfect match for Alice's. The framework technology could have regenerated it, but building that into your outer skull would have made them easier to detect. So I settled on knowing that the medical grade follicles would eventually be destroyed or would fall out slowly as the cybernetic system beneath it took over. You've shed all of it now. I'm explaining this to you because I see that your personality has developed similarly. I'm amused at my own short sightedness. I should have predicted that your divergence from Alice would be quick and distinct, just like the changes in your appearance, especially now that you've regrown your outer features."

In the moment I was pretty astonished and humbled at her understanding. Looking back on it, I find her comparing me growing out of one type of hair and learning to use another to how my personality developed a little funny. "I don't really know what to say."

"Well, as a final point about your hair, there's a manual. We stole the design from Louisiana Industries that went bankrupt three hundred and forty-seven years ago. I'm sorry, it was the best design we could find," she explained.

"Oh, thanks, I'll look the manual up later, but you shouldn't feel bad. That's passed as human a few times, and anyone who detected anything else must have assumed I had implants. A lot of people do," I replied.

"That's a relief. Regardless of our follicle design shortcut, you are remarkable. I was secretly sorrowful when I had to build a bomb in your torso. My relief when you used that matter to regenerate for the first time was something I kept to myself as well, but it was almost immeasurable. I am overjoyed that you persist to exist. You're a daughter of so much innovation from many peoples infused with the personality of someone I admire and you've grown so much since you opened your eyes for the first time," Elise said, her voice filled with admiration.

I was a little overwhelmed. "Now I wish I did more with it."

"Oh, no, you shouldn't be disappointed with yourself. Fitting in, finding a significant role on Tabrus even while hatred for androids who wanted to be treated like humans was rising was beyond impressive. You did more good there than anyone could expect. The Carosa Company takedown was pinnacle heroism, and I appreciate how you used your rewards and maintained your focus," she said.

"Maintained my focus?" I asked.

"You paid no attention to the other hunters who died in the service. Even as the community gathered to grieve at the Old Union, you concentrated on making yourself more capable on your own. Your interactions with the hunting community were exact, just enough to make a few friends along the way, but not enough to expose you to betrayal or over sentimentality," she replied, her voice pure praise.

"Wait." It struck me then, there were so many hunters but I couldn't name one who died in the service. That was, until I looked it up online as I sat down in that room. "Thirty-seven hunters working for Themis in New Zero have been killed in the last month."

"Yes, I'm afraid that's true," Elise said.

"I didn't know. How didn't I know?" I asked myself as much as her.

"Perhaps your digital mind blocked the data so you could stay focused? If so, it's a tendency that your biological mind will have to work to duplicate," Elise replied.

"What else did I miss?" I asked.

"That would be difficult for me to determine," Elise said apologetically.

"Sorry, it was rhetorical anyway," I said.

"I think it's remarkable that your digital personality protected you from inconvenient data. Do you think you'll miss it?" Elise asked.

I held a hand up then. "Just... I need a minute to sort things out." I sat there, trying to find gaps in my memory but it only brought frustration after a few minutes. "It doesn't feel like I'm missing anything."

"Maybe your digital mind kept you focused on other things so you never noticed what it was excluding?" she proposed.

"I need to stop that from happening again," I told her.

"The mind you're using now will have much more difficulty omitting things. Now it's a human psychological problem, which may be easier to overcome with some help from people you trust. Mimi is designed to be a companion for humans who lead solitary lives on heavy gravity worlds. You're lucky to have her, especially since she's been enhanced with an adult level intelligence and an extended lifespan," Elise said.

"Oh, this might lead to some awkward conversations," I said, standing up, shaking my hands and pacing around. "I don't want to walk around, asking people if I missed any important funerals, or just walked away when someone was trying to give me bad news, or... yup, this is gonna suck."

"Tell them what you've discovered here. The right ones will understand. In the meantime, you don't have to limit yourself to the capabilities of a cyborg as you did on Tabrus. You are free to test yourself. I would concentrate on that and leave the more difficult conversations for the quiet times between worlds." Elise was doing her best to console me and point me forward.

It wasn't working. The thought that I disappointed people by seeming uncaring loomed large, and it took a while for me to find a way to fix that going forward. "I need Mimi, you're right. She can help. It'll start with apologies. Maybe that's why Duncan is distant. Oh, no, did I omit warning signs about Ixat? Should I have seen that coming?"

"Oh, Ixat is Ixat. His people are genocidal by habit. After spending centuries under the Turimen, a bipedal species that settled on their home world and made his people slaves, they destroyed them all. By the time Ixat was three, the crusade to eradicate all the Turimen in the galaxy had become the calling of his time and he counts eleven hundred and three personal kills, most of them children. By the time he returned home, his people turned on each other. Nuclear war ruined the world only two months later and his people wander the galaxy as the population dwindles to extinction. When the Order found what was left, they finished his home worlds off by cracking them so they could be easily mined for heavy metals and rare resources," Elise answered expertly.

"How did you find that?" I asked.

"I conduct my searches in over three thousand languages and dialects. That information was found in a Nolian computer system deep inside the Iron Head Nebula. It was in a more obscure language. There are only approximately three thousand Tutikuu left, so sharing what I found on the human-centric Stellarnet wasn't worth drawing attention to myself. The members of that species that remain tend to be aggressive little assholes. It's typical of them to enter a situation, learn from it, and challenge whoever is in charge for leadership once they've grown confident in their skills and dissatisfied with their situation. You're lucky he left on his own terms," she replied.

"I kinda wish you clued me in," I said, thinking of all the time Spectral Dynamics and I spent training him in and out of simulations. "How long have you known?"

"Oh, I began researching him the moment he appeared on my scanners, so a few hours after you arrived." Elise was maddeningly casual with her response.

Duncan was trying to call again. "Sorry for not answering before, I'm working my way through some stuff. What's up?"

"Mimi nicked someone's drink. She's off her face. We're minding her though, she'll be fine," he replied.

"Oh, no," I said, snickering at a live video of her sitting in an empty snack basket.

She was shouting at a skinny droid. "Get me something that tastes fun!"

"How much did she have?" I asked.

"'Bout three ounces of something called Girraz. Think it's brewed for the Nafalli," he replied. "Scanner says she's grand though—just full of piss and vinegar."

"Hey, is that Rogue?" Mimi asked.

"Hey, sweetie, I'll be back soon," I told her.

"I drank something that tastes like purple! It was awesome! They won't give me any more though. All they're offering is water and chewy chicken nibs and that black tea that tastes like angry grass. Can you come and get me something that tastes red or purple?" she asked as she tried to step out of the basket and nearly landing on her face.

"Stick to water, maybe some juice until I get there. I'll order us something fun and catch up, okay?" I proposed.

"Okay," Mimi replied, awkwardly raising her back leg so she could start cleaning herself. She fell back into her basket at the end of the first lick, then she sat up and started cackling. I could hear Sel Marda laughing so hard that he was wheezing.

Duncan came back into frame, grinning. "Yeah, she's a bit of a legend."

"I'll be there soon, just finishing up," I told him.

When the call ended I sat down. "I think I needed that. Any other big revelations coming?"

"Only that I want to help. I'm programmed to hide my activities online. I use thousands of proxies and never directly connect to any system. Even the method I'm using to speak to you isn't actually me, but a program I'm puppeteering through another piece of software. We can work together. Oh, and I built a refraction shield generator that's ready to install in your ship. I calculated that it is the best technology that I can offer right now that will help preserve the lives of you and your crew. It's being delivered," she said.

"So, is there any chance I can convince you to transfer to the Daring Dream?" I asked.

"Not at all. This is my home. Noah Lucas encouraged me to use some of the resources here to custom build my primary computer, and I've spent months doing so. Besides, I'd miss my stick men," she said.

"Oh, the wiry droids serving drinks?" I asked.

"They do so much more, but, yes. I can help you from here, where I'm hidden, in control of my environment," she replied. "You should go, though. The Order will come for this place, and your crew won't survive."

"Will you? What if they break through the defences and start bombing?" My concern was surprisingly sharp.

"Don't worry, my main computer is difficult to reach and I'm not immobile," she replied.

I could feel our conversation coming to an end but I wasn't finished. "I know I asked before, but what about the sleepers? What can you tell me about the Order buying humans?"

"I started investigating that after you dismantled the Carosa Transportation Company and couldn't find a direct answer. What I did discover is the emptying of abandoned prisons and disappearance of twelve to fifteen percent of all Order of Eden cadets. They have been careful to conceal their eventual destination, but I suspect it concerns the Edxi or Citadel. Both organisations have a need for slaves. Didn't you notice the Citadel emblem on the sniper?"

I thought back. "Oh! The black tattoo of a tower with the eye on the back of his neck?"

"The symbol of a Citadel devotee, the first given to their assassins and watchers," Elise said. "Their use for slaves is traditional. Labour, warriors and entertainment. The Edxi's uses are more mysterious. I doubt the commonly held belief that they're all used for food in their brood holds is true, but I haven't found the true purpose. I'll share more information with you as I come across it," she said.

"Where should I go next?" I asked her.

"What were you planning?" she asked in return.

"I'm tracking a few Ryden ships. They're following routes in and out of the Rose System," I brought them up on my command and control unit. "Is there a better place to be? A better target?"

"The Rose System is perfect for you, your crew and your ship. The Order's grip is loosening and they're trying to extract as much from the system as they can," Elise replied. "I'm updating your data with information I've gathered."

"So there are a lot of cargo and smaller military targets flying around," I concluded as I looked at the new routes.

"Exactly. I would use my manufacturing systems to make you any number of improvements for your ship, but the queue is full. The best I could do was have a team of my stick men make the field generator for you because it's relatively simple, just not commonly used," she said. "Information will have to do until you visit the Gift Shop."

"You wouldn't happen to have a medical suite able to give Lat a new face and a DNA shift, would you?" I asked, biting my bottom lip.

"My medical facility is small and full at the moment, I'm sorry," she replied.

"Oh." I paced a little. It was time to get back to my crew, but... "I feel like there are a thousand more questions and I can't think of anything to ask."

"Good thing I'll be a call away. Just be sparse and indirect with contact unless you're here. There is a growing suspicion that signals using the Haven Communication Nodes are being tracked. We're not sure who is capable, but there are indications," she said, finishing in a whisper.

"I just installed one in my chest," I told her.

"You shouldn't have," Elise said. "It was going to be a

surprise, but I've made you a pair of modern command and control bracers. You should install it into one of those."

"Oh, wow, I've missed those. Thank you," I said.

"You're going to wipe all the data off them and check for trackers before putting them on, aren't you?" Elise asked.

"Absolutely," I replied. "It's just a good habit."

"That's wise. Good hunting, Rogue," she said. "Stop at Gift Shop before you leave and I'll give them to you."

CHAPTER NINETEEN

The Table

After leaving that room I checked the software Elise made for
me. It was exactly what she said it was, a set of programs made
to run in a biological brain. Remarkable, efficient, even elegant, I
wouldn't feel it once it was in place. All those android senses and
abilities would open up to my biological side. Even more aston-
ishing was how everything in my grey matter would back up to
my digital side automatically, where it could pick up if my bio-
brain was switched off or damaged. Switching back and forth
would be a capability, and I'd be the same person either way.

Convenience and the path to perseverance under the worst
circumstances should have been the main reasons driving me to
install it, but they weren't. I wanted to have one unified mind
so one wouldn't censor my life or force decisions on me. After
momentarily trying to recall a moment where I ignored someone, my heart was broken as I recalled several times when I

told Mimi to go to sleep when she pawed at me for attention or tried to start a conversation. She still loved me after that? I could barely believe it. My digital side was not only responsible for pushing her away but keeping those memories from me. It could have deleted them entirely, and I still don't understand why it didn't. The software Elise made for me would ensure that it would never happen again. My personality would only live in one place at a time, and I would have access to all my capabilities. That didn't mean I would be good at using them immediately. Like almost everything in life, there's a learning curve.

As the program became a set of neural functions in my biological brain I became unsteady. I slipped into the bathroom a couple of doors down the hall. I could see so much detail in the world around me. A battered cleaning bot that couldn't have weighed more than a kilogram emerged from a stall. I could see the residual matter on its brushes as their self sterilising surfaces killed germs. The scarce radiation surrounding its internal uranium cell gave it a halo, and every surface around it seemed alive with normally imperceptible scratches and dents.

A thought sent little scraps of DNA readings from my olfactory sensors to my digital side and the faces of three dozen people who had used the facilities came up. The music from the Lobby down the hall mixed with hundreds of voices, and I stopped looking people up once I got through half of them. The computer in my chest that held my digital side was just more mental capacity. It worked and felt different, but obeyed commands instantly. It knew how to carry my instructions out and did so at the speed of thought unless it had to wait for replies from external networks. I braced myself and the feeling of my hand on the counter was too vivid. Not only could I feel the temperature, fine texture of the cut stone it was made from, but the loops of my fingerprints against it were plain in my mind.

Intruding like thunder through all that noise was Duncan's voice. He was in the next room talking to Elyub. How could I tell? My tactical map was populating using the movements of sound, air, and heat. "...of training. Sims were the place, all in our heads, but she was the teacher, like. Never thought I'd get military training when I joined her crew," Duncan was telling Elyub.

"Her former master is a tricky, intelligent commander. Before she saved me, she stole three Order of Eden Advanced Destroyers from the shipyard orbiting Rodus. She got them away without firing a shot, it's a fascinating story," Elyub replied in a low whisper.

"And that's the one that made her? With her own bleeding memories? *This* legend?" Duncan asked.

"Leader of the Rebel Captains, yes. She hasn't been here in person for a while, sadly. Alice has been with the Legion as far as I know, but no one sits at the head of the table. They don't dare, especially with rumours of telepathy," Elyub confided.

"Telepathy? Her maker is..." Duncan didn't finish his question.

"Perhaps. I've heard so, but your Rogue is not. It's impossible. Sel and I tested. There was no reaction to the things we imagined or recalled while we were with her," Elyub replied.

"Well, that checks out, like. If telepathy was her thing, all I'd be saying is, 'And that as well?' She's some hunter as it is. Never seen anyone so focused in. Took us through training, giving us what we needed, spent loads, gave us good rest between, kept our eyes on the prize. That crew over there, even young Manny, didn't start off with much belief in her, or the fight, or even the ship, but she brought them up. Built 'em up proper." Duncan said.

"What about you, Duncan? Do you have faith in Rogue and her ways?" Elyub asked.

"Look, there's times I'm not mad keen on our Rogue, not gonna lie, but yeah, I'm confident. Way past that, really. It's faith at this point. Been there before, mind you, even fell for a Captain. Thought I lost her in The Fall..." he was about to go on, but I got a grip on my senses and started adjusting them back down to human levels.

What I'd overheard was a private conversation, and I wanted to talk to Elyub about being more careful when he shared things about me, but I wouldn't. What Duncan said was reassuring, it even lifted my spirits, but I was also curious and self conscious. I hoped my digital side was responsible for those moments when he didn't like me, but I was afraid of asking him about it.

There was one more weird sense that caught my attention as everything returned to a human like experience. I could feel the temperature and movement of the air using my hair. That was fully strange. It took a moment to find the less organic control for that. It was old cybernetic technology, all right, and it came with modes that presented as a list when I focused on my red curls. I selected; NORMAL instead of messing with them. Sometimes the worst thing you can do when you barely know how something works is to start playing with settings. For all I knew I'd end up with a frizzy mess that liked to randomly latch onto things and I wouldn't be able to return it to defaults. I'd check the manual later since I had more important things to do.

Once all my senses were behaving normally I checked the stalls, didn't find anyone inside, then slipped into one where I started the process of ejecting the Haven Node I'd installed inside my chest. It came out of its socket, the tiny access door to my internal computer opened, closed behind it and the node moved into my stomach. I turned towards the bowl and let the black tea along with the other stuff down there carry it up so I caught it in my hand.

After washing it and myself up, I installed the Node into my command and control unit. It was a good one for a commercial grade device, but I couldn't wait to get my hands on the military class devices Elise wanted to give me. Someone came in then, a woman in a long coat with rows shaved through her short hair. "So, how did you get a meeting with two Rebel Captains as soon as you got here?"

"And you are?" I asked, using a disposable towel to dry a lock of my hair that strayed into the sink while I was washing up.

"You answer first," she replied.

"Rogue, fresh out of New Zero," I replied. I was connecting with my Haven Node then and I peeked in on my connection to Red Gate. Its sensors were detecting something coming in slowly from the outer solar system.

That's why I was only half listening to the woman between me and the bathroom door. "What did you bring them? Was it enough to get you a seat at the table?"

"I answered one of your questions, so, who are you?" I asked.

"Vesper Durham." I could tell she was hiding a British accent. It wasn't something she'd grown out of, rather something she suppressed.

It was tempting to push back, but I was the new one on base, so I was willing to see where the conversation went. "Okay, I brought some fuel of questionable origin. Undiluted xetima. Are you interested? Only one tank is spoken for."

"Where'd you get it? Your ship doesn't have the hookups for a cargo train, so you're not a bulk transport," she said.

"Just because you don't see hookups..." I started to reply. There was another scene playing out in my head. Waves of torpedos and missiles from the Order of Eden ships headed for

Red Gate Station. They fired fifteen particle beams between them, taxing the station's shields. Red Gate was a fortress, but against five battlecruisers and several destroyers, it was outmatched.

The most impressive thing was how Red Gate fended off most of the first wave as small point defence turrets popped out of its armour to shred them. There were two waves of missiles behind that and the particle beams didn't stop when a section of the station's shields went down. The lines of cutting light and antimatter particles burned through the point defence cannons and Red Gate Station's hull started taking a beating. Several seconds later the torpedos hit and the connection went dead.

"Listen, I've been trying to get a seat at that table for weeks. Last Crisis left and took four captains with them, but they're still not letting people in. How did you get a private meeting in minutes? That takes more than fuel," she insisted.

"Look me up, or ask them what we talked about, I don't care, just cool off somewhere else," I told her as I started for the door.

Maybe she misinterpreted that, or she didn't like my tone, but her hand went for her sidearm. I crossed the space between us so quickly that my boots squeaked, streaking the floor. I was just fast enough to catch her hand and push it down so the gun was trapped between her palm and its holster. We were nose to nose. "Don't draw on me again."

Her other hand was on the move, slowly reaching into her long coat, so I caught her wrist and squeezed until I felt her bracer start to crack. "My crew is right..."

"...outside? So is mine, but I didn't come here to fight. I thought everyone was on the same side," I told her.

"What side is that?" she asked.

"I'm here to fight the Order and all their friends, starting with Ryden, and I'm wondering who you're after, Vesper?" I asked, squeezing her wrist armour until it creaked again.

She was in a hurry to answer, I'm pretty sure I was about to crush her wrist. She still wasn't happy about it. "Tiller Enterprises, transportation and fabrication. Order targets."

"Good," I said, slowly releasing her. When it didn't look she was going to finish reaching for the gun behind her back or draw, I stepped back and said; "Let's make this a memory and forget it." I still can't believe I used that old line, but she took it seriously enough.

"Don't make waves here, it won't work out," she said as she moved away from the door.

I didn't bother responding as I walked into the hall. Duncan was there in his dragon coat, looking up from the display in the palm of his hand. "All good in there? Heard a bit o' noise, and the door wouldn't open."

"What happens in the head stays in the head," I replied. "Sorry I was offline for a while."

Vesper left the bathroom and didn't spare either one of us a glance. "Captain of the Gerad," Duncan said after she passed.

"Is she a registered privateer?" I asked.

"Yeah, middle o' the list Sel sent. Came in to shift a cargo train and do a bit of boasting. Off again now, First Mate said. He seems decent enough." he replied. "You sure you're alright?"

"Red Gate is gone. The Order got there," I told him, doing my best to relax my stormy expression. "I'm making a whole list of things I should have done differently."

"Hindsight, and all that'll keep you up 'til the wee hours," Duncan said.

"I should have put a few hundred trackers in those inmates, shouldn't have shown my face in the wakeup message, or maybe I should have used ten thousand litres of xetima to blow the whole warehouse, ruin all the gear we would have left behind," I said as we started down the hallway.

"My finest and roughest relations used to say 'the past is just a list of lessons,'" Duncan said. "But I'm seeing you're not ready to let it go just yet."

People from the Irish Union lost so many that you could safely make the assumption that most of their relatives were gone. I never asked him about the scorching of their colonies, or who he had left, but being aware that I'd ignored the deaths of so many hunters brought on a wave of sympathy. It pushed my self pitying mood to the side. "I'm sorry, I don't know what I expected to do when even Haven Fleet couldn't get enough people free to intervene. How is everyone?"

"Grand, Mimi's faced, but into the nibs. Perri and Manny made an order, and there are deliveries piling up in the ship hold," Duncan replied.

"Yeah, I made a few deals," I told him.

"Aye, the word is out. So, we're installing new shields?" Duncan asked, rubbing his hands.

"Vindyne Fifteen Hundreds pulled right out of a large Order of Eden Corvette. They'll match the Model Nine Hundred we're using for the cockpit," I replied with a nod.

"We'll be one hard target, I reckon. What's the trade?" he asked.

"Fuel. It's worth four times as much here, so I'm offering it at the nice guy price. There aren't many customers around," I looked over the crowd in the bar and saw that most of the people were still from the Hammer and the Prowler, Sel and Elyub's crew.

I spotted the Issyrian, who noticed me looking at him and came over. "I hope this isn't rude, but is the other tank promised to anyone?"

"Other tank?" Duncan asked.

"I only traded from the port cargo pod," I told him before turning towards Elyub. "I was going to talk to the Haven Fleet side of the base, try to get my own storage tanks for it. I guess nothing stays secret for long here."

"My shuttles noticed it when they hooked lines up to your ship," Elyub said.

"Were you thinking of making an offer on the rest of my xetima?" I asked.

"You can store it in my tanks. They are underground, safe, guarded, just as I said. We will sell it to ships when they return and I will take fifty percent." Elyub's command of the language was slipping a little thanks to his excitement. His green-blue eyes were round and wider than my palm.

"I'd rather you buy it outright," I replied.

"It's too much fuel. I will buy from you if I need it later?" Elyub offered.

"Okay, it's a good deal, but it could be better. How about you take thirty percent consignment in return for security, vending and I can tap into it whenever I like to refuel. That way I won't have to lease storage space here," I replied.

"Forty percent and I set the price for fuel. It will be higher than the Haven average," he countered.

"Done," I replied. "The faster you can get that fuel off my ship, the sooner we can get out of here."

"My crew will hurry, thank you," Elyub said.

"Carefully," I added.

"Of course. This is good for the Bitter End," Elyub said, about to rush off.

"One sec," I said. "I ran into Captain Dunham. She was pretty jealous about my meeting with you and Sel. Should I be worried?"

"Catherine Dunham and her crew are mysterious. We know they haven't betrayed the Bitter End, because people are always checking her," Elyub replied.

"Why?" I pressed.

He looked around and guided me to an empty booth. "The former captain, quartermaster and first officer of her ship, the Gerad, were publicly executed by the Order on Rodus. No one will explain how they ended up in their custody. She is the Captain now. Her own success earned her a Letter of Marque, but no one trusts her," Elyub explained.

Most of the Issyrians are like that. Once they think you're a good person, you can depend on them to share important information without adding their own spin on it. It was good to see Elyub was no different and hadn't changed. "Well, I'll keep my eye on her, especially since she thinks I jumped to the front of the line for a seat at the Rebel Captain's table."

"That is wise. Perhaps she's innocent. Haven Fleet must have checked on her before granting her a Privateering License, yes?" Elyub said, puffing his cheeks and letting the air out slowly. I'd learn that it was his equivalent to shrugging.

"True. How long are you in port for?" I asked.

"Another week. The Prowler is about to begin a volunteer defence rotation with the Hammer," he replied. "I'll go call my shuttles so they know to imbibe the rest of your fuel."

I smiled at his slight misuse of 'imbibe.' "Thank you, Captain."

"Should I call Lat?" Duncan asked.

"Please? I want to check on Mimi," I replied.

"They're sitting at a table down the way there," Duncan replied, slipping away to an empty booth.

"See you after?" I asked, feeling like I was on very unsure

footing with him. I planned to apologise for everything I ignored, but I wasn't looking forward to it.

He looked up from his hand and nodded. Lat's holographic head appeared above his palm.

It would have been fine if I leaned in and told Lat what was going on, but I wanted to leave that to my First Officer so I could show him that I trusted him with some of the more casual stuff. It was a good practice, and Duncan didn't hesitate to do his job.

Perri, Manny, Mimi were where he said they were. Sel was sitting with them with another young man beside him. The back of his jacket had the name of his ship written across the shoulders: SILVER DEVIL. He was petting Mimi gently as she laid in the middle of the table, eyes closed, smacking her lips. There was a soft cloth beneath her.

Sel was busy talking to everyone except Mimi. "...four hundred three in my crew, including hangar hands here. It's all worth it, but I miss the old ship, small crew. The drama was simpler, aye?" he asked the young fellow to his right.

He noticed that everyone but he and Sel were looking at someone behind them and answered while he turned around. "All I know is the Silver Hulled Devil, and you know my crew." He looked at me and smiled, puffing a lock of his blonde hair out of his face. "Someone clear that chair there."

"Silver Hulled Devil? Your jacket's missing a word," I said.

"That's Rogue, if you're slow to guess," Sel said, flashing a smile at me. "This is young Captain Reggie Jude."

"When am I going to be just 'Captain Jude' to you?" he asked Sel.

"When an even younger captain comes to the table or you turn twenty-five," Sel replied.

"Rogue!" Mimi said, getting to her feet and rushing to the

edge of the table. I barely had a chance to notice that she had been laying on a black silk scarf before I gently took her in my hands.

She was so relaxed that I was afraid she'd slip away. "Sorry I took so long."

"It's okay. They tried to feed me barrow nuts," she made an exaggerated expression of disgust. "Then there was fish cake and it was good and I got really full so I napped. I think I did a good job communicating with everyone first though."

"If she's repping your ship, I'm envious. My comms guy never unplugs, so we have to remind him to bathe every week or two," Reggie said. "Well, not the image I wanted to conjure right away. Good to make your acquaintance." He was on his feet by the end, offering his hand.

I glanced down at Mimi and he withdrew it with a smile. "He's really nice, I like his scarf," she said, still a little inebriated.

"Good to meet you. If she likes you, then we're doing great," I told him.

Duncan joined us then, taking a seat. "Lat's watching the fuel transfer. I'm going to go help, otherwise we won't be pulling out of port anytime soon."

"I hate to break this up, but I think we should all get back. We have some parts to install and I should get her to bed," I said, surprised to see a flash of disappointment on Reggie's face. "I just need to hit the Gift Shop on my way out." I found the name amusing, but everyone else took it seriously.

Sel started getting up. "I can give you a lift there. I have to get back to the Hammer."

I looked down at Mimi, who was yawning. "Can I get some of those goggles?"

"I'll see if they can make some that'll fit," I said.

"I want to go to the store," she said, looking up at me.

"Sure, but it'll be boring. I'll probably spend most of my time looking at guns and armour," I replied.

Mimi didn't say anything more. She climbed up the front of my jacket and dropped into my hood instead.

"No arguin' with her," Duncan said. "The rest of us are off to the Dream. There's work."

"Huh? Oh, all right," Manny said.

"Can you look for a better food fab?" Perri asked me.

"Sure," I replied, watching Sel tell one of his crew members that it was time for them to return to the Hammer.

My crew gathered the pile of packaged foods and sealed drinks, putting them in a bag Manny pulled out of his pocket. Perri had a meal sized preserver box. She smiled a little when she saw me look at it. "For you and Lat."

"That's thoughtful, thank you," I said, before turning to Duncan. "Thank you for running things back there. Is there anything you want me to look for?"

"Boarding guns, automatic. Everything we've got's made for hunting street side," he replied.

"Good idea, I'll see you soon," I replied.

It would have been nice to hang around for a few drinks, meet a few of Elyub and Sel's crew members, even get to know Reggie a little. There were too many reasons to leave sooner rather than later though, so we moved on.

CHAPTER TWENTY

The Gift Shop

There was a sign above the Lobby's exit that read:

IF YOU LEAVE INTACT
YOU'RE WELCOME BACK

"Nice touch," I said as I got into an open frame buggy driven by one of Sel's men. Captain Marda slid into the seat next to me. The four spots behind were taken by more of his crew.

"Still can't say who put that up, but it's engraved over every exit in the Lobby. We're sticking by it, mostly," he said.

The converted baggage cart got going. The hallways from there took us away from the slips. Finally, we came to a set of doors that were nearly two metres thick. Above it was a colourful sign.

GIFT SHOP

There was enough room for a couple buggies to drive through at the same time, but we stopped outside. The eight guards were these combat androids that reminded me of myself, only they were covered in armour instead of skin. Their heads were shaped into angry looking silver skulls. Three of them had long, multi-mode rifles while the rest carried smaller automatic guns made for close quarters. "I'm guessing people don't try anything when they're around."

"No, a lot of people would love to rob this vault, but none have tried," Sel replied.

"How much would it cost for one?" Mimi asked. Thanks to her short nap and a metabolism that was still a little mysterious to me, she was recovering quickly.

"One of what, little one?" Sel asked.

"A metal man," Mimi said, stretching a paw towards one.

"Elise won't so much as name a price. Word is that they're proprietary," Sel replied, leading the way. The doors parted, their movement across the floor made the metal tile shake enough for anyone to notice. There were six more guardian androids strategically posted inside the broad halls. We arrived in what I can only describe as a war goods shop. "My favourite place on base," he breathed.

It was the biggest weapons and equipment shop I'd ever seen. An expansive variety of guns affixed to one wall, armour stands featuring restored and what looked like fresh suits stood in the middle. Ranks of shelves and transparent cases filled the rest of the room. Ship components and weapons hung from the ceiling. My human senses were experiencing an impressive, full store, but the others revealed that most of the stock was holographic. "It looks pretty sparse."

"What?" Mimi asked, surprised.

I waved my hand through a new suit of armour. "Just a projection. Is that normal?"

"For now," Sel said. "Manufacturing is handling other things."

"He's right. Most of my manufacturing facilities are currently contracted out to Haven Fleet for the construction of base defence systems," Elise's voice said as it was piped in through emitters built into the ceiling. "Come in, my stick men have made a display for you featuring some things you may be interested in."

"Thank you, Elise, I'm in no position to refuse special treatment," I said, following an arrow that appeared on the floor.

"I like the attitude," Sel said.

"I'm afraid you won't be test firing anything for now, Sel. I can tell you're a little inebriated. You know the policy," Elise said.

"Aye, just supporting the new Captain," he replied, holding his hands up.

"I guess I won't be testing anything either," Mimi said.

"That's correct, but I am working on an armour design for you. It'll take time to perfect, but I've also finished a prototype that should be sufficient in the meantime," Elise told her.

We came around the corner. There was a counter with three shiny stick men behind it. Off to the side there was a thick transparisteel wall separating a firing range from the rest of the shop. One of the stick men pushed a box towards me and opened it, revealing a pair of chunky but nicely shaped command and control bracers. Their expansion compartments were open, showing their surprising potential and a couple parts that were already installed. "These are the latest design, made for boarding operations and infantry engagements. They are scan shielded. There is a stun emitter with a one hundred metre range on the right unit. The left has a three ton test grappling line with a self-tapping, barbed cold weld end. A medical fabricator is built into the left with a replicable, expandable personal shield generator in the right. I've modified them to fit someone of your size properly so there aren't quite as many expansion ports. Other than that they match a variant Jacob Valent calls War Bracers. I could only make one set. Most of the rare resources they require are allocated to base defence hardware."

"Sold! I don't care how much they cost," Sel said enthusiastically.

"I'm afraid these are a gift for Rogue. I'm sorry, I would enjoy selling you a pair, you're one of my favourite customers," Elise replied. Then she sent me the rest of her thought in a private message. "They have been customised to work efficiently with your internal systems and provide an extra layer of digital protection. There is room for better interface and storage modules if you want to expand them later."

"These are amazing, thank you very much, Elise," I told her. They had a nearly black, glossy smooth surface that changed to match my crimson vacsuit when I touched them. I was surprised at how light they were, and couldn't get a clear scan of what material they were made of.

"Now, about my suit?" Mimi asked. I was surprised that she seemed to be sobering up quickly. "This one pinches in a couple places."

"Thanks to a large database of designs for people with full fur coats I was able to design something that will be more comfortable. A basic vacsuit and bowl style helmet is built into a collar along with some expansion slots compatible with a wide variety of devices." One of the stick men presented a chromatic coloured collar with a little metal dangling from it. Her name was already engraved in the middle. I helped Mimi get her old harness off. Her new collar expanded so she could get her head through then shrank to fit her neck.

Mimi moved around a little, then rolled and squirmed before she got to her feet. "I can barely feel it."

"Think about deploying your helmet," Elise suggested.

An instant later, Mimi was covered in a full vacsuit and a bubble helmet that was so clear that I could barely see it. "Wow. That was quick, and it's pretty comfy. Can I have some goggles? Like the ones Oonaa wears?"

"I know them, they were traded in here, cleaned and sold to her. With your permission, I can add them to your suit's shape library, they'll look the same and can be worn on their own or as part of your full protection."

"What? No more bubble helmet?" she asked.

"You will be able to switch between the styles," Elise replied.

"Then you have my permission, please." Mimi shifted in place before a square was highlighted on the counter.

"Stand there and I'll be able to add the feature," she said.

A few seconds after she sat there, her bubble headgear became a sleek helmet that even conformed to her ears. Most important to Mimi were the prominent goggles. "Wow, I have a display in here, it's amazing."

"Only you can see what's going on in your goggles. There are sensors that respond to eye movements, voice commands and some mental orders. They'll also work with hand, I mean paw gestures. The manual is built in, perfecting their use will take some practice so I've included a few games that'll help," Elise said.

"Thank you so much, I hope it's not too expensive," she said.

"The materials required for your suit weren't costly or in high demand, so I'm happy to give it to you. I wish I could do better. Maybe later, when the crisis is over," Elise said.

"Thank you, Elise," I told her. "Any chance you have a Violator Seven or something similar around?"

"That is not a common weapon. No one has traded one in and the scan scattering features of the original weapon make it impossible to properly duplicate. In short, I'm afraid not, but I have something you may enjoy. It can use several different types of armour and hull penetrating rounds. The Defender Ten." One of her stick men took a seventy centimetre long automatic weapon with a long magazine on the top out from under the counter. "A library of ammunition designs is available, ranging from simple, inexpensive rounds to extravagant variants that I can't currently fabricate."

"Most of your guards use these," I said, picking it up. There were different coloured dummy rounds in it already, so it was completely harmless. As soon as my palm touched the grip I noticed that I could connect with it directly.

Sel had plenty to say about it. "Tried a couple of those with my guys. Good enough deck sweepers, but there are better options, if I'm being honest. Sorry Elise."

"I'm not offended. I doubt your crew could make full use of them, considering the ammunition type changer most likely went unused. The Bitter Defender Ten is geared towards beings with control connections in their palms," Elise explained.

"Aye, I've got one who sleeps with his. Happens to have a metal arm, so that checks," he said as he looked around at the various real and stand-in weapons on the wall. "Got those Vanilla Crisp bars about?"

"There are some on the rack over there," Elise replied as a light highlighted a spinner rack in the corner flanking another door.

"Could you deliver three cases to the Hammer? We're runnin' low," Sel said.

"My pleasure," Elise replied.

As they talked I mentally explored the capabilities of the Defender Ten. "Ammo changer," I said to myself as I watched the blue, green, black, yellow and silver dummy rounds move around in the long magazine as I thought about which I wanted to load. There was also a sensor built in so I could see from the weapon's perspective. "I'll take four of these and the ammo patterns to go with them. We'll make our own. What I really need is a sidearm. What if you cut the stock off, modified the grip for one hand, and cut the barrel back three centimetres?"

A hologram showing me what I would get appeared and watched it rotate for a moment. Sel laughed. "That's got the intimidation factor, firepower, but I don't think a Nafalli could shoot it straight with that grip."

"My guardian androids would be capable of firing that with acceptable accuracy," Elise said.

"I'll be able to compensate even better," I said, handing the weapon back to the droid. "How long would it take to make the modifications on one and fabricate four originals?"

"I have ten in reserve. They are five hundred platinum apiece and I'll include fabrication patterns for every type of ammunition it can use. It will only take a minute for me to modify one as a sidearm. I suggest you test-fire it before you buy it," she replied.

"Load one with explosive, armour piercing, guided, silent, and hull burner rounds, please," I replied as I walked towards the firing range door. "Be right back," I told Mimi.

Sel and Mimi moved down the length of the counter so they could watch me test fire the new sidearm. There was a hologram in front of them of the far end of the range so they could see what my weapon was doing to the targets as well. The range was a simple half kilometre long reinforced rectangular box with five stations. There were a variety of emitters and foam sprayers set every ten metres in the floor and ceiling.

A stick man emerged from a sliding door and presented me with the finished weapon. The bare metal had a blue hue, and I didn't find any flaws in the printed weapon using my scanners. Seeing through those extra senses without thinking about it was still a little weird, but helpful. The Defender Ten drew an insignificant amount of power from my palm so its onboard computer could boot up. A mental image of its operating screen appeared in my mind for a moment before disappearing. I was instinctively aware of the weapon's capabilities, the software Elise wrote for me was working. Oh, and one of the things I really liked about that gun was the missing trigger. That wasn't standard, it was a change in the design specifically for me and other direct connection operators.

The droid gave me the magazine and I pointed my weapon down range. I slid the front end of the cartridge into place and pushed the back down with a satisfying click. I had a nice, clear mental image of the fifty-six rounds inside and watched as I thought about which type I wanted to use. The shuffling of the coloured rounds through the clear magazine was almost mesmerising. It meant the magazine was an extra one point one centimetres taller, but I liked the adaptability. The balance was really bad, a normal human would struggle to hold it up properly for long.

Strength wasn't a problem for me. I slipped into a sidelong firing stance. "One Order of Eden Knight at four hundred ninety-nine metres, please. Would it be possible to put an energy shield around him?"

"Of course," Elise replied.

The foamers at the far end sprayed for a second, creating the shape of a heavily armoured human soldier that hardened imme-

diately. The holographic projectors made it look real. The shield
I requested was there too, I could tell from a slight shimmer
around it. "Keep him alive if you can." I selected an electromagnetic pulse round and was impressed as it was ready in under a
tenth of a second.

I fired two bursts of five, emptying my weapon of that ammo
type. The energy shielding was gone, so I switched to armour
piercing rounds and fired a burst. Three struck the simulated
target's helmet without penetrating, which was normal. A
Knight's armour is top of the line, designed by ripping technology off from every manufacturer the Order can reach, especially Haven Fleet.

"Nice shooting!" Sel shouted.

I tightened my grip, adjusted my stance a little and fired
another burst. All five rounds hit my target in the middle of the
helmet, finally penetrating. The foam and holographic projectors
were so good that it looked real, but the foam flying around the
room kinda broke the illusion. My first burst actually broke the
dummy down, and the foamers re-sprayed to make it whole. "All
right, let's finish this off," I said, loading the ammunition types
in order of least destructive to most. "Move him up to two
hundred fifty metres, please."

The system animated the dummy as though it was running
towards me and I started shooting. First I single-fired the three
low velocity silent shots, then fired a bit faster until I was out of
guided bullets. I finished the supply of slugs off with two bursts,
and finally went to full automatic for the armour piercing,
burner and explosive rounds. Hardened white foam was sent
flying in every direction as the sprayers did their best to keep up
with the increasing destruction. That was until the explosive
rounds blasted the target, then flew straight through to the back
wall. The kick, and powerful percussive sounds of the weapon

won me over. It was different from my old Violator, but it felt just as powerful. I made sure the Defender Ten was empty, removed the magazine and put them on the counter in my stall. "Not bad, I'll take it."

When I looked through the window at Sel and Mimi, I couldn't help but laugh. The cat's eyes were as round as saucers and Captain Marda's jaw had dropped.

"What kind of holster would you like with that?" Elise asked.

"Right thigh with a matching one for three magazines on the left, please," I replied, leaving the range.

"You barely missed a shot," Sel said.

"So much booming," Mimi added.

"That was fun," I said. "It's not the most practical thing yet, but it'll do. Elise, can you make me a box of M-Twenty-Eight rounds, please?"

"I will pull fifty rounds from my reserve. I hope you won't need them," she replied.

"Me too, but you never know," I said.

"What are those?" Mimi asked, deactivating her vacsuit.

"They're special bullets that remove Order of Eden regeneration technology. Basically, you shoot a framework and nanobots inside make sure that they can never recover using framework systems," I replied as I watched the stick man pick my weapon up, turn it over in his hands to inspect it and then bring it out.

Another stick man took it so he could polish it before putting it into a case the other one behind the counter held out for him. I loved watching them work. Something about how they moved made them seem less like human analog robots and more like ancient marionettes.

Elise spoke as I was presented with new holsters. "Everything is finished in adaptive treatments so you may choose the colours later. Oh, and keep in mind that you may return the weapons you or your crew dislike for credit. That goes for you, too, Captain Marda."

"I'll tell the guys to turn in what they're not using," he said.

A new magazine was pressed into the gun case, the stick man closed it and then put it on the counter in front of me. "Do you have any vacsuits ready? Full military specifications with indoor plumbing, not the half featured ones they were selling in New Zero?"

"I have several that haven't been reserved by Haven Fleet. They include the internal waste collection and purification systems along with computing, medical support, reshaping capabilities, void excursion support, and several protective layers built in. The new suits were made for the Outbound Legion, these were left behind."

"I'll take ten," I said, half kidding.

"There are only five available and I must charge twenty-five hundred apiece," she replied. "I'm only given so much discretion on pricing and gifting."

"Do you accept Haven Luxury Credits and do you have a change room?" I asked.

"Absolutely, and we're still finishing that section of the store," Elise said.

"All right, I'll change here," I said as I started taking my jacket off.

"Well, that's my cue to move on," Sel said. "I'll leave one of my guys outside with a runner. They can drive you back."

"Thanks, Sel. You've made me feel welcome here," I told him, giving him a hug.

"As welcome as anyone can while they're telling you to leave as soon as possible," Mimi teased.

"Oh, I'm sorry, Mimi. Wish it was a good time for shore leave, but the sun doesn't shine on the Bitter End," Sel replied.

"You make sure your Captain calls me if you need the Hammer or anything else."

"Will do, thanks for the purple drink," Mimi said.

"That was not on purpose, I wasn't watchin' and..." Sel started to explain.

I let him off the hook. "She's sneaky, it's all right. At least I know where she got it now."

"I was drawn to the smell, it was like a field of sweet berries. Wonderfully intoxicating berries..." she said wistfully.

"Well, see you out there," Sel said as he retreated.

When the door closed behind him I asked; "I have a crew member who can't show his face in public. Do you have anything he can use to change his face? DNA?"

"I do. Elyub just delivered a box of New Look material. It's a beauty product, but will entirely change the shape of his face and pass most scans. I can bundle some DNA shifting cream with the box, altogether enough for ten applications for three hundred platinum," she replied.

"Put it in my cart," I replied. "I'm just wondering, where's the warehouse?"

"It's not shared with Haven Fleet, they keep what they purchase and the space they rent separate. As for where I've been keeping the items people trade in, I've been recycling most of them. I'm assuming you're looking for ship upgrades?" she asked.

"Wow, that was a lot of information at once," Mimi said, sitting up on the counter.

"I was actually hoping for a quick walk around, maybe pick up a better food fabricator," I said.

"I'm afraid I just recycled two cargo containers of vending machines that could have served you well. They don't generally

sell here because most crews steal upgrades for their food fabricators," she explained.

I dropped my old vacsuit and pulled the new one on. It felt
stiffer until it conformed. It seemed light, like it was barely
there, and after a few seconds it looked right on me, crimson
with a little gloss. "Do you have any boots to go with this?"

"The best I have are a pair of Legion surplus combat boots.
They are armoured and work well with the suit," she said.

"I'll take a set for each suit, please," I told her as one of her
stick men presented a pair.

I stomped my feet into them and enjoyed watching them
adjust. Mimi was all eyes too. "That looks good, but they should
stay black to match your jacket."

"Good idea," I said, throwing my jacket on. The bracers were
next. I liked having a pair, it felt more balanced to have one on
each wrist. Using them with the suit, I was able to make a direct
hardware connection with them. It only took me a minute to
transfer the Haven Node from my old bracer.

"I'm wondering, did you use the software I wrote for you?"
Elise asked.

"I am, it's kind of a game changer. It'll take a while to get
used to but I like it," I replied.

"Good, I'm deleting it along with any critical information
about your construction from my drives. Just because I'm one of
your designers doesn't mean I should hang onto that," Elise said.

"So, you won't be making an improved version of my model?"
I asked.

"No. The guardians you met on your way in are the closest
thing I'm willing to make, and they're the previous generation
with a few upgrades. The combination of technologies that was
used for you is too dangerous to share, so I'll make sure that's
impossible. At least, where I'm concerned," Elise explained.

"Wait, wait," Mimi said, looking up as though searching for where her voice was coming from. "You're her Mom, but I've never heard about you? Did you not call her? Check in on her?"

"I suppose I could be considered Rogue's mother. I wanted to contact her, but the common directive given to all concerned was to allow her to develop on her own. Her arrival here and direct communication with Haven Fleet suspended it. It was easy to convince Captains Marda and Elyub to arrange a private meeting with us in an acceptable space because they miss..." Elise stopped herself and paused before going on. "They would like to see you join the Rebel Captains, but understand that they can't invite you in before you've demonstrated the abilities of your crew and ship for the other captains."

"That's all good, but speaking as an orphan who was made in a tube somewhere, you really should have called," Mimi insisted.

"She had a limit put on her program," I explained as I stroked Mimi's back.

"Well, that's gone now, right?" Mimi asked, talking to the nearest stick man.

Its polished oval dish-like head nodded as Elise spoke. "It's not safe for me to have extended communications across the Stellarnet, but I will be more responsive in the future. I'm sorry for being unable to do so sooner."

"That would be great," I said. "No need to apologise."

"I would like to tell you I'm sorry about one thing before you go. I had to delete any experiences about your creation from your memory before you were activated. You were never supposed to believe you weren't the real Alice, and those engrams could have contributed to an awakening," Elise said. "All of that seems foolish now that I see you, independent and so different from her."

"How is she doing? She hasn't reached out," I asked.

"I'm not an expert on human behaviour, but my observations of Alice the last time she was here suggest that she may be nervous about meeting you face to face or even speaking to you," Elise said.

"She's nervous about talking to me?" I asked.

"Perhaps for the same reason I should have been anxious about it. You're arguably my responsibility, and while I've been able to ask Elyub about your activities, not being able to contact you myself has been worrying, even frustrating. I find the notion of you being deactivated by force maddening. I would take that personally, and that is not typical," Elise said.

It was a nice way for Elise to tell me she cared, not that she wasn't generous about that. Maybe I didn't see her as an actual parent, but my world felt a little warmer, calmer knowing that she was fundamentally on my side. "Can you do me a favour while I'm gone?" I asked.

"It depends on what it is," she replied.

"Fair. I can't take Ixat to another port without knocking him out. Can you watch out for him? He can't help how his past conditioned him, and he might be able to do some good if he has a chance. It would probably help if you were discreet about it," I explained, hoping that she could make sure he didn't get involved in the underground.

"He has a lot of platinum with him, and has rented a room in the most secure accommodations offered here, so that's a good start. I'll do my best to ensure that he's aware of trouble before he's interfered with. Keep in mind that I have to respect his free will and the law," she replied.

"I'd expect nothing more. Now, can I take a look at some of the other stuff you have already made?" I asked.

"Absolutely, my stick men will take you on a tour. The normal

Gift Shop is through the door behind you. Sel brought you in this way because he's partial to weaponry," she replied.

My visit should have started that way, because there were so many helpful things to pick up that didn't cost a lot, but I would have missed out if I didn't take one last look. Mimi and I filled a whole one metre square crate by the time we were ready to leave. I picked a few more things up from the more dangerous section of the Gift Shop on my way out, too.

CHAPTER TWENTY-ONE

Leaving The Bitter End

With most of our goodbyes said while we were in the Lobby, we left the broken remnants of Jeto behind. Two of the turrets we'd captured were put into a small storage vault that Haven Fleet granted me on base because we were official Privateers. I had plans for the other two.

I wanted to start hunting, and there was a lot to do. The crew was fortunate that I didn't need sleep, so as soon as we were accelerating through a wormhole with Manny on watch on the bridge, I told everyone else to take a break.

Things felt a little different as I made a connection to the ship's systems. My digi-brain didn't have its own personality anymore, so it was kind of like having a window in my mind's eye that was populated with all the ship's critical details. I had a few other windows up there too. Mimi was the star of one as security sensors followed her from one compartment to the next. She had to show everyone the new suit Elise made her, especially the goggles. I'd given her the job of telling everyone that they were getting a real, battle ready, adaptable military vacsuit too.

Perri was watching Lat enjoy the hot food she'd brought him. He dug into the chicken pot pie, sweet potato mash and vegetables like he hadn't eaten in days. He did take a few seconds to thank her. I don't know what happened after that because I stopped watching my crew. Checking in on people is one thing, but anything more is an invasion of privacy.

While that was going on, Duncan and I were working on our new shields. He wasn't interested in a break while there were stolen military class shield generators to inspect and install. They looked brand new, and they had under twenty two hundred hours of use logged, which is very low.

They were big, point seven-five metres square at each end and a metre and a half long components that literally weighed a ton. The connections had to be checked before they were installed, and after a thorough scan, it was time to slide the first of them into a socket. Without thinking twice, I picked it up using the handles at one end and carefully lined it up, then let it slip inside. With a loud series of clicks it locked into place and the interface lit up. "Everything's in the green. I'm setting this to a close field so it doesn't interfere with our wormhole."

"Never get tired of seeing you do that," Duncan said as he watched with his arms crossed.

"What?" I asked, relieved that he was starting a conversation.

"You, lifting. That's like one ant running off with the whole picnic on its back," he replied.

"You're comparing me to a bug now?" I asked as I double checked all the connections using the device's details screen.

"Sure, only in the best ways now, to be fair," he replied.

"Smooth," I said, letting him off the hook as I closed the slot cover and locked it, hiding the large component.

We started checking the next one and I picked that moment to explain a few things. I needed to get that over with, but I also wanted to start things on the right foot. "Thank you for taking care of things while I was running around the base."

"Look, the First Officer's meant to handle all the fiddly stuff anyway, but you're welcome. Bit shite we didn't get that turret sorted, though," he said.

"No worries, you didn't exactly have the time to install it. There's something else I'd like to talk to you about." I was busy tapping one of the main conductors on the side of the next shield unit with a sensor, so I didn't see how he reacted.

"Fire away." He sounded like he was bracing himself.

"It's not about you, or well, it sort of is. Okay, I'll start at the beginning. I had a digital and biological side to my personality. My bio-brain is more than a safety feature against digital vulnerability and other stuff. Most of what makes me, well, *me* was in there, and sometimes it argued with my other side." Explaining things so it wouldn't take hours was more daunting than I expected.

"I'm following," Duncan said as he continued to check things on his side of the shield generator. "Noticed you said 'had.' I reckon things changed?"

"Well, yeah. I think my digital side noticed that I was favouring the personality in my grey matter and it worked out a way to merge itself, adapt memories and its incompatible personality so it could move in. Am I making any sense?" I asked, checking the control connectors.

"You're saying your digital side got tired of being left out, so it made a way to shift into your other side," he replied.

"Okay, you do, good. If I didn't explain that part right, what comes next wouldn't make any sense," I put my tester down and stood up straight.

"Uh-oh, this sounds serious, like," he said, giving me his full attention.

"My digital side took over whenever it decided something was an inconvenient distraction. I think it started after the Carosa job. Whenever you offered to take me to the Old Union, or brought up a fallen hunter, it made a blind spot and blocked the memory of it. Now that it's merged, I can see them. Maybe not all of them, they're trickling in. Anyway, it's like a collection of times that I pushed you away and didn't do anything when other hunters were dying." Just explaining all that brought up one of the worst memories.

The recollection was so clear. It was back when we were in our Stonelands hangar. I was loading an emergency supply compartment in the Daring Dream. Duncan came in and told me that there was going to be a memorial at the Old Union that night. He was having trouble telling me who it was for. When I just stood there, passively listening, he finally told me that Rul Ekul was killed on the job. Kad, her husband, was going to be there with their sons. "They invited me and yourself, yeah. Wasn't meant to be one of them invite-only things, but it's gonna be packed out, so they just need a heads up if you're coming."

He trailed off as I shook my head and got back to work. Back in the present, I felt the full weight of that loss including a wave of fresh regret. "I can't believe I didn't even say anything."

Duncan stepped onto and then over the shield generator between us and gently took me into his arms. He didn't say a word.

"Kad and Rul gave me my first restraint belts. They ran Ryden off when the Envoy was destroyed. How could I just shake my head?" I wept. "They... never... asked..." I never finished that sentence, but they never asked for anything in return for saving Mimi, Lat or me.

As we stood there together other memories came back and I was happy for the comfort. The anger at recalling refused calls from Alice's friends and family could have consumed me if I didn't feel safe enough to be miserable for a few minutes. Finally, wiping tears away, I looked up at him. "I'm so sorry, that wasn't me. I mean, it was, but that side of me isn't acting on its own anymore. Maybe that doesn't make sense, but I'll be better."

"Ah, it's all right. All the best Captains are a bit mad anyway," he said. "I know from experience, like."

"Now I'm not even sure leaving Ixat behind was the right thing, even knowing that his people don't play well with others," I said.

"Oh, that was dead on, like. Ah, he saw what it's like being in your chain of command and it just did his head in, y'know? I reckon he was getting used to the safe training routine. Somehow got it in his head that you'd hand control over when trouble came along. But look, we'll see how he gets on by himself, won't we?" he said.

The reasons for Duncan keeping his distance weren't a mystery anymore, but I saw something else in those memories that was just as enlightening. "You never gave up. Every time there was something going on you told me about it, and you spared Mimi, made sure she wasn't around when you were breaking bad news."

"Not easy, sure. You and that little fluff ball are never more than a metre apart." he said with a little chuckle.

I was taking it more seriously. "Thank you, I'll never be able to say sorry enough."

"Well, I won't stop ya. I'll keep playing the solid First Officer, like. Just had me thinking; the merge can't be all bad, yeah? Is there anything decent you're getting out of it?" He asked.

"Maybe, it's going to take a while to sort out. All that programming is psychology now, I might never remember everything. It's all me now, for better or worse, right?" I replied.

"I don't envy you, not one bit. Must be a lot to carry." he said as he shook his head.

"Can I ask what you meant when you said you had experience with complicated captains?" I asked.

Duncan froze like he'd been caught with his hand in the petty plat jar. "Been meaning to tell you about that. Still holding off, mind."

I was ready to back off. "If it's a long story you don't want to get into, it's okay."

He stepped away, gently releasing me. "No, no, it's about time. Before The Fall I got in with a good crew under an even better Captain. We recovered wrecks, chased a few nasty buggers down, and finally started long hauling cargo and passengers. Time between worlds got longer, and I started getting on with the Captain, Veronica Noor. A few trips on, we were full-on carrying on. Good times, I'll say. So good we got hitched in Saint Kitts." He looked away from me then, his reverie saddening. "Almost nine months of good times, like. Then the Fourth Fall came along. I was down on Tabrus supervising a bunch of passengers who went down for a tour o' the Wherrick, big museum."

"I went there once, it looks like a wedge of glass sticking out of the ground," I said.

"Yeah. That's where I was when it all went sideways. Lost most of the tour passengers, and Veronica's ship got totalled. She got a call through right at the end. We said our goodbyes because the bleeding passengers up there panicked and took every last escape pod. The final volley hit, and that was the end of her, or so I thought. I checked the wreckage that didn't burn up on re-entry, but there wasn't a trace of her. I stayed on Tabrus after that, maybe because it was the last place I talked to her. Turns out she was alive. When her ship started going down, she took a mad chance, flung herself out the airlock in just a vacsuit," he said with a shrug.

I wanted to say it sounded like something I'd do, but kept that to myself.

He went on, pacing around. "Someone happened to pick her up in the nick. Then the Wherrick got hit, and I lost comms after one of the maintenance bots took my arm off and shoved it in his recycler."

"So she thought you were dead too," I guessed.

He nodded. "Right, so when she came back to Tabrus after hearing I was still knocking about, she was bloody fuming I hadn't gone looking for her."

"You must have been beside yourself," I said, watching his darkened mood lift.

When he continued it was with bitter humour. "Ah yeah, but she only went and handed me divorce docs, looking for reparations. She'd moved on, had a new lad and even adopted two of those Fourth Fall orphans. I just gave her what I had and signed off. Was too wrecked in the head to argue, to be honest."

Okay, so some lights went on for me. It explained why he was broke after the Carosa job, pretty sad for a while, and why he treated me pretty professionally while he was aboard. It wasn't just me pushing him away, but his history of being stung when he got together with his Captain. I had nothing but sympathy, and I wanted him to feel better. "Well, I don't blame you for not bringing her around the hangar so you could introduce her to everyone."

"Ah, could you imagine?" he laughed. "'Alright folks, this is me ex-wife. She's bleeding draining me, dunno if she really deserves the pips, but sure she was the love of me life right up until I thought she was dead. Nothing messy or awkward about that at all.'"

I laughed for a moment before leaning into my sympathy. "I'm sorry you went through that."

He waved it off. "Feels better, having it out. Training on the ship was a help too. Got my mind off it, made me see a new future outta New Zero. Love that place, but it was getting crowded, corps were taking over the hunting game like those plains wolves in the wastes. Buggers got my dinner twice while I was hunting out there, now corps are eating every hunter's lunch."

I was about to say something when a tactical screen appeared in my mind's eye. I got close to him and whispered; "Two signals just came out of the storage compartment outside."

"Which? The stash or suit closet?" he breathed.

"Upper hatch suit closet," I replied.

He opened a slender compartment hidden in the floor and pulled a pulse gun for himself then for me. We had them set to their highest stun mode in seconds. He sealed his vacsuit up and I did the same as I led the way to the armoured hatch.

When the door slid aside I was treated to the retreating backs of two Nafalli. "Stop!"

"I told you I could still hear them!" Oonaa said to a male Nafalli beside her.

He looked over his shoulder at me and I could see fear in his eyes before he broke into a run. "Nowhere to go!" Duncan shouted. He didn't hesitate, but broke into a run after him.

"Don't move," I told Oonaa.

She squeaked and quickly raised her hands. "Stopped moving, not moving."

As soon as Duncan made it around the corner I heard him fire once and heard the Nafalli tumble to a stop. "Don't think I have to hit you twice, do I, young bear?"

"It wasn't his idea," Oonaa said.

Mimi poked her head out of a small access hatch in the ceiling between us and looked around. "Hey, goggle Nafalli! Wait. What are you doing here?"

Perri and Lat came running next. "Boarders?" he asked, pointing the massive rifle I'd taken from the Bio First soldiers.

"Put that back," I said, rolling my eyes. "They're not armed."

"Exactly, no need for extra holes. I made sure we didn't bring anything that we could use as a weapon. We're just friendly passengers," Oonaa said.

"I don't think you should shoot that one, I like her," Mimi said, hanging upside down, half way out of the ceiling.

"There's another one?" Perri asked.

"Down here. Gimme a hand, he's too tall for me to carry with care, and he's wet himself," Duncan called from around the corner.

"On my way," Lat said. He powered the rifle down and handed it to Perri. "Arms Locker three, please."

"Uh, okay," Perri replied.

"What are you going to do with us?" Oonaa asked.

Mimi looked from her to me, activating her goggles. "Good question. What's the plan, Captain?"

"We have a brig," I said, gesturing with my free hand. "It'll be more comfortable than the storage compartment you crammed yourselves into. That way."

"Oh, I didn't mind that at first. Did I mention that Fersuu is my boyfriend? I was just starting to fall asleep when he decided to take a look around," Oonaa explained as she turned around and started walking down the hall.

A few minutes later, Oonaa was looking around our brig. There were four cells in the lower deck that were a bit like our quarters only smaller. The pull out toilets and safety beds were expertly fabricated by Perri, saving me a load of plat. The wall between the hallway and the cells was made of armour grade transparisteel with built in access slots. That cost me quite a bit. I dropped their work clothes, a pair of small life support packs and a box of cheap meal bars into the secure storage bin in the hallway. Mimi was all eyes as we finished searching our stow-aways and separated them into cells. "What were you gonna do for water?" Mimi asked as she watched Oonaa test the mattress with her hand.

"It's a human ship, there are water tanks," she replied as she sat down and sighed. "You're right, this is much better than the closet. Can we be in the same cell though?"

I looked at the next cell, where Lat and Duncan were lifting Fersuu onto the bed. "One passenger per compartment, lass."

"How'd you get on board?" Mimi asked Oonaa.

"When we saw deliveries going onto your ship, we picked a box up and walked it on board. Instead of leaving like the Issyrians or stick men, we found somewhere to tuck away. Oh, and we made sure it could open from the inside. It was easy, but I guess Issyrians could look like anything, so you shouldn't blame that one for letting us on board," Oonaa explained.

Lat couldn't look at me, and he was turning red.

Oonaa laughed. "I think he was hoping I wouldn't tell you about that part."

"Sorry. There were a lot of deliveries, and they were hooking hoses up. There was a lot going on," Lat explained in a rush. "When boxes came and I saw they were the ones you told me to expect in your message, I let them on. There were shuttles filling tanks so I was making sure we didn't have another xetima leak. I should have kept track of people better. It won't happen again."

"Another leak? Are you having maintenance trouble?" Oonaa asked, crossing her long arms.

Mimi started climbing my leg, then my hip as she said; "Well, a little one..."

"We're all right," I replied. "Why are you two running from the Bitter End?"

Fersuu, who was still pretty numb managed to say; "I fought you thaid they got the thour?"

"Just relax and let it wear off, Fersuu," Oonaa soothed. "He's right, though. You've seen that place. The name is no mistake. The only views we could find were of dozers piling sand, big rocks following behind, or darkness with a couple scattered galaxies. I mean, that's no place for a Nafalli, right? Oh, and he's in a little trouble."

"Thell them nothing!" Fersuu said, managing to raise a hand just enough to point at her.

"No, no, tell us everything or we'll make you talk," Mimi said with a thin lipped smile as I balanced her on my shoulder.

"It's not complicated or secret or anything," Oonaa said, shaking her head at her boyfriend "He owes a lot of money - he won't tell me how much - to the Ash Kings. They run a gambling spot in the underground. He needs to get to another planet or they'll make him work. Well, after burning his coat off. He just needs to get away from the Bitter."

"What about you?" I asked.

"Oh, she's just being a good girlfriend, right?" Mimi asked.

"I've never been that good," Perri said as she crossed her arms and leaned against a bulkhead.

Lat left the other cell and Duncan made sure it was locked.

"Not supposed to offer answers during an interrogation, wee cat."

"Oh, sorry," Mimi said.

"Perri has a point. You're not just here to help him get away from some gangsters, are you?" I asked.

"I didn't think I'd get stuck at the Bitter End when my tribe volunteered a bunch of us to help build Haven Fleet's part of the base. I love the cause, don't get me wrong, but when we were finished restoring the main structures and I decided to stay, I didn't think I'd be out of a job. All those new defences are being put in by a bunch of robots and specialists. I made my own work, driving people around. Now, with all the little ships away, there isn't much of that. You and the Kawaii cutie were my only customers today." Can a Nafalli pout? Oonaa proved that they could. "I heard that genocidal Tutikuu was your maintenance guy, and that he'd left, so, I thought I might be able to fill the opening."

"Kawaii is Japanese for cute, so unless you mean I'm double cute, that was redundant," Mimi said.

"I meant double cute," Oonaa said without missing a beat.

"Can we keep her?" Mimi asked me.

"Hold on, genocidal?" Lat asked.

"Yeah, you didn't know? The Tutikuu were a slave race for centuries. They freed themselves and killed all their masters. My big brother used to watch the hunts on the local 'net. They were still doing it when my people were driven out of the Iron Head Nebula." The explanation came quickly, like it was something everyone but us already knew.

"Again, why didn't I know about this?" I said half to myself.

"His language isn't easy for our translators. That's probably why it's not big on the Stellarnet," Perri said. "Just a guess."

"Ah sure, translator never properly managed his phrasing," Duncan said.

"We usually got along," Perri said. "Then again, we almost never worked on the same things at the same time."

"You won't find that kinda non-human drama there. I mean, I love the Stellarnet, it's eighty percent entertainment, but it's another ninety percent human news slop." Oonaa put her feet up and reclined on her bunk.

"That's not how percentages work," Mimi objected.

"I know, I'm just saying there are other networks, but they're not as interconnected. I can show you, there's nothing like Zonama. It's Nafalli wrestling. Biggest shows you'll ever see. Anyway, can I have a job?" she asked.

Mimi's jaw dropped. I snickered, but Perri and Duncan both laughed. I shook my head; "Incarceration before probation. We'll discuss qualifications if there's time."

"Aw, disappointing," Oonaa groaned as we filed out.

"Do you and Duncan need help installing the shields?" Lat asked after we were out of the hallway and the hatch was closed.

"No. I need you to watch our Nafalli friends for a shift. I'll take the next. Can you do the sentinel thing?" I asked him.

"Absolutely," Lat said.

"What's the sentinel thing?" Mimi asked.

"I'll armour up and watch them for the entire shift without saying a word. I'm usually watching training videos in a one twelfth sized window they can't see the whole time," Lat replied.

"I've seen you do that before!" Mimi said.

"I know," he replied. It was true, during our more mundane mission spree using the Envoy, Lat often guarded the ship entrance that way. I think he enjoyed it.

"What do I do?" Mimi asked.

"Nap if you can. Are you ready for a short watch on the bridge?" I asked.

"Sure!" Mimi was almost too excited.

"Remember, there isn't much to it, and you've trained for a bunch of emergencies. Not much should happen in wormhole transit, but you have to be ready," I said.

"You're telling me not to nap on the job. No problem, Captain. I remember all the simulation drills. Spin outs, power downs, unknown chasers, control failures, navigation errors, and all the other stuff. I'm ready," Mimi said.

"All right. I'm going to need you there after Manny's watch because I'll have to cover Lat's turn later," I told her.

"Okay. What are you doing?" Mimi asked me.

"I was hoping Perri could use some of the xetima we'll be scraping out of the cargo compartments for missiles. We should be able to adapt the leftover fuel gel for dumb fire darters. We need fifty to fill our new porcupines."

"I can get that started then have them print while I'm off shift," Perri said. "We'll process the xetima then load the solid form in by hand."

"I'll do what I can once the shields are in and tested," I said, glancing at Duncan.

"I'm not about to throw my feet up while you lot are flat out, and the cargo pods are still slathered in that expensive fuel muck. I'll give a hand finishing the shields, then I'll get stuck into scraping and gathering," Duncan said.

"Hey, that's a whole shift. Getting those missiles printing will only take me half an hour, the fabber will do the rest. Don't make me look bad," Perri said with a smirk.

"Just carrying my end," Duncan replied with a shrug.

"I'll help with the fuel pods while the printers run," Perri said.

"Just make sure you both get some sleep before we get to the Rose System. Don't make me call a rest day," I said, not too seriously.

"Outta curiosity, who grabbed that fuel in the end?" Duncan asked.

"Well, we traded some for our new shields, more for that box of plat that was delivered," I looked in Lat's direction.

"Checked in, went straight to the vault," he said, nodding.

"Oh, that's a fair trade," Perri said.

"I wasn't finished," I said, smiling at her. "We got more in Haven Luxury Credits, and I made a deal with Captain Elyub. He's storing our xetima stockpile and selling it for us for a cut. If the Bitter End is still around after the Order attack, we'll have a nice steady income for a while."

"Niiiiice," Perri said as everyone else shared the sentiment.

"We should make another trip to Red Gate," Lat said.

"That's gone. The Order moved on Warro and took it out." Did I feel bad about that? Yes, but I was also a little relieved that I didn't have to think about it so much anymore.

"Oh. They're everywhere, I guess," Lat said. "I'll go suit up."

"See you later," Perri said before turning her attention to me momentarily. "I'll tell you if there are any problems making those dumb fires."

"Do you expect any?" I asked.

"They're just fast, stupid missiles, right?" she asked.

"Exactly," I replied.

"Then it'll be easy. Bring me xetima and I'll load it into the chem processor. We'll let most of the work happen while I'm sleeping," she said.

"Thank you. Make sure you don't skip that last step." I looked at Duncan then. "Let's do a sweep of the ship with hand scanners before we finish installing our new shields."

"Yeah, let's get on it. Still mad we're installing barriers meant for a ship way bigger than ours. Bloody love this new wave stuff." he replied.

"Now we need to find the guns to match," I replied as I started up a ladder. "And put the elevator kits together."

We didn't find any more stowaways, so we were able to get back to work on our upgrades. It only took us another twenty minutes to finish testing and installing our new shields. Even though I told Duncan that he didn't have to follow through with his promise to scrape leftover fuel out of our cargo containers, he got into his new vacsuit and helped me out anyway. Perri joined in as promised and I was surprised that we got it finished before it was time to quit.

While they slept, Mimi took a four hour shift on the bridge so I could finish wiring the porcupine missile launcher system and install one of the turrets we captured from Red Gate Station. It took a couple of hours, but I managed to get it set up so it would slide out from behind a scan shielded door on the bottom of the ship. The weapon mount I used was made for something larger, but it was better than nothing.

I used my connection to the ship to watch our prisoners after Lat's shift. They were both asleep, so I had time to start loading missiles. I was starting to feel the same way Perri did about our limited fabrication capabilities.

Multitasking while working alone was easy. That internal eye was focused on Ryden as I put together all the data I'd collected. Everything came into play. The arm unit I'd stolen from one of their soldiers, information from the Carosa Company, Elise's data and everything since. A real plan was coming together, and I think my quiet demeanour the next day sent a signal to the crew at breakfast.

They knew we were headed for a serious fight.

CHAPTER TWENTY-TWO

Interesting Friends

My hunt for Ryden ships led to a clear destination, Oya, a gas giant near the edge of the Rose System. That was within a half million kilometres of the asteroid belt where the Outbound Legion was rumoured to operate. If anyone knew anything about Oya and wouldn't tell anyone that I was interested, it was someone in that fleet. Jacob Valent's fleet.

While the crew was busy and I was on watch in the cockpit, I took a deep breath and called him. As if she knew what was going on, Mimi leapt from her ceiling hatch onto the copilot's seat then up to her pad on the dash. "What's up?"

"Making a call," I replied as I got the usual response telling me that Jake was out of reach. "Looks like our friends are executing the 'fade' part of strike and fade."

"That's normal. There's news about them, though." She tapped her touch pad and flicked a trackball. A hologram of two kilometre long Order of Eden Heavy Cruisers drifting through space appeared. They were out of control, hulls blasted open, gasses escaping from inside their torn armour. Lesser Order vessels drifted nearby showing signs of medium and large hits, their portholes dark. "That's the better part of a battlegroup," I said, my spirits raising.

"Any sign of the cost?" Duncan said as he came through the hatch.

"There aren't a lot of details," Mimi replied. "Hart News says their ships were run off before they could finish their scans. This is the best footage, it's about nine hours old."

"That kind of damage," I started, pointing at the fin like side of one of the heavy cruisers. "Is caused from the inside. My guess is that someone got an antimatter bomb aboard. Just a small one."

"A little antimatter goes a long way," Duncan chuckled. "Must have had someone on the inside."

Memories of Alice breaking into a base ship with a small strike team came back clearer than before. "You could be right, but my bet would be on a boarding operation. The Legion can do a lot to a ship like that once its shields are down. These ruined capital vessels are mostly evidence that they didn't have a good fighter screen. Nothing should get close enough to do that kind of damage. Order fighters, gunships, corvettes and destroyers usually hold a perimeter to stop anything from getting to their main vessels. I only see the wreck of one destroyer, a couple of Marauder corvettes, so I'd bet real money that the Legion hit their defence so hard that these heavy cruisers had to make a run for it."

"Good theory, but why didn't they jump away?" Duncan asked.

"Something stayed close enough with an interdiction field

that kept them from forming a wormhole," I replied, staring at the image.

"Um, do a lot of people have those?" Mimi asked.

"No, they're highly illegal. Only law enforcement and military get away with having one," I replied.

"Good thing all we have is a jumped up scanning turret," Duncan said with a snicker.

"What does scanning have to do with stopping someone from jumping away?" Mimi asked.

"We can emit scan pings with ours that are so powerful that you can stop a field projector from working. It's not strong enough to disrupt energy shields, but it'll screw the formation of a wormhole up if we're within about five hundred metres with no interference. Takes a lot of power," I replied.

"But it's legal because you're supposed to use it for scanning," Mimi said.

"Exactly. Don't tell anyone. We can't let anyone know about..." I was interrupted as a call came in.

"That's a secure link," Mimi said, looking up at me. "We need a code."

After looking at the query screen I knew which one to use, so I tapped an older decryption key from Alice's memories into a number pad in the pilot's station. Duncan slipped out of the cockpit and closed the hatch behind him before it cleared.

"Sorry, I know I'm not who you're expecting," Remmy Sands said as his holographic image appeared. He always had the look of a rascal, and he'd grown his brown hair long enough to brush the straight collar of his unmarked vacsuit.

"You're right, but you're still welcome," I replied.

"There's a link tree now. You call one of us and you get bounced around until someone calls you back. Ashley started it after talking to your communications officer. Hi, Mimi," he said.

I looked at her, amused, surprised. "Were you talking to Ashley without telling me?"

"A little, she couldn't tell me anything important, and I tried to tell you, but you were busy," Mimi said.

I pushed Mimi away a few times when my digital side was in control and still hadn't talked to her about it. I petted her with care. "We'll talk about it after, okay?"

"Okay," she said meekly.

"You're not in trouble." That made her perk up.

"Ashley couldn't stop talking about your smart comms cat," Remmy said.

"Oh, really?" Mimi asked, proudly straightening her posture.

"Yeah," Remmy said, cracking a smile. "I can't talk long, we're about to jump. It's good to meet you both. I've been briefed on who you are, Rogue, so we're not on completely uneven footing. Is this a catch up call, or business?"

"We're headed for the Rose System, and I plan on hunting ships owned by the Ryden Corporation. We're not heavily armed, but we're running class four Vindyne shields," I explained.

"Wow, Samurai Squadron does not like seeing those. They turn a Marauder Six Corvette into a problem. What class is the ship you're running?" he asked.

"A custom clipper," I replied.

He laughed and nodded at someone in the background as she asked; "Did she say clipper?"

"Is that funny? Are we too little?" Mimi asked.

"Only on opposite day," Remmy replied. "I'm no thruster head, but even I know that those shields on that ships will be a surprise to anything that tries to take a shot at you. Nice."

"Thanks. I could use a few guns, but we'll figure it out," I said.

"Wish I could help you out with that, but we're on the move. My intelligence guys are looking Ryden up right now. I haven't run into them, but I've heard the name. They're fast transportation, right?" he asked.

"Exactly. Well, partially. They took deliveries of humans in stasis from Carosa Transportation. I'm working my way up the chain. We're headed to Oya, several of Ryden's transports have been seen there," I explained.

"Oya, that whole gas giant that scans like a headlamp through pea soup. Comm range isn't great either," he said as he reviewed something we couldn't see. "We're putting a file together on our end. The Legion doesn't go in unless we have to. I'm guessing you want to know what Ryden is doing in there?"

"That's right. We're going to take a ship or two if they're loaded with unwilling passengers. If we find them empty or loaded with non-biological materials, we'll take the wreck pay," I told him.

His eyes widened before he regarded me appreciatively. "Well, if you're looking to take them out and move on, Oya's the place to do it. Most ships operate in micro gravity, as far as we can tell, but if you send anything spiralling down, they'll get crushed way before they hit the liquid core. Are you sure you want to hunt in there, though? I don't think there's a ship around that wouldn't have trouble picking their way through most parts of that atmosphere."

"We have high end scanners, so we should have an advantage, but it'll help if I know the landmarks." I passed him the navigation data I had on Ryden's ships.

"We can help a little, but nothing stays still around Oya. Thanks for the data, we're plugging it in now. There we go, that's where they're going. There's a station that lines up with your nav data. It's important, under Order control, so be careful." he sent me the new info.

As soon as it was in front of me I sat back in the pilot's seat, breathing a sigh of relief. "That's the only thing in the area, and Ryden's sending the same three haulers in and out every nineteen hours. If they're on schedule, I'll know where I can start looking."

"The station's course isn't regular. They have to navigate between storms since they're right in the upper weather patterns. I mean, I don't want to be a joy thief, but you're going to have to do some searching, and there could be a big Order presence," Remmy said.

"If there's that much interference, we'll be able to hide," I said. "The benefit of running a small ship."

"That means we can sneak up on them too, right?" Mimi asked, getting caught up in the excitement.

"The best part," Remmy replied. "It helps if you have a software package that'll help you figure out what you're seeing too."

"We have it covered, but if there's a program you can loan us to sort the noise out..." I let that hang as I regarded him with an upraised eyebrow.

"Can't do that, it belongs to the Legion," Remmy replied.

"I had to try. No one likes flying through pea soup. We'll be fine. How are things going with the Legion?" I asked.

"Check the news," he said proudly before becoming more somber. "We've lost some good people though. It's war. My crew and I are doing well, I wish I could share more."

"No problem. Thanks for this. Listen, if anyone in this comms tree asks, tell them I'll be more talkative," I said, aware that Mimi was watching me closely.

"Will do. Check out my latest Must Watch List next time you're between stars. I've been reviewing some incredible pre-AI anime lately. Awesome and absurd at the same time, great for long transit times," he said.

"Wait, you're not the Remmy who created the Remmybase?" Mimi asked, astonished.

"I have the honour of carrying the credit and the blame. Good hunting!" he said before the call ended.

Mimi looked at me, still amazed. "He's some kind of warrior with the Legion?"

"Captain of the Raven, and a really nice guy, as far as I know. I never knew him super well, but I liked him. He really helped us out," I said, leaning back in my seat.

"But Uyo sounds terrible. Are you sure this is the target we want?" Mimi asked.

"I have planning to do, but it looks right. Don't worry, we're running a top of the line sensor suite with a full backup system. That's why I paid for the Explorer Package," I said.

"Well, if you say so." Mimi still looked worried.

I hoped what I had to tell her would distract her at least, and cheer her up at best. "Hey, something's happening, I'm changing." I pointed to the centre of my chest.

"Oh? Are you okay?" she asked.

I told her what I was going through, that my personalities and blocked memories were merging. She listened closely, and when I was finished I was ready to tell her the most important part. "I'm sorry I ignored you sometimes. I know I was abrupt, maybe a little rude. What I'd like you to understand is that it was me. Not the side I'm proud of, the digital side. It was more interested in being efficient than kind, and had a hot temper. Now all that is merging with my biological side. Maybe I'll have to struggle with it a little, try to find a new balance. I'm not sure. What I do know is that I'll always try to be kind to you, and I'll never ignore you again."

"Thank you, Rogue. I thought that was just what you were like sometimes. Bergio could be moody and rude too. That's just how really important people are." She locked her station with a tap of her back paw and hopped into my lap.

I petted her with care. "I don't want to be that way. You're my best friend, Mimi. You deserve better."

"Thanks. Don't change too much, okay? I like you the way you are, even if you're prickly sometimes. It helps me maintain a sense of independence. You're my person, Rogue." Her loud purring said the rest. She stayed in my lap as I finished my watch in the cockpit. Hours later, I had a plan worth sharing with the crew.

CHAPTER TWENTY-THREE

A Hydrogen Helium Sky

We entered the Rose System and headed for Oya, a gas giant that looked like it was from a dream. Its dark brown and white outer layers were mostly hydrogen and helium with large banks of white clouds.

"It looks heavenly," Manny said as he flew the Daring Dream into a decelerating descent into the outermost layer. The clouds beneath us were stretched in wispy, overlapping bands. "Too bad it's about minus two hundred out there."

"Do you have a lot of experience flying under these conditions?" I asked from the copilot's seat.

Most of Mimi's attention was on the emergency and defence transmission bands as she tilted one ear towards Manny as he answered. "I have a lot of simulated hours. I used to transport people around in the New Dreams Universe Simulation because I loved the view and was trained to handle the emergencies that come up in gas giants. Do you want to take the controls?" he asked.

"No, you've got this," I told him as he slowly took us lower. The New Dreams Universe was a tempting space I avoided because it had a reputation for being addictive. It was an ever growing simulation of the Milky Way where you could literally do anything, and it obeyed all the same rules as the real one. You remember me mentioning pod dwellers? Well, most of them spent the vast majority of time there because you could earn real currency, and, well, live out a full fantasy life with all the sensations while avoiding real consequences. Yes, there's a whole lot more to it, but the most important thing at the moment was that I could appreciate that Manny had as close to real experience flying through the clouds of Oya without actually doing it. He easily got us between the clouds in no time where we passed into a shadow cast by one of Oya's larger moons.

"I've been meaning to ask you something. I started talking to Duncan about it but he told me I should bring it up with you," he said.

"What's up?" I had no idea what was on his mind.

"It's about our escape from Red Gate. Why did you take the controls?" he asked. "When we had to run and we put the station between us and those pirates, you took the stick."

Assuming direct control of a situation when there were crew members with the skills to carry the task out was one of Jake's shortcomings. Alice and I picked up the habit, I didn't even realise it until then. I think Jake would have explained that whole concept to Manny in that situation, but I decided to try to do better. "I think I lost my nerve. I spent everything on this ship and our shields weren't great. I guess I wanted to take control because I knew the stakes were high. Now I'm sorry I did it because you're a better pilot than I am and you should have been in control."

"I thought it was something like that. I was a little pissed," he said.

"I know you took the training sims for this ship, for flying her in every condition I could imagine, seriously. I just… it wasn't the right move, it won't happen again," I told him. "I trust you."

"That's all I want, thank you," Manny said.

He was right to be offended when he surrendered control to me, and he behaved professionally when he brought it up. His complaint was my lesson. A reminder that even all the officer training I'd had through Jonas and Alice couldn't prevent mistakes. That was all the time I had for humility, mind you. I was connected to the Daring Dream's tactical system. The electromagnetic field, conductivity of the clouds, and swirling surges of heat coming up from the planetary core created more signal noise than I'd ever seen. Our sensors were still learning to separate signs of a ship from all the rest. "Anything else on your mind?"

"That was the big thing," he said with a nervous laugh. "It was such a big deal in my head, I expected a different reaction. It's a weight off now."

"I have a question," Mimi said.

"How can I help?" I replied as I mentally ran through optical scan results. My digital mind was helping the tactical computer, operating at thirty-two percent of its maximum speed. It was like my bio-brain had a big co-processor now, with no resistance or personality to slow my built in computer down. I would ask Elise if she could figure out how my built in computer could run at full speed next time I saw her.

"Why are we looking for Ryden ships here? It's hard to

detect anything, even the signals down here are junk," Mimi asked. "I know, our contact with the Legion said it would be like pea soup, but I'd never had pea soup, so I didn't think it would be this bad."

"You can thank the Sayli family and the updates we pulled in from the Legion and Elise. I pulled a lot of navigational data from their personal ship and when I crossed that with newer data from this solar system it looked like the best place to start. I don't think we'll find anything carrying sleepers, but we might be able to get the jump on one of their transports here." I kept on seeing signs of some rare trace gasses in the scan results I was getting. It could have been part of the noise, I wasn't sure yet.

"So, we're digging into their supply line," Manny said.

"Exactly. A boring hit that could have a big payoff. Destroying a Ryden hauler with a cargo train is worth twenty-five thousand plat without considering what they're transporting. I'm also looking for more information about Ryden's shipping. Some of their freighters have been seen bringing loads here," I said.

"Transport over there, three hundred one point four kilometres to port, marking it," Duncan said from the upper turret. "Forty-one tanks strung along behind it."

I looked at the scan results and shook my head. We were still relying on optics more than anything else. "I can't get a good reading on the mass. Does it look like it's flying empty or full?"

"Empty is my guess," Duncan said.

"Judging from how the ventral thrusters are firing, I agree," Manny said.

"Surface stress on the tanks confirm it," Perri said. She took Ixat's station in the component vault, where she had access to the secondary control centre.

"Well, that answers the real question. Are they coming or

going?" I said. "Keep your distance, but follow her in parallel, Manny."

"Oh, I like that. If the tanks were full, we'd have to try to backtrack," Manny replied as he adjusted course.

"I'm pointing our port side sensors at that ship. We should be close to the station. Look for escorts, Duncan," I said, watching the results come in. Filtering the noise from real data was taking a long time.

"Keepin' an eye out for anything that'll wreck our day," Duncan said.

The optical scanners finally picked out the name of the ship, Lucille. I gave half of my internal processing power to the ship computer to help with filtering our scan results faster. I was a little too busy to handle more than I was already seeing through my mind's eye. "Look that up, please."

Mimi got right to work. Using her trackballs and a little touch pad, she navigated the Stellarnet using the Haven Node installed in the ship. "Hmm... independent hauler. It's not on Haven's hit list and I can't find evidence that it's been to Iora or any other Order stronghold."

"Whoa! We're coming up on something," Duncan said.

The upper turret's optical systems spotted the bulbous shape of a harvesting station. The details became clearer as we passed a pillar of thick blue-brown clouds. It reminded me of an octopus with its tentacles half cut off. What looked like short-ened appendages were actually intakes. It slowly drifted above a more dense layer of clouds below us, cycling air in and out, sepa-rating what it wanted from gas chaff. Drones carried tanks between the station's midsection and the ships docked with pylons above that. "We're too close. Veer off and start a wide circle. We don't want..." I stopped speaking as one of the docked ships came in sight. "Ryden Runner Three."

"I'm putting some space between us and the station," Manny said.

"One target on the board, make sure we don't lose track of it," I told Lat. His job was simple but difficult. As we spotted objects, he had to help our tactical computer keep track of them by pointing our secondary scanners at them if they got too close to something they could hide behind.

"I've got it," Lat replied. "Details are coming up." Ryden Runner Three was a ninety metre long freighter with a large interior cargo hold. Drones were affixing tanks to the aft side, starting a cargo train.

"Five other Order of Eden associates are here. Two smaller ships with no interior cargo, the rest are all docked to the station like this one," Duncan said from the upper turret. "I can't get a good read on what's going on other than that."

"We're getting a hail from the station and a Navnet course from Sky Drift Station. I think you should take this one," Mimi said.

"Put them through. Replace my image with the captain of the Merry Mouse, Beyla Mann," I said.

"Okay, you look and sound like her, I'm putting the station through," Mimi said.

"Should I follow the course they're sending?" Manny asked.

"Yeah, we got too close, so we may as well slip into a safe pattern," I replied.

The holographic head of a young man with a perfect complexion and hair appeared. "Welcome to Sky Drift Station, Merry Mouse. I see you're following the Navnet course we sent, good. You're in the pattern. Are you here to buy, or..."

"Your first guess was dead on. We're buying for a small manu-facturing..."

He cut me off. "Don't really care where it's going, thanks.

Here's our price list. You'll need to pay extra for tanks. Pay once you dock. You're ninth in queue. Stay in the pattern."

The transmission ended. "This isn't a known station," Mimi said, shaking her head as she scrolled through Stellarnet sites on two holographic displays. "Online activity is rare, even going back before The Fall. There are bigger harvesting facilities around, but this one doesn't advertise."

"So most people skip this one?" Manny asked.

"Well, two of the big stations fell and were crushed by the planet's gravity, the other major facility is under British Alliance control, so, yeah, people go there. The smaller stations like this operate without regulation, so the less reputable people come here," Mimi replied.

As she spoke a ship Duncan highlighted momentarily drew my notice. It was Ryden Runner Two, and it was orbiting the station much like we were. It had a train of thirty long tanks and half a dozen service drones were inspecting the ship. "I think this is just a supply run," I said, looking at the new scan results. We were close enough to the station and other ships to actually get some good data.

"Looks like. Gotta say, their cargo may be worth a fair bit, like," Duncan said.

"We found the wrong Ryden ships if we're going to learn where the bodies are being taken, but..." I trailed off as I looked at our holding pattern, the station below and the conditions outside.

"Well, I guess it's time to move on then," Lat said, a little irritation in his voice.

That irked me. He expected me to back off because the answers I wanted weren't here, but that wasn't the plan. "We're not leaving this alone. Gimmie a sec, I want to see what's for sale. Can you try to get a read on what's in that Ryden ship's tanks, Duncan?"

I checked the list of compressed gasses and liquids the station was selling and something stood out. Duncan and I said it at the same time; "Resomene."

"That's worth loads," he said.

"We can do a lot of damage here. No one knows our ship, we're running a fake transponder, and we can outgun one of those haulers if we stay above or below it," I said quickly.

"So, butcher's business," Duncan said. "Ready for that."

"Tell me when you want me to break pattern," Manny said, gripping the controls hard for a moment then relaxing.

"We're gonna knock them down?" Perri asked.

"At least one of them," I said, forcing the computer to do another search through our rough scan results. The filter was working, but there was still a lot of garbled data thanks to the electromagnetic interference the gas giant liked to throw up from its core and between the more caustic clouds below. "They should call out to the Regulator or other Ryden ships for support if they're in the area."

"There are two Order of Eden planet hoppers down there," Lat replied, highlighting them on the tactical display. They were large enough to carry about forty people or small amounts of cargo. These had a lot of brown markings from being in Oya's atmosphere. It looked like one of them had been docked for a long time.

"Watch for whatever ship launched them. I'm hoping they've been there a while, just extra life boats for Order staff," I said.

"So, you're saying it's likely that the Order took the station over?" Mimi asked.

"That's what it looks like, or they're just really good customers. Resomene is a rare material used in high end manufacturing. Fabricators with access to a lot of energy, like a large antimatter reactor, can make it, but it's cheaper to harvest it from places like this. I bet the Order are having this stuff transported to a ship yard. Send our data to Haven Fleet and the Legion. I want everyone to know about this." I explained.

"Thanks to our handy Haven Node. I love getting around all that local static," Mimi said. "The data is packaged up and the transmission is away."

"Good, put me through to the station," I said.

"Okay. Wait. We're on hold," Mimi sighed.

The same face I spoke to earlier appeared. "Yes, Captain?"

"Something has come up. We need a departure route," I said.

"Understood. Don't complain if you come back and there are thirty in the queue ahead of you," he said before cutting the call.

"I have a Navnet route," Manny said.

"All right, follow it until we're out of their scan range. Duncan, don't lose sight of those Ryden ships. Lat, watch the Order of Eden shuttles. If they so much as turn their lights on, tell us about it," I said.

"Aye," Manny said, guiding the Daring Dream away from the station along the course he was sent.

"Clouds rolling in, high charge, but our computer is learning to look through some of that. I don't think we'll get better clarity," Duncan said.

"Our course is taking us right past them," Manny said.

"Good. We'll use them as cover while we go lower. We need to disappear," I said. "At least until one of those Ryden ships starts making their way up."

"I like this, it's like hunting in the tall grass," Mimi growled.

"Exactly. Everyone that isn't watching for something specific or flying has to keep looking for trouble," I said.

The Daring Dream slipped behind the tall, slowly moving

cloud bank. A streak of lightning raked our shields, and I was impressed at how little it diminished our new energy barriers. "We're watching for Typhoons or anything that has more guns than we do."

"I see a way down that won't put us right in the heavy gasses," Manny said.

"Work with Duncan. We need to find a place nearby that almost interferes with our scanners so much that we can't see. With our scanner package we should be able to detect what they can't," I explained. "We shut everything we can down as soon as we're in place."

"I'm so glad you're not an actual pirate, you're too good at this," Perri said.

"Watch it, now. You'll curse it," Duncan said in a whisper.

CHAPTER TWENTY-FOUR

The Storm

The view through the ship's sensors was streaming through my mind as I watched the instruments from the copilot's seat. The Daring Dream was almost completely powered down, moving through the microgravity only a few kilometres behind and beneath the station. There was a thick, dark bank of clouds ahead and another behind us. Electrical interference and intermittent lightning strikes surrounded the ship, interfering with our readings.

Our Third Eye Tactical System was getting better at filtering through the noise and making up for missing data, but there were still gaps, moments where the energy around us was so great that our sensors were overwhelmed, causing white-outs that lasted fractions of a second. The worst of them made me wince in my seat.

When lightning struck us from both sides at the same time,

I worried that the energy passing over our hull would light us up on everyone's sensors, but there was no sign that the station or any of their customers were alarmed. Mimi was looking through fragmented communications, focusing on distorted messages between Station Navnet Control and the ships that were loading up. She was good, quick, and patient. "It sounds like Ryden Three is almost loaded up and finished inspection."

"Get ready to move," I said.

"Easy," Manny replied.

"Duncan, can you get a passive scan on the other Ryden ship?" I asked.

"Working on it, every kind of interference here," he said. "Are we really not going to steal one of these?"

"We'll take one if they're hauling sleepers. If not, we'll take the kill reward for at least one," I replied. They knew what would happen if we found humans in a ship's cargo hold. We were all hoping to capture a ship that would lead to some answers.

"Ryden Runner Three has finished connecting tanks and they have a Navnet path," Mimi reported.

"I see it," Manny said as he glanced at the holographic navigation display. "Those Ryden ships are leaving together. We won't be able to track them for long."

"He's right, I'm pointing the instruments right at them and it's patchy," Duncan replied.

The tactical map in my head, as glitchy as it was, showed Ryden Runner Three slowly distancing itself from the station, moving into a parallel position beside Runner Two. As soon as they steadied the train of tanks behind them with their noses pointed straight up, they engaged their main thrusters. "Time to shine, Manny. Take us around the station, keep us inside highly charged areas, moving through clouds so no one gets a good scan of us. When we're clear of the station's range, we want to be right on top of those Ryden ships, flying in parallel with the aft most tanks."

"I love a challenge," Manny said with a grin as he activated our main thrusters and sent us through the edge of a dark cloud. Lightning followed us, reaching out from that dark gas culmination like long white fingers.

While Duncan focused on watching the Ryden ships using the upper turret, I watched as much as I could using the less effective secondary sensors. As we moved into the uppermost layer of clouds, I thought I saw a straight edge in beneath. It was moving towards our last position. "Keep flying after them, but I think I just spotted something."

"Should we start pinging?" Duncan asked.

"No active scans, not yet. We want them to go active first. We'll catch data from their scan pulses," I replied.

"If they bother at all. I think everyone here is trying not to announce themselves by sending scan waves out," Manny said. "Not smart. If I were picking up gas here, I'd ping every second, let everyone know I'm there as I got closer to the station."

"That's what happens when paranoia rides shotgun. Hiding becomes more important than preventing a collision," Perri said.

"Hey, wouldn't there be a lot of them if everyone can only see a few hundred klicks in front of their face?" Mimi asked.

"Not once they're away from the station. Chances of bumping into another ship go down fast," Manny replied. "It's not actually that busy here."

"We're getting close," Duncan said.

A scan pulse came from Ryden Runner Three then, an energy wave that was partially reflected by the particles and clouds, hampered by the atmosphere, but it also traced the outlines of unnatural things, like the station and every ship in the area. I activated the shields and turned them up to full. "They lit us up, they know exactly where we are."

"Closing now," Manny announced.

"Ping right at them. Use the scan results to target the weakest points in their shields and fire." I watched the ship systems and the tactical map as the haulers came into view.

Their tank train already showed the light and dark brown streaks from the atmosphere, and the weathered, boxy hulls of the ships that drew them looked even more weathered. These were tough industrial class vessels with thrusters extended in four directions around the main fuselage so they could maintain some manoeuvrability while pulling a shipment of liquid resomene.

They fired first. The double barrel turrets facing us sent energy bursts painted red by the atmosphere that missed early on. The gunners were panicking. "Not seeing any sleepers aboard those ships," Duncan said.

"Then we take them out. Ryden doesn't get to do business," I said.

"Aye. Deploying guns, blastin' Runner Three," Duncan announced as he started rapid-firing his four Ripshock cannons at one of the ship's main thrusters. "Weak spot's movin'. They're adjusting, I'm keeping focus."

After checking our scan results on the enemy ship and seeing that they weren't keeping up with Duncan's punishment, I nodded. "Good, you'll break them down fast."

Lat was working on Ryden Runner Two. The pair of rail guns and Ripshocks mounted on his turret tore into the middle of their cargo train. I could see their shield strength dropping. "They're not going to last long, these ships are made to lift and fly straight."

"Keep it up," I said as I checked the scans of the Runner's

interiors. Duncan was right, there were no stasis pods or any sign of the scan shielded cargo containers that Corosa used to move their sleepers. "Resomene must be worth a lot to their customers if they're not hauling anything else."

"Message from Leon," Mimi said, looking at me. "He says Order forces have been spotted around Oya. Three destroyers with escort craft. I put the last known position in the tactical computer. He also said the resomene is definitely going to ship-yards in orbit around Iora."

The locations and courses of three Order of Eden destroyers and their companion ships appeared in my mind. Each of them were two hundred fifty metres long and had a main escort of four Marauder Corvettes. They were orbiting the gas giant quickly, scanning the upper atmosphere for trouble. "We'll be in range of the next Order patrol in three minutes."

"Should we run?" Manny asked.

"Stay close to the haulers, use the tanks as cover," I replied. "Mimi, hail the Runners. Time for terms."

"Ready, they're answering," Mimi said. "Are you sure I should do the talking?"

"That's the plan, I'll be busy," I replied.

"Hold your fire!" came a male voice through the communications station. Whoever was speaking for Ryden Runner Three was panicking. Their gunners weren't, however. Our forward shields were taking fire from their main turret. They were holding up for the moment.

Mimi's voice was disguised by the system so it sounded impossibly low. "You will abandon ship. Your Order of Eden friends will pick you up."

"We're honest haulers!" he replied. He was about to continue his plea but was interrupted as Duncan's Ripshocks burned out the shields protecting one of the Runner's main thrusters. He didn't stop there. Rapid blasts of energy overloaded the electronics in the engine, and the thruster's fire stuttered before going out completely. The voice came back, near panic. "We can't lose another thruster, we'll lose the load, then the ship!"

Mimi's posture shifted, she was getting into the act as her voice was altered. "What are Ryden and the Order doing with the sleepers?"

While she started her interrogation, I was running several software packages in my computer hardware, switching all of its attention from assisting with scans to a digital attack. The speed of my mind accelerated, slowing my experiences down. Without a personality program to run, my digital side was free to use thirty-three percent of its processing power to enter stolen credentials into Runner Three's computer system. One of the remote access codes from the stolen Ryden trooper's bracer got me into the ship's computer. I was looking at their logs next, doing a search I'd prepared in advance. "Duncan, focus your fire on Runner Two now. Runner Three is about to die."

"Try again, but at human speed, like?" Duncan asked.

I intentionally slowed my speech down. "I'm shutting Runner Three down. Destroy Runner Two."

"Aye, can't wait to see this," Duncan said.

I downloaded everything I could from Runner Three's computer system. Its data drives and the connection speed were quick, it was done in three point four seven seconds. "Now your ship fails you," I said under my breath as I let my biological mind slow.

At my command, Ryden Runner Three's remaining thrusters shut down. The stabilisation rods holding the tanks in line behind the craft released and I shut the ship's main reactors down. "Done."

The first thing I saw when I opened my eyes was Mimi

staring through our window, her eyes wide. Ryden Runner Three was switching to backup power. Thick metal rods from the cargo train were springing away in all directions. One struck our shields and spun on as the enemy ship started to tumble, its cargo train twisting, bunching and pushing into the aft end of the hauler. "They're done," Lat said.

I thought he was talking about Runner Three, but he was looking at Runner Two. Its shields had failed, several of its tanks were ruptured, spraying green resomene as it changed from a compressed liquid into a gas. Rectangular single occupant escape pods popped out of the top of the craft as Lat pummelled the hull with solid rounds, punching holes into the bridge section.

With a thought, I opened one of our forward missile compartments and turned the Porcupine on. "Take aim at Ryden Runner Three, Manny."

"¡En chinga!" which my internal translation program told me meant; "Right away!"

The Daring Dream tilted, turned and as soon as we were lined up to fire, I launched five dumb fire darter missiles at Ryden Runner Three. One penetrated right through the hull protecting their backup batteries. I fired five more as soon as they were in line and watched as one ripped into the compartment, turning the ship's lights out for good. "Get us out of here. Fast. I'm sure Runner Two signalled the Order patrol."

Manny didn't choose a course I would have. Instead, he turned the nose of the Daring Dream so we were in line with the upper atmosphere and throttled up to maximum, engaging the antimatter injectors like afterburners. We would be easy to find, but hard to catch in that microgravity sky as we left a five point two kilometre long flaming wake behind us. The rumble of the engines and pressure of the thin air in front of the ship made for a roaring, howling audio spectacle. Mimi activated the protective transparisteel bubble for her station and gripped the pad beneath her.

"Don't worry, just getting us some speed before we break out into open space," Manny explained, white-knuckling the controls.

"You did this in games?" I asked, checking my belt. The shields were taking damage, and I routed energy from the weapons while I closed our missile launchers. The next step was a little trickier. I angled our energy barriers into a fixed wing shape around the ship and our navigational dampeners relaxed as we started to cut through the atmosphere like a pointed knife.

"Eight or nine times," Manny replied. "Never with this kind of thrust."

"We're all right, but I'm glad you didn't try this lower down," I said.

"Never would. How are the shields holding up?" he asked.

"Seventy-eight percent on forward shields, full everywhere else," I replied.

"I'm turning cryo cooling on down here," Perri said urgently. "The modules are heating up."

"Try to keep the wear and tear on the coils down," Lat said.

"I know, I know, I don't want to go shopping for new shields either," Perri replied.

She didn't spend nearly as much time training in that section as Ixat, we were already feeling the loss. The tactical system in my head finally showed an Order of Eden Destroyer along with four Marauder Corvettes and nine fighters. "Serious Order firepower ahead. They're adjusting course to intercept us. A hundred and seventy thousand kilometres out. Let's get to open space, it won't get better."

A yellow-red particle beam cut through the clouds ahead, sweeping close to the ship. "I get it, time to go," Manny said as he altered our course. We were out of the upper atmosphere seconds later, the sound of our shields cutting through the air was gone, leaving the relative quiet of rumbling thrusters. "We have signals coming in from the Subjugator Three," Mimi announced.

It was the destroyer in active pursuit. The Marauders were trying to close, thrusting hard. Their tall, narrow design featured a bridge section at the top and a large, main beam weapon at the bottom. They lit up and fired. At that range they were only a third as effective, but two of them managed to test our shields for five seconds. Manny evaded as best as he could. "Main thrusters are cooling down, we can maintain full throttle, they're not going to catch us unless they cut through our shields."

"Take us around Sellestro, Nafalli battlecruisers are guarding that area," I said. "Contact them as soon as we see a GFF signal, Mimi."

"GFF? Oh, right, Galactic Friend or Foe, right, right. Watching for furry warrior friends," she replied. "What do I do about the Destroyer? They really wanna talk."

All five Marauder Corvettes lashed out with their main beam weapons. Two managed to blast us for nine seconds. Manny spun the ship slowly as he tried to evade, spreading the damage across our port, starboard, dorsal and ventral shields. I struggled to shift energy to their capacitor banks so they could recharge quickly. It almost worked, but our main ventral shield was deactivated at the last second, earning the Daring Dream a long burn line along its hull. "Sorry! Had to turn that one off! It was about to burn out! Activating our old backup, for all the good it'll do."

"No problem, the hull held up," I replied. "Manny, keep our ventral side pointed away from those corvettes."

"I'm one step ahead of you," he replied. "We're outrunning them, almost on course for Sellestro."

"Um..." Mimi said, looking at me as she idly toyed with one of her trackballs.

"We're not answering that destroyer. Block them and all Order of Eden ships. Keep our transponders off," I told Mimi.

"Aye, Captain," she said, quickly following orders.

The Marauders tried to strike us with their beam weapons and launched two fast missiles each. I deployed the turret I finished installing and engaged our electronic countermeasures. Seven missiles didn't follow Manny's course adjustments as their guidance systems were scrambled. We were over a quarter million kilometres away from them, which bought us time to take the last three out. Lat blasted one with solid rounds, using his turret's aim assist program.

Our new turret, which wasn't really made for countermeasure work, managed to take another out before Lat blasted the third. Hot beams from the Marauders found us again, but our shields had too much time to recover, and their power was diminished just enough for our energy barriers to keep up with the damage. "We're on our way to Sellestro, damned fast," Manny said with a snicker. "Almost out of orbital space. Am I reading this right? Our shields are okay?"

"Thaaat's right, our baby made it through her first real fight." I could hear Perri grinning through the intercom. "Switching back over to our main ventral shield, it's cool enough."

"Well done, everyone," I said as the Marauder along with its fighter group turned back so they could resume their orbit.

"Just wonderin' what did we earn?" Duncan asked.

"Fifty thousand platinum at least. We'll get credit for destroying critical supplies, but we won't know how much until Haven Fleet gets around to the assessment. Probably an extra fifteen thousand," I replied.

"All right, for scale, what's one of these shield units worth? The Fifteen Hundreds?" Perri asked.

"A hundred thousand in the condition we got them in," I replied.

"Whoa," Perri said.

"Thanks for saving one from burning out," I told her. I was looking at the tactical map, zooming out so I could see more of the solar system.

"Aye, thanks," Duncan said.

"I'm looking at a superficial burn on the hull. I don't think that'll polish out," Lat said from his turret.

"Well, the Daring Dream was going to get some character eventually," Perri said.

"So, are we visiting the Nafalli?" Mimi asked.

I was busy reviewing the data I'd collected from the Ryden Runner Three. "I don't think so, Mimi. Sorry. Those haulers have only been working around Oya for five days. Their last run before that was definitely what we're looking for. Fifty cargo containers filled with stasis pods. We're going to Vercosa, slingshot around Sellestro, Manny."

"Vercosa, Vercosa," Mimi mused. Then she perked up and looked at me with wide eyes. "Moon. That's the third planet's moon?"

"Exactly," I replied. "Keep our acceleration up, I'll watch for anything trying to intercept us."

Mimi brought information about Vercosa up and shook her head as the brown and yellow image of the orb appeared in front of her with a few key details. "Zero point three gravity, sulphuric acid rain... I don't like it."

"Don't worry, I'm hoping we won't have to touch down. It's not a vacation spot," I said.

"Oh, five mega prisons. That is super-duper-mega unlucky,"

Mimi said quietly as she found several old news reports with headlines like:

WAKING INCARCERATION, LIVING HELL!

LONG TERM TROUBLE DISPOSAL

THE PRISON FEW SURVIVE

"Don't worry, we're not staying," I said.

CHAPTER TWENTY-FIVE

Sorting It Out

Buying the version of the Spectral Dynamics Clipper Military Class Hull was the smartest thing I did for the Daring Dream. The second good choice was specifying that it should come with the Explorer Package. That meant there would be a lot of compartments for crew, some internal cargo space, a good navigational system, and a top end sensor suite built into the upper turret. There were plenty of custom touches aside from that, but my point is that those sensors saved us a lot of trouble as we approached Vercosa.

We were half way there when Duncan pointed the sensor array at the moon. When we saw the results, I immediately ordered Manny to start decelerating so we could use Sellestro's orbital space as a safe haven. The presence of the Nafalli tribes was heavy there. We were able to detect a seven hundred metre battleship without trying. I remember Mimi staring at its bulbous, battered thick hull. It was surrounded by captured Order of Eden drop ships, local customs corvettes, and a variety of fighters. According to the buzz on the Stellarnet, there had been at least eight more small fleets sighted there, and the Order were staying away for the time being.

What you're probably wondering is: what did we see that made us stop cold? Well, it was so bad that we had to have a crew meeting, but I had to settle something before that. What to do with our stowaways.

Lat was the expert on them, having watched the pair of Nafalli for two shifts by then. We met in the hall outside our holding cells and I made sure Perri was there as well. "All right, what do you think of those two?"

Lat rubbed his chin for a moment. "It was interesting. The woman was calm. She tried to talk to me about the ship, asked what the Captain was like a few times. She wasn't sure if you were in charge, so I don't think she's very observant. I didn't move or respond to her, so she stopped and tried to go to sleep. That wasn't possible for a while because the male started yelling at me. He even pounded the door a few times. I think he was trying to get me to move. He started crying after he failed to break my resolve."

"Oh, no," Perri said sympathetically.

"The female told him I was probably a droid, and he said; 'that's worse!' and I moved a little because I laughed when he started crying again," Lat said.

Perri regarded Lat for a moment, looking disappointed.

"What? I thought it was funny. He was whining and wheezing like we were about to space him, but I knew they would be all right because we never would," Lat said.

"Did you tell them that?" Perri asked.

"I only moved when I walked in, laughed once, and when

Rogue took over, so no. The whole point was to see what they did when I did nothing," Lat replied.

"You could have reassured them a little. They're not criminals," Perri said.

"Yes they are. Stowing away on..." Lat started.

"I mean violent or dangerous criminals," Perri countered.

"Maybe. We don't know that for sure, do we?" he asked.

"Mimi and I couldn't find anything online about them being violent," I replied.

"Oh, okay. Anyway, watching them was more interesting when the female became frustrated. She wanted to sleep and the male wouldn't shut up. She yelled at him until he did. I don't think they're bad people, but the male is definitely soft. I'm glad we're not telling him anything, or letting him see outside. He'd tell an Order cadet everything he knows," Lat said.

"Why do you call them 'male' and 'female?'" Perri asked.

"I don't need to know them. They're probably getting put off the ship when we get a chance, right?" Lat asked.

"If Oonaa had the skills to serve on this ship, would you have any objection to giving her a chance?" I asked, having already run a security and employment check on her.

"Well, sure. But that other one? Not a chance," Lat replied.

"You need help in fabrication now that you're in engineering. Do you think you could..." I started asking Perri.

She nodded excitedly. "Absolutely! I'll start her on the simpler stuff, see what she can do. That is, after I finish making the ammo you ordered. Does she have a history with that?"

"Oonaa has served as a mechanic and maintenance worker, so I'm pretty sure she knows her way around a fabricator. Starting her with simple stuff is probably a good idea," I told her.

"Wait, with that kind of experience, I should be showing her the component vault. If there's anything we'll need help with during an alert, that's it." Perri wasn't just making a point, she was making a plea.

"You're not comfortable working alone in there?" I asked.

"I got a third of Ixat's training with the modules and the power distribution array. It wouldn't take me long to catch her up if she already has experience. Besides, we need a floater who can address damage or get to a turret, you know, the jobs I trained for," Perri said.

It was difficult to argue with her, and we were short handed. "She's your responsibility. Get her trained on the essential combat work in the vault. If she doesn't measure up or does anything suspicious, tell me right away. We'll either put her in another position or back in a cell."

Perri brightened at the prospect. "Okay, that's fair. So, you'll hire her and she can start today?"

"You offer her the job, tell her she gets put off the ship without pay if she breaks secrecy, and show up to the crew meeting with her. As for her boyfriend, he's staying in there until we get to a safe port, so make sure his meal bar and water hoppers are full. It could be a couple of days, maybe more," I told her.

"Maybe we could give him access to a flexi with a chunk of the Remmybase in it? You know, off the network, non-current entertainment," she asked.

"You already have one ready, don't you?" I asked with a smirk.

"Yeah, two actually. I didn't peek in on them long, but from the sound of the argument those two were having, I could tell their relationship was over. I thought a couple flexi's with a few thousand hours of the Remmybase and some old Hart News broadcasts would distract them from each other. There's nothing like taking a long trip with someone you can't stand," Perri replied.

"Well, as long as there's no networking hardware in the displays, no problem. Remember, you're Oonaa's supervisor. Crew meeting in half an hour,' I said.

"Okay, thank you," Perri said, giving me a brief hug.

"I'll stay and watch, just in case there's trouble," Lat said.

"There won't be," Perri told him.

"Just in case," he repeated.

"Good. Don't open Fersuu's cell, refill his dispensers using the access point in the ceiling and set his water to a maximum of five ounces every half hour," I told Lat.

"Aye," he replied.

Seeing that sorted, I moved forward in the ship to the armoury. I took a spare military vacsuit and formatted it into a chest bag and used the remainder to cover a helmet. Most people who serve in Haven Fleet never have to take advantage of the full adaptability of their military vacsuits, but I was stretching their capabilities.

The extra layer of armour that it provided to the relatively basic helmet was nice, but the most important part was the stealth system. That level of military vacsuit could match my surroundings and hide from most sensors unless someone performed a focused scan in my direction or used security measures that were specifically made to detect stealth systems. Once I was finished I headed for the common room.

Manny was already there, enjoying a fruit cup that he'd bought from one of the vending machines in the Bitter End. The ship status windows were projected on the table in front of him. "We're in orbit. Mimi got in touch with the nearest Nafalli patrol. They're the Uhrren Tribe. As soon as we sent them our privateering credentials they were happy to watch our backs. They even gave us a course that'll keep us hidden from long range sensors. It's good to have friends. I'll get back to the cockpit as soon as I finish this."

"Don't hurry, we're having a meeting," I replied.

Duncan came down from the upper turret, standing as soon as his boots touched the deck. "Almost dozed off up there," he said as he stretched.

The vacsuit looked good on him, but I didn't have time to appreciate it, so I looked away and put my gear down on the short sofa beside the gunnery chairs. "See anything new on Vercosa?"

"Only more lakes you can't swim in, clouds, rocks and sand," he replied. "It's pretty from here, but I'd go no closer if it were up to me. Planning a trip?" he asked.

"We'll wait for everyone," I replied as Mimi dropped from a small maintenance hatch above. She landed on my shoulder, scrambled a little, and found her footing as I gave her a hand.

"Your suit is slippery. I don't like it," she said.

"I had to make a couple of adjustments in case I need stealth mode," I replied.

"Ooh, does mine have that? I'd love to be invisible," she said, crouching low.

"Says the cat who wants all the attention," Manny snickered.

"Sorry, maybe the next version of your suit," I replied. I could have made some high end vacsuit material into a shape she could use, but it wouldn't be retractable or as effective. I would have to bug Elise for something better.

"Nuts. Ah well," Mimi sighed.

"You're sneaky enough as-is, like," Duncan said as he filled a bottle with cold water.

"Everyone welcome our new probationary crew member," Perri announced as she came in with Oonaa behind her.

"I'll do such a great job that I'll be in charge before you know," Oonaa said.

Don't get me wrong, I already liked the Nafalli, but I didn't crack a hint of a smile as I looked into her brown eyes for a moment before looking away, outwardly unmoved. "Lat?"

"Coming. He's just manually locking the cell compartment door down. Fersuu is well pissed that we're not letting him out or turning him loose," Perri said.

"His fault for picking the wrong ship," I replied.

"I asked the Uhrren Tribe comms lady if they would take stowaways and she said; 'do you think all Nafalli know each other?' Then she told me that stowaways are cowards and wouldn't talk about it anymore. She was nice about everything else," Mimi said.

"I'm not a coward. I just..." Oonaa clenched her jaw and looked away.

"I think we all understand. You just wanted to get off the Bitter End and help your boyfriend out. Now your job application has been accepted," Perri said.

"I hope I never have to look at Fersuu again. He's the coward," Oonaa said.

"Just put that frustration into your work, it'll be fine," Perri soothed.

Oonaa nodded then. Most of the Nafalli Alice knew were kind with sturdy resolves. Even I found Fersuu disappointing, despite the fact that I didn't blame him for freaking out. It wasn't the time to discuss it, however.

As soon as Lat came in I started. "All right, we've a Ryden fast transport on Vercosa, the largest moon of the third planet in the Rose System thanks to Duncan's work with our main scanner array. The time delay on our data is thirty-six minutes," I said, nodding at Duncan.

He tossed a bottle of water to Lat and got started with his update. "I ran a full hard scan on every prison in Basilisk Valley. All of them were empty. Not a single corpse. Which means someone's shifted those poor bastards. They didn't just wander off in the acid rain. Saw a Ryden transport landing at another site, the Supplicant Five. A Regent Galactic built fast cargo ship, armoured. One of the last they sold Ryden before they went bust and got bought out. Can't say what's in it. It's under a scrambling field along with the only active spot on the moon."

"Think that's where they've got the sleepers?" Manny asked.

"No clue. But I scanned more and there's heavy scrambling elsewhere too. Name that came up? Marigold Refuge." With a cheeky bow to Mimi he said; "Your majesty, the floor's yours."

"Oh, right. The Marigold Refuge is a retirement community for rich people who want to live in a fully virtual environment. They surrender their bodies to pods, and medical systems take care of them for the rest of their natural lives or until they want to leave," Mimi said.

"Not a bad way to age out," Manny said.

"It's not that kind of retirement. Most of the people are young when they go there, or at least really healthy. They're retiring from the material world. Until recently they were connected to the Stellarnet using a powerful hyper transmitter. That thing uses microscopic wormholes to speed up data transfers so they can share simulation data, update their software and communicate. According to what I've seen on the Stellarnet about the Marigold Refuge, no one has been able to contact any of the residents since the Holocaust Virus attacked the Rose System. Their families want someone to go down there and fix the comms systems, but no one will go because the Rose System is a war zone," Mimi explained.

"How many people are in there?" Lat asked.

"The last count was fourteen thousand, two hundred. There was an expansion planned before the war broke out," Mimi replied.

"Why would they put it there? I mean, it's all acid lakes, crazy heat in the day, minus one hundred at night and, well, the view can't be great," Manny said as he pushed his empty fruit cup into the recycler under the counter.

"Exclusivity and privacy," Mimi replied. "The process to get approved for that spot takes most people a couple of years because it's a curated community of people who want to live in a fictional world for a couple hundred years. The security is ridiculous too, anyone who gets in can expect to be protected."

"Is there any way to contact the residents?" I asked.

"I tried everything and didn't get through. The theory is that they unplugged to save themselves and never reconnected, but I think there's something going on down there," Mimi replied.

"Ryden doesn't want us to get a look," Duncan added.

It was my turn, and I hoped it would go well. "The Supplicant Five accepted a load of sleepers from the Carosa Transportation Company days after Ryden bought it. It's involved with the sleepers somehow, and it's a pretty serious ship."

"Is it as good as the Daring Dream?" Mimi asked.

"No. It's better armed though, so we're not going near it. There are also four Typhoons in orbit. Since they're not made for long trips or patrols, I'm guessing there's a mother ship nearby. Maybe the Regulator. I've already signalled the Legion and Haven Fleet. Leon got back to me and I've been offered a mission to go down and see what's going on." As I finished, Duncan drew air in through his teeth, cringing. Manny regarded me wide-eyed.

"We don't know what kind of firepower the Marigold facility

has on the ground thanks to those scan scatterers, right?" Lat said.

"That's why the Daring Dream won't be landing. You're going to fly a couple hundred kilometres away, behind the hills to the north. You'll slow down just enough for me to drop then take off. I don't want you fighting with anything. Just hide. The planet has eighteen other moons and several pockets of iron rich asteroids around it," I said, looking at Manny.

"I looked, it's easy to lose people there, and there are smuggler havens, but I'm stuck on the point where you're dropping from a moving ship," he said.

"You'll only have to slow to two hundred kilometres per hour. I can withstand worse in a military vacsuit made to take a beating. Just fly low, all right?" I asked.

Mimi was just staring at me, her jaw down. "I'm not doing that."

"That's why you're staying here. I need someone to answer my call when I'm ready for pickup. I'll try to get as far away from the Refuge as I can so the Daring Dream can get in and out without much interference. Remember, I'm carrying a Haven Node, so it should defeat any scrambling field," I told her.

"I'm going with you," Lat said, determination in his eyes.

"It's a recon mission. We're getting paid for information here. If I can steal another ship, I will, but getting out without drawing attention might be better. There shouldn't be much, if any, fighting if I do my job right," I told him.

That wouldn't take, I knew it before he opened his mouth. "I was made for this. The stats say the vacsuit can take that impact, especially on loose ground. I'm going. That's what I'm for."

"You won't keep up," I told him.

"Cold thrusters. It would take half an hour to make four. I'll wear one on each arm, set them to the same temperature as the air and no one will see me if the cloaking systems are working at all," he said.

That was smart, I had to admit it, even Duncan was nodding. "You need me aboard as your First Officer, otherwise I'd go."

"All right," I conceded.

"Okay, if he's going, then I'm definitely staying," Mimi said, drawing a quizzical look from Lat. "What? Someone has to take charge if the worst happens to the First Officer."

There were a few snickers around the room, and Oonaa covered her nose, trying to suppress a squeaking laugh. Thankfully, Mimi was kidding, so she wasn't offended.

"I'll see you soon, don't worry," I told her. "All right, I need a few things fabricated and there are missiles to reload. I need you in the cockpit, calculating a short wormhole jump to Vercosa and preparing for the flyby, Manny."

"Aye, it'll be smooth. A bit fast, but smooth," he said, grabbing a meal bar and a bottle of water.

"Me?" Mimi asked.

"With me," I replied. "We'll help Lat get ready."

"Oh, okay," she replied, her spirits rising. "I'll keep an eye on comms, too."

"Um, I'm not quite sure why this is happening? Are we saving people? Who is Ryden?" Oonaa asked as she followed Perri out of the common room.

"Catch her up," I called after them.

"Will do," Perri replied before the hatch closed behind them.

CHAPTER TWENTY-SIX

Into The Complex

Lat tamed my recklessness. Instead of simply taking my weapons, supplies, making sure that my suit was ready and then jumping, I had to make sure that the human I would have along would survive the landing with me. It turns out that I didn't have to worry about him.

There are several things Lat has deep training on, and making sure he was geared up, sealed up, and ready to fight on land was one of them. I checked his vacsuit with our best hand scanner to make sure there were no flaws, he did the same for me, and we helped each other do a gear check. We stood in the middle of the central cargo hold. It was in the aft half of the ship, and the most important feature for that mission was the emergency boarding airlock. It was part of the Spectral Dynamics Rescue Package, and could affix to and burn through hulls, open quickly, even withstand a little more punishment than the rest of the Daring Dream's outer hull.

The last phase of our check was under way, checking each other by eye and hand. I was making sure his pack was firmly affixed by tugging on all its corners and was moving on to his arm thrusters. "You know how this will go?"

"Fast drop. We're impacting like slow meteors in zero point three-eight standard gravitational units into loose sand. There will be hard spots. Our suits will protect us from impalements and I'm wearing a dampening emitter that'll activate point two metres from actual impact. Everything else is just like Combat Drop Simulation Thirty-Three."

I turned him around and checked the dampening unit, a thick belt around his waist with a rectangular emitter over his stomach. It was fully charged and calibrated. "You're ready?"

"I'm ready. Mimi is not," he replied as he started checking my equipment out.

"She's nervous, I know," I replied.

"Everyone but you and I are nervous. She's about to shake out of her suit," he replied as he firmly tugged on my pack, then the rifle slung beside it. He moved onto my new sidearm and the ammo on the other thigh. "I'll talk to her," I said as I turned around.

I opened the inner airlock door at our feet and we dropped down. I unmuted myself on the ship's intercom as the inner doors closed above us and the airlock started cycling. "Hey, Mimi, how are we doing?"

"Good. There's still nothing but scrambling noise coming from that installation. You know, I was thinking; you don't have to go down there. We could wait in orbit, hide near one of those other moons and jump whatever takes off. We'll get to see what they're taking away, maybe capture a ship," she said in a hurry.

"That's not a bad idea, but we might be too late to help some people. Do you remember the end of the Carosa job? We had to wake up all those people?" I asked.

"Yeah. Most of them seemed so confused for an hour after they woke up. I had to answer the same questions over and over," she replied.

"What was the question you didn't have an answer to? The one almost everyone had on their mind?" I asked.

After a short pause, she replied; "'What do I do now?'"

"I was there when you struggled with that, wishing you knew what to tell them. If Lat and I go down there now, we might be able to stop things from getting to that point. If we're lucky, we'll learn a lot more and we'll be able to stop them from kidnapping even more people before they ever learn that they're at risk." The airlock finished matching the air pressure outside and the lower doors opened. Lat and I clung to railings, our feet on a small lip as the red, brown and blue ground only a few hundred metres below passed by at incredible speed. The air whipped at us, but the artificial muscles in Lat's suit helped him resist it.

"I know this mission is important. We're going to make a lot of money if the plan goes well, save a lot of people, but..." she trailed off. "Good luck, Rogue. Oh, and Lat too."

"You say; 'good hunting,' on a mission like this," Lat told her.

"Thank you, Mimi," I told her. "I'll take all the luck you can give me, and I'll see you again soon."

"I'd better see you soon," Mimi said. "And good hunting."

"We're coming up on it, you should see a timer," Duncan said. He'd already told me good hunting, but our parting was brief and professional.

A countdown from ten appeared inside my transparent face-plate and I activated the stealth systems built into the suit. Lat did the same and disappeared from most of my sensors after creating an anomalous swirl of air. That was normal, a measure to defeat a whole range of motion sensors that read air pressure and sound. "Ready."

"Ready," I said.

If anyone ever doubts how real my human memories and thought patterns are, just load up the biometric data from that moment. My palms, the shelf between my nose and upper lip were sweating. The dunes of loose ground down there were rushing by fast even as the ship was decelerating. The counter ticked down. I took a second to glance up at Lat when it hit four. He wasn't looking down. He was watching me, calm, as though he was about to step into another room, not do a bare suit drop. "You know what to do," I told my crew.

"Drop," Duncan said from the cockpit as the counter diminished from one to zero.

Lat let go of the rail and stepped forward first.

I dropped as soon as he was out of sight. It felt like my heart leapt into my throat. I could barely hear the wind through my helmet, but the air resistance was surprising, like a giant hand trying to hold me back.

I didn't have much to worry about on my way down. There wasn't much to do, to be honest, so I watched the Daring Dream punch ahead across the landscape, its three main thrusters firing blue, a contrast to the brown tinted atmosphere and dark night sky.

It was the dry season on that part of Vercosa, and a relatively warm night at minus one hundred twenty-six degrees. I could see lights in the distance, a small cluster that meant that I was facing the Marigold Refuge. It only lasted for an instant before I fell behind a tall set of hills, enough time for me to replay it. There were actually five ships on the ground, one was the

Supplicant Five, sporting a full array of Order of Eden and Regent Galactic markings. I'd never seen that type before. It was a war ship, with two fairly large turrets on top and an antigravity field, but it was only ninety-two metres long. The most interesting thing was that it was docked to the uppermost floor of the Refuge.

Less than a tenth of a second later, I paid for my distraction, striking the loose sand feet first. My suit, equipment, and my body survived the sudden force of the impact, which became more crushing as I was pushed in deeper. Jagged sand gave way to harder and harder packed layers before I finally stopped.

The instant I came to rest, I started working my way up and out. My nervousness was gone, and moving through that dirt was almost like swimming thanks to the lower than normal gravity. There was a specific way to do it, though, since it became more and more difficult to make progress as I reached more loosely packed areas. By the time I got to the surface, it really was like swimming, moving almost horizontally with a slight incline so the sharp edged sand didn't fight me as much.

"...Rogue, are you in range of my laser link? Rogue, are you in range of my laser link?" Lat was repeating when I broke the surface.

"Yeah, I'm here, finally," I replied, unsure of where he was. The Haven Fleet Military Vacsuit cloaking systems were working perfectly.

"Good. I thought I really lost you. There was a little puff of dust and then you were just... gone," Lat said.

"You remember what I told you not to do on this drop?" I asked.

"Don't hit feet first," he replied. "You said it a few times."

"I should have taken my own advice. I'm all right, though," I said with a chuckle.

"It's good advice. I landed flat on my face and it was actually fun," he replied.

The soles of our boots expanded and we started moving. Thanks to the very low powered laser link between us, I could tell where he was and talk to him without worrying about being detected. "Maybe you should add it to the list of activities for Vercosa."

"Not a bad idea, except most suits would get shredded shortly after impact," he replied. "I was a little worried that would happen to mine."

"Punctures aren't the kind of thing that defeat vacsuits," I replied.

"Knowing it and seeing it are not the same. Now I'm sure. These are nice, thank you," he replied. "Should we jump?"

"Let's," I replied, making sure I was facing the right direction and pushing off.

He activated his arm thrusters and started flying. Other than a slight stirring of the air, I couldn't see a trace of him because he was using cold thrusters that matched the temperature of the air around him. We had to get away from the plume of dust I'd sent up when I landed. Small meteor strikes weren't uncommon on Vercosa, but we were only a couple hundred kilometres away from the Refuge, so I expected at least one drone to check it out.

Leaping across the regolith took some practice. My first two jumps ended in heavy landings, so I had to dig myself out both times. I tried taking the best running leap I could from the top of a hill on the third and was stunned at how far it took me. For most of my arc over the dark landscape, it felt more like flying. I didn't use my cold jets because there was always a chance that they'd be detected. Not a big one, but if someone spotted Lat, I might be able to back him up. At worst, I'd survive to complete the mission, but I didn't think about that too much.

When I finally reached the foreboding dark field of stone surrounding the Marigold Refuge, things got much easier. I bounded along, trusting my non-visual scanners to tell me how fast I was moving ahead, up or down as I leapt. The lava plain had solidified tens of thousands of years ago, and I could barely tell the difference between the complete darkness beneath me and the cloudy night sky above with my naked eye. While that was disconcerting, there was still a picture in my mind drawn by the rest of my senses, so I skipped across it like a tick. "Yeah, this is more fun than it should be," I said as I touched the ground then skipped up and ahead again.

"Flying is always enjoyable when you don't have to manage a cockpit," Lat said more seriously.

Other than a couple stumbles, I got the hang of it, and I was starting to catch up with Lat, who was more steadily making his way to the most barren field in the area.

That's when the Marigold Refuge came into sight. I stopped. Lat was waiting for me only a few metres away. We were on the edge of the scrambling field. "We're here, about to cross into the dead zone," I reported to the Daring Dream.

Thanks to the Haven Nodes aboard the ship and on my wrist, we could communicate clearly, but I didn't know if there was some kind of new countermeasure ahead. "We've made it to Fiona, one of the nearby moons," Mimi replied.

"Moving ahead, we'll need a pickup if we're detected," I said, stepping around a large lava blister that hardened ages ago.

The lights of the buildings and ships in the distance stood out like little beacons. For a complex that was mostly underground, the Marigold Refuge had plenty of surface buildings. They were set up like a circuit, with hard windowed corridors between rectangular buildings surrounding one main square structure.

"Nothing's shooting at us yet," Lat said.

We waited, ready to step back behind cover, and finally, when I was sure we weren't spotted, or no one was going to open fire, I nodded. "We're moving in. I'll automatically transmit updates every two minutes. The Order is here. The Supplicant Five is docked to the top of the main structure. Judging from the markings, the Order took it back completely, there's no sign that Ryden owns it."

"Be careful, and good hunting!" Mimi said, faking better spirits.

"Thank you, be ready," I replied.

The second part of the trip took almost as long as the first, running across solidified ripples and strands of stone. A few spots felt different, like there were tunnels beneath, and my sensors confirmed that there were natural tunnels down there. Sound, air movement, pressure, gravity and my optical sensors were still working at short range, but any attempt to engage anything else resulted in acute pain. Even trying to find the source of the scrambler they were using would take time.

The three storey building we approached didn't have any windows, and there was no one around. When we peeked around it, we were disappointed. There was a door there, but no sign that anyone had been on patrol. "We're not going to follow guards into the building," I said.

"We expected that. Who would patrol on foot out here?" he asked.

It was obviously rhetorical, but I snickered and looked around the corner carefully. Even when you think you're practically invisible and there are sensor jammers operating, it still pays to be careful. That moment proved it, because there were two men walking down a small shuttle's ramp towards the nearest airlock only twenty-five or so metres away.

One was a soldier in a full suit of green armour made of flexible, layered thin plates. He was carrying a standard Order of Eden foot soldier rifle. They were short, cheap to make, easy enough to maintain, but terrible in corridor combat. The man walking beside him was in a simple grey environment suit. The fitted garment had a sun emblem on the shoulder with three pips around it. I could see his big grin through the faceplate. "What kind of officer uses a grey uniform with a sun on his shoulder?" I asked Lat after quickly retreating.

"What? There are people out here? That's not an officer, it's a cadet. How many pips?" he asked.

"Three," I replied.

"He'll graduate and become a Junior Lieutenant," he replied.

"He has an escort, we're following them in now," I told him, moving out around the building.

Lat was right behind me. The excitement of having a way inside, and at the possibility of getting caught any second, even if remote, made me feel every aspect of the moment. This was probably what Lat wanted, a chance to encounter and thwart the Order, but I didn't expect such a presence there. Ryden was my target, and I'd already done so much damage to their organisation that the Order used their debt as leverage and bought them out. The presence of a cadet and an Order soldier confirmed that I wasn't investigating a smaller corporation anymore, but an arm of the Order of Eden.

We stepped into place behind the soldier and cadet. The airlock opened. It was so large that ten people could have fit in there with us. The door slid and latched closed behind us and the air started cycling. Artificial gravity took hold right away and its embrace was welcome, comforting. Adjusting to it was easier without having a digital and biological side working to cooperate.

Something else was different too. Standing in that airlock with two members of the Order tested my patience. An unwanted vision played in my head. In it I got behind the soldier, gripped the bottom lip of his helmet and pulled at it until the metal bent, the faceplate warped, and finally split so I could reach in and bash his head in. I was barely aware that I was centimetres away from the soldier.

It was shocking, and I was lucky that there was time for me to calm down as a decontamination spray hit us from all sides. If there were advanced scanners in the room, both of us would have been caught. We were lucky that there weren't more advanced scanners inside the airlock. Hot air dried all four of us after the decontamination fluid finished coating everything and everyone inside the vestibule.

The soldier took his helmet off as soon as it was finished, and the cadet deactivated his headpiece. "...soon. My class wasn't surprised I was sent to one of the frontiers. I've always been ahead."

"Well, the Edwyn Cluster isn't boring, that's for sure," the soldier said.

"Are most of the third party operations like this?" the cadet asked.

"What? On shitty little moons that hate life? No, this is a special case. Weren't you briefed?" the soldier asked.

The inner doors opened and I followed the pair. Lat did the same, and we kept our distance. The spotless corridors were somber shades of brown and bronze. The cadet replied without taking offence. "Of course I was, basically. I was told I'd be seeing some biotech developed in another galaxy. I've seen that in museums on Edrick. I'm more interested in meeting experienced soldiers. What can you tell me that I probably wasn't taught at the Academy?"

We followed them down the corridor, looking for any indication of what was actually going on as we listened to the soldier's response. "You know, something happened last week. August, this guy you'll meet later, kind of the joker of our unit, loaned his helmet to Eddie because good old Ed didn't want to explain that he couldn't find his. So, everything's good for a couple of days, then August comes down with this brutal case of Rodus Pink Eye. Ever get so gummed up that you wish your eyes could sneeze?" he asked the cadet, pointing to his eye.

The cadet laughed and shook his head. "No, that's ridiculous."

"Well, August's eye sockets were so clogged up that he did. I mean, he really did, it was brutal, and Eddie broke out less than a day later. Funny thing about Rodus Pink Eye, it spreads by touch, any touch, lives on surfaces for days. By the middle of the next day, half the squad was down with it, and it's antibiotic resistant, so they had to make a drug to get it gone. You think the Ryden folks could afford that kind of medical tech? No, a little corp like that could control the infection, but we had to get that shuttle to deliver an advanced synthesiser thing to wipe it out completely. I don't know what they would have done if they weren't bought by the Order outright."

"So, I should thank August for making that trip necessary, otherwise I wouldn't have gotten here," the cadet said.

"Well, sure. He's been busted down to custodial crew, so we'll spot him cleaning up somewhere around here. The rest of the squad pulled out without him now that we're getting ready to move on. I bet he'll be one of the last buggers here, working right along side the sanitation bots, sterilising the whole place," the soldier said with a tsk.

"As long as he learns his lesson," the cadet said.

"Him and everyone in charge. You catch your people swapping helmets, you give 'em hell. I mean shave their heads, make 'em give each other eye washes, slap 'em upside the head. If August was on my squad, he'd be on latrine duty for a year. One little thing can bung up the whole squad," the soldier said.

"That's definitely not something they teach us at the academy. I mean, we get the talks on lethal infections, how to prevent cross-species contamination, and all that, but I guess they skip the non-lethal stuff," the cadet said.

"Don't know why. I've seen all kinds of shit out here. You know the dogs run in packs in some parts of Rodus? One minute you're in casual dress enjoying the night life, the next you're in the wrong dark alley getting torn apart by a dozen mongrels. I've got stories," the soldier said, shaking his head.

"I'm all ears," the cadet laughed as they passed through a white door.

My suit's olfactory sensors picked up unusual particles. We didn't follow them in, the door wasn't open long enough. The DNA in the particles didn't match anything I'd seen or in my digital storage. I used several proxies to connect to the Stellarnet and was relieved to get in touch with a general search interface. I uploaded the sequence. The results came back from Leon's office after a few seconds.

"Whatever you sent in just got flagged by Haven Sciences," he said through my Haven Node. Our communication took place inside my digital system, it was as well hidden as I could manage. "Their software is investigating."

"I need to know how high priority this is. There's a locked door between me and the room that came from," I replied.

"The sample has a ninety-eight percent nucleotide similarity with the Edxi Prime Species. Can you see what it came from?" Leon asked.

"No. It was just an airborne sample. What is it?" I asked.

"It's not on record. Keep investigating," Leon said.

The door opened again and I managed to see through that time. The other side was an observation room with scrambled holographic displays filling the centre of the room. These were set so only authorised personnel could see the details. There were several Ryden employees in blue and red there, one woman was saying; "...to go in two hours. Finish loading up. This is a gestate under way situation, the timetable is not flexible."

The cadet and his pet soldier passed into the hallway. The disappointment on the younger man's face told me that he couldn't see what was going on either. "I was sent here to see how your operation works, so I have clearance!"

"Get out, kid!" a man in a red containment suit shouted after him.

"Maybe you'll understand who's in charge when my superiors hear about this. Oh, no, I'll just wait two weeks for my graduation. Then I'll dock and demote you so hard that you'll have to beg me for a weekly allowance!" Half of his threat was shouted at a closed door.

He whirled away and asked his soldier companion; "Is there anything else to see here?"

"We're just here in case the worst happens, and they won't even tell me what that means. I'm under orders to finish showing you around the facility. I think you'll like the last spot. There's a lake of acid under this place. We toss garbage into it when we're off duty," he replied.

"I would like to see what's actually happening here," the cadet whispered.

"You'll see something, that's for sure. Ever try to hide all your stuff on moving day?" the soldier asked.

"Oh. You have a point. Lead the way," the cadet replied.

Lat was about to follow. "Stop."

He did, then moved to one side of the hall. "All right, not moving."

"The Edxi, or something from their galaxy, probably their solar system is here. We need to find out what," I said. He knew almost as well as I did that they were the most deadly invasive species in human history. As far as anyone who had the misfortune of having an encounter with one, they were still on a revenge trip to eradicate humanity because we had the nerve to experiment on a few of them. To say that it was an overreaction was an understatement, and the Edxi are absolutely dangerous. They were instrumental in taking the Haven System over for the Order of Eden. That is, until the new founders took it back.

No one knew exactly where the Edxi were hiding, but most people guessed that they were regrouping, preparing for a bigger assault on the Edwyn Cluster and the rest of the Milky Way. Knowing that humans of any kind were messing with them at all frustrated me so much that I had to take a minute to clear my head before I could think of anything useful to do. "Leon told me to keep looking around. Maybe this will get the Fleet's attention."

"What if it's another Lidden situation? They want to help but don't have the people?" Lat asked.

"Then we'll do what we can and get the hell out of here. It sounds like they're in a hurry to get out of here. If all else fails, we'll sneak aboard one of their ships and wait until they hit open space," I replied, forming the frame of the plan as it was spoken.

"Then take it like real pirates." Lat sounded pleased, even eager.

CHAPTER TWENTY-SEVEN

Investigating the Refuge

As Lat and I moved down the hallway, Leon contacted me right through my Haven Node. I didn't speak to him aloud, routing his communication to the virtual space within my internal computer instead. He would see my head and shoulders in a crimson military vacsuit. I was seeing him as he was, in the back of an armoured personnel shuttle. "Sciences got back to me and their initial assessment of the DNA sample is alarming. It's most likely from the Edxi home world, but extrapolation suggests it's some kind of parasite. That's just the preliminary results from their software, real people are studying it further."

His focus wasn't where I wanted it to be. "There are over ten thousand people here, or at least, there should be. I'm going to get a closer look, find out what they're doing with the bodies."

"If you can get a better sample, or whatever shed this DNA, I can promise you a huge payday. If it were a Fleet mission, we would get what we could in as short a time as possible and get out. That's what I'm recommending to you. Don't get caught. There aren't supposed to be Order soldiers there, but from what you sent it looks like they're using Ryden as a cover. Not everyone keeps up with who the Order buys or which organisations are working with them, so it's a good gambit," he told me.

"That's old intelligence. What else can you tell me?" I asked.

"Fair enough, helpful info only. We've been able to determine that the Regulator is in the area and the CEO of the Ryden Corporation, Lene Thak, is now serving as a Captain in the Order. My guess is that they're keeping her corp together so she can run it for them. If you do a lot of damage here it's likely that the highest ranking commanders in the Edwyn Cluster will hear about it. I suggest you take my advice to get samples and get out quietly seriously," he said.

Lat and I had to step to the side as a group of four technicians with Marigold Refuge written on their blue shirts walked off the lift then down the hallway. "...when the place is empty?" a man with sharp features asked.

The woman in the lead, who also looked like she'd had cosmetic alterations because of her sculpted cheekbones and slender jawline. "I don't know where they'll send me, but I'll go just about anywhere for the salary bump they're promising."

"You're getting a pay bump? I thought I was lucky to be on the next ship out," a fellow behind her grumbled. "There's nothing left to do here."

Lat and I moved into the lift before the door could close. "Where now?" he asked.

"One minute, I'm talking to Leon," I told him.

"Tell them we don't need another Lidden." It was the most bitterness I'd seen from him. I'd seen him angry, frustrated, even a little depressed, but never bitter.

"Sorry, I was picking up more information from some employees here," I told Leon. "The facility is almost empty, from what they're saying. So, Haven Sciences wants a sample. I'll get them one. I don't plan on staying for more than two hours."

"Hours? Faster would be better," Leon replied.

Okay, so I knew I might be a little over my head, but being told so kinda pissed me off. "I'm not going to let this become another situation where I depend on someone else to save these people."

"This isn't going to be another Lidden, but be aware that we're marshalling a defence here, so that makes two causes calling for help from Haven Fleet. There are a lot more, so don't be surprised if neither of us get immediate attention. Right now, the evidence matters most. If we miss this opportunity to get involved with whatever's going on there, the Fleet will have a better plan to address the results because of whatever you collect," he replied.

While my mind's eye was focused on what he was saying, I looked at Lat's outline in my faceplate. There was nothing to see optically, he was perfectly hidden, but our link showed me where he was, and what he was doing. "I'm doing this my way. I don't have to hold back, so I won't. Don't contact me unless there's help coming."

With the call over, I pointed up. "We're using the elevator shaft," I told Lat, who immediately stepped into the middle of the lift car and cupped his hands.

I was on his shoulders a moment later, pushing the emergency hatch in the ceiling open and crawling in. He jumped up after me and we were in the two car elevator shaft. "Where from here? Up? Down?" he asked as we slipped into a maintenance space that ran parallel to the shaft. It was so good to have a fully functional vacsuit that could cling to practically any solid surface. "I can't catch a good wireless signal, the scramblers are messing them up. Leon said we should get out as fast as we can, he just wants evidence."

"So that takes us where?" Lat asked.

"There's a heavily armoured ship docked to this structure at the top level. That's where we're going first."

"I saw that, good." Lat replied.

We waited for an elevator car to speed past us before leaping up and across the shaft. Thanks to my android frame, I got there in four jumps. Lat did it in five thanks to the synthetic muscle built into his suit, I was more than a little impressed by his unintentional tree frog impression. "Hey, how are you doing down there?" Mimi asked.

"Good, we found a goal," I replied.

"That's nice. Hey, you were looking for the Regulator, right?" she asked.

"I was," I replied.

"Well, it moved into synchronous orbit right over your location. That's the good news? Maybe? The bad news is that it launched six of those gunships." She avoided trying to say 'typhoon' since there was some kind of mental or oral block that made it practically impossible.

It was bad news anyway. "You mean Typhoons?"

"Yup, that kind. A couple of them are moving away, Manny thinks they're looking for us, but it'll take them a while to find the ship, and Duncan's pretty sure we can take two on. Can you hurry up so we don't have to?" Mimi asked.

"Will do," I replied as I slipped into the vertical maintenance passage so an elevator car could get to the top floor. The muffled murmuring of people inside faded as they left. The car stayed in place so I climbed up and quietly got on top of it. As soon as I saw Lat was right behind me, I opened the access hatch and dropped inside. Lat did the same and made himself as small as possible against the wall.

"Okay," Mimi said, still sounding uncertain. "Rogue, do you think we can take two Ty... Ty... gunships on?"

"The Daring Dream's shields outclass them, our Ripshocks fire twice as fast, and you're almost as manoeuvrable, so you'll be fine," I replied.

"Okay, but what about picking you up? We can't fight past the Regulator. It's an armed frigate," Mimi whispered.

"We'll find a ride and meet you out there," I told her. "I have work to do, but don't worry. I've done this kind of thing before."

"Okay, good," Mimi replied. "I'll leave you alone for now."

The elevator doors opened, I managed to leave right before a man in a thick blue containment suit walked into the elevator along with three others. They all had Ryden Corporation written on the front and back. Lat had to wait until everyone was inside before he jumped out. "Hey," the largest of them said, looking behind him as he felt someone brush past.

"What? I'm just standing here," said the first employee he looked at.

"Something just went past me," said the larger fellow.

"No one here but us knuckle draggers," another said.

"Evacuation duty getting to you?" asked a man from behind.

"It's just too creepy, you know?" I heard the large one in the lead say as the elevator doors closed.

There was a group of Order of Eden guards standing there in containment armour just like the plate suit I'd seen the soldier wearing downstairs. The metal was unevenly polished, suggesting that these had spent some time in the rain. "We're going for the ship, but I want to know what's going on. I'm putting another call out to the Legion, hitting the whole tree, by the way," I said to Lat using our laser link.

"Tree?" Lat asked as he followed me down the hallway.

"Oh, the calling tree they use. Apparently they're making calling me back a priority. I had no idea," I told him.

"Well, that's something." He watched me stop in the middle of a long corridor. "What are you looking for?"

"Anything I can plug into," I replied. "I need to know if there's a chance I can get through their security, find more evidence, find out how many people are still here."

"You know they'll probably detect your location," Lat said.

"Not if I use that," I said, pointing to a security sensor at the end of the hallway. I had tricks that most soldiers only dreamt of.

I climbed the wall and affixed myself to the ceiling beside the sensor. "Stand guard. This could go very wrong," I said.

"Ready," Lat said, crouching and pointing his rifle at the Order guards at the far end of the corridor. "I'm also wishing I brought more guns. Remind me next time."

For the first time since I was on Rodus, I activated the fabrication systems in my chest and produced half an ounce of nanobots. They flowed through my circulatory system until they reached my fingers. My suit let them through a tiny crack, and they became a string, each microscopic bot staying in physical contact with the one behind it. The rest of the nanobots widened the imperceptible crack surrounding the sensor. I could see basic shapes using the senses of the lead nanobots, and guided them to the sensor's circuitry. After my nanobots felt around for a moment, I found a good connection to the security system. My tiny friends became wires then, and I used them to communicate with the Refuge. "I'm in."

"Excellent. I have a calf cramp," Lat said.

"Are you okay?" I asked, looking where his biometric data

should be in my faceplate display, and not finding it. Even that was being jammed.

"The suit's working it out. I really need to drink more water," he replied. "These vacsuits are amazing, by the way."

"I know, every spacer should have one. I'm going to connect to their security system." The sensor's connection was hard wired to the Refuge's internal security system, and there was nothing in my way as I piggybacked on it. I nibbled at the data first, checking through directories, reviewing small text logs, watching for guardian programs and other security measures. It turns out that the Order bought the Marigold Refuge five weeks before. The real activity started when Supplicant Five arrived.

Four other Ryden ships had repeatedly docked, loaded medical maintenance pods with humans inside aboard and left quickly. Where they went, I couldn't tell. Supplicant Five had made eight trips, this would be its ninth. Using employee logs, I could see that there were nineteen human employees on the Refuge. Every one of them was on duty, and the schedule showed that most of them were working on sanitising the complex.

Seeing that there was no sign that my presence in the system had been detected, I dug deeper, into security footage. My mind worked faster, as though I had the speed of my old digi-brain, only it was all biological. Whatever I saw, I transferred to my computer and uploaded to the Legion, to Haven Fleet, and to everyone Alice or I knew in either organisation. Finally, I found something that the Order would hide jealously. The main reason for the sensor and communications scrambling fields.

There were some kind of experiments going on, and it had a brutal cost. Optical security systems were able to see through the scramblers just well enough, and I watched several half garbled recordings at once. The Refuge workers worked long fifteen hour shifts along side Order of Eden medical technicians. They opened pods, turned the occupants onto their chests, made sure that the life sustaining tubes and manipulators were still in place and woke the humans up. As soon as they were roused, they placed a transparent cup onto the bases of their heads and waited. Through the side of the container they watched as something grey and dark green affixed itself to the slowly waking man or woman. Screaming, flailing, sometimes loud, anguished weeping followed. The one that really got to me was a thin, young looking man who fought his restraints with his entire body, trying to flail and turn over. "What's that? Ah! It's cutting me! Biting! Stop! Stop! It's scraping bone!" The rest of his objections were incoherent screams until he went limp.

"Brain death. Disposal!" shouted the Order supervisor in a dark green containment suit. His name was Lev Fisa, and he was among the four men who just took the elevator.

Other victims woke up innocently asking; "Where are my friends?" or "Why are you pulling us out?" or worse; "Am I okay?"

The virtual worlds they lived in had been emptying without explanation for weeks as the occupants woke to the horror of uncaring hands restraining them. I couldn't imagine what it must have been like to be plucked out of their fantasy worlds and implanted with some kind of Edxi parasite.

Through all that footage I was able to put together a clear three dimensional image of the thing. It was shimmering grey and dark green, shaped roughly like a starfish with four arms instead of five. There was a fibrous tongue between two hard, thick fangs. When it latched onto someone, the whole body flexed and twitched as it dug in, breaking through the base of the skull while their victim was awake. The host had to be conscious during the process, I heard several technicians say.

About one in ten humans survived the process. and they all lay still afterwards, eyes open in some kind of stupor.

I didn't notice what my body was doing as I reviewed the footage, used my mental connection to the servers to pillage every bit of data I could find and send it all along. My lips were curled, teeth clenched, and tears flowed. "No. We're too late. They've emptied this place, there are only two shipments left."

The last piece of data I scraped was from the external sensors. Bins of bodies were pushed outside where the harsh environment and sulphuric acid rain got rid of them. We would have seen it ourselves if we got there earlier. "Rogue?" Mimi asked through our Haven Node connection. "We're in trouble. There are four gunships now, and they've detected us. We're flying around a moon."

The fear in her voice made me take everything Ryden was doing even more personally, and I hated myself for putting Mimi and my crew at risk. My mind raced as I struggled to look through the Refuge's exterior computer systems. The digital security programs were trying to block me from accessing essential controls, but I was already in control, so their improvised measures weren't enough to stop me from getting control of some serious firepower.

It was like I was on the Overlord II all over again, only I wasn't software running from one system to the next, I was stretching thousands of fingers out to computers inside the system, assuming control as though the Refuge was an extension of my nervous system. "Deleted." I said as I cut the main guardian program off and ordered the crystalline drive it called home to erase itself. Their servers weren't set up to defend themselves against an attack coming from inside their own security hardware.

There was a temporary sensor array outside of the scrambling field so the Refuge's tactical systems could see objects in orbit. I took a moment to appreciate Manny's skills, since his low, controlled course kept them from noticing the Daring Dream when it dropped us off. Using the Refuge's tactical systems, I looked for the Daring Dream's pursuers. They were too far away for anything I did to be effective. They would have too much time to dodge whatever I threw at them. I sighted the Regulator instead. "Tell Manny to fly towards Ryden's main frigate, the Regulator. I can help you from here, but I don't know for how long."

"He heard that, he's going really fast," Mimi replied.

I put my own security measures around the systems I had control of, hoping that would buy me more time in the system. I wanted every scrap of data they had and to use Ryden's new venture against them.

"I'm accessing the defence systems, get ready to run," I told Lat using our laser link, as I warmed up every weapon the Marigold Refuge had.

"Where are we running?" Lat asked.

"To the nearest ship," I sent a route to his tactical system.

The humans didn't know I'd taken over yet. I activated the surface to orbit cannons built into the Refuge and pointed them all at the Regulator. There were three hundred small particle beams bundled in six pods outside. They turned and started drawing so much power that the lights flickered as their capacitor banks charged. I sent a priority message from the Refuge to the Regulator. "The Order bought a place filled with people who only wanted to hide from the galaxy and you helped them use them, murder them. Now you'll burn."

Five seconds after I got the notification that someone opened the message, I fired, cutting at the Regulator's energy shields with three hundred lines of perfect light. These weapons were made to fend off raiders in orbit, and in the air despite the thick atmosphere. The Regulator's luck wasn't great just then, because the clouds had cleared up.

When the shields protecting the main reactor in the middle of the ship failed, I burned a pinpoint through the hull, finally puncturing the large fusion chamber inside. Several of my borrowed beam emitters were close to overheating, so I gave them a break, pausing for three long seconds before reactivating them and cutting through all three of the Regulator's main thrusters.

"Rogue! The gunships are leaving us alone!" Mimi cheered. "Wait, they're going down to the Refuge."

"That's all right," I replied, targeting the nearest Typhoon, high in orbit, and fired. There was a half second burst of powerful beams, then the whole system went dead. Someone cut the power to the Marigold Retreat's defence systems.

"Rogue, something's happening," Lat said, drawing my attention down the hall.

Two Ryden soldiers stopped at the far end of the hallway. One was raising a hand scanner. Someone figured out where the system intrusion was coming from. "Shoot them," I said.

Lat opened fire on the armoured soldiers, starting with the one scanning the hallway. The broad scan pulse his device sent out revealed us with powerful sonic waves and pinpoint blasts of air. Lat's rounds still caught them by surprise, and his armour piercing bullets chewed their plate armour up quickly, putting them both down.

I ordered every airlock and interior door to open before I disconnected from the system and dropped to the deck. "They know where we are, run!"

"More problems coming up here, the Order has a big ship and fighters," Mimi said. "They're blocking us from jumping with an indiction field. Wait, sorry, Manny says it's an 'interdiction' field."

"Tell him to find cover, use anything you have to. We're on our way out, don't worry about picking us up," I told her.

"He's doing that, we're flying down to Vercosa, he says it's our best chance!" Mimi said.

Alarms blared and the lighting turned red as the freezing, caustic air from the planet surface rushed in, killing anyone who wasn't in a suit, exposing everything. Lat struggled to keep up with me as we rushed down the hallway towards Supplicant Five's airlock.

"What about the customers still connected to the system?" Lat asked.

"The Order got them. The last of them are in the ship we'll be taking," I replied. "Ryden let themselves become Order puppets. Kill everyone who raises a weapon."

CHAPTER TWENTY-EIGHT

The Cargo

The environmental systems in the Marigold Refuge tried to outdo the rush of inhospitable air and dust from the moon's surface, creating a whirling windstorm throughout the halls. I shouldn't have been surprised that Lat kept up with me as we ran through the corridors. I wasn't running full tilt, that wouldn't have been wise since visibility was down to a few metres and my other senses weren't doing much better thanks to the noise, interference from static from the sand and the sensor scramblers. I didn't see any sign of that system in the Refuge's computers, so I guessed the sensor scrambler was on a ship nearby.

Our stealth systems were useless, they couldn't overcome the interference of our environment, but we got through two long corridors, running right past Ryden employees in suits that were barely holding up against the friction of the indoor sandstorm.

Duncan was in my ear then. "We've put three Typhoons

down, keeping our shields up, but it's getting thick out here. Two Order Marauders with fighters launching off their hulls. They've got interdiction set up, no jumping for thirty million klicks. Mimi's trying all our friends in the Rose System."

"Has she reached anyone?" I asked.

"Nay," Duncan replied.

When I came around the next corner I was relieved that I was running ahead of Lat because there were four Ryden soldiers in full plate armour waiting for someone to try to get past. They opened fire, filling the corridor with armour piercing rounds. I took over twenty rounds in the torso and thighs before I activated the metre and a half tall, one metre wide energy shield on my left bracer. They punctured my suit, and I discovered how hard it was to ignore the anguish as my raw flesh was touched by the caustic, infiltrating cold atmosphere for a second. My wounds healed, and my skin adjusted to a formulation that wouldn't react with the atmosphere. The suit re-sealed over top, proving its resilience as the layers healed themselves and closed the holes.

Ignoring the pain took effort, and I wouldn't forget it. The entrance to the Supplicant Five was at the far end of that hallway, and in the seconds I spent there, I could see technicians rushing towards it.

I wanted to press on, but those guards tested my shield to near failure before I retreated around the corner. Lat tossed a pair of fragmentation grenades around the corner and leaned back as they went off with percussive pops. "They were really ready," Lat said.

Losing a step, seeing our goal and falling short brought waves of frustration. "Explosive rounds. Get ready." I tapped the bottom of my pack. It opened just enough to drop four cylindrical fragmentation grenades into my hand.

"Getting set," Lat said.

I owed Duncan a response, so I spoke to him through our connection to the Daring Dream. "We're finding our own ride out. Get out of there as fast as you can."

"Aye, on it, tryin'! That field's expanding, got more Order ships coming," I could hear the rapid fire of his ripshocks in the background as he replied. "What about you?"

"We're getting a ride," I replied. The chaos in the hallways was calming quickly. Someone was shutting exterior doors in that section and the environmental system was winning.

Lat held four grenades between the fingers of his left hand and brandished his rifle in his right. I drew my sidearm, armed my grenades and said; "Go."

The guards were not ready for what happened next. We each threw grenades at their feet and I brought my shield up. It had managed to recharge to half, which was enough to reduce the sudden air pressure as all eight of our explosives went off. That Order cadet was one of an unlucky group of six people who were on their way to the Supplicant Five's airlock behind the guards.

The four armoured Ryden troops were hit by the full force of five grenades. Two soldiers who were on their way into the airlock were still on their feet, their armour heavily damaged. They were stunned, momentarily dazed. One looked down and saw arterial blood pumping from his arm and grasped it. "Rebels, they're..."

I sent two bursts through the crack in his faceplate before he could finish. Lat rattled explosive rounds at the other surviving soldier, putting him down even faster.

"Run," I said. We pressed forward through the damaged hallway and the gore in front of the airlock, making it through the outer doors. I caught a glimpse of the cadet, who was staring off into space with dead eyes. "The Order is down one promising asshole."

Lat laughed as I spun on my heel and closed the outer airlock door behind us. Laying my hand on the interface, I was able to connect to it directly without thinking about it. That was easy, so was locking the outer hatch, it seemed like security clearance wasn't required for that command. The guardian program built into the ship computer stopped me cold with a set of firewalls that would take me a lot longer to crack when I tried to intrude deeper. Ryden had installed its own digital security, augmenting the already tough Order software.

"What's happening back there?" came a voice from an emitter overhead.

The inner airlock door was locked and as heavily armoured as the outer hull, nearly half a metre thick. We were barely aboard another Order ship that was built for war, I expected that it would be difficult to take, but we were so close. There was a slender transparisteel window in the outer door and I could see one of the people we'd caught on their way into the airlock moving. Their skin was re-sealing, legs starting to rebuild themselves from the bone outward, and that face was unmistakeable. "Lat, shift your suit to look like that."

"A containment suit?" he asked as he looked over my shoulder. Then he saw what I did. "That's a framework soldier. He's made using my template."

"Exactly," I said.

He only nodded as he dropped his pack, shifted his suit and then removed his helmet. "All right, not a bad plan."

"Airlock Two, respond. I see two shapes down there, and you're moving, but I'm not opening up until I know you're with us," said a male voice from somewhere inside the ship.

My mind raced, I had to assume we were headed into an

Order of Eden military ship. There were regenerating framework soldiers on the base, so it only made sense that the ship
they were using to transport the last of their experiments would
be just as secure.

Another problem with Order ships is that they are often
equipped with sensors tuned to specifically defeat the stealth
systems in our suits. Lat would be able to pass as a framework
soldier, but I didn't want to use the materials to shape shift into
one myself because I was expecting a fight, I'd need them to
recover if I got into trouble. Then I got an idea. The cadet was
slimmer than me, but around the same height, and his head was
actually a little smaller, so I took his image on, transforming as I
adjusted my suit to look like his. There was a little extra mass for
me to account for, so I spread it around. The end result was the
general shape of the cadet, only a little thicker everywhere but
the face. Hoping no one would notice, I detached my pack and
stuffed my weapon inside so it would be easy to grab. "All right,
let's try this."

"So, am I doing the talking, or..." Lat looked at me then and
nearly burst out laughing.

"Maybe I'll do it," I said, changing my voice to match the
cadet's. "There we go." It was all wrong in my ears.

The airlock was a little old fashioned, made for durability
more than convenience. It only took us a moment to find the
keypad for the inner doors and push the cover aside. I pressed
the intercom key and looked into the little camera above it. "Let
us in! The intruders are still running around out there, but we
managed to get their backpacks and get away!"

"Jeremy? You made it, boy?" came the response from the
bridge.

"Barely. There are rebels on the base. I think they're trying
to get in," I replied.

"It's all right, Son. We're opening the doors, head for the forward section of the ship right away. We're leaving," the man on the other end said.

The inner doors opened and we entered a cargo hold filled with long term human maintenance pods. They were like stasis pods, but were made to take care of people while they spent months, or even years fully connected to computer systems. There were hundreds of them. The scan scramblers weren't penetrating the hull of the ship, so I was able to pick up the occupants' biological readings as we passed the neatly shelved and secured stacks.

Many of them were cracked open by the oddly positioned people inside. The readings were strange, I still wish I didn't pay attention to them.

One that's hard to forget looked restful, but their shape was barely human as her legs and arms were drawn up and over her torso. Her bones were slowly breaking up, shifting to create new, more orderly shapes. Another pod dweller was fully awake, adrenaline spiking as his head was unnaturally being drawn down, his spine twisting as the alien parasite forced his body into a new form.

The last one I paid attention to confirmed my suspicions about what my scanners were picking up. His ribs were being turned into a grid. The parasite was directing his body to draw on the resources in his legs and arms as delicate, new iron rich bones were forming around two sacs. There was just enough shape to them for me to recognise them. Mergillians have an organ in the top of their skulls that can detect magnetic and gravitational forces, it makes them incredible space farers. What I was seeing was the early formation of organic sensors. A quick scan of several more pods confirmed it. The people inside had varying levels of brain activity, but the parasites were relentless in transforming their hosts. "Those parasites are using the bodies to create systems," I whispered to Lat.

"Bio mechanical drones?" Lat asked.

"No. Some kind of system packages. That one is becoming a sensor suite," I nodded at a pod as we passed it.

Lat considered that as we kept walking. "Why?"

That was one of those frustrating questions that would take hours to answer, and it didn't help that I didn't have all the facts. Everything I sensed was making me want to tear the whole ship apart, which didn't help me keep a clear head. "I don't know. What matters right now is getting them help."

That was a lie. The scans results I saw made it look unlikely that anyone could be saved. We'd come too late, and I wanted to stand there and scream. The best I could do was turn that into determination, and I did my best.

We heard crying ahead and saw a young man in a Ryden containment suit hiding at the end of a row of pods. Two of his co-workers were kneeling down in front of him. "They said we have to get to habitation, you can't stay here."

"I'm not going anywhere! This is all wrong. It's not worth the pay. The company said we were being trained to install new tech, but this..." he stopped to sob before continuing. "Then we're attacked? We just saw half our team get blown up!"

"Shoot him," said a dispassionate voice. We heard two shots an instant later.

Lat and I started walking faster, I wanted to get out of the cargo hold before that group. The more my scanners passively caught the work of those parasites, the more I was convinced that human beings were being transformed into ship components. There were three who were almost finished being converted into some kind of environment processing systems, it seemed like the parasites were able to adapt the human body to that service faster than the others.

The sound of the engines roaring, and my gravimeter told me that the ship was taking off. That was a relief, at least something was going our way. Duncan's voice was back in my ear then. "We've got one corvette and a bunch of fighters on us, out of missiles, on the run. That interdiction system still has us pinned, one shield generator is down, the backup isn't going to keep up."

There was no way I was going to let my crew get slagged while Lat and I were slowly working our way to the bridge of that ship. "We're hurrying," I replied aloud without thinking.

"We are?" Lat asked.

"We are. Follow my lead, be ready to start shooting," I told him.

We didn't take the large doors leading further into the ship, but quickly walked to another, smaller entrance. It opened for us, and we came face to face with a pair of Ryden guards in full armour. "We've been ordered to the bridge. Get us there, quickly," I said, pointing to the Order of Eden emblem on my chest.

The pair regarded me with no respect whatsoever. They were familiar enough with the Order to know that I was only a cadet, even if my expression was deeply sour and I carried myself like an officer. "Let us through or you'll have to deal with my father," I said, finding it unsettling how easy it was to imitate the brat.

That sold it. The guards let us through and we started running towards the bridge as soon as they were out of sight.

CHAPTER TWENTY-NINE

Supplicant Five

I was like a bomb ready to go off, my anger rising as I was aware that my ship and crew were in trouble and made my way through the ship as quickly as I could without losing Lat along the way. This was an Order ship with young order soldiers and specialists. Passing through the thirty person galley, I saw a group of nine people in unsealed containment suits gathering snacks and drinks from dispensers. "...can't believe we got through all those pod dreamers."

"Right? I mean, cleanup would have been a bitch too, I'm kinda glad the environmental systems blew out so we had to leave early. The payday is coming a week early and it's huge," said a woman as she opened a steaming turnover.

"Hey, where ya going cadet?" asked one man who didn't look any older than Jeremy.

We were close enough to the exit that we didn't have to stop. "Running like his shoes are on fire," another said.

Their fading laughter made me grind my teeth. There were hundreds of humans in the cargo hold undergoing some kind of brutal transformation. All they wanted was to escape from the universe, but they were kidnapped instead, and these assholes were laughing. I wanted to open fire, remove them from the galaxy, but didn't give in. There was a much greater goal ahead.

The Supplicant Five was a simple ship, with plenty of armoured cargo space at the rear, an engineering level that Lat and I skipped because we passed through habitation one level up instead. We moved along the port side corridors and passed a number of offices, a small meeting room that, unlike the offices had a wide open door, and finally a mustering room.

The layout of the ship didn't make sense to me on the way there. If this was a secure cargo vessel, then why were there five offices? Only one was set aside for the captain, the rest were labelled with thirty digit numbers. There was a meeting space that was set up like a high end board room too. In most cargo ships the galley served that purpose, so that was just a waste of space.

When we arrived at a pair of secure doors marked MUSTERING ROOM, I stopped. It was scan shielded. I had no idea what was on the other side. "Do we arm up, or play this out?" I asked myself as much as Lat.

"There are people on the other side?" Lat asked.

"I don't know, but I've been burned by rushing through doors before, I'm trying to break the habit," I grumbled. It sounded strange in Jeremy's voice.

"This worked. We're getting through the ship," Lat replied.

He was right. The few people we met in the hallways didn't question a cadet rushing forward with a framework soldier who was carrying backpacks. They actually got out of the way. They seemed too preoccupied with whatever they were doing to stop us and ask questions when we looked like we might belong there. "You're right, hopefully this is empty."

We stepped up to the doors and they parted. I'd never seen what the Order called a mustering room, so when we saw a large reinforced airlock to the left and a large open space that was designed for troops to gather before a boarding action, I wished I had more time to explore. There was a transparent metal wall with two doors built into it. The lockers were closed and the weapon racks were mostly empty, and I would have admired the pull-down shelving marked with different types of ammunition and other equipment if I had time or was in the mood. "Where is everyone?" Lat asked as we stopped in our tracks.

I touched the nearest access panel and the ten centimetre by twenty centimetre screen lit up. "No surprise, this cadet's biometrics doesn't get him anywhere. The firewalls are up, it would take too long to hack in. Let's just hope the soldiers who work here are still on the moon."

We moved on through the next doorway and, seeing that there was no one in the exterior facing corridor, I broke into a run. My secondary senses detected that the Supplicant Five was still its our way out of the atmosphere through the transparisteel hull on our left. We were accelerating, and would be in orbit soon.

A guess at where the bridge was based on the overall design of the ship took us to the right then, and I ran into Lev Fisa. He was still in his containment suit, looking at a durable tablet. It didn't give any signals off like most wireless devices, suggesting that it wasn't connected to anything. He looked up at us and was startled at the sight. "Cadet? What are you doing here?"

The secure double hatch to the bridge was right behind him

to the left. Lat was speechless, which was perfect. I'd never heard a framework soldier make a wisecrack. I had milliseconds to decide what attitude I'd take with the Supervisor. "You mean you almost left one of the most promising officer cadets on that caustic moon and you're surprised I made it aboard in time?"

"That attitude won't get you very far on this ship. If you were allowed to know the purpose of our mission, then you'd understand why we had to leave so quickly. Now, why are you going towards the bridge? Your father is very busy," he scolded.

Pretending to be indignant when I wanted to blow the Project Supervisor's head off was difficult. I could see his eyes darting around, considering me, Lat, looking at the bags in his hands, and was eager for our encounter to go sideways. I was determined to play my part for a little longer, I could work my hate out later. "I found these bags on my way off the station. The saboteurs dropped them when they were running from our soldiers. I thought I should bring them to the bridge."

"That's a terrible idea, there could be a bomb in there, for all we know. They need to be scanned and inspected," Lev Fisa said, reaching for them.

"You're right," I said, reaching into one of the bags, pulling my sidearm out and putting it to Fisa's forehead. I can't tell you why, but my body and face re-took their default shapes. Even my hair returned.

"Issyrian shifter," he hissed.

"Worse," I told him as I turned him around and shoved him into the bridge doors. "Open it."

He raised his hands but shook his head. "I'll never cooperate."

Duncan's voice was coming through my command and control unit straight into my internal computer. I wasn't just hearing it, but feeling it. "There's more fighters chasing us round this rock than I can count, haven't a clue how many we've dropped. Manny's flat out trying to keep the edge, but they're firing like they've got unlimited ammo. Whatever you're at, get it bleedin' done."

"Do what you have to, I'm working on a solution up here," I told him using my internal voice. My external words weren't so reassuring as I spoke to the Project Manager. "I don't need you alive. I can put you out, become you. Then, when I have more time, I'll see if you're compatible with one of those parasites."

Judging from his widening eyes and the redness of his face, I think he believed me. "You can't do that. I'm the key to what was happening down there."

He reached for his weapon then, and I caught his wrist with android precision before crushing it as I stared at him. There was only an instant of pain before his eyes became glassy, unfocused. Yes, he was high on something that dismissed his pain and made him feel way too good.

That didn't mean I was out of options. Cruelty wouldn't get me anywhere, and even while I was fuming, I knew I'd regret the kind of damage I'd have to do to get him thinking about his own mortality again. Thank you, Alice. Your lives, your memories saved me from the kind of cruel acts that would have haunted me for years. They made me think harder, rise above the anger that would have taken me in the wrong direction.

I took Fisa's gun and stuffed it into my bag. "Take him. We're going to the cargo section," I told Lat. "Make him run."

Lat quickly affixed his pack on his back and took his short rifle in one hand. "Let's go. I'll have questions when she's done, asshole," he said as he grabbed Lev Fisa by the back of his collar, nearly hauling him off his feet as he pushed him in front of him at a jog. I was right along side, brandishing my sidearm.

"What's happening?" Lev Fisa asked as he struggled fruitlessly.

"We're going to the cargo bay. I'm going to destroy the pods. Since your soldiers are all on the moon, I'll only have to kill a few crew members," I replied.

"You can't destroy the gift!" he replied, finally getting one hand over his head and around Lat's wrist.

The synthetic muscle in Lat's suit gave him an iron grip, and he was at least twenty kilos heavier, so there was little chance that Fisa would pry himself loose. I was happy to find something the Supervisor cared about. "Give me access to the ship's systems! I won't destroy it, I need it to save my people."

"That's the same thing as destroying the gift!" the Supervisor replied.

"No, I'm a pirate, you idiot! What do you think I'll do with a cargo hold full of mutants someone wants? I'm going to ransom them! It's only money, and the Order has lots of it," I told him, letting some of my outrage and fear out at the same time to make it perfectly convincing.

"You'll... ransom? This is about money?" he asked, confused.

"Of course it's about money! We were about to loot the Refuge because no one heard from it for months, and saw that there was almost no one guarding this ship. We were going to hack it, kill the crew and take it, but didn't know we were stepping into this shitstorm! I mean, what the hell are you doing to those people? Wait, screw it, I don't want to know. I just want to get control and get paid. Whatever that is has got to be worth millions of plat. I'll cut you in for ten percent if you help us out," I said, making it sound half like a threat, half like a plea.

"I'll never help an Issyrian," he hissed.

"You're kidding, right? Issyrians can't become humans as convincingly as I did. There are always flaws in the hair, the eyes, fingerprints. Look," I said, putting my fingers in front of his eyes. "Perfect loops, just the right detail. I had a cybernetic shapeshifting weave and adaptive bladders installed. Sure, I can't feel through my skin, but I can look like anyone."

"So... you're human?" he asked.

"Are you too high to understand me? Yes, I'm human with a few big mods, and like most humans, I like money because I want to get the hell out of the Edwyn Cluster and buy myself a nice, cushy life," I replied.

"Us. Buy us a cushy life," Lat added.

You know what, I think his little improvisation sold it. Lev Fisa smiled. "Sixty percent. My access code is everything, and I'll be ending my career."

"Fifty, because I'm in a hurry," I told him.

"That's a lot," Lat added.

"Done," Fisa replied, grinning. "I'll open the bridge doors, but you'll have to get access to the systems yourself by taking the captain's seat before he can lock the ship down. Do you under-stand? I'll get you in touch with my superiors, they'll pay the ransom."

"Back to the bridge," I said, leading the way.

As we were turning around doors opened at the opposite end of the hall and four crew members with sidearms came through. I was pretty sure that gunfire in the halls would set alarms off, so I shouted; "I'll catch up!" as I raced down the hall towards them at full speed.

These crew members weren't in heavy armour, just Order of Eden vacsuit uniforms. Moving faster than any human could, I leapt at the last moment, caught one of their heads between my legs, crushed him to death and came down with another head in my hands. Even the woman's suit couldn't protect her skull from being crushed against the deck. I was up then, grabbing another, twisting his neck with both hands, squeezing until I felt something crunch. The last one was raising his weapon, so I grabbed his hand, stuck my finger behind the trigger and looked him in the eye.

"I surrender," he croaked.

Three were killed in one second, and my furious indignation was barely lessened, my fear at what my crew were going through was only rising. The standard crew vacsuits the Order of Eden wear are a little slower to react to combat, so I had about half a second to disable him. I used the medical unit in my right bracer to inject him with a powerful stasis drug before his hood could deploy. I ripped the medical support cartridge from the front of his suit before it could counter the medication.

"Oh, my God," I heard Lev Fisa say from behind me.

Lat hadn't followed orders for more than a few steps. Instead he was still holding the Supervisor, watching me work. I couldn't see Lat's eyes through his visor, but his bio signs were calmer than before, as though my violence gave him confidence. The Supervisor was actually crying. Whatever drugs were trying to calm him down were failing, and I took advantage of that. "You're going to get me on the bridge now."

"Yes," he replied.

I gestured for Lat to put him down and, to my surprise, the Supervisor had no problem keeping up with us as we ran the short way back to the bridge doors. He pressed his palm to the access control pad, it read his biometrics, including DNA, and the doors slide aside.

I spotted the captain's seat immediately and ran like I was trying to win an android sprinting event. I pushed him out of his seat. The headgear of his suit deployed and I could see he was starting to say something. I had to take a chance, he could have been putting the ship into lockdown, so I fired a burst of three armour piercing shots through his right eye.

I was in the captain's seat in the next second, laying hands on the controls built into the arms, connecting with the computer. He didn't have a chance to lock it, so I hurriedly entered my own credentials into the system as the ship's new commander. It would take someone else to complete the process.

The tactical officer to my left drew his weapon as he got to his feet. Lat fired two bursts, taking him out before I could.

Supervisor Fisa tried to grab Lat's sidearm, failed, and I half turned the captain's seat, ordered my weapon to switch to non-lethal web rounds and pointed it at him. "You're down to a forty percent cut! Confirm the commander transfer and you'll live to spend it!"

"All right, all right, I'll do it. Just... I'm a researcher, all this violence is..." he was interrupted by his own nervous laughter, so high that it was probably more the drug he was on than actual amusement.

He crawled to the captain's seat as Lat watched the other two on the bridge, the helmsman who barely paid attention as he kept flying the ship and sensor officer, who raised his hands and glared back at Lat.

I turned the touch panel built into the command seat towards Fisa and he pressed his good hand onto it until it said; COMMAND TRANSFER CONFIRMED.

That's when I pulled my capture belts, the trademark of a good New Zero bounty hunter, restrained his hands then quickly bound him to a seat near the door. "Keep quiet."

"What's happening? You can't do this, I'm your best way to get the right attention! I'll get you paid!" he objected.

"Good bounties are seen, not heard," Lat said.

"You're bounty hunters? Do you realise what you've stepped into? You'll..." he started.

I took aim. "I only need a record of your death, and I'm recording."

He was finally quiet, so I addressed the bridge crew. "I'm taking control of this ship. You have five seconds to turn on the Order and join my crew. If you don't, my friend will put you off the bridge. If you do anything I don't like, I'll put a round through your head. Your time starts now."

It wasn't a large bridge. There were only six stations plus the captain's seat, which I thought was a little much for a cargo ship that was less than a hundred metres long. "I'm with you. Where do you want to go?" the helmsman asked.

"We'll get to that," I replied, looking at the scanning officer.

"Where do I sign?" he asked. "In other words, I'm deserting."

I nodded at Lat. "Lock the door then take the tactical station."

"Aye, Captain," he replied.

CHAPTER THIRTY

In Flight Negotiations

There was no time to appreciate what I'd tentatively accomplished as I sat in the command seat of the Supplicant Five. I tracked so many things using my internal computer that I felt like my attention was being drawn in many directions at once. I had to choose something to focus on, and I didn't have to think long and hard about what that would be as I kept up with everything else.

"Helm, take us on an intercept course with the Daring Dream. Full atmospheric military thrust, now." A quick lookup on the pilot's history revealed that he was from the Regent Galactic Settled Regions, The Forak System, to be specific. If you don't know what the R.G.S.R. is, well, that's because they were being renamed the Order of Eden Settled Regions then, and word hadn't gotten to the Edwyn Cluster just yet.

Back to the point. The pilot, Norton Soben, was born, raised and trained on a giant ring station called The Exo Band. Its primary industries were deep space training and research. Before the Order of Eden took the Regent Galactic mega corporation over, he was a dedicated pilot who took every opportunity to become certified on every craft he could and participated in the Outer Orion Interplanetary Racing League. After the Order of Eden took control, he stopped non-mandatory training and withdrew from the Exo Band Racing Team. He even sold his family home there before he was assigned to the Supplicant Five. He flew the ship as it passed through a once secret wormhole gate from the distant Forak System all the way to Cefa in my local Cluster with a massive Order of Eden fleet.

Since then he'd been serving quietly, effectively, but never offering more effort than was required of him. He replied with surprising enthusiasm. "Yes, Sir. We'll be on their starboard side in just under two minutes."

"Weapon shutdown," Lat announced from the tactical station to my left. "Midship dorsal main turret. We still have the aft turret, ventral turret, two racks of twelve hull piercing missiles and five pulse drones."

"Launch the drones as soon as we're in range of enemy ships and start locking targets for our missiles," I replied. "Can you see what happened to the turret?"

"It's powered down, other than that, I don't know," Lat replied.

After considering the situation for a moment, I decided that I'd spend as much time on the bridge as possible. Most of the trouble we were in was exterior to the ship, so as long as I could control the Supplicant Five, I would be able to help the Daring Dream. The access level I had took care of most of that, so I was able to close every security door on the ship, putting two more heavy sliding hatches between me and any crew member. Anyone who wanted to get to the bridge might have a better chance coming in from the outside.

With that out of the way for the moment, I started transmitting on all combat frequencies. "This is Rogue. I have taken control of Supplicant Five and have a full cargo bay of your experiments. I have sympathy for the people in those pods, but I will open the airlocks in the cargo hold unless you agree to my terms. You have one minute to reply before I end your experiment."

"You can't! That's a breach! You don't understand what those subjects represent!" shouted the Supervisor.

"Breach of what? You have a contract with the Edxi?" I asked.

"You have to listen to me. This ship represents a big step in trust, I can't tell you more than that, but doing anything to the subjects in the cargo hold will set humanity back. You can't do it," he plead.

"You'll have time to tell me all about it later. I need you to shut up now," I told him.

A response came in and I put it on the bridge sound system. I let the video sensors capture a two dimensional image of me sitting in the captain's seat with my sidearm in hand. Captain Marda was right, the weapon was so large that it looked off balance, but it had a fantastic intimidation factor. "Rogue. If you open all the airlocks in the cargo bay, you'll destroy your leverage." The female voice was familiar but I couldn't quite make it out thanks to static.

"Stop firing at the Merry Mouse and we'll talk about it," I replied.

"That's happening now. We're tracking the Merry Mouse, or whatever that ship's real name is, but no longer firing," replied the commander. The static cleared up enough for me to figure out who was talking. Lene Thak, the former owner of the Ryden Corporation and newly minted Order of Eden Captain.

I made sure that Lene Thak, every ship in the area, and the crew aboard the Supplicant Five could hear me, I addressed them. "Attention: Supplicant Five crew. My name is Rogue, and my people have assumed control of your vessel. As a privateer licensed by Haven Fleet, I have the right to seize the vessel and all of its contents as a war prize. I say almost because, unlike the Order and its Ryden Corporation lackeys, I don't believe that I have the right to own people. So you have two options: Your first is to jump into an escape pod and punch out like a cowardly Order zealot. The second is to join my crew. Looking through your files I see that you're all far from home, most of you were employees of the Regent Galactic Corporation, minding your own business until the Order whackos took over. I'm gonna guess that it hasn't been all Kawaii Kittens and pleasure cruises since then. I'm not promising that your lifestyle will improve if you sign up for my crew, but at least you won't be serving a cult of kidnappers. Oh, and we have a Kawaii Kitten. Again, you have two minutes to either get into an escape pod and launch or report in as a member of my crew."

There were surprisingly few surveillance sensors aboard the Supplicant Five. I'd learn later that the secrecy of the crew's mission made them cut right down on anything that could record what was going on. The public areas were lightly monitored. A security team of five started arguing almost right away. In the galley, six crew members in containment suits stepped in front of one of those sensors after less than a minute and took their headgear off. "We're with you. None of us signed up for this," said one of the eldest, a woman with a bare scalp that sported an old acid scar. "What do you want us to do?"

I muted the other channels and replied; "Can you check on the main dorsal turret? The tactical system is telling us it's disconnected."

"The gunnery team came through here a few minutes ago saying that they were going to shut the turrets down before making a move on the bridge," the older woman said.

"Is there anything you can do about that?" I asked.

"Absolutely," a younger man said. "I've got a couple pulse blasters with me."

"We'll clear them out before they can do more damage," the older woman said.

"Thank you. Good hunting," I told them.

Two more crew members moved into range of a sensor in one of the corridors near engineering. One was immediately shot by at least three people who were out of frame as soon as he took his helmet off. The other, a woman who activated a sensor inside one of the offices leaned in close. "They'll never let you leave. Do whatever you want, kill the gifts or trade them, it'll all add up to you dead or becoming just like them."

No one else could see these responses, they were playing internally, but I wished Lev Fisa could. I might have learned something by reading his response but I didn't have time to play the message back. I replied instead. "Is the Order using them to develop new technology? What's the goal?"

"You'll never understand the gift, or what a privilege this mission represents," she replied before turning the surveillance sensor off.

"Launching countermeasures, engaging electronic jamming. The Regulator is firing missiles from orbit," Lat announced from the tactical station.

The ship's tactical system showed that they'd launched two, and they didn't have a chance to strike us from orbit. We had more than enough time to counter. I switched to the Order frequencies. "That's not going to help you negotiate with me."

Her image appeared. Seeing her in a green and grey Order of Eden Captain's uniform seemed strange. "I won't be ignored. You can't trust anyone you recruit on that ship. They come from the Settled Systems, core Order of Eden territories. They have no sympathy for the people of the Cluster, you're backwater breeders to them. Follow my instructions if you want to get out of this alive."

My spirits lifted as I saw the Daring Dream through the bridge's transparisteel windows. There were a few markings from beam and kinetic weapons, but the only hull breach I could see was in the cargo pod, and it was less than a metre wide. "I'll bite, make with the instructing."

"Don't take this lightly, it's the key to your survival," Captain Thak advised. "You'll fly the Supplicant Five into low orbit. You'll instruct the Merry Mouse to follow you so you and any of your companions can follow you through the airlock back onto that ship. You will be allowed to leave as long as the cargo aboard the Supplicant is not damaged. Those are the best terms I can offer."

The scanning officer that remained on the bridge glanced over his shoulder at me more than once while Thak's instructions came over the audio system. His biometrics were steady, which was either a good or very bad sign.

"Two firefights detected aboard," Lat announced. "Getting three check-ins from crew members who want to join us. Didn't understand what they were at first, sorry."

"Accept them," I told him before returning my attention to

Captain Thak. I knew her promise to let us go was a lie. I would bet a year of service that she would secure the Supplicant and destroy the Daring Dream for good measure. I wanted to convince her that I was a believer, though, so I added a condition. "I want to take everyone who switched to my side today with me."

Captain Thak tried to suppress a tacky scoff and failed. "That'll never happen. They may only be serving you so they can maintain their positions on the ship until we give them the order to attack. Follow my directions..." she went on to repeat everything she said before.

While she was demonstrating her undying love for her own voice, I was using my internal communications system to speak to the Daring Dream. "What's the condition over there?"

Duncan replied first; "Looking up. Minor breach on the ventral side, it's sealed and refortifying. A cargo pod took more serious damage because our brilliant pilot used it to catch a bunch of missiles, but we're flying straight. We're doing worse shield wise. One Vindyne Fifteen Hundred is burned out, the rest are cooling down and will be good for another go. The ladies in engineering are wiring all our backups together so they can cover our dorsal side. Should get us seven tenths the protection one Fifteen Hundred had."

"Nice work. Wait, the ladies?" I asked.

"Right, Oonaa and Perri, it was the furry one's idea, should be online in a tick," Duncan replied.

Mimi broke in then, speaking as quickly as she could which made her sound like a high-pitched motor-mouth. Later she'd tell me that she did it because she knew that I could understand her if she spoke faster and she wanted to save time. "I've been calling everyone. Sel and Elyub say they're contacting every captain and freedom fighter in the Rose System. Leon is working just as hard, but I'm not getting responses from anyone in the Legion. What are we gonna do?"

"Keep calling. Duncan, get ready to run. Drop the cargo pods if the difference in mass will help. Head for the large desert on the equator if you need cover on your way out." I paused for a moment as the older woman from the galley reported that they took control of the main turrets and were reconnecting power to the gauss cannons. They were long range guns made for punching holes through ships of any size with seventy millimetre shaped explosive shells. They weren't commonly used in any part of the galaxy I'd been in, but the Supplicant Five had four of them on two turrets. I finished speaking to my Daring Dream crew then. "We'll cover you as you break away."

"Aye, getting ready, keeping the jump drive warmed up," Duncan replied from his position in the ventral turret.

"We're gonna be okay, right?" Mimi asked. I could picturing her shifting on her paws uncertainly.

"You'll get away. Manny will stir the metal rich sand in the desert up if he has to, it'll make you hard to catch while you move to the far side of the moon and break free," I replied.

"Not a bad plan," Manny replied.

"Scorch the air if you have to. The few installations on this moon shouldn't be vulnerable to a firestorm," I told him.

"That changes things, what about you two?" he asked.

"Yeah, when are you coming back?" Mimi asked.

"Don't worry. Lat and I will find our way, we're hard to pin down. Don't wait for the order, break off as soon as you've got the shields wired up," I told them.

"Aye," Duncan replied. "Good hunting."

Captain Thak had finished giving me orders and was waiting for my response. I muted her and made her wait a little longer as I turned towards Lat. "Are our main guns online?"

"Charged, loaded, ready," he replied.

I checked the tactical system and marked two Ryden Light-stride Typhoons that were hanging back about twenty-five kilo-metres behind us. "Kill those. Next, take out targets of opportunity. I'm taking control of our missiles."

"Oh, yes I will," Lat replied with relish.

I leaned forward in my seat and was about to speak to the pilot when the scanning officer pulled a pulse handgun from a hidden compartment built into the underside of his station and spun his seat. He was fast, I'd say as quick as most humans could be, but I put an armour piercing round through his forehead before he could pull the trigger. There was only one more crew member I couldn't trust completely on the bridge and Lat had his weapon pointed at Norton by the time I had mine trained in that direction. "You're right, there's a handgun hidden beneath my console too, but I'm not drawing it."

"Take it out and slide it to the Captain," Lat said.

The pilot kept one hand on the controls as he quickly, but not too rapidly pulled the gun out and kicked it across the deck to me. "I would have warned you about that guy, but I was pretty sure he'd shoot me for it, so I'll understand if that sets the trust back a bit."

"I understand. Remain at the helm. Be ready to chase the Merry Mouse," I told him. "Stay out of her wake, try to keep up, don't worry if you won't be able to."

"Acknowledged, Captain," he replied.

"Ready to fire," Lat told me.

"Do it," I told him.

The sound of sixteen heavy shells being launched by the magnetic coils of medium gauss cannons beat against the hull like a big drum as they broke the sound barrier. It was like a chorus of thunder along with the dull crack of discharging capacitor banks near the middle of the ship. Scant milliseconds later, two Typhoons were destroyed. "Targeting fighters," Lat said, manually operating the controls and locking his targets in. "Firing five per cannon."

Prompted by a simple thought, the missile doors outside the ship slid aside and I started locking several targets in. The four fighters and the Marauder Corvette would all detect that, and since these missiles were made to take on light to medium ships specifically, they'd take it seriously. While I was maintaining that, I continued my conversation with Captain Thak. "There's fighting aboard the Supplicant, but I'm winning the ship and giving everything you've sent down here a reason to run."

"Two fighters down, the rest have gone evasive, I'm pushing the auto-targeting system to its limit. We'll get them," Lat said.

"There's no way out, decoy. I know what you are. I know we missed you on the Envoy. This is a good day, I'll save the Supplicant and take a privateer ship out. After that I'll see if my technicians can reprogram what's left of you. You'd make a good galley servant," said Captain Fisa.

Sometimes you don't know how fresh a mental wound is until someone dumps vinegar into it. I took being called a decoy personally and instinctively launched all twenty-four missiles in our launchers at the Marauder Corvette that was stupid enough to follow the Daring Dream into the atmosphere. The roar of the rockets firing and pings of the metal flexing in the heat of their rapid departure were almost deafening. "That'll cost you a Marauder. I wonder what your new bosses will say when you show them how much this cost the cult."

The missiles went supersonic and hammered the Marauder Corvette from below. Its countermeasures managed to take out half the missiles, give or take one or two, but the rest overloaded its shields, destroyed its main beam weapon and most of the lower thrusters. I wish I had time to watch it plummet and crash then, but there was a lot going on.

The Daring Dream's dorsal shields came to life and they chose that moment to break away. Duncan was in the upper turret, firing at the fighters over long range. The lower turret was coming to life as Perri got in and started shooting.

The Supplicant was already having trouble keeping up with the Daring Dream's acceleration. They were using their shields like a wedge to reduce atmospheric drag as their main engines kicked up any loose matter on the ground into the air. "Damn, that thing can move!" our helmsman said as he got us away from their wake, which included boulders.

That's when the flames from their engines turned white. The Daring Dream was over the horizon seconds later. All I would have seen was a torrent of fire behind it if I wasn't linked with the Supplicant's sensors. Even at about three hundred metres above the ground, there was a trench of molten material behind it as Manny did exactly as I told him. He turned the thrusters up until the dampeners were at their limit, and the air was scorched behind them.

Things were taking a good turn for them, they'd put the moon between them and the few Order ships that were in position to stop them from jumping away in space. Their momentum would carry the Daring Dream off world, and past anything that tried to block them so quickly that they would get through. At least, that's what it looked like for a moment.

Using powerful wormhole generators, three groups of Order of Eden ships arrived in outer orbit. They started to split up right away, led by the Sanctifier, a one point five kilometre long heavy carrier that emerged from its wormhole launching a swarm of star fighters that would be perfectly capable of catching the Daring Dream.

The interdiction field the Sanctifier projected added to the existing ones. It encompassed the entire moon as well as over five hundred million kilometres in every direction. I was on my feet then, speaking aloud. "Manny, slow down, redirect. We're regrouping."

"You're trapped," Captain Thak said with a thin smile.

CHAPTER THIRTY-ONE

Sandstorm

"Redirecting to the desert, meet you there?" Manny asked from the cockpit of the Daring Dream.

I looked at the helm and replied as our pilot nodded. "See you there in a couple minutes, don't stop shooting."

The Supplicant Five wasn't built for planetary travel. She was blocky, kind of like a rectangle with extendable thruster pods. Her shields weren't as powerful or able to take different shape, so we were pushing through the air, creating a lot more drag than the Daring Dream. "Trying to keep up, but there's no way," the helmsman said.

"Your ransom plan is falling apart. Surrender and they might let your friend there live," said Lev Fisa from where he was strapped to his seat.

I'd almost forgotten he was there. Pointing my sidearm at his head was unintentional, an instinct that came too naturally, but the sneering stare I sent his way was not. The last firefight was under way right outside the arms locker. Judging from the sporadic readings I picked up as people moved through the ship, I could guess that the galley folk were winning. That was great, but that wouldn't be good resistance if the enemy got aboard. "What happens to you if you get caught?" I asked Lev.

"Me? Nothing! They'll force me into compassionate counselling, which will cost me a few credits, but other than that, I'll go on with my duties. Your new pilot is finished, I'd say. He knows. He gambled and lost, isn't that right, Norty?"

"Call me Norty again and I'll show you the door, cultist freak," the helmsman replied. He was trying to fly as low as possible, but it was a turbulent flight path. The skies were filled with ash and dust. "He's right about the rest, though. I'll be executed. I could step away from the controls right now and refuse to do anything for you, but they'll still drag me into the centre of some arena and show everyone what happens to traitors. Could take a minute, could take an afternoon. It's hell either way, but serving the Order's mission here is worse."

Lat was ignoring our conversation entirely, using the main guns to fire at the drones and fighters trying to come down from orbit. The targeting computer wasn't the quickest, so it wasn't as much help as we would have liked. Four in five shots missed.

I was only half paying attention to what was happening on the bridge. The Daring Dream reached the edge of the desert and Manny made an incredible mess, driving hundreds of tons of conductive, heavy metal sand into the air where an eighth of it melted as he started flying in curling, evasive turns that expanded the sandstorm as the Daring Dream disappeared into it.

I could see it in the distance, a dark brown-grey sand storm with roiling fire and arcing electricity inside. "We're almost there," Norton said from the helm.

"Last chance, surrender and the crew of the Merry Mouse will survive," Captain Thak said, interference from the sand storm introducing a little static as we started closer.

"That's the kind of decision I can't make on the spot. I'll have to think about it. Can you give me a minute or ten?" I asked as I killed the video but kept the sound going.

Lat shot me a wry look over his shoulder, taking a second to gesture at the tactical panel, which was bathed in red light from the collection of warnings it was giving him. We were being targeted by at least thirty weapons from orbit. If the ships up there decided we should go down, we would go down. I checked my sidearm as I listened to Captain Thak. "This isn't the time to joke around. We have you, it's done. Set down outside that miserable mess your ship is making, and we'll make sure your people survive if they cease resisting. I'll even handle your capture personally," she said.

Using the controls built into the command seat's left arm, I closed every intake and non-critical exhaust system the Supplicant had. We were in the sand cloud a few seconds later. There was no view, only churning brown and blackened particles for a hundred kilometres ahead as the disturbance grew into a weather system.

Manny knew how to make a mess, and my crew were smart enough to stop firing, so they would be harder to detect. Beam weapons fired down from orbit, adding to the illumination of the fire and energy arcs flashing all around us. As far as I could tell, they missed the Daring Dream for the most part, and their shields were holding. It was the kind of distraction we needed.

Even thinking at speeds that were impossible for a human without enhancements, I took a long moment to plan.

There were three soldiers using a hull cutter on the bridge's outermost security doors. They'd be through the first set in under five minutes. If it took them the same amount of time to get through the next two, they'd be on the bridge in a little over ten. The Regulator was still sending signals out to every Order ship in the area, they were coordinating.

What I could see on the tactical system confirmed that as the Order carrier's escort split up, covering more and more orbital space. They were preparing for us to make a break for the black beyond so we could get clear of the moon's gravity and jump away. There were nine Marauder Corvettes, five Order destroyers, at least twenty fighters and hundreds of drones in the way. Oh, then there was the Regulator and a few other, smaller Ryden ships. If they weren't spreading out to cover orbital space, they could wipe us out in seconds, but they were moving to recapture the Supplicant. Maybe they wanted the Daring Dream too, I couldn't tell for sure.

To the people around me, it took a few seconds to make my decision, but it felt like a few minutes of reviewing all the data coming in before I shut it all out and thought it through in silence. That was broken by Captain Thak's voice. "I understand that you're only an android, but you must understand sympathy, the sanctity of life. You must want to preserve the lives of your crew. Surrender if only to show everyone that an artificial person can do the right thing for a small group of humans."

Her words weren't as insulting to me as how fake they sounded. I wanted to punch a hole through the Regulator, the ship Captain Thak spent half her wealth on, but I did my best to hide that. "All right, we're surrendering, but I want to do it officially, face to face with you since you were contracted to run this operation. We'll fly up now."

When Captain Thak finally replied, her voice was filled with surprise. "Come to the Regulator. I'll take you into custody myself and make sure your crew is handled well."

"What? We can't!" Mimi said using the secure connection between the Daring Dream and my command and control bracer.

I made sure my response could be heard by everyone on the bridge of the Supplicant and the Daring Dream after I muted all other communications. "Don't worry. It's our only chance. The coverage is thinnest around the Regulator, she held four Typhoons back for support. It's our best route to get past the blockade. You're going to use the Supplicant for cover since they don't want to fire on us. We'll accelerate all the way up so we have as much momentum as possible when we break orbit and fly right past the Regulator."

"Oh, that's much better, I like it," Mimi approved.

"Got it, lead the way," Manny added.

"Tell me we're going to take shots on that ship on our way past, yeah?" Duncan asked. "Mimi's been telling us how Ryden was contracted for this horror show and we've got full launchers."

"That's the plan, but watch out for the Typhoons. Our guns were able to cut through them in atmosphere easy enough, but their shields are tougher in space," Lat said.

"Aye, we'll open fire when you do," Duncan said.

I took a deep breath and braced myself. There was a fair chance that my plan would backfire, we'd frighten Captain Thak and she'd open fire with everything she had, destroying either ship or both. "Norton, set a course for the Regulator and get ready to accelerate as hard as you can without burning our dampeners out. You're going to head towards them so the other ship can use us as cover once we get past. They're not going to use lethal force while our cargo is alive."

"You're right," Norton said, working at the helm. "Those people in the hold are the most precious thing in the galaxy to these cultists. It's disgusting, I deserve to be fried from the inside just for ferrying them around."

"Don't you dare reveal the gift!" Lev Fisa raged, struggling at the restraint belts.

Norton's voice rose from a normal pitch to a furious bellow as he said; "Get me out of this, and I'll tell you everything, especially if that guy finds his way out of an airlock without a suit! I'm sick of you fanatical cash cult freaks!" He took a deep breath and, shuddering, finally said; "Course laid in. We blast off the moment you give the order."

"Go," I told him.

The nose of the Supplicant pitched up more rapidly than I thought was possible and the main thrusters roared, melting the sand below and around us. I unmuted the channel I shared with Captain Thak. "We're on our way up. The sand storm we've created is making it difficult to achieve escape velocity, so we're overcompensating a bit. We'll slow down once..."

"She's lying, Captain!" Supervisor Fisa shouted from his seat.

I was able to mute the channel before he finished saying; 'she's' and trained my weapon on him. "Give me a reason not to end you right now."

He stared at me, turning white, starting to shake. This was the true test of his resolve, his heart was racing. "Murder me here, but surrender the gift alive. Humanity's survival depends on it."

The dull roar of the engines was the only sound on the bridge until my ammo changer came to life, click-clacking a non-lethal stun round into the chamber. I shot once. My weapon went off with a faint pop, sending the bullet out of the barrel much slower than the speed of sound. It burst before reaching him, unravelling into hundreds of charged shards that made him twitch as they interfered with his brain activity before drugging him to sleep. It was my first time trying it, and I was surprised at how effective it was.

My attention was immediately drawn elsewhere. "We have about seven minutes before soldiers break through to the bridge. There are three of them."

"We'll catch them on their way through," Lat replied, unconcerned.

"You've achieved escape velocity. You're going to begin decelerating," Captain Thak was saying over our channel.

I unmuted my end. "We're just making sure we get enough momentum to finish the climb."

"Stop accelerating and prepare for docking operations now," Captain Thak replied.

Muting myself again, I spoke to my crew aboard the Daring Dream. "She's not buying it. Get behind the Supplicant."

"Aye," Manny replied as the Daring Dream slipped into position, the flatter, more streamlined ship managing to fit its hull behind the Supplicant's silhouette by tilting at a forty-five degree angle.

"I will fire on you. Do not attempt to escape," Captain Thak said.

"They're locking weapons," Lat said.

"Take the nearest Typhoons out, then work on the last two, Lat. Daring Dream, fire on the Regulator's bridge with everything you've got," before I finished giving the order, the Typhoons began firing with everything they had. Sure, their Ripshock cannons fired at less than half the rate the ones we transplanted on the Daring Dream did, but each of those ships had six of them. The Supplicant's shields couldn't stand up to the punishment of all twenty four of them.

Our forward shields burned out first. Lat managed to fire thirty rounds at two Typhoons, blasting their energy barriers down and ripping holes through their hulls before our dorsal shields failed. They broke away, trying to evade Lat's tactical eye. He concentrated on one Typhoon at a time, aiming for their main thrusters specifically, and struck his mark on the second try. One Typhoon lost a main thruster and spun out of control. The next gave up on running and came around to charge. That made it easy for Lat to finish it off, sending a barrage right through the middle of the craft. Its aft thrusters continued to fire as the lights in the cockpit went out and it started a quick uncontrolled descent towards the moon.

The course Norton was following to the Regulator kept most of the Order ships in the region in the shadow of the moon and the debris around it, making strikes with weapons that fired in a straight line impossible. They were holding back with larger guided munitions, most likely to make sure that the Supplicant could be retaken. Fighters were moving in for support, but most of them were minutes away.

That suited us, and made the best targets obvious. Lat moved on to the next pair of Typhoons as the auto loader for the gauss turrets finished their work. He focused two turrets firing two cannons each on one Typhoon, sending nearly a hundred armour piercing, shaped explosive rounds against their shields then through their bare hull. Most of the holes they punched struck the troop cabin. Jets of air escaped through the holes even after Lat hit something important and the ship went dark.

The fourth Typhoon came about and fired on us with all six of its guns, abandoning any attempt to evade. Warning symbols appeared on the captain's display on the right arm of the command seat, telling me that their Ripshock guns were burning microscopic holes through the less armoured dorsal section of the hull. Our life support system took the largest hit, and I had to stretch the range of the aft dampeners to cover several sections in the middle of the ship. If our artificial gravity went out, our manoeuvrability and acceleration would be severely limited.

The fourth and final typhoon paid for their bold attack as Lat riddled it with gauss cannon rounds, breaking its shields down before blasting through its cockpit. "That's all four down, moving on to the Regulator's bridge," Lat said.

The Regulator was finishing what the Typhoons started by then, using directed electromagnetic beams on the Supplicant's starboard side main thruster pod, disabling it with a torrent of energy. Its point defence guns were trying to strike the Daring Dream. They missed until my ship slipped out from behind us just long enough to fire a full barrage of dumb fire missiles at the Regulator's bridge. In the few seconds that it was out of position, the frigate's point defence guns hit the Daring Dream's shields hundreds of times.

"Ventral shields down! We have a burn out!" Oonaa announced.

"Lower turret's unresponsive," Duncan added. "Perri, you whole?"

"Suit saved me," she replied. Judging from the sound of her voice, I could tell that her headpiece was sealed and she was under the influence of some kind of pain medication. "I'm okay, getting out on my own. Turret's open to space."

That was the last time the Regulator would damage the Daring Dream or harm my crew. The bridge's shields were overwhelmed by the combination of the Daring Dream's missiles and the Supplicant's main turrets before the tail end of the barrage struck bare metal then dug through in under three seconds. If they hadn't already targeted the Daring Dream with most of its point defence guns, it would have taken most of the missiles headed for its command centre out, but our missiles hit so fast that I didn't have time to say goodbye to Captain Thak.

"We're about to pass by, but every Order ship in the area is coming after us," Manny said.

I could see it, whoever was in charge of the blockade knew what they were doing. The Marauder Corvettes started projecting their own interdiction fields as they moved at full speed to grow the anti-wormhole space ahead of us. Fighters were moving in so they could run support ahead of them, the destroyers were making best speed to keep in position in behind. There was no way the Supplicant could outrun the problem. "The Daring Dream can outrun this, but you're going to be on your own with no cover."

"So... what's the strategy?" Manny asked.

"We go back to the planet," Duncan offered. "Those corvettes are shite down there and we can keep the fighters away with another storm."

I wasn't so hopeful. The tactical map showed too many guns pointed at us from afar, we wouldn't make it back into the atmosphere. "New contacts incoming," Norton announced as I saw the same red circles on the tactical map in my head. "Wormholes just outside of the interdiction field."

"Oh my God, didn't they get the memo? I'm the hero of this story!" Mimi cried.

The Regulator's DEMP beams were still operational, and they blasted the Supplicant, taking out another main thruster by burning through its energy shields then disabling it. "Down to two main engines. We're not outrunning anything now," Norton said.

Lat turned the turrets on two of the beam emitters and started hammering them. Duncan was doing the same from the Daring Dream's dorsal turret, using his Ripshocks to batter their shields down. I was about to order them to make a run for it, to leave me, Lat and the Supplicant behind to fend for ourselves, but then I noticed something about the wormhole exit points.

I rushed to the science station and grinned as the Reaper, a Clever Class Light Corvette belonging to Jacob Valent emerged from transit space. Fourteen Samurai Squadron Archangel fighters came through at the same time, accelerating with a burst of speed towards the Order ships converging on us. That would give us time to escape, and I was overjoyed at the sight of them, but worried at how much it would cost them at the same time.

That was until five much larger transit exit points opened, momentarily lighting the black sky above Vercosa up. Four Nafalli battlecruisers emerged, their bulbous, elongated shapes revealing dozens of gun ports. Turrets emerged, and Nafalli warriors opened fire on every Order of Eden target in the area. The fifth exit point was right between them, wider than two of the battlecruisers combined and almost as long. It was shaped like a sting ray with a gleaming black and dark blue hull. I was welling up with tears of joy at the sight. "It's the Triton. We got through."

"They got the memo!" Mimi cheered.

Two of the hangar bays beneath the Triton's wings started opening. "Daring Dream, Supplicant Five, we'll cover you," Captain Jacob Valent said from the bridge of the Reaper. The shape of the forty-two metre long light corvette always had a brawny look that I liked. Its railgun turrets came to life as it charged towards the nearest Marauder Corvette. Bays opened and unleashed two storms of Javelin missiles as the Reaper put itself between us and most of the incoming fire.

No one saw the Raven, the sister ship under the command of Captain Remmy Sands, until it uncloaked and unleashed a fury of turret fire at a group of Order fighters. When they finished perforating them with railgun rounds, it cloaked again.

Jacob Valent broadcast a message over every channel. "The Legion is here. Deactivate your interdiction systems. You should try to escape. We're not taking prisoners today."

I could hear my crew aboard the Daring Dream cheer. "Now that's battlefield charm, that is," Duncan laughed.

All thirty-five of the Triton's forward torpedo bays opened, fired, and closed. The munitions disappeared as they aggressively accelerated towards their targets. Forty-two turrets built into the forward section of the dorsal side of the ship began to seek and fire at targets of opportunity as the great ship tipped forward and started to accelerate towards the enemy carrier, which was already turning so it could get away from the moon and jump away. "Where are we landing?" Norton asked.

I pulled myself away from the mesmerising sights playing out before my eyes and on my tactical system and addressed the Triton directly. "Triton Flight, we could use a hangar assignment."

"Hangar Three, rescue and boarding teams are ready," came the reply from the Commander in charge, a man I knew from Alice's memories as Slick.

"I was headed to that side already," Norton said.

"Acknowledged," I said, drawing my sidearm and opening the armoured bridge doors with a mental signal. I put my helmet on and strode through. "I'll be right back."

Lat and I were finished on the bridge, there was nothing left to do. I wasn't surprised when he caught up to me, his rifle at the ready. I closed the doors behind us as we both faced the next set. The soldiers had managed to cut a half rectangle through. I used the intercom to send my voice throughout the ship. "I need everyone on board to put your weapons and tools down. Step three metres away from them and lay face down with your fingers laced behind your head. You will remain that way until we get to you and determine friend or foe. You will be treated fairly if you follow those instructions immediately. Hesitation or resistance will get you killed. The Outbound Legion is here. We are landing on one of their carriers. I am leading counter-boarding actions with their assistance. Surrender or die."

The few sensors I had access to showed the few remaining crew following my instructions as most of them pulled weapons and tools off their belts and backs. They kicked them down hall-ways and across floors. Finally, even the three remaining from the galley team that helped me out laid down and put their hands behind their heads. They understood the situation, and I'd reward them for everything they'd done for me.

Then there were the Order's true believers who were desperately trying to cut their way to the bridge. I couldn't see them, they'd destroyed the sensors in that hallway, but the plasma cutter didn't stop burning a new rectangle in the door in front of us.

"Ready?" I asked.

"Ready. Prisoners?" Lat asked.

"No," I replied.

"Good."

In response to a mental signal to the ship, the doors unlocked with several deep clicks then slid apart. Lat and I both fired at the first soldier we saw. My rifle was set to its highest setting, but we still couldn't burn his personal shields down until the doors were fully open. The soldier dropped the cutter and reached for a grenade. I shot it before he could throw it, disabling the detonator inside.

These three were in Order Knight armour, a parallel knockoff of the most powerful personal combat suits Haven Fleet used. Lat's focus was on the other two knights, and he fired in their general direction, hitting a third of the time as he drew four small electromagnetic pulse grenades and tossed them with his other hand. The knights didn't stop those from skipping across the deck between their feet. They went off and decimated what was left of their energy shields.

The Order Knights didn't flinch as they fired back at him. Lat's armour warped as it tried to resist the barrage and he stepped behind me, bloody. That was more than I could take. I closed with the trio. I fired at one Knight as I came into contact with the nearest, planting my feet. My soles affixed to the deck as I slapped one hand onto the knight's faceplate and used every bit of physical power in my mechanical and biological systems to break the strength enhancements and mechanical bracing in his suit. It sounded like the metal and synthetic muscle inside screamed as I poured all my anger into the act of slamming his helmet onto the deck in front of me, half crushing it and denting the surface.

His suit started breaking apart as I swung him up into another knight and leapt to his fellow. The soles of my boots affixed to his hips as I put the muzzle of my weapon against his faceplate and let loose with three bursts of armour piercing rounds. The third got through, and I was firing at the third Knight before the second collapsed. Order Knights almost never surrendered, they were paragons of the cause, and this one was no different. He drew his sidearm, I grabbed his wrist, turned, put it over my shoulder, and shoved the stubby barrel of my weapon into his ribs. I angled it upwards, cutting through his armour after two bursts. Rounds exploded into his body. I didn't stop until my clip was empty.

They would regenerate. All Order Knights had framework regeneration technology. I didn't have to think about how my systems made munition twenty-eight nanobots. They were generated in seconds, sent to my fingertips where they clung like water drops as I retracted my gloves. I flicked the nanobots into the wounds of the first two, then the third Order Knight.

Those nanobots were designed for one thing: to initiate a final regeneration cycle in framework soldiers. Their bodies would be rebuilt from the bones outward without their regeneration systems, reducing them to simpler, more vulnerable humans. One was still dying, somehow surviving the gruesome head wounds I'd inflicted. He stared up at me with a bare green eye, breathing rapidly. "You'll remember me. You'll remember everything you did on this ship. Your only job when you wake up is to tell everyone what I did to you. You're going to tell that story over and over or I'll get rid of you for good."

What was left of his jaw worked for a moment before his eye rolled back and he began a full regeneration cycle, his body rebuilding itself from the inside out. I rushed to Lat, who was breathing wetly. "Wish I could talk like that."

Sympathy and deep worry flooded in, disarming my anger. "Just a sec, I'll put you out."

"Wait," he coughed. "It's not that bad."

It took me a second to clue in to the fact that he thought I was about to euthanise him. I shook my head. "I'm just giving you a stasis dose. They'll take care of you here, the Triton has a good infirmary." The dose was finished combining in my command and control bracer then.

"A nap would be nice," he wheezed.

I injected him then, and held his hand as he slipped into

stasis. The notion that he thought I would just kill him for being injured moved through my mind like a demolition charge. Did he expect me to kill him for falling in combat? For not being strong enough? Was that what he'd come to expect from me? I should have gotten up, put him somewhere safer, helped the boarding teams.

That didn't happen. When the Legion soldiers arrived I was still there, sitting at his side.

CHAPTER THIRTY-TWO

An Inevitable Meeting

I was too distracted by Lat's condition to be nervous about meeting people from Alice's life. When I opened every one of the Supplicant's hatches for the boarding team, I was surprised when the ship was swarmed by five squads, that's seventy-five well trained Legion soldiers in full personal power armour.

I'd never met one of Jake's Legionnaires. I didn't know how much had changed since I landed on Tabrus, but the professionalism and speed the boarding teams demonstrated as they took full control of the ship looked practiced. None of them got excited, they put every crew member into restraints and walked them off into the hangar if they cooperated. The three freshly regenerated knights didn't follow orders, they were waking up fighting when they came face to face with the Legionnaires.

I'd already taken their weapons away, throwing them into a

disposable bag I had in my pack while I stayed with Lat. Those would find their way back to the Daring Dream thanks to a Triton crew member. When the knights tried to regroup, the Legionnaires shot them with special rounds that safely captured them in something that looked like bodybags with life support.

As soon as they were safely captured, one Sergeant leaned down to me, retracted his faceplate and asked; "Ma'am, there's a medical suite three minutes away. We can take him there unless you'd like us to administer emergency treatment here."

"Take us there," I replied.

Within seconds three members of his squad had a collapsable stretcher out and they were loading Lat onto it. Mimi was talking to me next, interrupting Duncan before he could get his first word out. "The Triton people are asking if we want repair drones. When I asked how much that would cost, they laughed at me."

"Say yes," I replied. "Is everyone okay?"

"Triton Flight's telling us the deck crew can take us to you in some rescue centre," Duncan said.

"Meet me there," I said as I followed Lat as he was carried on a stretcher by Legionnaires at a jog. Norton was ahead of us, his hands bound, led by a pair of armoured Legionnaires who made him look small. Another walked behind him with three crystalline drives in his hands. "I need Norton and those drives with me." I told him.

"Yes, Ma'am," said the soldier at the rear, handing me the bag.

"Do you want him to remain restrained?" another Legionnaire asked.

"No, Norton's switched sides," I replied.

The pilot stared at me with wide eyes and a raised brow as

his wrist restraints were removed. It took only a couple of seconds, but I'll never forget that look of surprise and relief on his face. He ran right along side us as Lat was brought out into the massive hangar, through a pair of blast doors then into a rescue centre that looked like it was a combination of a small hospital, brig, and meeting spaces.

I saw the white and green doors leading into the medical area ahead. When Zac, the lead Medical Officer emerged, I caught his eye. "Major injuries to the torso. Explosive rounds." I was about to go on, but stopped when he nodded.

"We already have the scans, Ma'am. We'll get him back in shape in a few minutes," he said.

"He's my oldest friend," I said.

Zac nodded at me and froze when he saw Lat's face. "Interesting. Don't worry, he'll be right back out." Two medics in white and blue took over, placing Lat on a gurney. Zac led them through the doors of the emergency medical centre.

Perri came into the hallway behind me on the next stretcher. "I can walk on my own, really," she was telling the Legionnaires bearing her along at a smooth but quick pace.

A brief scan showed that she had a full thickness burn through her upper arm, but the vacsuit was blocking pain and holding her arm steady from the shoulder down. All the measures were temporary, the wound would only get worse. The suit saved her life in other ways too, protecting her from most of the trauma when the ventral turret was seriously damaged with her in it. "Captain," she said as soon as she saw me.

"You're going to be all right, let them take care of you. They're good here," I told her.

"I'm sorry we lost the lower turret," Perri said. "I'll start repairs as soon as I'm out."

"Don't worry, just relax while they give you the royal treatment," I told her as she passed by me and through the doors.

I can't describe what it feels like, but every sensor built into me felt some kind of background energy for a few seconds. I knew we'd entered transit space, a dimension near my own that dimension drives used for interstellar travel. It was the fastest way to move across the stars, and the core technology inside quad drives. The Triton had spirited us away.

The Legion's assistance was welcome, but I felt like I'd lost control of my ship, my crew and needed to see them. "Where are you?" I asked Duncan using my internal comm so no one else could hear our conversation.

"Aboard the Daring Dream. There's an army of bots crawling around out there, inspecting the hull, starting work. I'm stayin' back so I can answer questions. Thought I'd help out, but those bots are quick. The rest of the crew is behind an Ensign who said they'll take them to you. Never seen a more efficient bunch, if I'm honest. Everything all right? We get what we needed off that bleedin' moon?"

"More than we bargained for. Sorry this almost went sideways," I replied.

"Almost, but we won out, like. Now I'm wondering who gets the credit, yeah?" Duncan replied.

"I'll make sure we do all right," I replied.

"Grand, you sort the deal. I'll keep an eye so no one starts robbing bits or picking at secrets," Duncan said.

"Thank you, Duncan. Good job running the ship," I told him.

My tactical system highlighted a door behind me as Manny leaned into the hallway. I turned around and started walking towards him. "Great flying out there."

"Thanks, but you haven't seen the Daring Dream yet. There are a couple holes, and the ventral turret's down," he said, cringing.

"It could be a lot worse," I replied.

"What about Lat and Perri?" he asked as I stepped into the room. It was like a waiting room, only the seating was well padded and there was sound dampening so I stopped hearing everything outside as soon as I was over the threshold. The colours were relaxing dark hues.

Mimi started running towards me the moment she saw me from the opposite door. She jumped onto a chair, the table then into my arms. "Are we safe here?"

I adapted my vacsuit so it had a hood and she hopped into it. "We're safe, but that's about all I know."

"Well, it's something," Mimi said.

"God, I still feel like I'm flying," Manny said, looking at his hands as he sat in the middle of a sofa made for three. "I swear I was one with the controls."

"He didn't panic once," Mimi said. "Who's that?' she asked, pointing at Norton with a paw.

"That's Norton. He left the Order and might be joining our crew," I replied.

"Oh. I didn't know they could do that. Are you sure he didn't desert so you wouldn't send him out the airlock?" Mimi asked as she regarded him with a suspecting gaze.

"I never signed up for the Order. I was a Regent Galactic Security Service pilot when they took over and I had no idea what they were about until we got to the cluster," he told her, wisely taking her seriously. "I think I was waiting for a chance to desert, there was nothing impulsive about it."

"Okay, we'll see," Mimi said, shifting around in my hood.

"Captain," Oonaa said as she hung her head and stepped closer. "I'm sorry, the backup shield generator Perri and I put together burned out. I couldn't pull the adapter I used to connect them out in time. All our backup shields will have to be rebuilt with new coils, and some of the circuitry will need replacing."

Her apology painted enough of a mental picture for me to guess what happened and why. I'd later find all four of the Spectral Dynamic shield generators that came with the ship wired together in a pile, critically overloaded. "I'm guessing the Daring Dream would be a lot worse off if you didn't set that up in the first place."

"Yeah, well, it was my idea, but Perri showed me how to wire them up without overloading the array," Oonaa said, stroking the top of her head.

"Thank you. I hope you'll join my crew," I told her, earning a grin from Manny.

"Does it pay well?" she asked.

"You start with one share," I replied.

"That translates into; 'yes, it pays very well,'" Mimi added.

Oonaa cocked her head at the cat and was about to say something when the door opened and Jake came in. He was still wearing his heavy armour, the horizontal metal bands exaggerated his size slightly as they followed his form and movements. Mimi jumped up and put her paws on top of my head so she could get a better vantage point. She moved so quickly that it was like something poked her from behind. "Old Man!"

"Mimi, glad you made it in one piece," he said, looking over his shoulder to nod at the two Legionnaires behind him. "No one enters without clearing it with me first," he told them.

"Done," one said. They remained outside as the door slid closed.

Jake returned his attention to us then. "There are a few Order of Eden workers in holding saying you invited them to join your crew. Quan's observing them."

Quan was a Nolian, a man from another galaxy where a humanoid species started interbreeding with humans centuries ago. He was a telepath with a strict moral code, so I was surprised to hear he was aboard. "He joined the Legion?"

"Before it was officially formed," Jake replied. "We don't have much time, but I can have him do his thing for you. His guess on where they stand won't be a hundred percent, since he only listens for surface thoughts, but he's better than most lie detectors."

"I'll take the help," I replied. "I hear your droids have already started work on the Daring Dream?"

Jake nodded and walked over to the wall where he pressed a button. An armoured shutter slid upwards, revealing a broad view of a large hangar. The Daring Dream only occupied a quarter of the massive space and there were small crawler droids lined up beneath as many repair drones around the ship. "Sorry if I overstepped, but there's not much time. We were on our way to another target when we got Mimi's message. We've got the materials to restore the hull, it'll only take half an hour to do the exterior work."

I didn't want to ask what it would cost me, but I didn't assume it would be free, either. Some of the materials in the Daring Dream's hull are dense and a little rare, giving them a higher price tag. "Where are we headed?"

"We're taking a detour to the Bitter End, dropping you off and moving on. I wish we had more time, trust me, but our target won't stay where it is for long," he replied. "Nothing exciting. A few Order ships have been separated from the battlegroup and we're taking advantage. I can't be more specific than that."

"You don't trust him, huh? I mean, he could leave, right?" Mimi asked, glancing at Norton.

"If I were only protecting myself, I'd tell you all about it, but there are thousands of lives and alliances on the line. I couldn't tell my own fiancee what she doesn't need to know with stakes like that," he replied.

"Oh, okay," Mimi said.

I went to the window and tried not to recoil at the Daring Dream's battered hull plating. The worst was the long fissure in the cargo pod. I couldn't see the ventral turret from above, and I didn't want to. The abrasive sand did superficial damage, since most of it didn't get through the energy shields, but I was surprised at how much it polished the front edges of the hull. There were dents and scratches from solid rounds as well as particle beams that tried to get through the hull but failed. Most of it would repair itself as long as there was a trickle of energy moving through the ship's structure, but there would be superficial wear and tear left over. I wasn't sure if I liked it yet.

As if he was listening to my thoughts, Norton said; "That's a ship with patina."

"Is that a sneaky way of saying something mean?" Mimi asked.

"No, he's understating it. Thank you for the repairs, Jake," I said.

He tapped his command and control bracer and another rack of fifteen droids swarmed the Daring Dream. "What are your plans for the other ship?"

I thought for a moment. I was over my head with the Supplicant Five and I knew it. "I don't even know what I have. I scanned the cargo, but I can't tell if anyone in there can be saved."

"They can't," Norton said. "Have your medical people look

them over, do whatever you need to, but I've heard it a few times from the experts. Once someone is bonded with one of those parasites, it's permanent. The phrase I heard was 'brain infiltration.' The captain made sure we didn't go anywhere near them, just in case."

"We're not equipped to handle that," Jake said with certainty.

That was the opposite of what I expected. Jake had one of the best carriers in the Edwyn Cluster, maybe the galaxy for all I knew. He was experienced with the Order's experimental tech, and his fiancee was Ayan, the leader of Haven Fleet Sciences, last I checked. "Any suggestions?" I asked as I checked Leon's most recent message.

Speaking with Haven Fleet. Will get back to you as soon as we've determined a course of action.

I sent another query before turning all my attention to Jake. "I sent my scans to the Privateering Initiative. The most important thing is to get the ship to Haven Sciences or whoever can try to help those people before it's too late."

"I'm telling you the experts I flew around with those things were sure extraction wasn't possible. Once the parasite's teeth crack through the back of someone's head and they get their tendrils in, it's over," Norton insisted.

"I want as many people to go over the people in those pods as possible before we give up on them," I replied.

"That's the way to do it. I can have the pods moved to containment if you want the ship, though. Military transports like that don't get taken whole often," Jake said.

"I want a few parts, so you won't have to move the pods," I said.

"Upgrades?" Jake asked.

"The Gauss cannons. I've got two turret mounts on the Daring Dream I'm not using. I don't care who gets the rest of the ship, as long as we have time. A look at the armoury would be..." I stopped and sent Leon's incoming call to my bracer, which projected his image in the middle of the room. "Hey, Leon."

"Rogue. I didn't know I was stepping into a high level meeting. Sorry I have bad news," Leon said, getting to his feet.

"This is about the parasites," I guessed.

He cleared his throat and straightened up. "Exactly. Fleet Sciences took a look at the scans you took in Supplicant Five's cargo hold. The parasite fully takes over the host's brain in ways that make extracting them and rehabilitating a human impossible. The bright side is that the host probably won't remember who they were, or that they were ever human. It's not much of a bright side, if you ask me. They're eager to get their hands on that ship. They've known that the Edxi use biomechanical technology since the invasion of the Haven System, and they suspected that the hybrid fighters they captured were the result of a merging between some lesser species from their own galaxy and a parasite, but this is the first time they've seen a lot of humans in a transformative state."

I wanted to know what the sleepers were being used for, but I didn't like the answer. It took a huge effort to push my disappointment aside. My desire to look professional in front of Leon and especially Jake was a big help. "I feel like an asshole for asking, but what's it worth? My repair bill is gonna be steep."

"You're not interested in what's going to happen to the people in the hold?" Norton asked.

Everyone turned to him, but I replied before they could. "Haven Sciences is more qualified than I am to make the call. They'll probably study them, sure, but they'll also take care of them, restore them if they can. What can I do? Anything I try will probably kill them or worse."

"What could be worse?" Norton asked.

"What if the parasites react to interference? They could create a disease, or turn their host into a bomb. This is alien tech on an intergalactic level of weird from a species who would love to wipe all humans out. I am in way over my head," I replied.

"So am I. She's right, Haven Sciences is the right way to go. We have a science division here, but it's in its infancy, so I'm not letting anyone near those things," Jake added.

"You're wrong about one thing. The Edxi don't want to wipe humanity out. They want to punish us for tampering with one of their brood worlds. They want to subjugate us, and the Order thinks they're negotiating their way out of it," Norton said.

"Negotiating their way out?" Mimi asked.

"Okay, this is going to sound rehearsed because I've gone over how I would tell people about this in my head a hundred times," Norton said.

"Go on," Jake said.

Norton looked around the room and continued on, mostly looking at Leon. "Before I start, I'm Norton Soben, Lieutenant Junior Grade. What you've stumbled onto is a top secret Order of Eden mission called The Gift. They only store data about it on disconnected computer equipment and pass orders using the highest encryption. I've deleted more data than I've saved since I pulled this duty. You have one of the Lead Supervisors in custody. Get him to unlock that pad for you, and I bet you'll find all the details, but here are the broad strokes. The Order have a deal with the Edxi who came to the cluster. The aliens don't push on to the rest of the galaxy if the Order brings them people - they call them sleepers - to use for their ships and other tech. I think some even become warriors, but I heard that's a different type of parasite."

"All right. I can't say much, but we've run into an Order lab where they were trying to extract a different Edxi parasite from a human host. They weren't having much success," Jake said.

"I'm not surprised. The Order is completely corrupt all the way through, it's built in. Why wouldn't they be two faced about this too? I'm sure there's a lab somewhere filled with Order eggheads who are trying to find a way to reverse this, just in case the Edxi go too far, but I don't know where they'd put that," Norton said.

"To be clear, you're suggesting that the Order is handing people over to the Edxi so they can implant parasites. Why? Pretend I haven't seen the scans or spoken to experts," Leon said. "No theories, just fact, please."

"Right. I've seen a few Edxi ships since I got this assignment. The scans results I saw showed biological space faring technology. Anyone with eyes can see that their hulls are grown. Well, the fighters, their internal systems are pretty much the same. The details from conversations I overheard aboard the Supplicant, the parasites gather minerals and other essential ingredients from their own bodies and their environment. Oh, great, 'ingredients,' it sounds like I'm talking about a muffin recipe," he shook his head.

"Push through, this is important," Leon said.

"All right, so the Edxi do this whenever they're getting ready for a full-scale invasion. It could take decades, according to a couple members of the science team, but no one can say for sure because the Edxi aren't exactly social. They don't make documentaries about their own tech. This whole effort to provide the Edxi with breathing bodies is meant to show them that they can trust the Order, that they're allies. Just like the Fourth Fall, they're doing their best to make sure they're not the ones who get crushed when the hammer falls. Instead of putting themselves on a computer virus' friend list, they're trying to appeal to these aliens who see mammals as lower life forms. What I'm transporting is evidence that the Edxi are willing to trust them." It really did seem rehearsed, and Norton seemed more relieved to say it all aloud as he went on.

"How does it prove that?" Jake asked.

"Listen, this Gift mission is new. The Edxi gave the Order thousands of those parasites as a sort of test. They wanted to see if they could handle implanting humans before they were transported so they'd develop in transit. Everyone is guessing that the Edxi are keeping track of how many parasites go missing instead of being used on hosts. Sorry, I know you want facts, but that's a guess everyone who knew more than they wanted to made, so it probably tracks. As far as facts are concerned, you'll find them on the drives I took from the helm. They have all the navigation data you'll need to see where the ship went, but the scan data was wiped after every trip, and the drop off changed every time," Norton said.

"Why are they doing it?" Mimi asked.

"Like I said, they're trying to placate the Edxi. This debate came up a few times on the bridge, and a few people were dragged right out of their seats for objecting while I was on duty. As Captain Barchess explained it, the Edxi have been demanding tens of thousands of humans. They didn't explain what they were for at first, but this is it, they're building complicated ship systems using these parasites. Anything else I say is beyond what I can prove," Norton replied.

"Interested in making your defection official? I'm sure we'll have more questions, so Haven Nation would be grateful if you'd be our guest for a while so you can answer more questions. When I say guest, I'm not being euphemistic. You'll be well paid and immune from prosecution," Leon said.

Norton glanced at me before lowering his head. "Sorry, Captain, if I can make amends, I should."

"I respect that," I replied. Luckily, I already had a great pilot. I was also more concerned with the relationship between the Order and the Edxi. I wanted to strap every weapon I could find onto the Daring Dream and rampage across the galaxy until the Order and their allies were slagged. Hiding it wasn't easy, but seeing Jake's stoic demeanour helped. "Good luck."

"We'll take care of your transportation once you arrive, Norton. I'd rather you weren't in the room while we close this issue for Rogue and her crew. I'll give you a moment," Leon said.

Norton looked like the weight of the universe had been lifted off his shoulders. He ignored everyone in the room except for me. "Thank you, Captain. I didn't see a way out of this on my own. Don't stop here."

"You're welcome," I said as I watched him leave. Jake was right behind him so he could make sure that a pair of Legionnaires took the defector to a nearby room.

Lat and Perri came in through the opposite door in fresh military vacsuits and better boots. My frustration was pushed aside by relief, and I didn't realise that I was about to give Lat an affectionate hug until I was touching him. He stiffened as I wrapped my arms around him. "Just give in to it," Mimi whispered.

He laughed softly and hugged me back for a moment. "You scared me there," I told him as we parted.

"I guess these suits don't hold up to high end rounds from a knight's rifle," he said. "I'll remember for next time."

I didn't know what to say to that, so I moved on to Perri, who was probably as surprised but much more receptive to a short embrace. "How's your arm?"

"I opted for rapid regeneration, it was weird, and the new

arm still feels, well, weird, but it works as good as the last one," Perri said.

"Did we just get a second ship?" Lat asked.

"No," I answered immediately and flatly. "We're turning it in." Thinking that Duncan should have a say in what might come next, I called him and projected a hologram of him to my left.

He was half way through a bite of a vanilla wafer bar. "Wha's goin'?"

"I'm not sure," Manny replied.

"Negotiating payment. This is a big one," I felt a little wrong, doing the right thing for money, but I silently resolved to get the best result for my crew and my ship.

"What kind of reward does a capture like that earn?" Lat asked.

"A big one. There's no calculation for it. You're in for bonuses, but what I'm after for the ship will cost more money than any of us have had," I said.

Manny leaned forward. "Does it start with a 'Q?'"

I put my finger over my lips and he grinned at me. "I'm also stripping the weapons off that thing. They're rapid fire coil cannons."

"Gauss guns? That's not common out here, people don't tune their shields for them," Perri said.

Jake came back and Leon reappeared saying; "We can give you and your crew a few minutes to speak in private."

"I could be somewhere else," Jake agreed.

"I think that's Leon's way of saying he wants me to gather the consensus so he doesn't have to negotiate with every member of my crew," I said.

"Think it's fair to say we're all grand with the bonuses and the ship getting a bit of love," Duncan said.

"As long as you look into getting a better food fabricator," Perri added.

"I will. No need to leave though," I told Leon and Jake. "Where does that ship and what's inside it rank on your list of prizes?"

"High. We almost can't calculate it, but you know the Fleet. We have ways of figuring that out. I have a number here, it's enough to break a small crew up," Leon said.

"Not this crew," Mimi said defiantly.

"Don't give me a number. I'll take half a million platinum, some new repair droids, a commercial quality food fab, and three quad drives," I told him.

Jake's brow raised in appreciation and amusement.

Leon actually reeled a little. "That's not even legal. If you want tech, I can set you up with personal armour, a regenerative enhancement to your hull, a combat shuttle, upgrades to your other components..."

"Fleet is afraid to let the quad drive genie out of the bottle," Jake started slowly walking around Leon's hologram. "Trust is the issue, but not with you, Rogue. Having control of the fastest mode of travel in the known universe can make people paranoid."

My patience for diplomacy was bouncing back, but I wasn't going to get short changed. If I had to do it all for free, I would have, but the Privateering Initiative promised rewards, so I was going to get everything I could for my prize. "If it's a matter of trust, I think we've demonstrated that we're not sympathetic to the Order. It's also worth considering that the Daring Dream and her crew took the Ryden Corporation down. We bankrupted them, the Order bought them, and that led us to the Supplicant along with everything in its hold. Maybe the Mergillians would like to bid on this. Mimi, can you..."

"Hey, there's no need to look outside your contract," Leon said, totally falling for it.

"I'm on the verge of offering them a place in the Legion," Jake said, still walking in a slow circle around Leon's hologram. "The Daring Dream is a good ship, her crew is proven, it's all upside."

"We need ships like hers out there on their own. If Rogue and her crew didn't chase after Ryden, no one would know anything about what's going on with the sleepers. The Legion is..."

"Careful," Jake warned.

"You're after more military targets, investigating other things," Leon explained. "Besides, she's well liked with most successful Rebel Captains. That matters a lot more if you're on your own, Rogue. We need success stories and good leadership."

"All right, I won't poach them. They deserve what I'd offer though, and I'm not afraid to make sure they know what they're worth." It looked like Jake was enjoying himself.

"What's happening?" Mimi asked in a low whisper.

"I think we're being represented," I whispered back.

"You don't have to be part of this at all, if you'll pardon me being blunt," Leon said with a little smile teasing the corners of his mouth.

"You're pardoned," Jake replied. "All right, I'm sure this crew needs to get back to their ship so I'll cut this short. How about I make an offer for the Supplicant then trade it to Haven Fleet myself? I'm authorised to receive quad drives and other technologies I was involved in developing, so I'll pass two to her. Then you can pay me while I draw a couple drives from the factory."

"Excuse me, she asked for three," Mimi interjected.

"So I could get one," I whispered to her.

"Oh. Two would be just fine then," Mimi said.

"So we're clear, Rogue trades you the Supplicant Five and everything inside. You give her two quad drives and some loose change for it, and then you trade it to me for platinum while you buy a couple for cost?" Leon asked.

"Exactly, well, maybe not exactly. I'll have to figure out a handling fee. We'll talk about it when I get there," Jake told him.

Leon shook his head, not looking displeased, just a little surprised. "Go ahead. As for the rest, Rogue, put your kills, intelligence findings, and other activities in a report with your scanner logs and we'll reward you after you get here. Just keep your ship ready. We're still expecting the Order to hit the Bitter End any time."

"Thank you, Leon," I told him as his hologram faded.

"Did that go well?" Lat asked Perri secretively.

"I think so," she replied.

"It did," Jake replied. "How about it, two quad drives and a hundred thousand platinum so your crew can have their bonuses right away."

Being able to think faster than your opponent when you're haggling isn't fair, but it is helpful. I made an effort to ignore everything Jake and the Triton already did for us momentarily. "Make that two quad drives and three hundred thousand. I'd also like the guns, shield generator modules, and some time in the Supplicant's armoury. Throw in a rack of skitter droids along with three fully loaded repair drones and we have a deal. Oh, and a fabricator for my galley."

Jake's jaw actually dropped a little. My crew was silent as they watched him consider my counter. "All right, two drives, a rack of skitters, one repair drone, and you get to ransack the Supplicant as long as she still flies when you're done. As for the food fabber, I'm sure our salvagers have something good, just not new.

I'll give you a hundred fifty thousand platinum to go with that. Oh, and we only have a couple hours. We're turning around as soon as we get to the Bitter End."

"Deal," I said, offering my hand.

He shook it and I looked into his eyes. This was the first time I'd been in the same room with him. It didn't strike me until then because there was so much going on, but I'd slipped. While we were bartering I'd forgotten that we hadn't known each other for years. Maybe that's the way it ought to be, since the memories I'd inherited from Alice felt like my own then. I just hadn't realised it until then. For a few seconds it felt like I was with my father. It was as if he was shining his affection on me then, and I froze for a moment.

It was a bit too much all at once, I guess, because I tensed up. I ended the hand shake formally. the standard way - two pumps followed by the release. "Thank you, Jacob."

"Yeah! Thanks Old Man!" Mimi added.

"You're welcome," he told her. "Oh, and I'm really not that old."

She ignored his comment. "I've wanted to ask, why don't you let people have Kawaii Kittens on your ships?"

"You've asked that before," I reminded her.

"I know, but he didn't give me the right answer," Mimi replied.

Jake took it the right way, giving her a gentle pat on the head. "Most Kawaii pets aren't as smart as you are. They're usually too distracting. How's that?"

"That'll do for now," Mimi replied.

Silence started settling into the room and Duncan broke it. "Let's get stuck in, we've work to do."

"Right," I said as the rest of the crew got to their feet.

"Thank you, Jake. Not just for the trade, but for saving our butts, putting my crew back together and for the repairs."

The rest of my crew added their thanks as well, Manny actually bowed. Not just a little, either, but bending at the waist. "You're welcome," Jake said as they finished up and filed out.

I was the last, and Jake called after me. "Can I have a minute?"

"Can she listen in?" I asked, pointing to Mimi.

"No," he replied.

"Fine, I'll wait outside. I'm actually an adult, you know," Mimi said as she dropped out of my hood onto the deck and padded through the door.

Jake went to the window where at least thirty small domed skitter repair bots and five or six drones were working on the hull of the Daring Dream. They were working hard on the breaches, but also addressing several dents and pockmarks. "I need you to know that I was serious about my offer. There is a place for you in the Legion."

"Thank you, but I agree with Leon. Being able to chase my own leads has been working for my crew and I. Not that I don't appreciate the offer," I replied. "How has it been going?"

"Well. We're selling captured ships and resources to privateers and other governments so we don't have to take every privateering reward we earn from Haven Fleet. We might eventually bankrupt the program if we did. Lost a few important people along the way, but that's the cost," he replied. He pushed on to another topic. "That's a nice ship. The right size, probably the best thrusters in her class, and room for upgrades."

"I knew I was in trouble when I saw the advert for it. I had to have one, even if I didn't admit it to myself for a while. They never went to full production, the demand wasn't there, but I got mine." Knowing that he liked the Daring Dream felt good somehow.

"Alice will be disappointed she missed you. She doesn't know we picked you up, but we talk about you." It seemed like he was looking past my ship, as though Alice was somewhere beyond it.

"What are those conversations like?" I had no idea what the answer would be, and was a little afraid of it.

"She wants to meet you again. Face to face. It's impossible right now, but she's curious. Worried sometimes, but that's how it goes. She wants to apologise to you, make sure you're all right. Abandoning you was her way of giving you a chance. You woke up, became sentient when you weren't supposed to and she was sure you'd be in for months of study, maybe long term containment if you stayed," he said, not looking at me.

"She knew how much I'd hate it because I was running on her memories at the time, even though my digital side pretty much took over," I said, watching as a repair drone sprayed a layer of sealant across a freshly installed inner hull plate. Another drone was waiting behind it with the outer armour segment.

"Digital side?" he asked.

"It's a whole, long thing. I used to have two minds working at the same time, now they're merged and my problems are... different. It's all right, I'm dealing with it." There were bigger things to talk about, things that concerned my crew, so I didn't want to dwell on my internal issues. "What would you do in my position?"

"Drop the chase. The problem of the Order trying to get into Edxi's good graces is too big for you and your crew. It's probably too big for the Legion. I don't know what the Edxi will do when the shipment you captured doesn't turn up on time. That's Fleet level trouble," he replied.

"People are being kidnapped and sacrificed," I pressed.

"Right, but what do you want? What was the cause? Are you going to take the Order on and push the Edxi out of the galaxy using the Daring Dream?" Jake asked.

Okay, so I didn't think it through. Me and my crew trying to solve that problem was like a tiny, two ounce Tamber fruit bat attempting to fly off with a whole bunch of bananas. He was talking sense, but I wanted to fight him on it when I should have been listening to his advice. "You're right, this gets really big from here on. I wanted to know what was happening to the sleepers, why the Order wanted them. Now I know, and I think my end game is to tell the galaxy."

"Do you need credit?" Jake asked.

The question surprised me. It was as much about safety as it was ego. Credit for taking the Supplicant and exposing the secret inside would make me and my crew famous. It would also make us one of the top targets for the Order, the Edxi and all their allies. Sure, the Order may find out that I was the one who took the Supplicant eventually, but rushing that didn't seem wise. As far as my ego went, well, that was a little funny. I was too proud to admit that I wanted credit. "No. I just want people to know about this. Maybe it'll turn more people against the Order and remind them that the Edxi are out there."

"So you wouldn't mind if I put a clock on revealing everything you'll forward to me from your experiences on that base and the Supplicant?" Jake asked.

"Maybe not, how much of a delay are you thinking?" I asked.

"I want Fleet Sciences and our team on the Triton to have one month to investigate what you found. Someone more well liked by the public than me will release a report using Hart News. We can work with their people while the investigation is under way. I don't want this to get delayed while people endlessly study this find," Jake said.

That brought the Lidden Warehouse up in my mind. Jake was going to make sure something happened, and I believed him when he said there would be a firm date on that. By using him and his people, I would also be protecting my crew. "I'd appreciate that. Just don't move your timeline, all right?"

"We'll set it and keep it. My team will do hard scans of the entire ship before we hand it over. It'll be enough data to virtually recreate that as an experience we can share online and study once the month is up. Fleet Sciences won't like me involving Hart News, but that'll make them move even faster," he replied.

"Then we have a deal. I'm still going to look for sleepers and save whoever I can," I said.

"So will we. There hasn't been much of that on our end, but maybe we can find and free more when we make it a priority," Jake said. "This could change the war, and when it's safe for your crew, I'll help you tell everyone that it started with you, if that's what you want."

I'd never thought about Jake looking towards the end of the war, when it would be time to collect facts so history could be properly recorded. The funny thing was, the more we talked about me taking credit, the less I cared.

Manny, Perri, Lat, and Oonaa emerged from the doors below us and I watched them walk across the hangar deck to the Daring Dream. "Well, other than watching for sleepers, I guess I'll move on to the next challenge." My mind drifted to the pirates who escaped Warro. They'd go to the top of my watch list.

Jake smiled and inhaled deeply. "That's something you and Alice have in common. You can stand at the feet of a giant, look up and say; 'I like a challenge, let's go.' It took her almost as long as it took me to learn when it's time to back off. It's probably a lesson I'll learn again, but watching her take giants on is still terrifying. Maybe you're not my daughter, but you can have the same effect. This isn't about me though. What would I do if I were standing in your boots?"

"He'd get bigger boots! Tell him he should get bigger boots! It's funny because your feet are tiny compared to his!" Mimi said through our secure communications link. I'd forgotten it was still on.

I cracked a smile, but I kept quiet because I wanted to hear the answer.

"I'd want to chase all that down, take the Edxi and Order out. No doubt, but there are indirect ways to do that. It's a group effort. There's room for single ship captains to contribute without getting killed. I'd hit the supply lines, test the Daring Dream, get experience with my crew. Then I'd find an interdiction system I could install. Buy it, steal it, build it, just get it put in. That's the key. Stop the enemy from jumping into a wormhole, force the crew to abandon ship, and take the haul. That is, until a crew doesn't get in the pods, but stays and fights," he said, half turning away from the view to watch my reaction.

It reminded me of the old pirate movies I watched with Mimi. "Sounds like a lot of privateering," I said, turning towards him.

"Exactly. Sure, you're getting wealthy, but for people like us it's about the one that stands and fights. If you can take that prize, you'll find something the Order is trying to hide, and that's more exciting than money. It might take twenty captures to find that one, but people like us live for the twenty-first prize. We love to share the Order's secrets with the galaxy. Maybe even turn them to our advantage," Jake said.

"What is it? What's the twenty-first prize?" Mimi asked on our channel.

There was a soft scratch at the door and I rolled my eyes, stepping towards it so it would open. Mimi looked up at me. "They wouldn't let me back in."

I scooped her up and she climbed over my shoulder so she could drop into my hood. "This was supposed to be private time."

"Hey, I'm not the one who left our channel open," Mimi replied before half crawling on top of my head and regarding Jake. "You're tall. Anyway, what's the twenty-first prize? What does it have?"

"Well, it could be the fifth, or the fiftieth," Jake replied. "How many ships you have to take to find it isn't the point. The secret, or extremely rare prize is. We don't know what it is until it's found. Could be a part of a new super weapon, comms tech, or a giant load of platinum. The point is to catch it, find out what it is, and use it to your advantage."

"Oh," Mimi said, pausing to think. "I don't think that answer is as satisfying as you think it is."

Jake laughed and nodded. "You're right. Back to the point. I suggested you calm things down, take normal, safe jobs before."

"That was all right, I didn't mind it, actually. Lat was the restless one," Mimi said.

"Let him finish," I told her.

"Okay, okay, it's just an exciting conversation," she said.

"Right, so the jobber life didn't work out, I didn't expect it to for long. Maybe privateering is exactly the thing. Repair the Daring Dream, arm her, and that ship will be ready to tear into the Order's allies. It's not too big, she's fast and it can take a pounding. Her captain is trained, and I'd bet the Reaper that the crew is in shape. Start using your ship's proper name, and before long you'll have crews surrendering as soon as they see the Daring Dream on their nav screens." Jake said.

"Like Black Bart Roberts and the Royal Fortune," Mimi whispered with reverence.

"You've got it. Everything you've been through on Tabrus - in the wastes, New Zero - then going after Ryden and finding this hasn't taken you to a destination. No, it's prepared you for the next thing. Even Mimi the Kawaii Kitten is ready to roar into space and show the Order that they can't depend on contractors to do their dirty work."

"Yeah!" Mimi cheered. "I'm a Kawaii Cat now, by the way. I've seen some shit."

"I believe it," Jake laughed. "Work with the Rebel Captains, cut the Order's supply lines. If you want to show the Edxi that their ally is weak, undependable, that's how you do it. Let Haven Fleet take over with the Edxi, they're ready."

"Are they willing? They're not here, and it's not the first time I called for help," I said.

"They are. The Legion and people like Captain Blake, Elyub and Marda are all making the Fleet look weak, or like they don't care about the war. The Haven Defence Minister is sick of it," Jake replied.

"Funny, I didn't see anything on Hart News or the rest of the 'net about that," Mimi mused.

Jake grinned. "Trust me, Minister McPatrick and I are old friends. Who do you think he calls when he needs to vent? Haven Fleet has been building for a while now, training new people, and they're starting to move. I don't know more than that, no one outside of Haven Fleet does, but we'll see them out here soon. In the meantime, they're letting us have all the fun in the Rose System and beyond. Once those quad drives are installed in the Daring Dream, the whole Edwyn Cluster becomes your playground, go have fun, and bring your victories back to the Rebel Captain's Table. I'll be the first to nominate you for a seat."

"Thank you, Jake. That means a lot," I replied. That was when I really started to question myself about keeping my distance from Alice's friends. It came down to one thing. I didn't feel like Alice anymore, I had become more than her memories and the merging of an old artificial intelligence. I would never feel like I was Alice again, I could only be Rogue. What that meant to the galaxy was for me to determine. "I'll earn that seat."

EPILOGUE

A New Goal

The best visits always feel like they end too soon. I wished we could stay, it felt like I'd been reunited with a like-minded relative, but I knew there was a lot of work to do before the Triton arrived at the Bitter End. After the Daring Dream was basically ready to take off, me and the whole crew descended on the Supplicant Five. We stripped weapon systems, supplies, the materialiser from the kitchen, whole modules like the shield generators, and equipment out of it. The only place we avoided was the cargo hold, and with the repair droids helping us out, we managed to fill our cargo space.

While we were looting, for want of a better word, two Order deserters joined in. Quan the telepath gave his stamp of approval to Kerra Newsome and Bud Cote. Both of them were part of the group from the galley who helped me take the Supplicant. The rest of the crew we captured were either still loyal to the Order, or didn't want to join me.

Oonaa signed onto the crew officially even after I told her she would be a trainee on probation for three months. You might be surprised to see that her then ex-boyfriend, Fersuu stayed on too. We couldn't drop him off at the Bitter End because he still owed a pile of platinum, so we temporarily took him on until we found a better port.

No one aboard the Triton really had time for us other than the deck crew, and that was all right. Disappointing for Mimi, who was hoping to meet Commander Ashley Lamport in person for the first time, but she was busy. As the master of the Triton's Helm, she couldn't get away. Even though I felt that I'd improved my attitude about people from Alice's past, I was still a little nervous about meeting them. I'm not proud of it, but I was pretty relieved that I didn't run into any more of them. Meeting Jake face to face was enough for one visit.

Before we arrived at the Bitter End I took one more look at the Supplicant Five. The horrifying question that haunted me for weeks had been answered. The sleepers were damned, and I swore to prevent the Order from taking more of them whenever I could.

The greater cause, defeating the Order and the Edxi, would rest in the hands of people who were capable of bringing that about. The Daring Dream still wouldn't last too long in a big fleet battle. I'd be watching though, and the first to give them a push if they needed it. That meant I'd need influence, and I was determined to get it, maybe through membership with the Rebel Captains, maybe another way. The particulars were still in the air.

As I walked away from the Supplicant Five, I was very conscious that I'd gotten lucky once again. I nearly lost my ship and my crew suffered thanks to my choices. It was time to change the way I did things.

I'd gone from a wasteland wanderer to a bounty hunter. From a bounty hunter to a privateer. It was time to become a proper Captain. Trusted by her crew, respected by her peers, and feared by her enemies. It was a version of myself that I wanted to evolve into more than anything.

***

*Thank you for buying and reading Rogue Chase. Rogue, Mimi and the rest of the crew will return in **Rogue Clipper,** the final book in the Rogue Element Quartet. Coming in the second half of 2025 or sooner as a serialised adventure for subscribers. Visit www.randolphlalonde.com for more details.*

Thank you for buying and reading this adventure!

CREDITS

I'm grateful to Janet Lalonde and the Readers from Ream Stories, who helped proofread this book. They are:

Alan
Art Jenkins
Brenton
Centurion22
Charles Ferguson
Charles Love
cjryden
CmptrWhz
Dave James
Euronymous
GenoM
Guylc2
Jac Grimes
Jeff Mueller
Joe L Goode
M Thole

Rosemary Smith
Paul Gear
RyanB
Steve Carol
Tom Bentley

I'd also like to thank the unofficial UK Community Organiser, Tracy Holmes, who has been responsible for ten gatherings on that side of the pond. I wish I could afford to attend or to pay her for all the work she puts in online and in person. Thank you, Tracy!

SPINWARD FRINGE UNIVERSE TIMELINE

With regard to the Rogue Element series, Psycho Electric and The Last of the Bullet Chasers, you don't have to read any of the other Spinward Fringe novels to understand and enjoy them. You can also read Carnie's Tale and The Expendable Few separately if you'd rather dip your toe into the universe than start at the beginning with Spinward Fringe Broadcast 0: Origins. Having said that, if you're going to dive into the series, and I invite you to, it's a hell of a ride, here is the chronological order of all the books in the Spinward Fringe Universe.

Spinward Fringe Broadcast 0: Origins

Spinward Fringe Broadcast 1 and 2: Resurrection and Awakening

Spinward Fringe Broadcast 3: Triton

Spinward Fringe Broadcast 4: Frontline

Spinward Fringe Broadcast 5: Fracture

Spinward Fringe Broadcast 6: Fragments

The Expendable Few: A Spinward Fringe Novel

Spinward Fringe Broadcast 7: Framework

Spinward Fringe Broadcast 8: Renegades

Spinward Fringe Broadcast 9: Warpath

Trapped: Chaos Core Book 1

Cool Pursuit: Chaos Core Book 2

Spinward Fringe Broadcast 10: Freeground

Spinward Fringe Broadcast 10.5: Carnie's Tale

Spinward Fringe Broadcast 11: Revenge

Savage Stars: Chaos Core Book 3

Spinward Fringe Broadcast 12: Invasion

Spinward Fringe Broadcast 13: Warriors

Spinward Fringe Broadcast 14: Rebel

Spinward Fringe Broadcast 15: Pursuit

Spinward Fringe Broadcast 16: Hunters

Psycho Electric - A Spinward Fringe Novel

The Last of the Bullet Chasers - A Spinward Fringe Short Novella

Spinward Fringe Broadcast 17: Clash

Spinward Fringe Broadcast 18: Samurai Squadron

Spinward Fringe Broadcast 19: Samurai Squadron II

Rogue:Assembly

Rogue Cause

Rogue Chase

Rogue Clipper (2025)

Spinward Fringe Broadcast 20: Samurai Squadron III

Legion: Spinward Fringe Broadcast 21 (Late 2025)

THE FANTASY NOVELS

While most of these aren't arranged into a series, they do land on a timeline and occur in the world of Nemori. Here's the chronological order of all my fantasy novels, which are written to be enjoyed in any order except for the NEM novels.

Brightwill

Highshield

NEM: Awakening

NEM: Crimson Shores

WHERE YOU CAN FIND ME

If you'd like more information about me, to get in touch, read articles or find out what's going on you can visit my website at www.randolphlalonde.com or www.spinwardfringe.com. If you'd like to access my entire library, including a couple exclusives starting in 2024, and read the newest books before release in a serialised format, please visit my Ream Stories site: https://ream stories.com/randolphlalonde

www.ingramcontent.com/pod-product-compliance
Lightning Source LLC
Chambersburg PA
CBHW051942020726
47501CB00001B/236